THE WINTER MARINES

Far to the west, perhaps ten miles into the hills, the glow of flares dropped by plane showed faintly. *So that's where they're shooting. Recon must have found something. Charlie must be crawling all over those fucking hills.*

A movement caught Haney's eye and he turned and saw the lanky, angular form of platoon sergeant Larret approach. The man slapped Haney on the arm and leaned against the sandbags, lighting a cigarette, his face showing concern in the glow of light. "Get your boys up, Joe," he said quietly. "We're mounting out. You can guess why."

Haney motioned toward the hills. "Something's on the move out there."

"Yeah. Recon stumbled on a potful of gooks. Maybe a regiment of regulars. Our whole damned battalion is mounting out, even the companies down the line —I'm gonna roust the rest of the platoon. Get 'em up, but no lights. There's no point to making it obvious till the choppers get here."

"Are we going in first?" Haney asked.

Larret shook his head. "India company gets set down at first light. We'll be right behind them—Let's get crackin'. As soon as your squad's up, go over to the skipper's tent for a briefing." As he left, the sergeant again gripped Haney's arm. "We're in for a real donnybrook, Joe. Keep your head on straight."

THE WINTER MARINES

Allen Anthony Glick

(Formerly titled *Winter's Coming, Winters Gone*)

BANTAM BOOKS
TORONTO · NEW YORK · LONDON · SYDNEY · AUCKLAND

This low-priced Bantam Book
has been completely reset in a type face
designed for easy reading, and was printed
from new plates. It contains the complete
text of the original hard-cover edition.
NOT ONE WORD HAS BEEN OMITTED.

THE WINTER MARINES
A Bantam Book / published by arrangement with the author

PRINTING HISTORY
Formerly published as Winter's Coming, Winters Gone
by Eakin Press 1984
Bantam edition / October 1987

ISBN 0-553-26799-X

Published simultaneously in the United States and Canada

PRINTED IN THE UNITED STATES OF AMERICA

O   0 9 8 7 6 5 4 3 2 1

THE WINTER MARINES

*To those mourned on the black stone, and
those who grieve before it.*

1

South of Tam Ky, Vietnam, 1966

In Vietnamese, the word kill is spoken *giēt*, a swift and
guileless sound, kin to the word *chēt* which means to die. A
man might know the meaning of these words yet only guess
their substance.

David Schrader sat that night on the hillside, the rifle cold
in his grasp, the heavy infra-green scope cradled in his lap.
He had scanned the slope, testing; had seen through the scope
the glowing of another marine's head over in bunker six. Now,
adjusting, and still peering through the infra-green scope, he
refined the silhouette: broken nose, hard jawline, deep-socket
eyes all glowing jade green, from body heat. About sixty yards.

Then he sat there, goldbricking, and turned off the scope's
battery, his stomach fluttering as he tried to imagine his first
ambush.

A breeze was wafting up the hill. It carried the smell of
fecund earth, and Schrader savored it. He was a farmboy, a
tall and towheaded midwesterner, and he grinned secretively
when the others complained the Orient smelled—well, stank.
The plain seemed to shimmer in the light of a moon that was
dropping behind the mountains, with its paddies shining silver,
and the dikes crisscrossing neatly, a vast jewelled chessboard.

The fields lay all around the hill, which was steep and
draped with barbed wire and its top was bulldozed to barren-
ness, so that the red clay festered in the sun like a wound, and
hemorrhaged into the paddies whenever it rained. A road was
graded all around, a man's height below the top, which was
flat and featureless except for the tents and bunkers.

The sound of hurrying footsteps crunched on the road,
yet even in the moonlight Schrader could see nothing against
the backdrop of the hill. Turning on the scope again, and keying
on the noise, he spotted what seemed to be a jade figurine

1

coming down the road. He knew that movement, the easy crouching lope of their point man, Calderone. Time to hat.

Schrader stood and slung the battery in its case over his shoulder. He put on his helmet, hefted the heavy M-14, and stepped onto the road.

"Schrader?"

"Yo!"

"Let's hit it, man."

"I'm ready, Mingo. What's the rush?"

"We're pulling out early. The squad's at the south gate."

"South gate? The river ford is north of here."

Calderone barked a hard, short laugh. "Figure it out, boot."

"We circle around the hill. So what? We won't fool anyone in this moonlight." He felt a blunt finger poke his skull.

"Think harder, David." Calderone was muscular and quick-handed. "The moon's low. This hill throws a long shadow to the east. Maybe it will work for us."

"Maybe. Who knows?"

"The shadow knows, boot. Don't doubt it." He began to quick step along the road and Schrader followed. The camp was blacked out, razor thin glints of light shooting from one tent or another, muffled laughter bursting from behind heavy canvas.

There were men milling about the gate, talking low, moonlight fracturing their paint-streaked faces. Now and again a rifle bolt would snicker as a round was chambered. Schrader loaded and locked, the smooth action comforting.

Calderone punched him lightly. "Watch yourself," he muttered, then slipped away and was wrapped in darkness.

"Over here, Schrader." It was Corporal Haney, the squad leader.

"It checks out okay, Corporal."

"No fuzzy images? The crosshairs are bright enough?" Haney was a few inches shorter than Schrader, lean as a post, a measured and deliberate man.

"Yeah. She's a beauty."

"And you're firing only tracers, right?"

"Every round."

"Time for you to break your cherry, Schrader. I've made a last minute change. I don't want you on point with Mingo.

There'll be enough moonlight for awhile, and he's got eyes like a cat anyway. I want you to bring up the rear. I'm as nervous about gooks slipping up behind us as I am gooks in front of us."

Schrader caught his breath. "Sure. I can do that." But he felt a frost in his chest.

"It will get pretty thick sometimes, but you can follow us with the scope. You'll have to guard both directions. Anyone behind us gets powdered. Don't hesitate. Blow the suckers away. You got that?"

"Yes sir."

"When we clear the paddies and get into the trees, you drop back about thirty yards. Try to keep that distance. Don't panic if you lose sight of us sometimes. There's no telling how far body heat will penetrate the brush, but we'll take just the one trail and there ain't no crosstrails to throw you off. I'll come back to check on you after we clear the jungle."

"Don't worry, Corporal."

Haney stepped close. "Look, you got the sauce for this or I wouldn't trust you with the scope. So stop bracing like I was your DI. You call me sir one more time on patrol, some gook might shoot me for a shavetail."

"Okay, Joe."

"Burgess brought your gear from the tent. Remember. Thirty yards." He turned on his heel and strode toward the gate. Two short whistles brought the fireteam leaders running to him.

Schrader followed, slower, angling off toward a familiar figure.

"This my shit, Calvin?"

"Yeah. There's cold coffee in one of your canteens."

"Ugh."

"Hot java steams, man. The gooks can smell it." Burgess was a black man, not tall, but thick and heavy-armed and his skin was very dark.

"What do you think our chances are tonight?"

"Chances for what?" Burgess scoffed. "For living?"

"I mean — hell, Calvin, you know what I mean."

"Let me tell you, man. The chances look good we'll lay on our fuckin' bellies all night and feed the bugs. Anything else happens, then the chances look bad."

"You don't like any of this, do you?"

Burgess snorted. "Where you from, chuck?"

"Missouri."

"It figures. You must not have anything better to do at night."

Schrader grinned foolishly.

"Look there. Haney's waving us up. You gonna carry that scope on point?"

Strapping on his cartridge belt, Schrader answered: "No. Haney wants me to bring up the rear."

"Better you than me, man. That's some spooky shit."

"Yeah," Schrader said as he fitted the battery into its harness, then slipped the harness over his shoulders like a pack. "Yeah, I'll bet. Some spooky shit."

The night was vibrant with marsh noise, a dissonance that feathered down his spine. Once sound becomes a presence you can feel, silence seems like a withdrawn touch. Stepping along the narrow dike, craning his neck one way and then the other, Schrader winced when the tiny creatures down around his feet fell quiet. Then the stillness would spread outward, as would the ripples in a pool. The wider the pool, the more visible Schrader became.

He turned around slowly, listened as he had never in his life listened. He would silence his heart, muffle his breath, still the icy stream tumbling through his veins. One by one he heard a hundred tiny voices. *You're alone*, they sang to him; *you're alone*.

He could not see Casey, his fireteam leader, the next man up the line. But Casey was a stick-carrying, slouching, viri-descent ape, viewed through the scope.

They had been twenty minutes on the narrow dikes, Mingo setting a cautious pace, and Schrader had stopped often to keep his distance. The moon sank lower, and the moonshadows cast by the dense treeline grew longer, until, one by one, the men began to disappear among the trees. Then Casey was the last, bits of emerald light splintering as he vanished. On their own, Schrader's feet began to race for the trees, his knees weak with panic. *Stop!* a voice shouted in his mind. *Wait*, it said gentler. Schrader waited. Then he stepped to the edge of the dark, black jungle and, with a last glimpse at the open sky behind, plunged in. The air was heavy and as moist as a sticky tongue on his neck. Vision became a dozen shades of black. The path was blackest of all, an inky ribbon kept to as much by touch as by any other means. His face and hands were scratched by brush. A slither or flutter set him to thinking of snakes, and his bowels went cold. Through the scope, Casey was a comforting fragment of light. Yet in the time it takes to cut a throat, thirty paces might as well have been the distance to the moon, dropping lower now, behind the mountains.

Progress was slow. He kept edging too close to the patrol. Then, abruptly, they passed from the smothering jungle into more open country; some fields, some orderly groves. It seemed much brighter, though the moon was only a glow over the horizon.

When the patrol halted, Schrader was within spitting distance of Casey before he saw him. Casey's arm was a gray blur waving him to a crouch. Schrader was down in an instant, the rifle in his shoulder, his eyeball straining through the scope. He counted the squad—little foetal monkeys growing smaller and smaller—one of them hurrying down the line as though hunted; pausing, sniffing, feeling, the night. Joe Haney. He was quickly beside Schrader, kneeling, patting him on the shoulder as an invitation to whisper. But Schrader had nothing to report.

Gently, Haney took the rifle from Schrader's grasp and put it to his shoulder. The battery cable tugged. Haney squirmed closer and peered through the scope, then he gave the rifle back.

"Too slow," he whispered tersely. "Can't check on you again. At the site, Mingo will bring you in." Then he was gone.

The pace was quicker after that. On the edge of a field they came to a steep-banked stream, cold from the recently-ended monsoon rains. Schrader gritted his teeth as the water rose to his crotch. The bank was slick and he slipped to his knees, holding the rifle high. Once up, he used the scope. When he began walking his boots squished water and he shook them out, then ran to catch up. It went on like that—stop-and-go, hurry-to-catch-up—for half an hour, until the lay of the land changed. They patrolled an area of waist-high grasses, marshy, the ground spongy as they neared the river.

The men began to disappear into another dark treeline.

Schrader paused and used the scope, scanned the fields and stands of brush in every direction. He stepped along cautiously. Three men remained in the open, then two, then only Casey remained. Schrader watched him kneel by the trees, joined by Calderone, luminescent monkey heads briefly touching. Casey moved off, dissolved to jewelled drops through the eye of the scope, then disappeared. Calderone waited. Schrader moved along and came to the edge of the clearing. He could hear the river.

"Come on," Mingo hissed, and they crept through the treeline. There was the river, a stone's throw away, across an apron of white sand. The trees made a crescent of the clearing. The narrow trail came out near the center, where a big log was rotting, and Mingo pointed. Schrader scurried to position behind the log. Cocking his ear, he heard the faintest of rustlings as the men settled in. Then all was still, the squad invisible against a darkened skyline.

Wet and shivering, David eased the packboard from his back, setting it aside, trailing the power cable carefully. Using the scope he slowly scanned the far bank, perhaps two hundred feet away. It was a tangle of jungle that spilled to the very edge of the river.

Someone tugged on his leg and he reached for the twine handed him, looping it about his ankle. Whoever spotted the enemy first, gave three sharp tugs on the twine, passed along by each marine. Schrader squirmed loose from his cartridge belt, sipped stale coffee from his canteen. The sand flat was littered with brush — he counted seven clumps and fixed them in his mind. Now that he was still, mosquitoes swarmed him. There was repellent in his jungle jacket and he smeared himself with it, clothes and all, while keeping his eyes on the river bank.

An hour passed. Two hours. Staring too hard would make the clumps of brush seem to move. He counted them over and over. Wriggling a few feet to the side, he scooped a hole with his knife, pissed, filled in the hole and wriggled back to position without yanking the cord that looped his ankle. Every few minutes he would scan their front, but after three hours it became routine and he expected to see nothing. When the scope flared suddenly with a show of body heat, Schrader's heart skipped awry. He fumbled to tune the silhouette more distinctly, but it hung to the brush and all he saw was a dis-jointed mass of glowing meat. He thought to grab the twine, three hard tugs—but wait, it could be an animal, an ape or a hog—. A minute passed and Schrader's eye burned into the scope. Goddamnit! What is it! When the creature moved back into the brush and vanished, he wanted to bellow his disgust.

Grimacing, wiping sweat and sand from his face, working the cramp from his neck, he locked his eye once again to the scope. Seconds later the creature returned with two others, and suddenly Schrader was very sure. He grabbed the twine and yanked it hard, three times left and right, unlooped the twine and yanked it hard, three times left and right, unlooped the twine and then jammed his eye back to the aperture. They were there, joined by a fourth hovering back in the thickness. Oh fuck! he worried. What if it's a reinforced company!

Haney slithered to his side and took the rifle, peering through the scope some seconds then setting it aside. They hunched down behind the log and touched heads, whispering with lips hard against cupped ears: How long? Three minutes. Are there more of them? Don't know. It doesn't matter, Haney told him. We're committed—you know what to do. And he slithered away to prime the trap.

When Schrader looked again, there were still only four. He watched the scout slide into the water, heard no splash above the murmur of the river. His mind raced. When the gook came ashore to scout the treeline, Haney would kill him. Schrader was to cut loose on the others, his tracers burning red, marking a killing zone for the squad to raze by fire. As close as the other three huddled, Schrader knew they would get them all.

His heart thumped in his ears. He breathed finally, fogged the lens, tried to swallow but could not. His tongue tasted of the wood and steel he gripped and, teeth bringing blood to his lips, he slipped off the safety catch. His finger danced beside the trigger.

Come on, gook!

The scout had wavered some time in the middle of the river. The waist deep water furrowed about him. When he waved his comrades into the river, Schrader's mouth turned to an ugly skull's grin, smirking—so this is ass-kicking Viet Cong!

They trailed single file from the water, a few steps apart and in no seeming hurry, the scout bearing toward Schrader.

Not yet . . . not yet . . . He centered the crosshairs on the enemy's face, huge features aglow, a face that abruptly became human. With a shudder, he tipped the muzzle to the man's chest and the recoil slammed into his shoulder. The stillness exploded as he watched an emerald silhouette suddenly become a man in one thrashing spasm—everyone firing then except Schrader, seeing the bodies fold and collapse, pieces of flesh trailing away, little chips of jade . . . A hand flare whooshed above them, then another. The screen on the scope flashed uselessly as the landscape erupted in light. Haney was shouting "Cease fire! Cease fire!" and it was over, with a silence dropping so heavily that the ringing in Schrader's ears pierced like a toothache.

Perhaps the ambush lasted eight seconds.

A hurried voice barked jubilantly into the radio: "Kilo one, kilo one this is hawk's foot. We have contact. I say again, we have contact. Request immediate eight one illumination, over."

The light came in seconds, white hot flares from mortars, and instantly it was almost day bright: colors shifted, red tinted, harsh and glaring. Schrader looked at the bodies, saw the blood and scraps of flesh sprayed across the sand. Haney talked on the radio and listened to squawking replies. Nobody moved. Nobody spoke but the corporal.

As the flares fell more would burst above them. The parachuted cannisters whistled as they plunged to the ground. They sizzled and crackled and cast dancing shadows as they tossed in the breeze.

"Calderone!" Haney called. "You and Schrader check out the bodies. S-2 wants to know what weapons."

Schrader stood on rubber legs, feeling numb, and Mingo came up beside him.

"Let's hurry it up, man. I don't like standing in the open."

The first one lay forty feet away, sprawled across a rifle. He was a boy, maybe sixteen or seventeen. When Schrader turned the body with his foot, to retrieve the weapon, he saw spinal cord and ribs and lung blown out a gaping hole in his back. He turned his head as he took the rifle. The next soldier was a teenaged girl. Her jaw was blown off, her head hung by shreds of muscle to her shoulders, and there were pieces blown off her torso. She had no weapon, only a pack on her back.

"See what's in it," Calderone told him. "I'll check the others."

Schrader knelt slowly. He took his knife and cut the pack from her shoulders, got some blood on his hands and tried to wipe it off, but it only smeared. He opened the pack and lifted the contents. There were some rations, but mostly it held medical supplies: bandages, dressing, some liquid antiseptic —and a book of poems, its pages worn and soiled. In the book was a picture of a family: peasants, two adults and four children standing stiffly. Schrader's hands shook. Bile rose to his throat. After a few seconds it passed, and he placed the picture back in the book. Then not knowing why, he tucked the book into his shirt.

Calderone walked back to him, carrying two rifles. They were antiquated models that neither of them knew.

Madre de Dios! Calderone muttered. "They're only kids."

Schrader couldn't reply, and Delgato slapped him on the back. "You'll get used to it, David."

Haney hollered out: "What ya got?"

"Three rifles!" Calderone called.

"And a pack full of medical supplies." Schrader mumbled.

"And a pack of med supplies!" Calderone echoed.

The radio was squawking. Finally, Haney shouted: "Mingo, take your team and stack up the bodies. They're sending a forty-six to us. We fly back."

There were some ragged cheers. At least they wouldn't carry the bodies back over their shoulders. Spurted conversation began:

"Not a bad night's work!"

"Never seen 'em so easy before!"

Then, voice like a rasp: "Somebody get an ear! Hey Schrader, lop off one of them ears!" It was Mathis, hulking and mean. Schrader didn't like Mathis.

"No one's takin' ears!" Haney barked angrily. "And no goddamned chatter! Quiet down and listen!"

Someone touched Schrader on the shoulder. It was Burgess, come out to stack the bodies. His black skin shone like onyx in the flare-light. "Don't listen to that jive about the ears."

"I wasn't going to," Schrader muttered.

"It's funny what a dude will do sometimes, thinkin' it's cool."

Schrader stood dumbly as Burgess stooped to grab the heels of the girl. The rifle slipped from his shoulder, so he handed it to Schrader and dragged the body to where the others were already stacked. When Schrader took the rifle, he reached unthinkingly and grabbed it by the barrel. But his hand wasn't burned. The barrel wasn't even warm. Schrader put his nose to the breech and it smelled clean of oil. Calvin didn't fire, he thought. But his mind was foggy and he made nothing of it.

When he glanced up, Burgess was in front of him, staring coldly. He jerked the rifle from Schrader's hands, saying nothing, and trotted back to the trees.

Everything was seeming far away to Schrader. Even Burgess's reaction registered little on him. He looked around slowly and saw he was the only one still standing in the clearing. He thought it might be a good idea to get to cover, so he walked clumsily to his place and lay down on his belly.

Distantly, he heard the radioman tell company to cease the illumination. The helicopter would need a clear air zone.

In a couple minutes, the last flare sizzled to earth and burned out. The landscape went black and they were awhile getting their night vision. They heard the chopper: *Whop, whop, whop*— Some green flares were tossed onto the sand as the pilots' chatter came over the radio. The double-rotored machine drifted in deafeningly, throwing debris and dust everywhere.

They were no time loading the bodies, and the last of them dashed up the ramp. As the helicopter lifted, it tumbled the sand violently, leaving little trace to tell the story.

Burgess was fidgeting. The sun was bright and warm on the hillside and he watched the farmers in the paddies below, saw a child herd some ducks along the barbed wire at the base of the hill.

Calderone handed him a cigarette. "What's the matter with you, man? You're steppin' round like an alley cat."

"That was a slaughter last night, you know that?" Burgess replied. "That was like pushin' meat through a grinder."

"Might've been us," Mingo shrugged. "I don't like zappin' kids but they got rifles, you know. They can shoot the suckers, too." Mingo Calderone, lance corporal and fireteam leader, purple heart, Bronze Star, was only nineteen himself.

"What do you think of that dude Schrader?" Burgess asked. "I can't make him out."

"He's okay, Calvin. He showed some stuff last night."

"Yeah, but he's so damned straight. Duty, the Marine Corps, all that crap. I'm not sure I trust him."

"He ain't no lifer," Mingo said. "The kid's goin' back to the farm. Besides, he didn't like that shit last night, either."

"I didn't fire my rifle," Burgess suddenly confessed, looking Calderone straight in the eyes.

"You dumbass!" Mingo said coldly. "What's gettin' in your head? Man, I seen this comin' for months, you gettin' all worked up about this bein' the *Man's* war, not yours . . ."

"Well, it ain't mine!"

"So what?" Calderone said. "You'll get killed in it just the same if you start foolin' around!"

"Wasn't any point joining in last night, Mingo. I knew we'd shoot those poor bastards to pieces."

"Hmph! And what if we really need you next time, man?"

"You know you could count on me."

"Sure, Calvin. Now or tomorrow. But if you get any crazier, I don't know—." Mingo lit another cigarette and scuffed a rock down the hill. "I hope you get your head on straight, brother. You're makin' me nervous."

"Schrader knows," Burgess said.

"Oh yeah? I wonder what he thinks of it?"

"That sucker better not say anything."

"Naw. He won't say nothin'. I'm tellin' you Calvin, the kid is okay. He wouldn't fink on you."

"He bothers me," Burgess replied. "He's too damned friendly. Makes me suspicious when a chuck gets that friendly."

Mingo laughed. "He's a farmer. They're all that way. Not everyone grows up in Chicago or San Antonio, you know."

"Ohhh Chicago," Burgess said slowly. "It's changin' every day and I ain't there to see it."

"If you don't smartin up, you ain't never goin' to see it," Mingo scoffed. "Just keep your head on for eight more months, and no more of this layin' off the trigger crap . . . You comin' to chow?"

"What are they having?"

"Who cares," Calderone replied. "Just hold your nose and swallow."

"You go on, Mingo. I ain't too hungry."

Burgess stayed there in the warm sun and watched the valley. Off in the distance at the edge of the fields, nestled in the green jungle, the thatched huts of a hamlet shined yellow-gold. It seemed such a neat and ordered little world. Burgess wanted to go there unhindered: without a weapon, in no uniform and under no flag and shout Hey! I'm your brother! Look at me! But it would never work, he told himself, I'm something I don't want to be, something they got no use for, another grunt with a gun and they couldn't see me any other way . . . God in Heaven, I don't like killing these people. But I can't let them kill me, either. Mingo is right. I gotta stand with my own.

The sun made him drowsy and he was lost in his thoughts, and he did not hear the other man approach. Burgess started when the shadow fell across him. "What you mean, sneakin' up!"

"Sorry Calvin," Schrader apologized. "I wasn't sneaking."

"What do you want, man?"

The farmboy shrugged and looked embarrassed. "Just wanted to talk with you a minute. Didn't mean to break in on your privacy."

Burgess looked at him hard. "You gonna tell Haney 'bout last night?"

"I don't know what you mean?" Schrader looked puzzled.

"Come off it! You know I held my fire."

"Oh, that. I didn't think much of it, Calvin. Figured your rifle jammed. To tell you the truth, I was too sick to my stomach to think much of anything . . . I'll leave you be. Maybe we can talk later." Schrader turned to go.

"Wait a minute, man," Burgess said. "That ambush made me touchy. I don't mean to jump on you."

"Yeah, it affected me, too. I was expecting some grizzled old jungle fighters, armed to the teeth. But that girl was about my sister's age."

"I thought you farmboys was used to a lot of blood."

"I guess so," Schrader replied. "Hog and steer blood, butchered chickens, that sort of thing. Not human blood. Hell, the smell is even different."

"You want a smoke?"

"No thanks. I did something dumb last night."

"What's that?" Calvin blew smoke out his nose.

Schrader looked doubtful a second. "I kept something that should have been turned over to S-2." And he reached under his shirt and removed the book of poems.

Burgess looked it over, stared long and quietly at the picture of the peasant family, the children all smiling stiffly. "You found it on the girl?"

Schrader nodded.

"There's notes all through the margins. Could be code, David. The intelligence people will want this."

"I know," Schrader replied. The Marine Corps had sent him to language school. "But I looked up a lot of those words. I can make some sense of it."

"And you think they're just school girl notes?"

"That's what I think."

"What are you going to do?" Burgess asked.

Schrader swallowed. "Try and get the book back to her parents, the ones in the picture. That's what my folks would want if—if it was my little sister who got shot."

Burgess began to think of the white boy differently. He whistled low. "You could make a lot of trouble for yourself, man. They might call it collaboration with the enemy."

"I don't see why," Schrader protested. "It's just a little book of poems."

"My man," Burgess admonished, shaking his head. "Nothing is nothing over here till the Marine Corps tells you. If they wanta call that little book the master plan for the seige of Danang, they will. And you'll be bustin' rocks and none of your good intentions will mean shit."

Schrader set his jaw and looked stubborn. "I'll have to figure a way to do it without being caught . . . Maybe I can just leave the book in that hamlet over there, the next time we patrol. Put a note in it and explain about the girl. Then the local VC will sort of parcel post it for me."

"Mmm hmmm. And if the hamlet guards find it instead?" Burgess asked. "And if they hand it right back to us with your note inside? They'll parcel post your ass straight to Leavenworth."

"Maybe there's another way," Schrader persisted.

"I don't think so," Burgess replied. "We're a half-step out of place here, man. Maybe you ain't noticed that yet. But we can't go anywhere or do anything without bein' seen and suspected of something."

"I'll think of a way," Schrader replied.

"Best thing to do is burn that book," Burgess told him.

Schrader just shook his head and tucked the poems into his shirt. "Thanks for talking to me about it, Calvin."

"What's Missouri famous for?" Burgess laughed. "Mules?"

"Yeah. Mules and Jesse James."

Burgess saw someone approach down the road. "Quiet now. Here comes Haney."

"Crap," Schrader said. "It's working parties for sure."

The corporal stepped close and smiled tightly. "You fella's had chow?"

"Not me," Burgess said.

"Better grab a bite. The Skipper gave us a firebase security job, up to Tam Ky."

"How many days?"

"Three. We'll be with the cannon-cockers."

"Hot damn!" Burgess said. "Three days off this fuckin' hill!"

"You'd better go eat. We're pulling out in an hour. Field marching pack, me and Schrader will bring the ammo around."

Schrader followed the corporal across the crown of the hill and through the neat rows of bleak squad tents. The ordinance bunker was heavily sand-bagged and it was dark and cool inside.

"You did okay last night, David," Haney told him, letting his eyes adjust to the dimness of the bunker. "I didn't expect the gooks to fall into it like that, and then I wasn't sure how long you could hold off the trigger. But you cut loose at just the right time."

Schrader saw the bodies tumbling again. "I didn't expect them to be kids."

Haney barked a short, harsh laugh, ringing with the things Schrader knew of him: second combat tour, silver star and purple hearts, busted from sergeant.

"How old are you, David?"

"Nineteen."

"Hell, I'm only twenty-four. We're both still kids—don't

waste pity on these gooks just 'cause they're a few years younger. They'll kill you dead. War grows these kids up fast."

Schrader thought about the children in the hamlet. "I've heard that before. I don't know if I believe it."

"You damned well better believe it. You get soft on these people you'll end up in graves registration, wrapped in a canvas bag. You'll be a memory and a purple heart stashed in your mother's dresser."

"Do you hate them, Joe?"

"The gooks?" Haney looked at him for long seconds. "No, I don't hate them anymore. They do what they have to do, just like us . . . We better hustle now, get this ammo to the tent. We'll each take two cans, and send Mingo's team back for more . . . Think about what I'm saying, kid. You want to go home to that nice farm, don't get soft on the gooks."

Schrader hefted the heavy ammo cans and did not reply. He was getting ideas of his own.

2

They tried not to think of mines, or of being exposed. They were just out in the light of day and having a good time with the wind rushing in their ears and escaping the basecamp, the officers, and the drudgery of the bull-dozed hill top. It could be such a bore when the war slowed, nowhere to go and nothing to do but a work detail.

They were all standing as they rode in the bed of the truck, a five-ton the cannon-cockers dispatched for them, big-wheeled, heavy-girded, but a big mine could throw it like a toy.

The road to Tam Ky ran due north and was alternately paved or tarred, hard to mine except in the chuckholes. The land was flat coastal plain, stretches of jungle broken by ordered paddies and grasslands, the jungle sometimes growing right to the road and then quickly retreating beneath the flashing knives of the farmers. Occasionally, they would rumble through a village, thatched huts next to old French two-stories, the whitewash fading and vines creeping up the walls and the peasants would look up and wave or maybe frown but the truck wasn't slowing and the scene would disappear behind them.

Schrader watched the farmers. They were plowing fields with hulking water buffalo they somehow tamed like puppies. Schrader's father had once used a team of mules, but it had been awhile. Some of the peasants were knee deep in the paddie mud, planting rice shoots, stooped and patient and seemingly ancient. The monsoons had only just ended. Schrader had joined the squad when it was ass-deep in mud and in two weeks it had disappeared everywhere but in the paddies. As the land dried up, the war would shift gears again and they all knew it. Haney better than any.

They were bouncing along pleasantly and Schrader was leaning on the rail of the truck bed, his rifle slung over his shoulder. Duffy, (Schrader's fire team leader) was beside him. The short, stocky redhead was watching the peasants too.

"Ain't like farming in the states, eh Schrader?" Duffy was a rodeo rider from Oklahoma.

"You're from wheat country," Schrader had to shout over the rush of wind. "We still see horse and mule teams at home. Hard way to farm, though."

"You said it, man. But there ain't no easy way," Duffy shouted back. "My daddy gave up when I was six. We moved to town."

"Doesn't rain much out there," Schrader replied, shaking his head. "I always feel bad when a farmer goes under."

"Daddy felt bad a long time. Now he never goes past the old place anymore. Funny how a piece of land gets under your skin. How much land does your daddy farm?"

"Half a section. Good land, Duffy. River bottom and gentle slopes. Dad's trying to lease some more, wants to expand when I get home."

"Soybeans?"

"That's the coming thing," Schrader replied.

Duffy nodded with a tight smile and looked away. Schrader knew how fortunate he was that his father had managed well and had luck and was making it.

Traffic was light on the highway. There were cyclists and motorbikes, and occasionally a French bus bursting with passengers—even on top and hanging off the sides—the little bus swaying and tipping under its load. Most of the traffic was military: drab green trucks and jeeps contrasted with the gayly colored buses and the bicycles with pretty girls in their flowing white gowns.

They came to a cluster of huts and shops at a crossroads, enclosed on three sides with a woven bamboo fence, the tiny ville looking fragile as a paper fortress. There were fields behind the ville and then the jungle. Schrader caught a faint salt sea smell on the wind, as it blew from the east. To the west toward the mountains, the open fields stretched a mile without a sign of a tree. The truck slowed and stopped and was quickly besieged by the worldly-wise urchins that seemed to be everywhere in this country.

As Duffy arched and stretched with the rifle over his shoulder clunking, flack jacket clinking, helmet clanking, canteens ringing, bullets rattling he sounded like a medieval knight.

"Tighten up over there!" his buddy LaRosa shouted from the rear.

"I'll tighten your head about two turns, guinea!"

"You limp wrist!" LaRosa laughed. "We'll arm wrestle for the beer."

Duffy turned and winked at Schrader. "This'll be a snap, boot."

They clambered out of the truck, thirteen young men with enough ordnance to destroy a small town, and the urchins clustered around, touching them, their begging and laughing blending musically. Duffy handed out chewing gum; LaRosa gave away his chocolate rations. Burgess dug into his pack for the tins of fruit he'd been hoarding.

The motor pool corporal who'd been driving the truck walked around to the rear. "I'm havin' a couple beers," he told them.

Haney took him by the arm. "How much further?" he asked.

"We gotta go through the city yet," the man said, pulling his arm free. "About ten miles, then north of there we turn west and that's where the guns are."

"Another hour?" Haney asked. The squad was bunched all around the motor pool corporal.

"That's right."

"Don't take too long," Haney told him.

"Wait a minute! You don't outrank me."

Haney put his face close to the other man's. "The afternoon's getting on. When we get to the battery park, our work's just beginning. So you do what I say, buster. You're going home to a nice billet tonight."

The truck driver looked around at the lean faces. "Okay, man. Don't get a hard-on." And he hurried off to have his beer.

"We'll stay with the truck," Haney told the squad. "Two beers apiece, no more. Nobody's punking out when the work starts."

Duffy took off his helmet and handed it around. His short red hair shining in the sun. "C'mon gents, a hundred *dong* each . . ."

"Beers are only thirty-five *dong*!" Mathis growled.

"A little something for the kids, Mathis."

"Screw the little gooks," Mathis said. He'd been with them a month, transferred from another company, and he had his collection of ears. He counted out seventy *dong* very carefully and dropped it in the helmet. The thing was full of tattered, sweat-stained bills.

The urchins smelled a deal brewing and clamored even closer, maybe twenty of them, and Duffy knelt and motioned, "C'mere kid," and a quick-footed rascal of six or seven barely three feet tall came scampering up.

"What you want, fella? Me get," the boy said.

"You got some buddies with you?" Duffy asked. The urchin signalled and three others stepped up, two boys and a girl, ragged, dirty-kneed but pretty and bright-eyed. "We want twenty-six beers," Duffy told them. "Cold beers. You know how much twenty-six is?"

Hai müdi sáu, Schrader prompted, leaning close.

The urchin nodded. "Sure. Me know."

"Make sure they're cold," Duffy told him, handing the helmet to the boy and he plucked out the bills and handed it back.

Lành! Em hieü, không? Schrader repeated.

Da phai, the boy replied. He understood. Cold beer. Those *Nguoi My* and their passion for ice! The four of them scurried to a shop nearby; the interior looked cool and there

were a few young whores, and souvenirs hung from the ceiling.
Outside the other urchins were not dismayed and stayed close,
little groups hanging around one marine or another, but Mathis
leaned against the truck and glowered at them so they left him
alone.

Duffy stepped over to LaRosa. They were both sturdy,
one fair, the other dark.

"You ready, guinea?"

LaRosa grinned. "You dumb Okie, this time I'll have your
ass."

"Come on," Duffy chuckled, laying on his belly. "Muscle
talks, bullshit walks."

They lay flat and squirmed around for position and put
out their arms. LaRosa tried to get the jump but the cowboy
was ready and it was a puffing, red-faced contest in no time.
The urchins got around in a circle and cheered them on and
a couple of the merchants and some of the young whores came
out and laughed and shouted and everyone picked a favorite.
One little whore who was dressed in pink and about seventeen,
jumped and squealed and pointed excitedly to LaRosa. LaRosa
held his own for awhile, looking like he might get the edge,
but Duffy was holding back and when he turned it on LaRosa's
arm slowly began to go down, the man grunting and straining
and thump! The back of his hand hit the dirt.

The small whore in pink made a face and poked LaRosa
with her toe, and said something disdainful. She promptly
walked back to the shop.

"Wha'd she say?" LaRosa asked Schrader.

"Couldn't follow it," Schrader replied.

"She said you got no *cojones*," Calderone laughed, standing over them. "Some Latin! Lettin' a Okie whip you."

"I'll get his ass next time." They got to their feet and
dusted off, and the urchins came back with bottles of beer in
baskets and were delighted when no one asked them for change.
The marines sat around the truck drinking the ice-cold beer,
local beer, *Ba Muoi Ba*, which was the number thirty-three.
They called it tiger piss but it was good. When the truck driver
returned they climbed aboard and were off again, the tiny ville
disappering behind them and the countryside rolling by. But
the traffic was heavier as they neared Tam Ky, and the going
was slower.

Haney was impatient. He stood with his rifle propped on the cab of the truck, the wind in his face, his eyes forever flicking and searching. He was never comfortable on the roads. He felt too exposed. The squad was in a skylarking mood and Haney knew that later he would have to sit on them. They were fine infantrymen but their attention would wander and Haney could not tolerate carelessness. He was remembering what green-assed boots they were, when he first took them over. Five months now he'd had them; pulled most of them through but he remembered the ones they had lost: Harper, Michaels, Lippman and Ferris. Haney didn't want to lose anyone else, but deep inside he knew that he would. The monsoon was over. There would be trouble soon enough.

They drew to the edge of the city and the thatched huts of the country became tin and cardboard shanties jumbled together on the roadside, long stretches of wretched slums, the people dreary and listless as they stared at the passing marines. There was a faint odor of foulness, and Schrader was uneasy at the sight of such misery. He glanced down the length of the truckbed at Burgess, who shook his head sadly.

In a couple miles they came to a nicer part of the city. The road broadened to an avenue and the shops were stucco and brick with open fronts, with the merchants all in western dress. The pedestrians and cyclists were not the poor of the slums, but well-paid workers and the middle-class. The willowy school girls in their white *ao-dais* were startingly pretty and they looked at the marines shyly and the marines gawked back. The traffic was slowing them down. It took ten minutes to go a few blocks, and then there was a traffic circle bordered by Mediterranean-style buildings in pastels and a militiaman whistled the truck through and that was Schrader's blurred view of the center of town. And then the traffic was faster and they were moving again out of the city, past the respectable quarters and fine homes and through a new set of slums. They were north of the city and it was rice paddies and fields and jungle again, and after the city slums these country peasants did not look so poor.

At another crossroads, the truck turned west towards the foothills. The road was macadamized a way, but soon it was clay and the jungle seemed to sweep down upon them from nowhere and close them in. The skylarking ceased without

Haney saying a word. The cameras were quietly put away and they all had their rifles ready and stood at the rails, the truck bouncing and jarring in the potholes, the jungle sliding past them on both sides so close they could reach out and swat the leaves.

They drove about three miles through the thick of it, the sky sometimes blotted by the trees, when the truck suddenly emerged into a large open plain. The deep grass rolled like a green sea in the breeze, dotted here and there with thickets of bamboo and brush. Schrader was good at figuring acreage. He thought the plain was at least a section, a square mile, though it wasn't square at all and the jungle was a thick green line all around. The foothills were so much nearer, the plain seemed almost hard against them. It was rough country. In the middle of the plain squatted the artillery battery, six big pieces of 155-millimeters, a typical high explosive round weighing ninety pounds. The big guns could easily shoot them seven or eight miles.

Haney called to the squad: "Listen up fellas . . . These cannon-cockers are easy to get along with. If we do a good job, maybe we'll get an afternoon off on the way back to basecamp, maybe get a look at Tam Ky, seeing as how you all brought your cameras . . ." The truck was bouncing along and they were almost at the battery park. "We'll be patrolling new country," Haney continued, "best to pay attention and keep the wreath off momma's door."

"Amen, brother," Willie White said.

"Hallelujah," Duffy echoed.

They passed into a hastily made encampment; rolls of concertina were like acccordian reels around it, the big howitzers parked in an arc perhaps ten yards apart, snouts pointed threateningly at the foothills and the grass trampled down all around by the trucks. Men were busy everywhere, stringing more barbed wire about the camp and building bunkers from sandbags.

The big truck squealed to a stop and the squad climbed out and began to stack their gear and ordnance. The battery commander hurried over to them, a tall skinny captain with graying hair. Haney saluted.

"Glad you boys got here," the captain drawled. "Hope you're ready to go to work."

"Yes sir," Haney told him. "We've been sitting on our butts."

"How many machine guns did you bring?" the captain asked.

"Two, sir. And five thousand rounds. Just tell us where you want them."

"My boys got two of our own. We're putting them in those bunkers we're building—I'll tell you what," the captain said, turning, "you build me a bunker there, about ten yards left of the gate, and one over there. That will give us fields of fire all around the camp. Get your boys started on that and then come and see me. I'll show you the area maps."

"We'll get right on it, captain."

"See that pile of sandbags over there?" the officer pointed. "Those are yours. We gotta hustle, corporal. There will be fire missions any time now."

"Who's out in the hills, sir?" Haney asked. "Our boys?"

"Shit no!" the captain hawked and spat. "It's a South Vietnamese operation. Those fuckin' Arvin are out there tripping over each others feet . . ." and the officer turned on his heel abruptly and strode away, mumbling and shaking his head.

Haney got them to work and they were at it for three hours, getting the bunkers built and setting up the machine guns. Then they strung barbed wire until the sun went down, and Haney posted guards and they settled down for the night. There were only a few fire missions, the cannon thundering in unison, the gunners moving like well-drilled machines and the projectiles slicing the air and trailing away with a sound like a fast train moving off. Except for the exploding howitzers, it was a quiet night.

Early the next day there was a patrol.

They had the reconnaissance maps, and Haney worked out the route with the captain. The officer was sorry, but he could not send the battery's only corpsman with them. But they sent one of their radiomen, and by seven o'clock the patrol was pulling out.

Mingo took the point, his fireteam spaced behind him, and they trailed out the encampment through the makeshift gate. Duffy's team was next in line with Schrader, Cezeski and Willie White. LaRosa's team brought up the rear: Naylor, Mathis, Perry Jackson. There should have been a fourteenth infantryman, a grenadier to carry the short-snouted grenade launcher, but they had been short that man for a month, and Haney carried the launcher with his other gear.

Up and down the line of patrol there were vendors dangling wares in their hands, haggling with the marines in pidgin. They were from a nearby hamlet and they appeared at the crack of dawn, risking the nervous fingers of the machine gunners. A few of them trailed after the patrol and Haney brandished his rifle and chased them away. A few of the boys were taking pictures, and Haney barked at them to put the cameras up. *If they want to clown around,* he thought, *I'll make their tongues drag.*

Haney was in the center of the line with the radioman, the squad strung out a hundred and fifty yards in column. The corporal flashed Calderone the handsign to speed it up. Ahead lay the jungle. They would sidle the trees until they found a certain trail that was marked on the map. It was almost a mile in the open, moving fast, and Haney knew it would sweat the clowning out of them, though they were traveling light — only thirty-five or forty pounds of gear.

After half a mile he heard Ceseski bitch: "Haney's got a hard-on!" and the corporal grinned meanly to himself.

They halted when Mingo found the trail leading into the jungle.

"What's the hurry, Joe?" someone called out.

"Yeah. What's the rush?" They were all sweating.

Haney glanced around wide-eyed. "What rush? We're just shaking out the ants."

They all knew what he meant. "They're shook out already!" LaRosa said.

Haney gave them five minutes before they pushed on, taking the strange, spongy trail into the tangled matte. The trail was wide and well-traveled, and mostly open to the sun. There was the sweet musty odor of blooming flowers, and the air seemed tinged a faint green. They could not see three feet into the thickness on left and right. Except for the buzzing of insects and the twittering and rustling of tiny birds, the jungle was very still. Haney drew the squad closer, six or seven yards between men, and they stepped along quietly, peering into the thickness.

In the distance, the howitzers resounded, shaking the

ground, the rounds shrieking overhead. The guns fired three booming salvoes and then were silent, the jungle falling hushed as a tomb a few seconds before the little noises started again.

They had just passed through a small clearing, edged by bamboo and colored with a hundred blossoms, when Calderone held them up. Haney trotted to the point. They had come to a side trail not shown on the map, one that was a good bit narrower than the one they were on. With the jungle hanging heavily over, this new trail seemed like a long green tunnel.

Haney glanced at his map. "If it doesn't peter out, it should exit somewhere around here." He pointed on the map for Mingo. "Maybe we can work along the jungle till we come to where the main trail breaks out—What do you think?"

Calderone shrugged. "Might as well look and see. Nothing going on here."

"You and Duggan nose it out," Haney said. "Check it out a couple hundred yards."

Mingo nodded and gave a sign to Duggan, who was farther down the line behind Burgess. They plunged down the trail and were quickly gone from sight. Haney whittled a stick of wood until they returned.

Mingo was puffing. "Looks okay," he said.

Haney nodded and walked back down the line to the radioman.

"Get your skipper on the hook," he told the man.

The operator talked into the handset and in a few moments handed it to Haney. The corporal gave a precise explanation, giving their map co-ordinates and a promise to call again when they were clear of the jungle. The captain gave them the go-ahead, and Haney waved up the line to Calderone. The patrol began to snake along the crosstrail. The air was sticky and still. Here and there a patch of light would glimmer through the canopy, but there was no other sign of sky.

A green viper, coiled lazily around a limb, watched them pass, flicking its tongue to discover what they were. The small and colorful birds still flittered about, but Schrader saw nothing exotic: not parrots or macadoos or anything like that. He'd seen monkeys and mongeese and black scorpions that would cover a man's hand. But no tigers or elephants or pythons. It occurred to him that the war was driving the animals inland, where the mountains gave them more protection. Schrader had heard of the standing orders to kill elephants on sight, because the Communists used them for transport.

They were half an hour on the trail before it led them out of the jungle, and they winced at the bright morning light. There was a wind and it was cooler. Haney talked on the radio. When their position was cleared, they moved on, skirting the dark line of trees.

Initially, the patrol had headed due west toward the hills, and under the artillery fire. They had worked their way in an arc and were then two miles south of the guns. By midday they would trail back to camp, and after chow they would patrol the northern half of the route.

Haney thought it was time to break clear of the jungle. The treeline continued south beyond their sector, and they had to cross the plain of waist high grasses. Calderone led them cautiously along a path, searching hard for trip wires or even a length of grass laying out of place. The Viet Cong had a thousand ways to do you in. Mingo had seen a lot of them.

The wind was tossing the grasses and they rippled from light to dark green, sometimes flashing with sunlight. The grasses were thick on both sides of the path, though the growth was still young and later would double its height. The plain was dotted with strands of trees and bamboo, like islands in a bay. The squad was spread out again, fifteen yards between men.

They were approaching a fortress-like strand of bamboo, about half a mile into the plain, when the artillery began to crack and thunder. It was the noise that stirred up the warthog.

The animal had heard and smelled the patrol for some time, lying low in the bamboo, beady-eyed and aggravated by the pounding of the cannon. It was a big tusker, fierce and scarred and not easily driven from its range. When the cannon cracking started again the hog burst from its cover toward the marines, snorting and squealing, and trampling the grasses in its wake. Schrader knew the sound and his rifle was up as the hog rushed onto the trail taking White by surprise; Willie hot-footing it, the hog then charging down the line, swiping at Cezeski who was highstepping toward Duffy, who was back-pedalling and shooting from the hip, Crack! Crack!, Schrader shot it through the head. The beast shuddered and squealed before it died.

"Oooooeee!" Duffy hollered.

"Look at that ugly bastard!"

The men began to cluster around the hog.

"How big you think it is?"

Schrader eyed it judiciously. "Maybe two hundred eighty pounds—three on the outside."

"Man, I didn't know *what* the fuck it was!" Willie White said, shaking his chocolate brown head. "Look at them teeth!"

Schrader stopped and grabbed one of the tusks. It was six inches long and its tip was sharp. "It would have sliced you to the bone, Willie."

Duffy was taking pictures. So was Burgess.

Haney laughed at them. "Mom will be glad to know the war is over."

"C'mon, Joe! Just a couple pictures."

The patrol was bunching up. Haney signalled down the trail for LaRosa to hold his team in place. Calderone and Duggan had remained at the point.

"What we gonna do with it?" Burgess asked.

"Let's dress it out and take it back to camp," Schrader suggested.

"Yeah!" Duffy added. "Maybe the captain's up for a pig roast. Nothin' much happening . . ."

Haney scratched his jaw and looked at the beast. "The captain must be sick of rations, too." he replied. "But I want to get out of the open like this." He took his cane-knife and tossed it to White. "Cut a big piece of bamboo. We'll carry it to those trees up ahead."

Willie White trotted to the cluster of bamboo and brought back a length six inches in diameter, and they trussed the hog safari-style. Schrader and Cezeski hoisted it up, and the patrol got underway. It was a quarter mile to the trees where they gathered under some hard woods. Haney tossed parachute cords over a limb and they spread-eagled the animal in the air.

Somebody asked if it was a razorback. "Naw!" Cezeski spat. "A razorback is just a barnyard hog that goes wild."

Schrader grinned. "I didn't think anyone knew about hogs in New Jersey."

"Are you kidding me?" Cezeski laughed, his grey eyes going wide. "My neighborhood is pollacks and guineas. We eat pig from end to end . . . You krauts think you have a monopoly on sausage."

Schrader stepped to the hog and sliced the throat deeply, and the blood that had swelled its insides began to spill out. Then the farmboy made a cut just below its anus. Placing the blade between two fingers, he lifted the hide from the bowels and sliced neatly to the hog's sternum. The hide was thick and tough, even tougher than the Hampshires they raised on the farm.

"When I cut around the asshole," he said to Cezeski, "you start pulling the guts out, and I'll cut the tissue as you pull . . ." In seconds the bowels were dangling out. Duffy's bullet had gone through the lungs, and it was pretty messy. Schrader's hands were bloody almost to his elbows, but soon the heart and lungs were loosened with a sucking, slurping sound and the whole mass of innards was lying on the ground, and in moments, covered with flies.

Later, when they trudged into camp like something from a Tarzan movie, the captain and his cannon-cockers whooped with delight. The South Vietnamese soldiers weren't stirring much up in the hills, and the gun crews were playing cards. In a twinkling they were digging a pit for the carcass and someone was passing a helmet to buy wood from the peasants.

The squad ate their lunch and lounged in the shade of the trucks. By one o'clock they were patrolling again. The sun beat down on them all through the afternoon. Sweat stung their eyes, and the landscape shimmered in the heat. It was an uneventful patrol. Coming through the grass towards the camp, they could smell the pig roasting. The captain, with a wide smile, met them at the gate. "We buried that sucker in coals," he told them as they gathered round, shucking gear on the ground, their clothes soaked with sweat. "We won't be able to eat him for awhile, though. You fellas are doing a great job. Take the rest of the afternoon off, lay in the shade if you want." All the grunts grinned. The artillery was okay.

It was well into night and the stars were gleaming when the pig was finished cooking, and they ate it down to bones, sitting around a small fire, the fat glistening on their hands. The captain had stretched the rules and let them buy two beers per man from the peasants. It felt good under the open sky, a wind blowing on them, while Willie White played sweet

sounds on his mouth harp. Even Haney looked relaxed. But
something nagged at him. They had been too loose on patrol.
Something would have to happen to tighten them up again,
to shake the over-confidence that the ambush had given them
two nights before.

That's what nagged at Haney: what that something might
turn out to be.

But the next two days were quiet and uneventful, as well.
The patrols were routine and the operations in the foothills
were just firing practice for the artillerymen. On the morning
of the fourth day they were packing it in: rolling up all the
wire, dismantling the bunkers, hitching the howitzers onto the
trucks for towing.

The squad loaded their machine guns and gear and were
climbing in the back of a truck when the captain approached
them, walking with another man.

"Sergeant Brown here will drive you boys back to your
unit," the captain told them. "I've told him to give you a few
hours in Tam Ky, for the good work you did."

"We appreciate it, sir. Maybe we can do it again, sometime."

"Good luck to you fellas." They saluted and the sergeant
drove them from the now barren campsite out of the grassy
plain and through the jungle again. In an hour they had another
look at the slums of the city, Schrader not wanting to look that
time but there was nothing else to see. They passed a boy on
crutches who stared at them with hollow eyes. The boy's limbs
were like sticks and he was losing his hair. Duffy tossed him
a can of food, but the boy was too slow and other children
snatched it away. An old woman hunkered in a doorway, swat-
ting flies and spitting and looking like a corpse that did not
know it was dead.

Schrader fastened his eyes on the blue sky until they
were through it and into the city, where there were pretty
girls to see.

"Shit!" Cezeski suddenly shouted, snapping his fingers.
"Did anybody bring any rubbers?"

Everyone shook their heads but Duffy, who smiled and
patted his knapsack.

"How many did you bring, Duffy?"

"Just enough for me."

"Oh yeah? How many is that?"

"A dozen."

Cezeski laughed. "You limp-dicked Okie, you couldn't get a dozen hard-ons in a week! Lend me a couple, eh?"

Duffy grinned. "Do you promise to wash them before you give them back?"

The truck turned off the main road, down a narrow street and stopped at an old stucco building, windows boarded over and painted pink. There was a big sign in front.

"The Cha Cha Club," Calderone whistled. "Hot damn, *hombres*! We're gonna get laid!"

And they did. All but Haney who stayed with the truck, writing letters to his wife.

3

Schrader was crouched over and running hard, the canteens slapping his ass and the sweat blurring his sight as his legs churned across the field, Haney in the distance waving with impatience. He reached the shade of the trees and dashed past the corporal who was signalling the next man on. Schrader was gulping air as he trotted up the trail, getting distance from Duffy ahead, who was panting too. So was Willie White as he slowed up ten yards behind Schrader.

Duffy glanced back at them and shook his head, sweat dripping from beneath his helmet. They were all hang-dogged. Haney had been on them for three days, since the spree in Tam Ky, since they were drunk and passed out on the return trip, only Haney alert. And he was drilling them that day on patrol like they were recruits. It's what he had told them: you're acting like boots! I try to treat you like professionals, trust your judgment, and you're puking over the sides of the truck!

He said something else: I'll be goddamned if I'm getting killed because one of you is screwing up!

And three days later he was still on them, pushing them,

the routine patrol they'd looked forward to had become a tongue-dragging infantry drill.

Schrader slung his rifle as he walked and reached behind for a canteen. The water was piss-warm and heavy with chlorine and it spilled as he drank and walked, running down his chest, too tepid even to cool him. For the hundredth time he touched the lump beneath his shirt, the book of poems wrapped in plastic, his little secret mission. Schrader was thinking that Haney would hang him from a pole if he knew, the mood he'd been in.

At that moment Haney went trotting past him, up the trail, and Schrader dropped his hand from the book guiltily. He did not have a plan. He was simply going to leave it by the village well and hope for the best. He had labored long over the note, embarrassed by his rough grammar. It said simply in Vietnamese: I am your enemy, but I do not like to kill young girls. Please return this book and picture to her parents. Her name and home are written inside . . .

Schrader's hope was that the hamlet soldiers did not find it before a peasant. For some reason—barely thought out and which he could not define—he was counting on the sympathy of the peasants.

Haney halted there on the trail for lunch. There was a collective groan. The hamlet was only a half hour's march, and the villagers sold good food and cold beer. But Haney nixed it so they took rations from their packs and ate on the trail, Haney sitting off by himself and oblivious to their gripes. There was another half day's patrolling. If they angered him anymore, they knew what to expect.

Schrader opened a tin of chicken and a tin of fruit salad, sitting on the cool ground beneath the canopy and leaning against a tree, his legs sprawling and helmet off, the rifle laying carefully by his side. He ate woodenly, automatically, to quell his fluttering muscles and silence the growling in his gut. But the food did not spark one shred of appetite. In the hamlet he might have had fresh pineapple and rice and chicken cooked with peppers . . . He glanced up the trail at Haney, who was studying the map as he ate. Schrader knew he liked to vary his routes. Their corporal's first Purple Heart had come on a booby-trapped trail, a trail too frequently used. But sometimes there was no way to avoid it.

Among the men there was little chatter. The line had clustered tighter for lunch, and looking up and down the trail Schrader could see the whole squad, but they were too tired to talk. Schrader leaned back and closed his eyes and dozed. Far away he heard the rattle of metal and when he opened his eyes, the men were on their feet putting on packs and helmets, resuming the war.

"Sweet dreams, kid?" Duffy asked, slinging his rifle.

"No dreams, Duffy. I was absolutely nowhere and it was fine." Schrader stood and slung his pack, slapped on the helmet and stooped to pick up his rifle. He smashed the empty tins and kicked them into the brush.

Duffy stepped over to him and looked closely at the hand grenades safety-pinned to Schrader's flak jacket.

"Those are taped down good, Davey boy, maybe too good. Back at camp, you might re-wrap 'em. Just twice around. I used to wrap 'em three times and couldn't get the suckers undone when I needed."

"Okay, Duffy."

The team leader looked up the trail. "Haney's signalling to us. C'mon . . ."

There was a wide spot in the trail and the squad gathered close around Haney, faces tired and eyes expecting rebuke. But the corporal was smiling slightly. "Everybody had enough of this crap?" he asked, looking at them one by one.

There were nods and mutters of assent.

"I've had enough too," Haney told them. "You boys keep it good and tight and I'll lay off. You start fucking up again, I'll be on you even harder . . . Some of you know I'll be a daddy in a couple months. I want to see my kid. Anything wrong with that? No? Then we all understand each other. When we get to the hamlet we'll take a beer break. Two beers. Don't try and guzzle anymore when I'm not looking. Calderone. LaRosa. Duffy. I expect you to start leaning on your teams. Don't leave the heavy hand always to me. You understand?"

"Sure, Joe," Calderone told him. "We were feelin' cocky 'cause of the ambush. We're okay now, right *hombres*?"

"That's right man."

"You know it."

"All right," Haney said. "Back to the war . . . Slow the pace down, Mingo. We're ahead of schedule."

The squad spread out and the patrol went on. They came to the edge of a large clearing that jutted south for half a mile, between two neat lanes of forest, the clearing sharply quilted with paddies and fields. Calderone called a halt and Haney joined him at the point, looking long at the treeline on the other side of the fields, easily two hundred yards away. Mingo was smoking, and studying the trees too.

"We'll send Rosie's team across to work that side," Haney said at last. "Keep the same pace, but start spreading the men out more."

"Want us to check IDs?" Mingo asked, thinking of the peasants he saw working in the fields.

Haney chuckled as he lit a cigarette. "How many of those have you looked at?"

"Couple of hundred," Mingo answered.

"You ever know what they said?"

"Shit no! Coulda been their memberships in the Communist Party."

Haney shook his head. "Let's leave the gooks to their farming. It's hard enough for them to fill their bellies." Haney trotted down the line and waved up LaRosa's team, the men moving quickly across the field, smartly, glad to have the corporal off their asses. When the fireteam was in place, they began to edge along the length of the clearing. The peasants paid them little mind and kept to their stooped labor, accustomed to these daily patrols. The heavy-headed buffalo showed no interest, not a raised snout or a snort, pulling plows somnolently, urged on by their masters but seeming to set their own paces, heedless of the men.

The columns walked enfilade to the end of the fields. They smelled a wind from off the ocean miles to the east, a salt wind they could taste and think of the surf pounding in, and the lucky mothers at Division on the beach, with the beer and the round-eyed women and the movies every night with no face in the mud motherfuckinghumping, but that's the grunts for you and they reached the end of the fields and regrouped, Rosie's team again bringing up the rear. The jungle ended abruptly east of them, toward the sea, and they saw the basecamp and the scarred, bull-dozed hilltop two miles away. Rounding a bend on the west, they came to the cart path that led to the hamlet, the huts and pole homes visible then for the first time, a quarter mile in the distance. A bamboo hedge grew dense and tall west of the path. At the sight of the hamlet, Schrader had become apprehensive. He was determined to see the book of poems returned. The girl had been too child-like, too much like his sister and he dreamt of her. But in his young life he had seldom been so disobedient, and the Marine Corps was an awesome authority to him. He touched the book again and glanced about furtively as if someone might guess.

Duffy was twelve or fifteen paces ahead. He turned around and called: "Time for a cool one, eh Davey boy?"

Schrader grinned nervously and was about to answer when Duffy stepped on the mine. There was a sharp blast and the ground erupted and one of his legs just seemed to disintegrate. Duffy was twisted and tossed in the air, landing in a heap, his clothes smoking and blood spurting from the stump like water from a hose. Something wet struck Schrader in the face and knocked him to the ground. In a blur he saw Haney dashing past him, then the corpsman, and Schrader was on his hands and knees crawling for Duffy because his legs wouldn't stand. Haney was grabbing for the artery, slick and warm and he tried to pinch it off with his fingers, but Duffy was thrashing about screaming horribly, the corpsman grabbing for a clamp while the screams echoed back at them and he and Haney tried to hold Duffy's arms, then two others, but four of them couldn't hold the terrified man still, and the blood gushed brightly across the path, beading in little pools and finally the corpsman got a clamp on the artery but it wasn't enough. Shrapnel had ripped into Duffy's groin and the shock was killing him. They could all feel him going. He sobbed wretchedly and his chest heaved like a buck deer Schrader once shot and then he was gone, the eyes rolling back in his head with an awful finality.

For long seconds it seemed like nothing in the world was moving. There was no wind and no sound, and the blood-spattered men clustered about the body gaped at one another as if in a grim vacuum.

Time for a cool one, eh Duffy?

Some of the marines had gathered around, silent and hard-eyed, muttering their first anger. Calderone stayed at the point, waving away the peasants who had run from the hamlet, and the radioman had contacted basecamp. Haney stood up stiffly, reeking of blood and it dripped from his fingers as he spoke numbly into the radio, while LaRosa put his poncho across the corpse and the corpsman looked at Rosie helplessly. Schrader still had hold of the body, on his knees with Duffy resting against him. Schrader stared unbelievingly at the poncho-covered face and when Rosie nudged him gently he staggered to his feet and turned his back on the sight.

Calderone got them moving, deployed them up and down the trail and then stepped over to Haney, hard-faced Haney who was saying words automatically over the radio but inside there was a voice telling him: one too many will break you Joe Haney, break you Joe Haney, break you . . . and Calderone lit two smokes, his hands shaking badly, putting one in Haney's lips and the look that passed between them was like the knowing and resigned glances of two very old men.

"They're sending the rest of the platoon," Haney told him, wiping his bloody hands on his shirt. "The choppers have to come all the way from Division. We're supposed to deploy and wait here."

"There's mean talk coming down," Calderone replied. "*Los hombres* wanna go into the ville and shoot things up."

Haney glanced around and shook his head. "We do nothing till the skipper gets here . . . Schrader! C'mere!" he called, and the farm boy hurried over unsteadily, rifle gripped tightly and his face pale. "You and me are gonna have a talk with the hamlet chief. That's him in the crowd, up the trail. Wipe some of that blood off you. Mingo, take some green smoke from my pack and send Cezeski and Willie out in the bean field to signal the choppers. Then you stand by the radio . . ."

He and Schrader cleaned off as best they could, and then strode menacingly up the cart path, past the marines who stood there with readied rifles, bayonets fixed, and bitter eyes in young faces. They were certain of one fact: the peasants had been aware of the mine, and they'd kept the knowledge mutely to themselves. Haney guessed the mine had been placed less than half an hour before. In his mind he saw a slight, dark figure coming from the jungle to dig the hole and set the bomb, smoothing over the diggings, replacing the turf . . .

A crowd of Vietnamese had gathered nearer the hamlet, a safe distance from the hulking *Nguoi My* with their sharp bayonets. The hamlet chief stood nervously in front of them, a handful of his militia around him, their M-1s held awkwardly and fidgeting at the approach of the two marines.

The chief was middle-aged and graying and he wore a service revolver. He bowed politely to the young corporal, because he smelled the trouble coming. *"Chao ong,"* he said. Good day sir.

Haney nodded curtly. "Tell him they're sending more marines in some choppers, David."

Schrader looked hard at the chief and spoke tersely: *"Nhieu hon Thuy quan luc chien dang den o trong phi-co truc-thang."*

The hamlet chief nodded.

"Tell him our captain is coming with Major Ky," Haney said. "Tell him Major Ky will want to question him right away."

Schrader nodded. These were easy translations, the military phrases he'd been taught by rote. But Schrader did not know the words for flower or peace. *"Dai uy Bullock dang den voi Truong-thanh Ky."* He saw the chief stiffen at the mention of Ky. *"Nguoi truong-thanh se muon ong hoi."*

The chief bobbed his head stiffly and spoke sharply to a militia sergeant, who hurried off to the hamlet. Without a bow or the courtesy due him, the two marines walked rudely away from the chief. Yet he was one of the few men without knowledge of the mine. He and his soldiers had been imported by the government only a year before. They had no family ties in the hamlet, and little affection.

Haney was back with the radioman. He struggled to avert his eyes from the poncho-covered corpse and his gut knotted again. LaRosa stormed up to him.

"What the hell's going on? LaRosa demanded, his eyes hot. "Are the fucking gooks getting away with this?"

"Wait till the skipper gets here," Haney said wearily.

"Wait! What the hell's Bullock gonna do? Pat their asses?"

"Go on down the trail to your team, Rosie."

LaRosa stood his ground. "They gotta pay, Joe! Me 'n Duffy go back to boot camp. The gooks knew about the goddamned mine and they kept their slant-eyed faces shut!" His voice broke then and he had to look to the ground.

The corporal, who was losing count of the friends he'd lost, put an arm roughly around Rosie's shoulders. "Keep yourself together, man. Duffy would want you to keep yourself together—go back to your team. The farmers will want to use the path when they come in from the fields. Make 'em go the long way around."

LaRosa nodded glumly and jogged back to his post, the anger churning in him. Many of them felt betrayed by the peasants. They had been through long indoctrinations telling them they were protecting the peasants from the terriorists, and a few of the marines had taken it to heart.

Long minutes passed before they saw the banana-shaped 46s land on the hilltop in the distance. In minutes they were lifting off again, whopping angrily toward the hamlet and Cezeski and White tossed out the green smoke and the helicopters bounced heavily onto the field of soybeans, their first green tips showing life in the bleak aura of death surrounding the squad. As the ramps dropped and the engines whined down, the hamlet militia appeared on the run behind the chief, and they fell into ranks. A squad of marines charged from each ship, Duffy's buddies, and Sergeant Larret was with them, halting them in two columns, awaiting the command of the man who stepped down the ramp next, Captain Bullock. With him was a slight, mustachioed Viet, Major Ky, the district commander.

Bullock nodded to the sergeant, and Larret moved the squads quickly past the militia who were in formation, ran them to the fringes of the hamlet and deployed them in a line. The two officers strode toward Haney, who waited by Duffy's body, there on the ground.

Haney saluted.

"They got poor Duffy, eh Joe?" Bullock was of medium height and stout.

"Yes sir. You want the details now?"

Bullock waved his hand. "Later Joe. They killed one of my best men, Major. We don't plan on taking that lightly."

Major Ky smiled thinly, showing a line of white teeth. "We do not expect you to, Captain. We cannot allow such occurrences in our secure areas." He had a soft voice. Haney thought he sounded like a snake.

"Then we're of the same mind," Bullock replied.

The major nodded slowly. "Let me talk to the hamlet chief."

"You go ahead, Major," Bullock said. "And maybe you

should send runners to all the fields, get everyone here, and then the chief can count heads."

"Of course," Ky agreed as he parted.

Bullock waited until Ky was out of earshot, then turned to Haney. Schrader was standing off to the side. "Get the body loaded, Joe. Then get your boys together and throw a picket line around the gooks as they come in from the fields. I'll sweep the other squads through the hamlet and round up everyone there—then we'll search their homes." The captain rumbled off toward the village.

Haney and Schrader carried the body up the ramp into the helicopter. Schrader reached for the poncho to look at Duffy's face one more time, but Haney held his arm and shook his head. When they stepped down the ramp, they could hear Major Ky's voice. He was shouting at the hamlet chief who was standing mutely in front of his troops. Schrader strained to translate and follow a few of the words. The insulting tone was apparent.

"You are a fool!" Ky spat at the chief. "And the people in your hamlet are fools if they think this ruse will succeed. They knew, did they not? Did any of them use the path in the late morning?"

"I do not know, Major," the chief said glumly.

"You do not know! Were you asleep?"

"Oh no, Major! There was much to do. I was very busy."

"Ahhh . . . You were busy. Too busy no doubt to have the trust of your people."

"I believe they are beginning to trust me, Major."

"Then why did no one come to tell you of the mine?"

"They are afraid they will be killed if they inform. You know the peasants are always afraid of that."

Ky smiled meanly. "And I also know it is your job to protect them. And if they are afraid, it is because you are not doing your job."

The chief only looked at his feet, making no reply.

"When the hamlet is assembled, you will account for everyone," the Major continued. "Then I think our American friends will want to search the houses. You will keep your people in order, do you understand?"

The chief bobbed his head vigorously. "Of course, Major. There will be no trouble. The people listen to me."

Ky spun on his heel and spoke over his shoulder. "Be prepared in case you are needed." And he walked scornfully toward the hamlet. The peasants, in the meantime, were coming in from the fields, finding the marines waiting and seeing their own militia stand by as the Americans shoved and harried them into a group, surrounding them with bayonets. More and more of them straggled in and were handled roughly. The crowd swelled, and there were children looking tiny and very frightened, and fathers shamed by their helplessness. But when they saw the marines in the hamlet going through their homes, the crowd suddenly got noisy. The Americans were dragging things outside and dumping them, overturning mats and cooking pots. Some of the men tried to break through the picket line and there was scuffling and the marines cracked some skulls. An old grandfather with hate in his eyes charged at Schrader and he hit the old man hard with his rifle butt, making him bleed, and his terrified wife ran up screaming and dragged him away. But it only got more unruly. The hamlet chief brought his soldiers on the run and began loudly to berate the crowd, his face reddening with the effort to outshout them. Peasants began to argue with him, shaking their fists, their eyes bulging with anger. The chief stomped his feet and shouted louder than anyone else, but it did no good. The crowd was about to charge the line of marines and they were ready to pull some triggers, when Major Ky came storming from the hamlet. His eyes were smoldering as he snapped his pistol from his holster and pointed it randomly at a man in the crowd.

"I will kill this man now if you are not silent!" he shouted. And he was not joking. Among the peasants he had a reputation for extreme viciousness.

The hubbub ceased immediately, and he began to harangue them: "It seems that this is not a patriotic village! You have allowed traitors among you to place a mine! And now you rebel because the Americans are only doing what they must. You are shaming your government, and I will not allow it!"

The major turned and barked at the hamlet chief: "You will order your men to shoot any who object. Any soldier who refuses will be shot!"

The chief nodded submissively, and his soldiers looked nervously at each other. It had become very still. Captain Bullock walked from the hamlet with Sergeant Larret, and he eyed the scene impatiently.

"Did you find anything of interest?" Ky asked demurely, holstering his pistol. He was smiling thinly and his eyes had lost their darkness.

"Naw. No arms or countraband," Bullock replied. "But I'm not satisfied, Major. It would have been nice to find some clues. But now we got no one to punish. And if they get away with it, it'll happen all over again. You know how these Commies are."

"They are dogs," Ky assured him. "And neither am I satisfied. We will of course replace the hamlet chief, but that is of little measure. What else should we do?"

Bullock tossed the question back. "What do you think we should do?"

Ky shrugged.

Bullock spat and looked disgusted. Each was of the same mind. The captain turned to his sergeant. "Burn the goddamned village, Mike. And everything in it."

Larret was an old Korea hand. He didn't even blink. "Aye aye, sir." He turned and trotted away.

The captain spoke to Haney: "Take your squad and give Mike a hand. These Vietnamese can guard their own. Ain't that right, Major?"

"Certainly." Ky spoke sharply to the militia, and a wail went up from the peasants when they heard their homes were to be burned. But Ky ignored them and continued to address the soldiers: "Is any one of you not loyal to the government? Good. Then you will all do your duties." And with that, Ky glared menacingly at the crowd, and the militia rifles clicked as bullets were breached. Fathers and uncles looked angrily at their feet, but the men were helpless and the crowd became stoically subdued.

Schrader found himself on the run toward the hamlet, his mind a little numb around the edges, struggling to piece together the morning's happenings. But he could only see the picture in fractions. He had hit an old man, one Wilbur Steuber's age and about his size too, and mom wouldn't like that but the dirtyfuckinggooks killed Duffy, killed him like the sneaking bastards they are and they could have warned us, but the children in the crowd looked so afraid and frail and mom wouldn't like that either.

When they reached the hamlet, some of the huts were beginning to smoke and crackle into flames. Haney assigned a few huts to each fireteam and the squad split up and Haney was left standing there. But Calvin Burgess stayed there, too. He looked at Haney and shook his head. "Not me, Joe," he said simply.

Haney didn't give a damn, one way or the other. What was one more burned village? What was a man, who decided to say no? Would it cost them the war? "Go stand around somewhere, Calvin. Don't look conspicuous."

Burgess nodded gratefully and walked away, thinking he never quite knew which way Haney was going to jump: would he be a stiff-necked marine or a human being? Burgess walked to the edge of the hamlet and slipped behind some trees that grew there. More of the huts were burning then, some hot and thick black smoke billowed into the air. All around, marines were throwing the searched belongings back into the flames. Burgess watched Schrader and Cezeski and Willie White torch a hut, fanning the flames angrily, their faces hard. Willie White was a brother and Burgess watched him and shook his head sadly, thinking someday Willie would know, too. Schrader was throwing furniture and clothing into the home, which was burning strongly then, and Burgess saw him reach into his shirt and pull out the book of poems. Burgess knew about Schrader's plan. He thought it was foolish but he admired the kid and then he saw Schrader throw the book into the flames and he understood that the boy had tossed part of himself in there, too. *There's no going back now, Davey boy*, Burgess was thinking. *Welcome to the war*.

All the huts were ablaze then and Larret signalled for the platoon to assemble and they double-timed out the hamlet and past the defeated and homeless peasants to the waiting helicopters, engines warmed and rotors turning, drowning out the crackling and popping of the big fire. The ramps closed and the choppers lifted and they never saw the hamlet again. In a day or two, they got a replacement for Duffy. But no one really got a chance to know him . . .

4

Haney slept restlessly, his mind filled with moving shadows and pulsing lights that imploded from bright, viscous spheres to dull, barely glowing embers then to nothing. He felt himself recede with the dimming lights, drawn along, folding upon himself and becoming even smaller until he was sucked into the nothingness.

Then the explosions burst on his dreams and Haney bolted upright in his cot, a low moan passing his lips. The sound was heavy with fear, and it grated along Haney's spine and he was ashamed.

To the north, the big 155s had begun to pound heavily, the salvoes thundering one after the other in a rumbling sustained fire. It was nice to have the cannon-cockers at hand. Haney recalled his first tour of duty, the sweep through Happy Valley with the Vietnamese Marines, when they walked into the pincers ambush, all of them pretty green. The enemy fire had slashed through them like a scythe through wheat, and they were scattered into pockets with little cover, losing the initiative to the Viet Cong. Combat inertia. Once your face is in the dirt, it's hard to get moving again.

But the artillery had saved them, had held the enemy at bay while the company regrouped and got off their bellies. But a lot of them had fertilized that valley. Blood rice.

Haney had his war the first time around and, coming home short-sighted, he'd thought the war was winding down and once would be all for him, and that was in the summer of 1965. He wasn't going to reenlist. He and Helen really wanted to live another life, and her pregnancy came and then his orders for Vietnam, and it was a bitter pill for the man, because he'd looked around in the civilian world and seen all the shirkers.

There in the darkness of the tent he felt the trembles come on him again, so he sat on the edge of his cot and held his stomach, his head between his legs. *Oh no! Not now! Who*

*are you? goddamnit! Who are you! Joseph Alan Haney, cor-
poral, silver star, bronze star, two Purple Hearts . . . no No
NO! That's not who you are! You're just Joe Haney and it's
okay if you're scared. Just hold it in, push it deep inside, bury
it, stuff it away with everything else about this stinking war
because you can't go home like this, all brittle inside like dried
reeds, you can't go home to Helen and frighten her or build
any kind of life with this fear-crud that keeps seeping to the
surface . . . Seven months and it's all over. You'll go home—
you'll live, Joe Haney. You'll live!*

And he sat there in the darkness for a long time, telling
himself he was not going to die, while in the distance the sounds
of war continued to rumble: booming, booming ponder-
ously . . .

Haney dressed quietly and glanced at his watch. The
numerals glowed. It was four o'clock. He slipped from the
tent into the cool, early morning air and sat on the sandbags
around the tent and smoked, trying to find a rhythm to the
sounding of the cannons: Boom! . . . Boom!Boom!Boom! . . .
Boom!Boom! . . .

Far to the west, perhaps ten miles into the hills, the glow
of flares dropped by plane showed faintly. *So that's where
they're shooting. Recon must have found something. Charlie
must be crawling all over those fucking hills.*

A movement caught Haney's eye and he turned and saw
the lanky, angular form of platoon sergeant Larret approach.
The man slapped Haney on the arm and leaned against the
sandbags, lighting a cigarette, his face showing concern in the
glow of light. "Get your boys up, Joe," he said quietly. "We're
mounting out. You can guess why."

Haney motioned toward the hills. "Something's on the
move out there."

"Yeah. Recon stumbled on a potful of gooks. Maybe a
regiment of regulars. Our whole damned battalion is mounting
out, even the companies down the line—I'm gonna roust the
rest of the platoon. Get 'em up, but no lights. There's no point
to making it obvious till the choppers get here."

"Are we going in first?" Haney asked.

Larret shook his head. "India company gets set down at
first light. We'll be right behind them—Let's get crackin'. As

soon as your squad's up, go over to the skipper's tent for a briefing." As he left, the sergeant again gripped Haney's arm. "We're in for a real donnybrook, Joe. Keep your head on straight."

Haney watched the man's retreating back, felt his own pulse throbbing in his temples and knew that it was starting then, that pinprick of chemicals that put him on edge and made his head and arms feel suddenly light. He thought quickly about the fitness of his squad. He had no grenadier. The new kid, Duffy's replacement, was eager enough but he had not even been on a combat patrol and Cezeski was green as a team leader. Mathis had been a pain, not pulling with the others, going home in a month and not giving a damn. He'd bitch about this, Haney knew, bitch that he wasn't pulled off the line with only a month to go — *Still, Haney was thinking, we're sharp enough. I wish to hell I had a grenadier, though. The extra weight is gonna slow me down.*

Then Haney stepped into the tent and woke Calderone, told him the news. Mingo was up quickly. Together, they went from bunk to bunk. " — Get up, LaRosa, there's trouble . . . out of the rack, Mathis . . . wake up, Willie . . . C'mon Schrader, get up . . . Up, up, up! No lights . . . I said no lights! Find your gear in the dark!"

Haney told them the little he knew, then gathered his own gear and stacked it outside. "Mingo! Get everyone out and check their gear. Make sure all the canteens are filled — I'll be at the skipper's tent." Then Haney hurried away.

"Hey Calvin!" Mingo shouted in the dark.

"Yo!"

"When your stuff is outside, get the canteens and fill 'em at the buffalo."

"Okay," Burgess yawned, fumbling with the laces of a boot. He had to shake his head to make his fingers work. Across from him, Schrader was having the same trouble.

"Time for the war to start," Burgess mumbled, tongue thick with sleep.

"They could have waited till I finished my dream," Schrader replied.

"Then you'd all be wobbly-legged, Davey boy. No good to us then." Burgess laced his boots and stood, calling to the tent at large: "Anybody with empty canteens, toss 'em on my rack." Then he gathered his gear and walked outside, Schrader a few steps behind, and they stacked it like good troopers and stood and smoked, listening to the thunder of the artillery.

"I knew this was coming," Schrader said quietly. "I've been dreading it."

Burgess shrugged. "Don't worry about it. When the time comes, you'll know what's coming down. You'll do like you've been trained."

"I hope so. I'm shaking already."

"Come on," Burgess smiled. "Give me a hand with the canteens."

They gathered them from the cot and walked to the buffalo, the wheel-mounted water tank, and filled them quickly, other marines standing in line. The camp had come awake, and men, low-voiced and scuffling, milled about outside. Back at their tent, Haney was just returning, and he called the squad to gather around him.

"Listen carefully," Haney told them tersely. "There's only time to go through this once. There's a force of regulars— maybe North Vietnamese—we don't know yet. But they're on the move, could be a regiment. No one's sure we can get to them before they vanish, but the Colonel wants to try. My guess is they'll stand and fight, or they would have vanished already. Choppers are on the way to us and the other companies down the line. Should be here about the time dawn breaks, in half an hour. We're going in with a full marching pack, two-hundred extra rounds, four grenades per man, and three days rations. Sergeant Larret is driving a mule around, and everything will be on it. Get your packs together quick. Any questions?"

"How's the Recon team doing out there?"

Haney shook his head. "Who knows? Maybe they've been spotted."

"Poor bastards."

"Are we the only battalion on this?"

"Right now we are," Haney answered.

"Jesus fucking Christ! We'll be outnumbered two to one!"

"I guess if we catch a tiger by the tail," Haney shrugged, "they'll send us some more help."

Somebody snickered. "Where have we heard that before?" And a few of them muttered agreeing sarcasms.

Haney could only smile bleakly. "Let's just pull together. We'll get by okay. Now let's move!"

Soon the sun was peeking like a fiery crystal just above the horizon, and they could feel the air pop as the morning mists began to burn away. Overhead, still at a distance and competing with the thunder of the artillery, could be heard the *whop! whop! whop!* of the helicopters.

The machines dropped almost vertically, in groups of three, like great spiders on threads of silk. The company formed in ranks and the lead platoon immediately began to enplane, filing by squads, running low and fast up the ramps. The noise was deafening.

Burgess, his body taut, watched the lieutenant for a hand sign. He glanced at Calderone, then over to Schrader, and they began to move, dashing for the ramp. Burgess found himself inside and the ramp closed. Then the chopper lifted and they all dipped at the knees, sagging with the weight of their packs.

They rose perhaps a thousand feet and began to circle, waiting for the other ships to load. Kilo company would go in as the second wave. India company was already on the ground. Burgess remembered what Haney once said: better to be in the first wave, and get on the ground while the enemy is surprised. *If*—Burgess mused—*if they're surprised.* He peered through a port and saw the sun splash a countryside patched with earthy greens and browns and reds. It was too beautiful. It did not register on him, except that it was the ground and he wanted to be back on it. He felt the fragile craft lurch in the air like a wooden raft bobbing and dipping on a pond. They were over craggy hills heavily carpeted with mute and sinister jungle. There were valleys lying long and narrow at the foot of the mountains, occasionally marked by streams that vanished under the mantle of forest.

Burgess glanced aft, toward the ramp, and saw the sergeant hold three fingers aloft. Three minutes. India company would be catching it. Burgess closed his eyes and leaned on the thin shell of the ship, and suddenly the gunner fired a burst that vibrated the bulkhead and jangled into his brain. He and Schrader bunched together, straining to look out the porthole. The sister ships were firing, too, and the tracer rounds arced downward like angry hornets, the brass from the machine

guns streaming behind the ships, flashing in the sun. And they
were taking fire, the enemy tracers rising sharply. Then from
the jungle canopy erupted a single huge shell, glowing red-
hot and stabbing at them effortlessly, coming straight at them
and Schrader and Burgess ducked ridiculously, their eyes wide
and frightened as the monster shot whooshed past them.

Burgess felt like a bird on a wire.

The helicopters began to descend, sharply at first so that
Burgess felt the shift in his loins. From the porthole he saw a
broad valley, dotted with brush and jungle outcroppings. The
green valley-floor was pockmarked with shell craters, and there
were the red-gray flashes of explosions and men scrambling
frantically. At the edges of the valley, gunships were darting
about like dragonflies, firing heavily, the blasts from their rocket
tubes billowing in the air.

Lower and lower they dropped, the hydraulics groaning
as the ramp opened, and everyone turned aft. They were raked
by fire, and shrapnel whizzed through the cabin. Burgess saw
a man from another squad grab his throat, blood pulsing through
his fingers. Then the helicopter bounced on the ground and
the running began.

Crouching low, Burgess scrambled down the ramp and
away from the chopper, following Haney's lead. His heart
pounded in his ribcage and his lungs heaved after a very few
yards. His legs were like noodles, and though he drove them
against the ground with all his might, it seemed he was hardly
moving. He tried to run faster, rounds crashing about him,
the whipcrack of rifle fire everywhere on the air.

He began to see in sharply etched impressions, frag-
mented scenes branded into his mind: an airstrike to his right,
not far, the jet diving insanely low and pulling out steeply, an
orange-black ball of napalm erupting like fiery jello . . . someone screaming "Corpsman! Corpsman!" the voice raking his
spine. Mortars dropping on them suddenly, Burgess hitting
the ground, panting like a dog, then on their feet and moving
again . . . the whopping roar of gunships overhead . . . artillery
smashing the side of a hill . . . All of it came in one great jagged
blur.

Burgess found himself flat again, gulping air and hugging
the ground, and he fought to slow his heaving lungs. The
adrenaline flooding him began to dull its razor's edge and the

jangled, out-of-control, pit-of-the-stomach fear began to lose its grip. He was left with a dawning distinctness, the havoc beginning to seem comprehensible, and a certainty of function came to him and he was better then.

Lifting his head, Burgess saw the line of trees that marked the bases of the hills: thick and dark and ominous, laced with the flashes of rifle fire. Three gunships darted in and began to work the treeline with their rockets and mini-guns. They flitted down and up, down and up, dipping their bloody beaks and the jungles shredded and came apart as though it was thrashed. The groundfire about the squad slackened, but behind them exploded the fire meant for the choppers still landing troops.

Burgess knew they would move. He looked to his left and right and saw a ragged line of men, fewer than should be, all eating dirt. He saw Calderone crooking his neck to watch for a signal from Haney, who had gotten behind them. *Come on! Come on, goddamnit! Do it now while they're pinned down!* Then Haney signalled fireteams on line, and Burgess scrambled to his feet, guiding on Calderone as they sprinted forward, legs flying, heart pounding, twenty, thirty yards and doing a nose-dive. Calderone was a dozen yards away and they showed each other hard lines of teeth from cottoned-mouths, bits of spittle foam-flecked around their lips.

The other fireteams came on line, and other squads, and the platoon and then the company was re-positioned. The gunships were still raking the treeline, and in the thickness little could be seen but flames and smoke. Squads at a time, the company advanced twice more — forty yards — eighty yards. The closer they came to the trees, the more fire they took. When there was less than a hundred yards to the brush, the gunships drifted down the valley to support other troops.

The fire became murderous.

It whined and cracked around Burgess like hail, and he felt this cringing urge to curl in a ball and hide his eyes away. But his rifle began to slam into his shoulder as if someone else was pulling the trigger. At first he shot wildly at the trees ahead, then a flashing muzzle that winked out and did not reappear. He rammed another magazine into his rifle and fired on another muzzle flash, then a third.

They moved again: two teams charging while one covered with fire, halving the distance to the trees, where the darkness now seemed not so dense. Once more they were up and on their feet. Burgess fired from the hip, fired and charged madly, not even hearing the animal growls from his own throat, knowing only that in a moment he would have blessed cover. But when he crashed into the brush, sucking air through parched throat, the covering foliage was little comfort. It was dim and he crouched low, squinting to separate shadow from real. Sweat burned his eyes. His chest ached. Ahead, he could see perhaps thirty yards, more where the brush was blown down. Somewhere beyond his sight, a hill began to rise meanly. He knelt behind a fallen tree and fired a magazine into the jungle. All along the line, men were doing the same.

But the firing died down quickly, the echoes faded away, and all along their front it was still. Behind them, in the open valley, the last troops were set down, and the big choppers hovered about, machine guns spitting. The gunships and jets were chewing up the jungle across the valley, supporting another company. Word was passed to hold up and dig in, but they'd all done that anyway. Burgess saw Calderone to his left, through the brush, and Willie White to his right.

"Mingo! You shovel and I'll look out!"

"Okay!" and Calderone shucked his pack and began to dig furiously, chopping and cursing at the red earth with his entrenching tool.

Burgess called to White: "Willie boy, where's Schrader?"

"Somewhere off to my right, man. The brush is too thick to see."

"And Duggan?" Burgess called.

Willie kept his eyes to his front. "He didn't make it, man."

"Oh Christ . . . Mingo? You hear about Duggan?"

Calderone's voice was rasping as he threw dirt furiously. "Yeah. I saw him get it. He just—"

It was then that Burgess saw the brush stir, knew what was coming and was raising his rifle when he saw the thing lobbed towards him. He fired blindly as he was dropping, screaming "GET DOWN! GET DOWN!" and it landed and exploded, the concussion slamming his eardrums. Suddenly there were two little men coming up on him, their rifles smoking, and he shot one down, saw the red holes punched into the man's chest and crimson foam in his mouth as he fell. The other one was coming on and Burgess's rifle empty, *Click!* —

a hollow sound like eternity but Mingo was firing and the man was killed.

All along the line the marines were charged with a fury that carried the fighting back into the open valley. Fierce, clawing, close-in combat. Burgess fumbled his magazine, caught a glimpse of Willie, tumbled to the ground, finally rammed the magazine home and fired a burst in front of White, fired to his own front, ripped a grenade from his jacket and yanked the tape and pin, threw it wildly into the jungle: *Carump!* He threw another: *CARUMP!* Then he saw Mingo rolling on the ground, legs locked about a man, down and up in a flurry, knife flicking in the man's eye and Mingo was on his feet scrambling madly for his rifle.

And as quickly as the attack came, it was over. The enemy melted into the jungle and the cries "Corpsman!" stabbed through the air.

Burgess staggered to Willie White. The man was breathing raggedly, blood bubbling from a wound in his shoulder and Burgess knelt over him, trembling, wanting to cringe again and hide his eyes away. *Oh shit oh shit oh shit!* "CORPSMAN!" he screamed . . . "CORPSMAN!" He found Willie's pack and yanked out the blanket and a skivvy shirt, and as gently as he could, he wrapped the half-conscious man in the blanket. Then he pressed the folded shirt over the wound, beneath Willie's flak jacket, all the while babbling to the man and to himself because the sound of his own voice was soothing: "Hey Willie boy, you gonna be all right. You gonna be just fine—This wound ain't much. You'll lose some blood, feel some pain but you're strong, brother, and you'll make it okay—Pretty soon the Doc will shoot you with some morphine and the pain will go away and we'll load you on a chopper and they'll fly you to Japan or maybe Hawaii. Pretty soon after that they'll ship you home—Hey! You hear that, brother? You're alive and pretty soon you're going home!"

White could hear the words faintly. Home sounded good to him. He tried to talk, but it was all he could do to nod his head.

"CORPSMAN!" Burgess glanced about frantically for the doc, and saw for the first time the extent of what had passed: the battalion was split in half, two companies along each side of the valley, the hills looming over them darkly. The plain was smoking in the bright sun. Napalm billowed about the fringes and helicopters were landing to load the wounded, the wounded that littered the field everywhere. Burgess was stunned by the numbers of bodies he saw, and he shook his head dumbly, his mouth open and dry.

The helicopters loading the wounded drew fire, erupting in plumes of earth and dust that whirled away thinly in the rotor wash. Burgess flinched and hunched over his friend, then scooped the man up, grabbed his rifle and lumbered to Calderone, Willie feeling like all the weight in the world to his spongy muscles. Mingo had dug an oblong hole, and they laid Willie in it just as the mortar fire began to traverse the line. The rounds crashed at them like giant's steps, crunching the earth and tearing the air with shrieks.

The pair threw themselves across White, huddled together and tried to worm as low as they could. The rounds exploded all about and they choked on their fear as though it was a squirming ball of muck right in their throats, clenching their eyes tight so the darkness would keep them safe. The rounds walked down the line and then past them, and as the explosions receded, they lifted their heads cautiously, and Burgess rolled to one side and lay flat, straining to see into the jungle.

"How's Willie?"

"He's out," Calderone gasped. "Still bleeding—I'll get something clean. Shoot any fucking thing that moves, Calvin! They might come at us again."

Burgess nodded and gulped water from his canteen, keeping his eyes on the jungle. "We didn't exactly take 'em by surprise, eh?" he tried to joke to Calderone.

"At least they wasn't dug in, man—*Madre*! If we come off those choppers against bunkers, it would be worse now."

Burgess snorted. "It's bad enough. They shot the motherfuckin' Jesus out of us—and you know they're diggin' in, higher up."

"Then they better send us help," Calderone told him, trying to dress Willie's shoulder as best he could, with the bulky flak jacket in the way but he did not dare remove it. So he wedged a skivvy shirt into the gaping hole on Willie's back, and bore down on the wound in front with another shirt. "CORPSMAN!" he screamed.

Haney came scrambling down the treeline, sideways, blood streaking his face from a gash on his forehead. "How bad's Willie?"

"He's lost a lot of blood," Calderone said. "He'll be okay if they can lift him outta here."

Haney handed him some syrettes of morphine. "Stick two of these in him : . . All the corpsmen got their hands full. Where's Duggan?"

"He's dead, Joe."

Haney grimaced and looked away. "So are Jackson and that new kid. Goddamnit! I can't even think of his name— Lewis! Rosie is wounded as bad as Willie, and Naylor, too. There's gaps all down the line, everybody's shifting left. Can you move Willie?"

"As soon as we stick him with these."

"How's your ammo holding out?"

"I got maybe two hundred rounds," Calderone told him.

"Me too," Burgess added, glancing at Haney quickly. "Got a little heavy-fingered, Joe."

"Schrader's got a couple cans down the line" Haney said, eyes darting about. "Take it easy on the automatic fire, Calvin. They might have trouble resupplying us."

Haney left them and hurried down the line, thinking of Duggan and what a quiet kid he was. Anger seared in him, anger at their own stupidity, at being set down inexcusably in an open valley against an enemy who held the heights. *I know what they want us to do, goddamnit! They want us to chomp on a leg and hold 'em like good dogs, hold 'em while they make their plans instead of keeping us back and sending two or three battalions in at once . . . Shit no! Just shove us right in there, Colonel! We don't mind . . . The bastards! Look at this! My God, I've never seen anything as bad as this. Not at Happy Valley, not going into those paddies west of Quang Tri or those hills near Dai Lap . . . Christ! The gooks are gonna be a motherfucker to pry out of these hills . . .*

"Hey, Joe! Over here!" Larret was waving at him, crouched low behind a fallen hardwood, the two other squad leaders with him.

"How bad, Joe?" the sergeant asked, as Haney panted over to him, the four of them hugging the shelter of the tree.

"Three dead: Jackson, Lewis and Duggan," Haney told

them woodenly. "Three wounded: Naylor, White and LaRosa. They'll need to be evac'ed."

The other corporals muttered and shook their heads. Haney did not have to ask how bad it was with them.

"That makes eight dead and eleven wounded," Larret said, his eyes red and hollow. "God in heaven. Forty percent casualties in the first hour."

"Somebody should have their nuts cut off for this," Haney said.

Larret only shrugged, and everyone was quiet for a time. The companies across the valley were being mortared, and artillery was smashing the hillside high above them. In the plain, choppers were still loading wounded. Still, it was more quiet than it had been, and they could be heard without screaming at the top of their lungs.

"Let's get the wounded together," Larret finally said. "This is a good spot, with these big trees. Detail one man from each squad to dig holes for them. Might be awhile before they can all be lifted out, or an aid station set up. Let's keep the line tight. When we're done shifting, space your men and have 'em dig in good. I don't think we'll move again until another battalion sets down, then we'll push up in the hills. Reissue ammo and grenades—no automatic fire unless absolutely necessary —and let's take it easy on the water. There ain't much else to say, now . . . The lieutenant is dead, Joe. So is the exec and two of the platoon sergeants, Smith and Kowalski . . ." Larret looked at the ground as he spoke the names. Kowalski had been his buddy since Korea, ". . . so I may have to move up and let Joe, here, run the platoon. Who will handle your squad?"

"Calderone," Haney replied. "He'll do as good a job as I would."

"Okay."

"Sorry about Kowalski, Mike."

"Christ, man. I'm sorry about them all—now let's get moving." And the Communists obliged him by shelling them again.

It was later in the day and Haney was checking on his men. Things had changed little, except that the aid station was set up and the wounded had been evacuated. They were mortared now and again, but the marines were well entrenched and the line was secure. When two patrols were pushed up into the hills, they took heavy fire from bunkers. Charlie had dug in for a fight.

Schrader was lying on his belly, staring at the jungle and wolfing down cold beans, the earth damp and cool and the smell of urine was not so strong then, hours after he'd pissed his pants running and fighting across the plain. He'd never been so scared in his life. He didn't want any of the guys to know.

Haney came up on him quietly. "How's your water holding out, David?"

Schrader started. "Jesus, Joe! You oughta make a little noise . . . I got about a canteen and a half . . . Did Willie and Rosie get off all right?"

"Yeah. They're in good hands now."

"We gonna move out soon?"

Haney lit a smoke. "Probably. When second battalion comes chargin' in, we'll have to make room for them. Maybe we can divert the small arms fire to us."

"I'm scared to death, Joe. I can't help it . . . The thought of getting out of this hole and going up that hill scares the . . . Well, I already peed my pants."

Haney slapped him on the shoulder. "Join the club, grunt. Hardest part's over, though. Those little yellow bastards up the hill, they're scared too. Thought they could keep us from getting a foothold. Now we're gonna chew 'em up!"

"Come on, Joe. Lay off the pep talk."

"Maybe it's for myself," Haney laughed, starting to move down the line again.

Schrader gripped his arm. "I hope you get to see your kid, Corporal Haney. Don't take any chances, eh?"

"You neither. Now keep a sharp eye . . ."

Cezeski was the next man down the line. Haney chatted with him a time, smiling, talking easily behind the facade he put on for the men. Then he moved on and came to Mathis, who was surly and angry he'd been ordered on the assault.

"I'm re-shuffling the squad," Haney told him. "Brown is working with Ski and Schrader. I'm putting you with Calderone and Burgess."

Mathis sneered. "That's just peachy, Corporal. Why don't you put me to guardin' the aid station or something safe. I done my fuckin' time in combat. You know how short I am."

"And I'm short-handed, Mathis," Haney replied. "I'd do you the favor if I could . . ."

"Yeah. Right. Some favors you do me. Put me in with a nigger and a greaser. You know I don't like those two."

"Gee, that's too bad, Mathis. Because right now they're your best ticket out of this place alive. Maybe you could at least work up a little respect for them."

"I'm in tears, Haney. Cut the bullshit."

"Take your gear and move up the line to Calderone," Haney motioned sharply with his head. "If you give me any crap, I'll have your ass. And don't smirk, you son of a bitch, or you won't be on any plane going home."

Mathis glowered at the ground and did not reply, and Haney spun around and hurried back up the line; he felt Mathis glare at his retreating back and his spine began to tingle. But Mathis only gathered his gear and, muttering curses, began to scurry up the line of men, past Cezeski, past Schrader and Brown to where Calderone lay stretched out in his hole, rifle propped on the hard-packed berm of earth in front.

"I'm supposed to work with you," he growled to the Chicano.

Mingo nodded wearily. "Stay behind Burgess," he told him. "When we move out, we'll start in column, and if we draw fire, we'll get into wedge formation. Burgess takes the point, you keep to his right and behind him. Not too far behind, Mathis. And keep your fire to the front and right. Remember that."

"I've done this before," Mathis spat, curling his lip.

"But not with us, *hombre*. Calvin is quick. He'll get ahead of you more than you think, and you can't see shit in this brush. You shoot to the left at all, you could be shooting at him. You *comprende*?"

"I don't speak spic, man. Wha'd you ask me?"

"I asked you if your mother would like to suck my dick. I ain't circumcised Mathis, but I think she might like it."

"I'll remember that, chili-gut."

"Right. Now move on down past Calvin, and start digging yourself a new hole, asshole."

Mathis stepped past Burgess and shucked his pack, but before he could begin to dig, Sergeant Larret hurried by, waving everybody up: "Platoon in column! Let's move it! Platoon in column!" And glancing behind, Mathis could see waves of helicopters coming over the hills, dropping into the valley and the enemy shelling picked up and the valley floor again began to crash and explode. He lurched to his feet and double-timed behind Burgess as the men scrambled into squad lines, thirty yards apart, and pushed into the jungle. There should have been forty-four men, but there were only twenty-five.

Soon they were at the base of the hill, peering up through the torn foliage at the slope thick and steep, and looking left and right Mathis could not see the other squads through the brush. He heard them, faintly, and they were trudging up the slope, leaning forward to balance the weight of their packs. But when the bunker opened fire on them the weight was forgotten. Calderone, Burgess and Mathis all spun out to their right and humped and gasped into line, the rounds snapping over their heads, drowning out the mayhem back in the valley.

Mathis was on the ground, crawling forward, seeing the hillside above only through patches in the brush. It was steamy and he was breathing hard. Straining his eyes he saw muzzle flashes side by side, shrouded in grays and greens. About the bunker were smaller flashes winking and blinking.

Spider holes around the bunker, Mathis was thinking, *but they ain't seen all of us yet . . . Maybe I can keep from being spotted . . .*

Looking to his left, front, he saw Burgess ahead of him and waving him on. *You first, nigger,* and he lay still until he saw Burgess raise up and dash forward. The brush was too thick to see Calderone. Finally Mathis heaved himself up and half crawled fifteen, twenty yards and threw himself on the ground.

He could see the bunker clearly then, but he had less cover. To his right lay a thick clump of brush and some shattered trees and Mathis crab-walked frantically and threw himself behind the trees. Burgess was out of sight then, though Mathis knew he was firing on the bunker and would draw fire in return. *Now the nigger can't bring it down on me.* He held his fire and wormed his way low against the fallen logs. He smoked a rumpled cigarette down to the nub, and flinched when bullets whined too near; but he was determined to stay there until it was safer.

A gunship came whopping low over the trees to work the slope, guns spitting, rockets whooshing and the bunker was blown apart. The squad began to move again, Mathis hurrying forward to catch up, finally seeing Burgess to his left front. Then he disappeared again, swallowed in green, and Mathis edged forward cautiously, thinking of the spider holes. Suddenly he saw a patch of ground move and he swung his rifle and fired a burst, then snatched a grenade and jerked away the tape and pulled the pin, let the spoon fly dangerously, counted two, then tossed the grenade and hit the dirt. It landed on the patch of vines and exploded before it could roll down the slope. Mathis was up quickly and running forward.

The camouflaged cover was shattered and peering inside cautiously, Mathis saw a twisted figure, dripping red, and he shot the moaning thing through the head and was about to move on when he noticed the other chamber, smaller and hidden by the body. Something stirred in there. Mathis tried to shoot at it but his rifle clicked on empty, and he was jamming home another magazine when the figure showed itself, and Mathis froze.

She was a woman, maybe a young girl, bleeding from her nose and looking stunned, reaching up with her hand. Mathis stared at her coldly, everything around him seeming to stop as a rolling, quaking heat shot his loins and he grabbed the woman and dragged her from the hole, slapping her to the ground beside the spider hole still smoking and smelling of flesh scraps and the girl looking very scared then with the air cracking and whining and the ground shaking from the explosions of battle.

Mathis shrugged off his pack, his eyes heavy on the woman as he tore off her clothes fiercely, punching her face when she resisted, beating her down and forcing apart her legs as he dropped his cartridge belt and undid his pants, all the while squeezing tighter and tighter on her throat with the hand that held her down. When she went limp he did not notice, knowing only a come-rush that grabbed at him as he tried vainly to push inside her, and he cried hoarsely as he spilled over the lifeless girl, and lay over her gasping.

Then he bolted up and looked around wildly, eyes wide

and nostrils flaring. There was nothing but trees and brush and no one had seen. The crash of battle again pounded at him, farther up the hill, and he hurried to put himself in order, knees weak and hands shaking badly. Then he shot the corpse three times, the last bullet smashing the nose and a hemorrhage squirting from the eyes. Mathis kicked the corpse into the hole and tossed in a grenade. He was zig-zagging from tree to tree when it exploded.

They fought through the afternoon, cursing and gasping up the hill, jelly-legged a hundred times, on their knees and panting, heads shaking dizzily, up on their feet and moving again, moving at them, always at them.

A gray and heavy dusk was falling when the two companies linked atop the hill, hollow-eyed and bitter boy-men, feeling betrayed by their own. They dug in wearily, fearfully, amid the broken and tangled brush and shell craters, and the scorched ground. The men were afraid of booby traps and the falling night, afraid of dying in the dark alone.

It was a waning moon that set early, and clouds covered the stars and the late night grew black and choking as a velvet bag. Few of them could sleep, though they altered the guard, as one post after another was probed and sharp, brief firefights erupted, with searing flares, and explosions of sounds raping the silent night.

They were mortared before dawn and when the sun finally arose it was seen through bleary eyes in foggy heads. As the first light grew, small fires cropped up everywhere. Schrader, Calderone and Burgess were squatting in a circle, cooking their breakfast in cans. Calderone took an onion and a bottle of hot sauce from his pack, and diced some onion in his ham and eggs and mixed in the hot sauce. He was grimy and his clothes were torn. "Wonder what's happenin' today?" he asked.

Burgess shrugged. "I guess they're still out there," and his eyes swept the green hilltops all around.

"Maybe we'll come across a stream and I can take a bath," Schrader said.

The other two laughed. "We'll just stop the war so you can lather up."

"You mean there ain't tropical waterfalls out there, with native girls waiting for William Holden?"

"That was the other war, fool. The real one."

"Oh. I guess we were born too late."

"Ain't it the truth, man."

Burgess pulled a can from the fire and hot-fingered it, thumped it, and a steaming ball of bread popped in his lap. He smeared peanut butter all over it and wolfed it with his ham and eggs. "I could eat a day's rations for breakfast."

"You know it. They'll have to fatten us up when we get back to camp."

"We'll have it easy for awhile," Calderone guessed. "Gotta take on replacements."

Replacements? New ones coming in wide-eyed and respectful, uniforms shiny-green, working into the pecking order of the old ones who had been there. Nobody said anything. Each in his own way, that unreal morning after, was saying some good-byes.

Haney found them there, eating in silence, and he squatted beside them wearily, trying to smile. The gash on his forehead was one long scab. "You ready to go home?" he asked them.

"What?" They all turned their heads.

"They're pulling us out," Haney told them. "We're shot up too bad to be any good. The other battalions will finish the sweep, but I don't think they'll find much. The gooks made their point. I bet they're miles from here."

"You mean leave now? This morning?"

Haney nodded. "The captain wants us off the hill in a couple hours."

They stared at each other dumbly. Was it only yesterday that it began? Could that be? ". . . won't catch any flak going down the hill," Haney was telling them. "But let's be careful just the same. I'll go tell Brown and Mathis and Cezeski."

They scrambled and straggled down the mountain, footsore and aching, and into helicopters and the valley sank tiny and dreamlike beneath them, a scarred, tortured waste land, and soon they were at the foot of another hill, the one they called home, and the dry red dust of the landing zone was stirring and whipping around them, and they trudged up the hill grimly, with bowed heads.

Schrader kept looking around at the men, again and again

as if just then realizing how few they were. The vexing feeling that he had seen it before came to him, and he shook his head in confusion. Salt sweat burned his eyes and the feeling was gone. But it came again when they reached the tent. Schrader was inside, standing by his cot and dropping his gear when someone rolled up a side of the tent and light fell on Duggan's cot. It seemed the emptiest thing he had ever seen. And that sight prompted again that taste of foreknowledge. Schrader glanced about the tent, somehow familiar with its emptiness as if he had known all along that there would be so few of them left.

There was little talk as one by one the men shucked gear and clothes and wrapped towels about their waists. Then in a group they walked to the showers, groping among the soap-slick weary bodies to bathe. And then to sleep. No one bothered to clean a rifle, not even Haney.

It was the next day that they heard about their change of duty.

5

From the mountains that jutted north to south, courting the coast, fingers of hills would stray now and again toward the sea. The valleys that lay between were lush and prized and in the war, which was a game of real estate, they became particularly valuable. The hamlet of Ap Do lay in just such a valley, and it became a focal point of the war. It lay furthest inland of the many hamlets in the valley, closest to the mountains, and anyone passing from the dense and rugged interior first passed through Ap Do.

In this hamlet lived Kinh Van Li, a respected man, one to whom his neighbors deferred in the everyday business of their lives. To a good listener, stories of Li might be told, stories about a soldier and a farmer, stories of a man who had come home and wanted only peace.

He awoke that morning before dawn and felt the mat

beside him empty. It was damp, and a breeze blew through an open window. Faintly, over the lilt of crickets and frogs, Li could hear his woman moving about the house. Light shimmered through the doorway from the lantern she had lit. He smiled. His father had once told him: of all the virtues of women, consistency was the first to seek. And Li thought it was true.

Sitting and stretching, he turned aside the netting and climbed from bed. Li was taller than the average Vietnamese, and his thick black hair was streaked gray. On the right side was only the stub of an ear and his front tooth was chipped. He dressed in his black peasants' garb and stepped into his sandals. Padding to the lantern-lit room, Li found a basin of water and splashed the sleep from his eyes. His wife was there, knife in hand as she hunkered over a chopping board, the blade tick-tick-ticking as she worked.

Each glanced at the other with little expression, nodding slightly, the woman looking back at her work at once. Li wiped his face and turned from her, stepping into another room, a tiny one with tapestries and no windows. He lit two candles and some incense. The room shimmered in the dim light, showing the object it housed: a tall and ornate altar, hand-carved and deeply polished, the candlelight refracted and reflected in its surface.

Li knelt before it. As was his custom each morning, he talked with his father. Li revered the man. And he knew this: each good son to have a good father becomes an extension, and as a generation will turn, that son becomes the father. It was as simple yet as profound a tenet for living as Li knew, it was the ethic which guided his conduct with family and neighbors. A sound family continues where a weak family fails.

So Li spoke with his father, whose name was Vo, and he was not the stern and distant figure that many fathers could be. Rather, Vo had been a compassionate man, one who took great interest in the doings of his children. So Li's talk was familiar: talk of crops and crafts, portents and doings. And when he finished, Li bowed and touched his forehead to the floor.

Back in the lighted room he ate his morning meal: rice cakes and salted fish, duck eggs and mangoes. His wife squatted across from him, stabbing with chopsticks, *các đủa*, at the bits of food in the common bowl.

"I talked with Mrs. Kim last evening," she said.

"How is the woman?"

"Well. But frightened. The American Marines will come tomorrow, and she has that daughter, you know."

Li knit his brows. "Americans! That is all I have heard for days now. The whole village is like a flock of quacking ducks."

"Can you blame us? What defense have we?"

"No less than ever. At least they won't steal our rice."

"But to live with us? Every day, prying into our business?"

"The village will prosper."

"And our young women?"

"Wait and see," Li replied. "The times I have worked with them have taught me some things. They can be terrible, yes. But not like the *Phap*."

"So now you love the Americans!" But the woman no sooner said that when she clamped her hand over her mouth and looked at the table.

Li was silent, swallowing his anger. So many times he had tried to explain to her. But his wife was younger and many things she did not see as he did.

"Would you have me fight them?" he finally asked.

"No, husband. I would have you here in this house."

"Do you know I might still be fighting if it were only a little different?"

"Yes, husband. I know."

But Li did not know for certain himself. Perhaps he just told himself that in his dark moods . . . He had fought a long time. He had fought the French, then the French and Japanese, and then just the *Phap* alone again.

He had always hated the French, and then they were gone.

But the Americans? Li saw them as inevitable. A man does not stop the wind with a fishnet.

"Luc will depend on you much," Mrs. Li was saying.

Luc was the hamlet chief, and he spoke no English. Li spoke the language well.

"We will profit," he replied simply.

The gray haze of first light was showing through the window, and people could be heard stirring outside. Some dogs were barking.

Their oldest son walked sleepily into the room, rubbing

his eyes and yawning. He was ten, and named Vo, after his grandfather.

The boy bowed politely and washed his face in the basin.

"Come and eat," his mother told him.

"Are the children awake?"

"Yes, father. Tran is sitting up and I twisted Lim's toe."

"We have much work today. Do you feel strong?"

The boy grinned. "Yes father. I am strong today."

"Good," Li replied, smiling. Then he rose and walked out of the house; past the small altar room and through the short hallway to the porch. He had built the home himself. Beside the average three-room hut, the house was elaborate. It sat high on poles, and was built of hardwood and bamboo, sturdy and open to the light. The well-thatched roof did not leak, and the house was comfortably furnished.

In fact, Li was considered well-off. He had a water buffalo bull and two cows, and some pigs and a healthy flock of ducks. He owned six paddies and two fields. Their yield was ample, and fed his family, with much to sell in the market.

His prize possessions though, were his tools. They were the means by which all the other possessions were obtained, even his family. Li was a carpenter. He was a master, as his father had been. When he was still a youth in 1931, the remnants of his family had fled to Hong Kong during a nationalist uprising against the French. Li remained in China, apprenticed to his father, until their return to Vietnam in 1940, to fight in yet another rebellion that would fail. Fourteen years of warfare would come before Li could again take up the tools of his trade.

But he had returned to his craft. And later, when the Americans came, he found the things they wanted built to be absurdly simple.

Standing there, on the porch of a house built with the money of foreigners, he contemplated what it meant that these same foreigners should come to his home. Li might have hated them. But too much of his life had been given up to hate, and it could no longer sustain him.

He heard a familiar voice, "*Chao*, Li," and he glanced and saw the hamlet chief standing at the foot of the steps.

"*Chao*, Luc," and he gestured that Luc should come up.

"You are on your way to the fields?" the chief asked.

"Soon," Li replied, touching the man on the arm.

Luc was shorter than Li, and a little plump, and he stretched and breathed deeply the morning air. "I cannot help but feel that it is a good thing the Americans are coming," he announced.

Li laughed richly. "Certainly good for you, my friend. Maybe now the Communists will not have your head."

The chief touched his own neck fondly. "It is such a little head," he grinned. "Why should they want it?"

But both knew the gravity of the jokes. The valley was fertile and the Communists had been making encroachments. That was why the marines were coming to stay.

Li looked serious. "Men like you are doubly dangerous to them, Luc. The good ones always are. The government is so corrupt that it is easy for the Communist to preach piety. But when they are confronted with a good man they cannot convert—" and Li drew a finger across his throat.

"What of you, my friend?"

Li shrugged. "I do not trouble them. I am not a chief."

"You might have been."

"And my head might have been on a pole, too."

Luc made a face. "It is not pleasant talk for morning."

"I agree. Have you eaten?"

"Yes, thank you. And I must go to inspect the troops."

"*Chao*, Luc."

Li stood there awhile watching his friend walk down the lane that divided the village. A neighbor stepped outside and waved to him. Then Vo came out on the porch with a water jar, and together they went down the steps and around to the back of the house. Li took a wide-bladed and blunt knife and two thatched baskets from his tool shed. Then they stepped past the vegetable plot and clump of banana trees, past the water buffalo tethered with ropes through the rings in their noses, past the hog pen with its fat sows.

A little beyond the pen the yard ended in a thicket of towering bamboo, deep and dense, with a small path leading through. The hedge bordered the hamlet on the long sides as it sprawled along the small road. From the air, the hamlet had the shape of a fat and stubby cigar. Around it like spokes lay the fields.

They walked through the hedge. Li stopped a moment to

look at what lay before him. There was nothing to excite the eye, except the hint of forests that lay in the distance. The land was flat and distinctly divided by the dikes. Green new shoots winked from the paddies, tossed by the breeze and washed by the murky water.

But Kinh Van Li saw things that were no longer there.

Like the jungle he helped the men of the hamlet clear over thirty years before. And the rocks they hauled and the dikes built by hand. Still the jungle retreated before the men, year after year.

Reaching with his hand, Li scratched the nub of ear that always tingled when he thought of those things. He was ten years old and working near his father, hacking with a knife at the brush, his arm weary and his mind wandering to other things. The brush had been thick all around him, and when he first felt the prick of those fangs so sharp and clean on his ear he thought he had been stung. Gasping, Li had turned to see the snake poised on the limb, and it was then that he screamed and his father saw. Li remembered his father beside him in a flash, and the icy burn of the blade and the blood gushing into his father's hand, the man clutching Li and weeping he was sorry as he carried him to old Tuc the healer.

Li stopped and looked down and drew his own son to him. He thought how different it would be for the boy. There was little tradition left, and the future could go but two ways. The Communists could win and restore some of the old ways, true, but bring a new dogma as well. Or they could lose and there would be little hope for tradition at all. Saigon was corrupt. Li had worked there and had been disgusted. The old were ignored, there was no charity, every virtue had a price. And it was the way of the future.

But the cities were far. He hoped the war could be weathered and some sanity in peace could help to keep his family about him. Family was everything to Li. Each member had the strength of them all.

He sighed at the memories. They treaded the dikes, the boy a few paces behind, looking at his father's back and trying to imitate his walk.

Li's plots were spread about; a few paddies there, a field and a paddy here. Rice shoots had been set in four of the paddies, and the fields were planted in soybeans.

The pair had zig-zagged along the dikes almost half a mile before they came to one of the fields. Two-thirds of it showed in new beans, and the rest was set off by a very small dike; his rice bed. The shoots grew thickly like turf, showing eight or nine inches above the ground. There were even cuts in the earth where they were taken for transplant.

Li removed his sandals and stepped into the mud at once. It was cold and he made a funny noise, twitching his torso. The boy laughed. Then he was in the mud, too, hunkered beside his father. The man had the blunt knife out and was cutting evenly at the earth, lifting the shoots in rectangular chunks and placing them in the shallow baskets. Vo took the first one and started off for a paddy. His father loaded the other somewhat heavier basket and followed behind him.

The jungle was close and the birds were singing. In the distance, unseen, a tribe of monkeys was screeching noisily.

At the paddy, Li stepped into the muck gingerly and felt around with his hands. The mud was loose and soupy, with two inches of water on the surface. Recently he had turned it with the buffalo and it was just right for planting.

They set to work.

In the course of an hour, one might see them stretch or sip some water, but mostly they stooped and planted. There was little talk. The sun rose and it grew hotter. They had to squint against the light reflected from the sheen of water.

Sometime in the late morning Mrs. Li arrived with the younger children, hearth chores done, and there were more hands to plant rice. She brought food. They ate a midday meal hunkered in the shade of the jungle. Then back to work through the warm afternoon, bending and stooping and uncomplaining, their crop too important, and even the youngest children were subdued.

Li was infinitely proud of them, this family that had come so late, after he had warred long and so futilely, losing everyone, seeing so much hope come to naught for the treachery. French treachery, and English and Japanese and American treachery, and of course the treachery of their own. Li had dreaded the day when the war would come to Ap Do, and now it was coming. The Communists wanted the valley. The marines were coming to stop them, and the people of the valley were caught between. In his life, Li had been both spider and fly, and standing there with the breeze in his face and watching his family, aching at the danger to them, he could only shake his head sadly in acceptance. Li knew he could never escape the war. His fate was bound up in it. For so many years he had brought the plague of battle to others, that to think of escaping the plague himself was folly. All deeds come back to a man, regardless of how righteous their guise, and the best he hoped for was to place himself between his family and the violence.

Li was lost in thought, staring at the sunlight shimmering in the paddies when he heard the children giggling. Shaking himself, he saw them all looking at him, grinning. Even Mrs. Li the perpetual worker had ceased planting and was watching him.

"What are you dreaming, father?" Vo asked, squinting in the light, and Lim and little Tran giggled again.

"Shhh!" Mrs. Li clapped her hands, a square-faced and handsome woman, and the children covered their mouths. "Back to work now. Let your father be." And the three of them turned to planting shoots again, but young Vo waited respectfully for an answer.

"I was thinking of your grandfather," Li answered, taking the cone-shaped peasants' hat from his head and wiping the sweat with a sleeve. "I was thinking it would be fine to have him here, now. He was a wise man . . ."

"More wise than you, father?"

Li smiled. "Oh yes. Much more . . ."

"Would he have killed the *Phap*, father? The *Phap* who killed grandmother and my aunts and uncles?" The boy looked very concerned, and Li saw his wife glance at him sharply.

"Yes, son. If your grandfather had been here, he would have killed the Frenchmen. Now back to work. Your mother is shaming us." And the man and boy stooped together and set the thin rice shoots and there was no more talk.

But later, in the hamlet, talk abounded. By dusk they had washed and the children were playing and Mrs. Li was talking with her neighbors. The houses were huddled closely and the ville hummed as small groups hunkered or stood together, and laughed and chatted busily. Most of the talk was again about the *Nguoi My*, the Americans, and Li stood with the village chief and a few others and listened politely, but he said little.

He was more interested in how the soybeans were doing, or when the people of the hamlet would begin to build the dikes in the fallow fields to the south. But there was time for all that, he knew, and it was the first time in history that marines were coming to live in Ap Do, so he understood his neighbors' desire to speak of it. Still, he would rather be in his house, reading.

When Luc invited them all to his home for some *roui nep*, some rice wine, Li begged off and climbed the stairs to his house, and put the village talk out of his mind. He read into the night, the hamlet quiet then, and the children asleep, and Mrs. Li was mending clothes. Then they went to bed and another day ended for them, another peaceful day, or so Li thought.

But that night the Communists came for him, quietly, and not even the dogs noticed. Home guards patrolled inside the bamboo hedge, and these were either part of the scheme or outwitted, because the first Li knew of it was the scrape of a chair that woke him, and two shadowy figures shrouded in a faint light.

Li sat up quickly. "Who are you?" he demanded, and his wife gasped in fear.

"We would speak with you, Mr. Li." The voice was young and hard-edged.

Li tensed himself to spring from bed. "What do you want?"

"Nguyen Tri Phan sends his respects," the voice muttered in the dark. "He asks if twelve years have changed your mind?"

Li's memories raced back over the years. Nguyen Tri Phan. Once, when he was wounded, Li had carried Phan on his back to safety. Phan was a party member even then, and when the Communists killed Li's uncle for speaking against them, Phan had counselled Li to do nothing rash. "We are the only ones who can win," Phan had told him, "but we cannot do that with all this divisiveness. If you would continue to fight, Li, it must be with us. What do you say?"

Li had said no, and his refusal made him suspect. They might have killed him too, but Phan had spoken in his favor. So Li quit the fight and went back home. Now the man was cropping up again like a ghost.

"The years have given me a family," Li told the shadows. "More than ever, I mind my own affairs."

"We would speak with you anyway," one of them said.

"Of course!" Li half laughed. "Should I light the house and serve you a meal? Will you drink with me face to face?"

"Do not treat us lightly, man! We intend you no harm, but you must come with us!"

Mrs. Li grabbed her husband's arm. "Do not go! They will kill you!"

The voice in the dark was impatient. "We would kill you as you lay there, if that was our purpose! You know that!"

"Only too well I know that . . ." Li replied, holding his wife. "But I will come with you . . ."

His wife pulled at him. "No! Li!"

"Shhh . . ." he whispered. "You will wake the children. Keep to bed and do not show any lights. I cannot hide from these men if they want me. But I will return safely, you will see . . ."

Li rose and hurriedly dressed, and like wisps they slipped from the house and down the stairs, where they hid beneath the shadow of the house as a pair of guards strolled by, talking and smoking carelessly. Then, with Li between the two intruders, they darted out the back and through the gap in the bamboo hedge. And pausing only a second, they began to run along the narrow dikes, crouching low, the man behind Li pushing and urging more speed. It was half a mile to the forest that lay west of the hamlet, and when they reached the edge Li was roughly blindfolded and spun around in circles. Then they set out through the jungle.

For a wearying hour Li held a man's hand and trotted along, sometimes on narrow trails, sometimes in the open, and occasionally he stumbled with a groan. At one point they spun him around again, and a little later they began to move uphill, their pace slowing but still stiff enough. Li was lost in his own thoughts, blinded like he was, when they slowed suddenly and came to a stop, and Li could hear many people moving about. His head was forced down and he was pushed through the flaps of a tent. Light glowed dimly through his blindfold. The air was stale and thick with smoke. When the cloth was dropped from Li's eyes, there before him stood the man whose life he had once saved.

Li blinked away the brightness of the lantern and locked his eyes to the other man's, each seeing the changes in the other; the graying and the weariness. A faint smile showed on Phan's lips.

Li remained expressionless. "I hope at least you have something to drink," he said at length.

Phan smiled with his eyes then, too. "Yes, Li . . . and food. You look good, old friend. Here, sit down." He gestured with his hand.

There was a folding chair at a cheap card table and Li sat there. "You have frightened my wife half to death."

"I am sorry. We must be careful, you know. I wanted to see you and this was the best way."

Only then did Li smile. "It is good to see you, Phan. The years are heavy on us both."

"Have they been good years, Li?"

"If you could see my family, you would not bother to ask."

"I, too, have a family. They are my pride."

"In the North?"

"Yes. Perhaps I will not see them again."

"What was it that crazy Thu was always telling us?" Li asked. "That old soldiers cannot complain."

Phan shook his head. "I was not complaining. My family is here," and he touched his heart. "Will you eat, Li?"

"Of course. Was I not just dragged through the jungle?"

Phan poked his head from the tent and spoke a few words. Shortly, rice and pork was brought in, and wine and cups and chopsticks. Phan sat opposite Li and they began to eat.

They were alone in the tent. Their shadows were thrown on the thin and dingy walls.

"We eat simply here," Phan said. "You must be used to better."

Li jabbed the bits of food into the crock of *nuoc mang*. "Why do you say that? Have you heard I am a rich mandarin?"

"I have heard little of you, Li. I was sent here with a task, and I recalled that Ap Do was once your home."

"So this is to be only a friendly chat?"

"Yes. Of course I will try to pick your brain. You know it is the Americans that have drawn us here."

"Drawn *you* here, you mean," Li told him. "If it was only the Ap Do militia and Saigon's soldiers, there would be no need for a big gun from the North—you are that, eh Phan? High in the party I would guess."

Phan's eyes went to the table, then back to Li. "I am a servant of the people," he said.

Li grinned. "The pure altruist? Really, Phan—I remember your ambition, your dreams of glory in the Revolution. Can you still see your old self, from so high on the ladder?"

Phan grimaced, but courteously filled their cups. "What do we learn, from young to old? Must we always carry the flaws of our youth?"

"Always."

"Then they are grown over and changed. Do not judge me so quickly."

Li nodded his head. "That is fair. But do not feign humility to me, Phan. I knew the seed from which you grew. A good seed, but always too proud."

Phan protested, "The pride has been transferred! It is no longer so personal. It is pride in a struggle, the sacrifices of many."

"And many sacrificed," Li retorted mildly. "Some not so willingly."

"I was hoping that the years had tempered your grief for your uncle."

Li shook his head once, vehemently. "It is tempered, but not forgotten. He was a strong man. A patriot!"

"But he misjudged the times, Li! We could allow no opposition, not in the rank and file. The Viet Minh was our child. We fed it, we—"

Li slammed the cup onto the table and his eyes grew hard. "Do not tell me myths! I am not a schoolboy hearing your written-again history! The Viet Minh was not yours! It was ours, the whole nation's! *We* put heart and mind in it, *we* gave it strength, a strength that your Party used but did not own."

The two men stared hard across the table. But Li softened.

"There, you see?" Li said. "You have brought out old passions in me. The flaws of youth we cannot cast off."

Phan relented and grasped his friend's hand. "You were a good soldier, Li. One of the best."

"It is behind me."

"Would you be a soldier again?"

"No. Never."

"You answer so quickly—you think the Party has not changed, that we have not learned from our mistakes?"

"Ahhh! So now they are simply *mistakes* that can be righted. I suppose you can bring the dead back to life?"

"We can make a decaying and corrupt regime into a government that responds to the needs of the people!"

"There you go, flaunting the people again," Li laughed. "Which people, Phan? Not all of them care for your Party."

"We can educate them. Our system works, Li. If you were in the North you would see."

"I do not doubt that it works. But you cannot educate everyone. Some have reasons to hate the Party and its methods. And I do not speak of the bad ones, either. Do what you want with the bad ones. I have no love for corruption."

Phan sipped at his rice wine. "What do you love, Li?"

"My family and my friends. Once I loved a whole nation, and I tried to embrace it. Remember? Vietnam for Vietnamese! And we fought so hard and endured so much. For just that— a country ruled by our own—well, we have that now. And it has turned out badly."

"Nonsense!" Phan barked. "What you have now are lackeys—greedy men who dance for the Americans!"

"That is true. But they are ours, Phan. Our very own. We cannot disclaim them."

"But we can throw them over. We *will* throw them over!"

"Go ahead and do it. I believe you can. But do not expect me to help you. I have seen your two-headed Party at work. I do not agree that your transgressions will be justified by your success . . . You have killed many good people. And you will do so again."

"Yes." Phan agreed harshly. "Individuals count for nothing, not you, not I, nor our families. The Revolution has its own needs and we are all its servants."

"But you said you were a servant of the people. Which do you ultimately serve? The people? The Revolution? They cannot be the same if one rolls over the other."

Phan watched him closely over the edge of his cup. "You are still clever, Li. But sometimes words are only a trap and they mean nothing."

"My words only reflect what I have seen," Li replied. "If ever the answer comes—which of the two is ultimately served —perhaps I might change my mind. But you cannot explain away the terrors and the murders. You can only say that the end justifies the means, and I would not rebuild a nation on such a moral."

"We will rebuild a nation any way we can. That is the first task. Later we can mend the wounds."

"And if they run too deep?"

Phan only smiled. "Time heals all," he said.

Li kept silent.

"Perhaps tomorrow you will see things differently. After the Americans come and take away your home."

"If they harm my family I will fight them," Li shrugged. "But not under your banner."

"I was hoping you still hated the oppressors, Li."

"Which oppressors do you mean? They seem to be everywhere for the simple man. Did not your Party oppress my uncle?"

"Will you never be reconciled of that?"

"No, Phan. And as for my hatred, it was for the French."

"French! Americans!" Phan spat. "They are one and the same. Mark my words, you will come to see that."

"Perhaps—"

They lapsed into silence and picked clean the bowl of food. Phan poured more wine and offered Li an American cigarette. They smoked and kept their thoughts to themselves, listening to the hum and scuffle of soldiers outside in the camp. Even in the late night they worked and toiled with a dedication. They wanted to whip the giant. Finally Phan asked, "If I cannot enlist you to fight, can I at least use your eyes?"

Li sipped the wine slowly. "Use them how?"

"To watch the American marines. Perhaps you could tell me how they are armed, when and where they patrol, the usual things."

"Understand me, Phan," Li began cautiously, "of the people in Ap Do, I and my family will not hinder you. The others will take the safest path, as you know. The home guards you can frighten off unless the marines can make something of them . . . And that leaves one man to stand against you, and he is my friend. Because of him, I will tell you nothing."

"You speak of the hamlet chief?" Phan asked, raising his brows.

"Yes. What do you know of him?"

Phan made a dismissing gesture with his hand. "Luc is known by some."

"Then it is known that he is a good man. He—"

"Spare me the platitudes, Li!" Phan said harshly. "He is a lackey for Saigon, and you know we have marked him."

"So. Because you must kill him," Li replied, "you refuse to look at his soul. Don't you weary of being the soldier, Phan? Doesn't it seem to crush you sometimes, to be the perpetual killer? Luc cares for the people, and you the fighter in the Revolution for the people, you count his caring for nothing."

Phan was gripping his cup tightly, and Li could see the muscles of his jaw work. He wondered how far he could push the man before the friendship collapsed. But the lines of severity began to leave Phan's face, and he sighed and appeared to be suddenly tired.

"It is war, Li. Sides are chosen. Once we find ourselves bloodied, it is too late to ask what we have in common with the slain. Those we slay must be foes or we can no longer fight. You know that. Luc might be a good man, but he stands opposite me and I have my duty. It is often an ugly duty, but a man makes choices and must stand by them. Beyond that, words soothe nothing."

Li reached across the table and touched his hand. "It is crazy, is it not? We have our ideas of peace and justice, and in order to attain them we reduce ourselves to animals. Once, I cut a young French soldier's throat. He could not have been more than eighteen. In his wallet was a picture of himself and his sweetheart, and I remember asking for the first time: was he not human, too? But I could not bring myself to admit it because I had to hate them. It is madness, Phan. All the more so because we see ourselves rational and sane as we do the insane. I am glad I am no longer a soldier."

Phan sighed. "I see now I had no business trying to involve you. Forgive me my foolishness. Keep to your family, and I will not trouble you again."

"Seeing old friends is no trouble. But I will not feel better knowing you are behind the violence that is about to begin. And I must tell you, if my family is harmed you will have me for an enemy."

Phan stood abruptly. "I would expect that, though it would

grieve me." He pulled at a bell that hung in the tent, and the two soldiers ducked inside. They came around behind Li and prepared to blindfold him. "Keep your children away from the Americans as best you can," Phan continued, "and do not ride in their vehicles. You know this meeting must go undisclosed."

"Of course," Li replied, but he knew it would trouble him.

Phan smiled. "You were always discreet."

Li stepped around the table and embraced him. "Goodbye, old friend. Maybe there will be better circumstances another time."

"Let us hope so."

The cloth was tied about Li's face and he was led from the tent into the night. The guides seemed gentler with him on the return, and the trip was not as arduous.

After a time, they halted and let go of his hand. Li stood there quietly waiting to continue, and it was a minute before he realized he was alone. Quickly he undid his blindfold, only to find himself at the treeline, before the paddies of Ap Do. He looked around and saw no sign of anyone, and muttered to himself.

It was in his own backyard that he scuffed a rock and set the dogs to barking. In seconds, a pair of homeguards were running toward him, rifles at the ready.

"Who is there!" one of them demanded.

"It is only I."

"Oh, Mr. Li. What are you doing out?"

"I thought I heard a noise. I came to investigate."

"Did you see anything?"

Li chuckled low. "Only a ghost, it seems." And he stepped past the puzzled guards and into his house, to calm his frightened wife.

6

The convoy came rumbling and clanking through the valley, down the narrow road with peasants scurrying sidewise, the big groaning trucks looming monstrously over the pushcarts and spider-legged farmers. The marines were armed and armored, only the flash of faces beneath helmets and the bare arms showed them to be flesh and blood, and the faces were jaw-jutted and hard. The platoon was now mostly replacements, unseasoned, only three weeks after the bloody debacle in that *other* valley, the one that had no name. But the new men were quick to convey the mood of the veterans, and there was no skylarking in the trucks that looked like plated porcupines with the rifles poking out.

It was April, 1966, and the ground was drying out and the convoy was tossing dust lightly. They saw the red cloud from the open end of the hamlet, by the roadside, Luc the chief and the headmen and the militia all lined up neatly, the women and children standing behind, the small crowd buzzing with talk. Li was with the elders, amused at their nervousness but too polite to show his amusement. Li was prepared to like the Americans, but not to court their favor. Like Luc the chief, Li could smell the changes on the winds, but unlike Luc he was not so certain just how the new winds might blow. So he stood calmly amid the apprehensive mutterings and listened politely if he was addressed, but his mind was on other things.

The morning sun was climbing high when the convoy slowed and halted before the entrance to Ap Do, two jeeps in front, five big trucks, and a jeep in the rear. A straight-backed lieutenant and tall, skinny sergeant stepped from one jeep as the men jumped smartly from the trucks and fell silently into ranks with rifles slung on their shoulders. Quickly they were a grim and deadly phalanx, with eyes staring sharply ahead. For weeks they had been coached on the importance of military bearing while they were among the Viets, and the native militia could only gawk at them and squirm restlessly. They looked puny and ineffective alongside these giant marines.

The lieutenant saluted politely and little Luc returned the salute sternly and proudly and all the elders bowed. The militia clumsily presented arms in the American fashion — Luc had drilled them for a week — and they stood there awkward and grinning, with their rifles canted at any angle.

The lieutenant muttered something to the sergeant who called out, "Lance Corporal Schrader!" and Li watched as another tall marine stepped from ranks and hurried forward. He was younger than the lieutenant, but there was a difference between them and Li sensed it right away. This lance corporal was no green recruit. Li watched as Schrader saluted the lieutenant and then Luc, and then he began to speak in Vietnamese. "This is Lieutenant King and this is Staff Sergeant Larret of the United States Marine Corps. They would like to say that we are very proud to be in Ap Do. And we are ready to help Ap Do to remain free."

Schrader had practiced hard with his language books and the dialect was almost right and all the Viets in earshot beamed and nodded approvingly, disarmed at the little speech. But Schrader stood there stone-faced.

"We are pleased to have you among us, lance corporal," Luc bowed. "I am Tho Ban Luc, the village chief, and these men are the elders." And Li bowed slightly with the others and the three marines bowed stiffly in return and Schrader translated for the officer.

"Tell them the district commander will arrive tomorrow," the lieutenant said. "Tell them he is coming with a marine major, to explain how we will, uh, work together."

Schrader did pretty well. He botched the phrase "to work together," *lám viec cúng cá*, but he talked around it until Luc understood.

"Your Vietnamese is very good," Luc said to him, being polite. "It will be useful to have you here. We have a translator, too."

"A man who speaks English?" Schrader asked, looking suddenly relieved.

"Yes."

"One of the Viets speaks English, sir."

The young lieutenant raised his brows. "That's good news. Who is it?" and his eyes swept the crowd.

But Li kept his place until Luc gestured, and then he stepped forward, putting his hand out first to the young lance corporal. "I am Kinh Van Li. I am pleased to meet you."

Schrader, surprised at the western gesture, took his rifle sling with his left hand across his chest in order to shake Li's hand. "How do you do, sir . . ." and he introduced the others, somewhat stiffly, the proper Midwestern boy with Sunday's guests.

Li spoke with them, small talk, and his English was quite good and none of the Americans knew what to make of him, obviously an educated man in peasants' garb and with mud on his feet. If Schrader closed his eyes he could still smell the powder from the battle in the valley. He could hear the cries and smell the blood-sweet ground, and the gooks had done it—the slant-eyed little bastards—and here was this gook smiling openly, and his handshake was strong, and Schrader's dad always said to judge a man by how he held your gaze. There was no deceit or retreat in Li's eyes. Schrader was confused. He had been a good kid and he did not want to hate anyone. But the war was forcing it on him. As he glanced around as the bosses made their talk he saw the hard-working faces of people who lived an iffy-chancy life, and he knew then that he had come to live in another small farming town, and the talk around the square would be just like the talk in Otterville or Carrollton. All of a sudden Schrader did not feel such a stranger. But it passed. The faces turned dark and foreign and Duffy was screaming and the mine would be there beneath his own feet someday . . .

"Schrader!" The lieutenant's voice snapped at him.

"Sir!"

"I said fetch me the maps from the jeep."

"Aye aye, sir," snapping to attention, smartly about-facing, Schrader double-timed to the jeep glancing sidewise at the squad standing tall, Haney half amused, Calderone wanting to laugh because Schrader was caught doping off. He hurried back to the group of men. "Here's the maps, sir."

The officer was now speaking to Li, who was translating to Luc, and Schrader stood aside mutely, not knowing whether to stay, or return to his place in ranks. The morning sun was climbing high and he began to sweat beneath his helmet and his eyes salted, but he would not wipe his eyes or shake his head because that would not be soldierly. Schrader did not think the protocol was a lot of bullshit. He liked being a marine. He was proud. And though he could not see it or begin to understand it, the protocol—the hardnosed bearing—was a shield that kept these foreign people and their strange ways at arm's length. He was tired of seeing their women squat and shit in the fields, he was tired of betel-nut stained teeth and old broken bodies that could barely get around, he was tired of watching children dig through garbage dumps and fight for scraps and he was oh so tired of the big-toothed grins and bobbing, smiling cheerfulness that held who knew what kind of lies and treachery.

Once before they had protected a village, not like this exactly, not living with them but they had chased Charlie out so he couldn't steal their rice or their sons but the gooks had stood by in silence and Duffy went home in a body bag and this place would be no different. Schrader was sure of that. Three months in the country had taught him that much. Yes, they were farmers and he was a farmer, but he did not understand them. If thieves had come into their valley back in Missouri to steal their corn and wheat, his family would fight them and they'd be damned grateful to anyone who lent them a hand. These people have no fucking gratitude, Schrader was thinking, his eyes sweeping the crowd. Where were the whores? he wondered. When would some wrinkled *mama-san* set up shop with cold beer and only lukewarm pussy from boom-boom girls whose breath was fish and chewing gum. They were pretty enough, sure, sleek and fine-boned and they made you want them. But they delivered like robots. Not like Becky Chaffee who loved to do it in the back of her dad's pick-up with hay down her ass and who threw you about like Mr. Leutweiler's steers on a chilly morning.

The group of bosses began to walk around the perimeter of the hamlet and Schrader stepped along with them.

"Put the men at ease, Sergeant," the lieutenant said. Then he continued speaking with Li, and they all relaxed a little. Schrader mopped his brow with a regulation green handkerchief.

"I understand there's a hill that juts out apart from the mountain range, west—northwest of here," the officer was saying as they walked.

"Yes. We call the hill old woman's back," Li replied, Luc standing close and straining to understand. "*Gai cua dan-ba gia . . .*" Li told him quickly, and Luc nodded understandingly. The marines would be nervous about the hill.

"It is perhaps four kilometers," Li said, and he pointed, but they could not see the countryside for the bamboo hedge that encircled them. The hedge was so tall it hid even the mountains in the background.

"That'll have to come down, Mike," the lieutenant said to Larrett, nodding at the hedge.

"Yes sir. We'll need fields of fire."

Li perked his ears at the remark but said nothing. The *Phap* had burned down the hedge in 1931, along with the hamlet. Both had grown back.

They made a quick circuit of the enclosure, Schrader noting the neat gardens and ordered huts and the water buffalo and hogs sleek and healthy. Maybe three hundred peasants, thirty or forty militia and four hundred acres fallow or under plow. Schrader had guessed that much coming in on the truck. The hamlet itself took up no more than five acres.

"Tell the chief," the officer said to Li, "tell him we will start work now on a temporary camp outside the hedge. We'd better be dug in by dark. Tomorrow, I'm afraid that nice bamboo will have to be cut down. The barbed wire we put in its place is better protection anyway."

Li nodded and spoke to Luc, who smiled hugely and replied that anything the marines needed to do for defense was okay. Go right ahead. Li told the lieutenant word for word, but he did not feign Luc's enthusiasm. He knew the hedge must go, but it saddened him nonetheless. Barbed wire would not shade his sows in the afternoon.

"If you'll excuse us, sir," the lieutenant said, after saluting Luc, "I'll call on you later in the day," and they all saluted and bowed and Schrader smiled wanly at Li who was complimenting him on his Vietnamese. Then the marines strode away and Sergeant Larret marched the platoon away from the hamlet and the trucks groaned along behind. Immediately the *Nguoi My* set to work and the peasants who had come from the fields to see the fire-breathing marines went back to their tasks with new gossip and portents. They would have a lot of money to spend, yes, and they will trifle with your daughters another said. But no. Madame Xiap was bringing some girls from Danang. The daughters would be safe. Yes! But will our husbands, another wailed? And they laughed at the joke. No one but the *Nguoi My* could pay Madame Xiap's prices.

Luc took Li by the arm and led him off to the side. "They are not monsters, eh Li? I do not think they will eat our babies."

"No, my friend. But they will devour your esteem if you let them."

Luc glanced at him sharply. "What do you mean?"

"I mean that the people will continue to respect you only if they see that the Americans respect you."

"And you think they will not?"

Li pursed his mouth in thought. "There was disdain in their eyes. They will try to always have their way. Sometimes you must say 'no' to them."

"Yes, and each time I refuse them they can go to the district commander."

"So?" Li replied. "You have stood up to the government many times. When they want too much rice, you tell them no. When they want men we cannot spare, you tell them to look elsewhere. Why should it be different with the Americans?"

Luc lit a cigarette and inhaled deeply before answering. "Times are changing," he finally said. "Once I could defy the district government, it is true, and they would gnash their teeth but leave me alone. I have been as popular as most chiefs have not, nowadays. And there has been little intrigue here. But now there are soldiers pouring down from the North and their supply trails are not far west of here. This little valley has become important. You can see the shapes of things. Only the Americans can keep out the Communists. They are the big bosses now. To defy the little bosses of the district is one thing. But to defy the Americans is now an affront to Saigon."

"Saigon is far away," Li commented.

"Yes, it has always been too far or too close," Luc told him. "When they are poking into our business they are too close. But when you are alone at night, and your ears are straining at strange noises and your guards are poorly trained and you never know where the enemy is—then, my friend, Saigon is much too far away. And lately I have been afraid."

Li nodded silently.

"You think I am a coward?"

"No, Luc. We all know fear."

"But all of us are not chiefs."

"We are all human, though. If the times must change, then there is no blame for changing with them."

Luc smoked the last of his cigarette and dropped it on the ground. "Blame is like a vulture," he said. "It always lands on the losers."

* * *

It was late and the frogs were croaking and the night breeze was stirring gently. Mrs. Li was snoring and her husband lay smoking, the ash glowing faintly in the soft darkness and Li there with an arm propped behind his head could not sleep. He was thinking about Phan, out there somewhere on the slopes of the mountains, out past old woman's back under the dense and protecting forest in their quiet, disciplined camps with their fanatic zeal and the way they had learned to fight. The way the Europeans with their extravagance in arms had taught them to fight—quick jabs, nothing wasted, back-pedal and dance away, saving the flat-footed, toe-to-toe brawling until certain you could win. Phan would not wait long, Li knew that. He would not let the Americans march into Ap Do and the surrounding hamlets uncontested. With Russian supplies, they were not so lean and hungry as in the old days. But Phan would fight the same way.

Li's body was tired from an afternoon in the fields, and the crickets were lulling him to sleep when the sounds drifted to him distantly and touched old places in his mind—Whoomph! Whoomph! like a giant whuffing a flame—and Li was suddenly awake and rolling from bed, shouting to his wife, "Quickly! Quickly! The children! Under the house!" And together they were running and snatching up their family as mortar rounds tore the air overhead and began to explode. But not in the hamlet. The Communist gunners were shelling the marine camp further away, along the road, and as Li raced down the steps clutching his daughter with his heart in his mouth, he saw the flash of explosions in their camp, through the gateway in the bamboo.

They hurried under the house and into the dug-out shelter, the little girl Lim whimpering and clutching at Li as the barrage continued. Li held her tight and stroked her hair, listening and counting the rounds and guessing six gunners, very good at their craft, and firing from atop the old woman's back. He knew the marines could see the muzzle flashes from their camp, if the officer was any good and not cowering in his hole. They would already have the co-ordinates of the hill and soon enough the *Nguoi My* would reply with artillery. But the gunners on the hill could still fire many more rounds. And Li was still counting and the little girl still clutching and the whole family squeezed and breathing in the cramped dug-out when there came a ponderous silence and the barrage was over.

Li then began to count the seconds, imagining the gunners frantically grabbing up baseplates and red-hot mortar tubes, hurrying, hurrying to get off the hilltop before the heavy-handed *riposte*. He had not counted to thirty, hearing faint shouts from the marine camp. when the reply of artillery shrieked above and thunder sounded distantly from the slope of *gai cua dan-ba gia*, the old woman's back.

They stayed crouched in the shelter, the children silent but trembling, the hamlet silent, all the Viets huddling here or there except Luc the chief hurrying about, ordering the militia back to their posts, urging courage and watchfulness, going from hut to hut to reassure folks. All the militia was called out and they posted around the hamlet while the artillery wailed and crashed. This was their reintroduction to the war, having lived somewhat secure for a decade, putting up only with occasional government troops sweeping through and leaving their marks like dogs pissing, putting up only with the Communists passing through sometimes and stealing food or lopping off a head, someone else's head, or shanghaiing a few young men, someone else's sons. And huddling around the hamlet, many of them were thinking that the old trade-off wasn't so bad. Much better than a full-scale war. That's what they would have now, a full-scale war if the marines stayed. But others in the hamlet were more stout-hearted than that.

The American artillery ceased thundering and the night became heavily quiet again. Long minutes passed before muffled voices could be heard about the hamlet, people scuffling restlessly and the muted cries of infants. The dawn would bring a hard day's work and the peasants needed their sleep. Leave the worry to Luc and his soldiers. If the Communists came, theirs would be the heads they wanted. So one by one, the families returned to their beds and mats. Luc let them go. He recalled half his militia and reposted the rest, checked their rifles, buoyed them up with confident talk. Li could hear him chattering with the guard behind Li's house. There were a number of pathways through the bamboo hedge and Luc would keep two men at each one. His best men tonight, the ones who would not shirk or fall asleep.

In the darkness, Li could make out his wife looking at him questioningly.

"It is over for now," he said to her and gathered his children close. "Go with your mother, back to bed. The war tonight was for the Americans. Good little children are safe." He hugged them and squeezed his wife's hand as they stepped from the shelter. "I'll come to bed soon, Nhi. Do not worry." He pushed them along gently and listened as they padded up the steps, thinking that the danger was not really past. The Communists could attack the hamlet, but this was not likely at this stage. First, they would try to win over the people. Yet, if they attacked the marine camp from the Ap Do side, the effect would be equally bad. The American ground fire would tear through the hamlet and later, of course, the Communists could righteously claim that it was not *their* bullets that did the damage.

Li was thinking this when he stepped behind his house. Beyond the hog pen and staked buffaloes, the big bull was nervous and nuzzled at him, and Li stroked the soft nose as he walked past. Luc was still talking with the guards, there by the hedge tunnel where the prior night the Communists had slipped into the hamlet. If two had sneaked in, why not twenty? Who were their men inside the hamlet? Perhaps in the militia? Li knew that he must break his pledge to Phan, and tell Luc some things. He knew also, despite his hopes, that he could not remain neutral. Only three options faced him: join the Communists, join the government, or take his family to a safer village, which would really be only a postponement of choices.

Li could not forgive the *Cong* for killing his uncle, for murdering so many of their own in 1946, when they actually joined with the hated French to purge other Nationalists groups from the Viet Minh. Other patriots! Proud fighters! Li's throat tightened at the memories. He once had friends in a secret camp that was massacred by the French, after the Communists had revealed the whereabouts of the camp. He once had friends who had gone to a truce and been shot down by the French, while the Communists turned their backs. He once had friends who the Communists had betrayed to the French for torture and mutilation, and they were left in the sun to rot with their genitals crammed in their dead and gaping mouths.

There was no end to the treachery, all in the name of the

peoples' revolution, and even the blatant and disgusting corruption of the Saigon government could not push Li back into their camp. He and remained, it is true, for seven more years after the purges, masking his feelings, speaking no politics and he was always suspect, but the French had still been there and Li hated the *Phap* more than anything, and he ached to kill them, to cut their throats and watch them kick like dying pigs. He had been a fine and fearless officer, but when the French were broken at Dien Bien Phu, Li quit the Viet Minh in disgust. At one tense moment, Phan had spoken for him, Phan whom he had carried through a swamp, and Li was allowed to leave because even back then Phan was gaining respect. And now the man was back again, a shadow from the past, but to Li he was no longer a friend. Not when Li must clutch his own children in the night. So Li's choice of sides seemed clear-cut and simple. Except nothing in war is ever really simple—certainly not the events in Li's life, which had brought him to this point; not the aching fear for family that he had just passed through, after twenty years as a soldier and bearer of death. And he thought he had known it all, every emotion, every aspect of war but he had been a fool. Losing an uncle or a friend was not like losing your own child. Oh no. His children were all that remained of *him*, Kinh Van Li, the man who had killed and warred and smelled nothing but sickly-sweet decaying flesh, the man who was only a brittle shell without his family. What a fool you were, Li, to speak with Phan so removed from feeling. Who did you think you were? The proud young captain who strode from their camp in 1954? You are that man no longer. That man had no weaknesses because the years of war had taken them, one by one. But you have many weaknesses now. And you are a different man. Best you stand with your friends, or the tiger will pull you down alone.

Li waited a discreet distance while Luc instructed the guards, the young men nodding tersely and gripping their carbines.

Luc slapped one of them paternally on the back. "Is your rifle loaded?"

"Yes sir."

"Is the safety on?"

"Yes sir."

"Don't shoot yourself in the foot."

"No sir."

"And don't fall asleep. If anything goes wrong, shout your lungs out." Luc stepped away and walked over to Li, both of them old soldiers, and Luc lit a cigarette in cupped hands. "They're nervous as birds," he chuckled, "and scared enough to keep awake, I think."

"You had better hope so, my friend."

"What? You don't think I'll sleep, do you?" Luc rubbed his chest and breathed the night air deeply. "I like it better this way, out in the open now, the lines drawn. I have been nervous for months. But now the marines are here and tomorrow we'll circle the hamlet with wire and mines and let the Communist bastards come for us, eh?"

Li smiled mutely in reply and Luc gripped his shoulder tightly. "I know what you feel, Li. You've had enough war. You only want to raise your family well and die peacefully in bed. But that's not for us. Not yet. Without the Americans we would all be Communists within a year, or dead. But now there is a chance. It will be better for your children, if only we fight a little longer."

"And you think the Americans will save us?"

Luc spread his hands. "Look what they did for South Korea. They have remained all these years."

Li shrugged but made no response and they were quiet for a time. The night was very still. There was no sound at all from the marine camp, and no lights, and Li could imagine them straining their eyes in the darkness, listening for sounds and waiting for dawn.

Finally Li broke the silence. "There is a matter we must discuss, Luc. I was going to keep silent, but I changed my mind tonight."

"Oh? What is that?" Luc was still smiling and feeling expansive.

"I had some visitors late last night. I think you should know about them."

Luc suddenly sobered, furrowing his brow. "You mean here? In the hamlet?"

"Yes, my friend. They slipped right through the hedge and past your guards."

Luc put a finger to his lips, the implications coming to

him immediately, and suddenly he was glancing around suspiciously. "Say nothing here! The dogs! Right under my nose!"

And he led Li somewhat ferociously to his own house, and they talked in hushed voices and drank *roui nep* late into the night, and Kinh Van Li made his choice. It was only a very tiny decision in a big war. But it was all the trust and hope one man had.

7

"None of us like to patrol without a corpsman," Larret was saying, cigarette poking from his pointed face, smoke-slitted eyes blinking. "But it can't be helped . . ."

Haney was looking at the two other squad leaders, and the three of them in unison stared at the sailor, Doc Shelton the senior corpsman, who shook his head and muttered at the ground.

"I'm sorry boys, but there's only me and Hennessey. Between treating every cyst and sore in the hamlet, and vaccinations, and making rounds, we just ain't got the time to patrol."

No one doubted the Doc. Corpsman in the F.M.F. — the Fleet Marine Force — were tough and reliable, but the idea was hard to swallow. Haney had never liked to patrol without a corpsman.

". . . maybe in a few weeks they'll send us more help."

"Hell, Doc, it ain't your fault," Carter told him, Carter who just returned with his squad from the old woman's back. They had found nothing on the hill but powder-burnt and trampled grass, and Carter was still sweating and stinking.

When the lieutenant walked into the tent they all got to their feet. "At ease, men," he said jauntily, a young fellow not long from college. The grunts were withholding their judgment. "First, I want to congratulate all hands for their conduct last night. Pass that along. Not one damned casualty! That Viet who speaks English, what's his name? Li? He told me he counted over seventy rounds, but nobody got hurt. The men worked hard and dug in deep and by God it paid off! What was the final equipment tally, Mike?"

"Two rear tires off one of the 5-tons, sir. And a personnel carrier had the engine blown up. That's motor pool's worry. We lost four cans of ammo, a case of grenades and I'm afraid your jeep is beyond repair . . . And there's one other thing, sir."

"What's that?"

"They blew up the beer ration. Fifty cases of brew on that pallet and every goddamned can is burst."

"Crap!" the lieutenant spat. "I promised the men beer after they got the bamboo down and the wire strung."

"You want me to go supervise the work, sir?" Larret asked.

"No. That little chief has his militia out, and they're busting ass. What the hell are we gonna do for beer?"

The NCOs only glanced at each other saltily. "The gooks will see that there's no shortage," Larret explained. "I'll guarantee that, sir. The tiger piss is pretty damned good. And the gooks got the only ice, anyway."

"Arrange that for me, will you Mike?"

"Yes sir."

"You told the men about patrolling without a corpsman?"

"Yes sir."

"I'm sorry about that, men. I've bitched about it to headquarters, but so has every other platoon leader in the battalion. We'll just have to do without for awhile."

Haney raised his hand. "Will we get quick med evacs, lieutenant? Or will we have to go up the chain to battalion?"

"No, Joe. You get on the hook to me or Mike, and the choppers will come on our say so. I promise you."

"How many patrols each day, sir?" Carter asked.

"Just one. But a long one, a real mother! We've worked out a half dozen circuits on the map, but none of them are shorter than ten miles. You'll have to carry rations and three canteens, anyway."

"Any time off, sir?"

The lieutenant shook his head. "Not much. As best I can figure, one fireteam can take a day off in every nine. The schedule is roughly like this; every third day a squad pulls recon patrol, or guards the farmers in the fields, or drills the militia. And then on market day, a reinforced squad will escort the natives to the main village."

"And the mine-sweeps down the road every morning, sir?"

"Battalion headquarters takes care of that. Their troops guard the sweep and we keep off the road until they reach us."

"Strung pretty thin, ain't we, Lieutenant?"

"Corporal Carter, are we *marines* or are we dogfaces?"

Haney wanted to fart, then. The others felt the same.

"What did the hill look like, Carter?" the lieutenant asked.

"A gradual slope up the southeast face, sir. But the other side drops away steep, and all you can see is jungle clean to the mountains. The base of the nearest mountain is about two miles away from there."

The lieutenant nodded. "If we had one more squad, I'd keep men posted on that hill 'round the clock . . . But wishes are like assholes, eh Mike?"

Larret looked a little pained. "Yes sir. Everybody has one."

Nobody laughed. The officer stalled a moment. "Well now . . . we only have three radio operators. One will be in the command bunker at all times, one on the recon patrol, and one will be a floater. I want one good man from each squad to learn some radio procedure—give Mike their names— they'll need to learn spot reps, sit reps, med evac's and saluted reports. Not your team leaders, either. One of your riflemen. What else, Mike?"

"The M-60s, sir."

"Right—we have only four teams of heavy weapons men, but we've got six guns. So everyone gets a refresher course on the M-60. And I mean everyone. A complete field stripping and cleaning in quick time. We'll have to train the militia on the guns, too. You have anything to add, Doc?"

Shelton shook his salt and pepper head. "No sir. We hashed it all out before you got here."

"You're not treating any clap now, are you?"

"No sir."

"I want to know about any cases. No penicillin under the table."

"Of course not, lieutenant. That's SOP."

The fuzzy cheeked officer looked at all of them sternly. "Warn your men. Any malingering rates an Article Fifteen.

That includes venereal disease, chronic sunburn and drunkenness. We're too short-handed for any bullshit. That's about it for now. Your squads have their assigned details. The quicker it's finished, the sooner we take a breather."

They all stood up to leave.

"Corporal Haney. You stay a minute," the lieutenant said.

Haney remained standing while the others filed from the tent.

"Sit down, Joe—how about a smoke?"

Haney took the offered Chesterfield and drew on it slowly, eyeing the lieutenant through a haze of smoke. He had been with the platoon only a week and he was younger than Haney.

"Sergeant Larret tells me you're the best damned squad leader in the battalion."

"It's my second time around, Lieutenant. You learn the ropes, you know."

"How long have you been a marine?"

"Five and a half years."

"You reenlisting, Joe?"

"No sir. Not on your life."

The lieutenant chuckled. "Our advisor status is over, you know. We're running the show now, and there will be some good careers built on this war."

Haney looked bored. "If this is a re-up lecture, Lieutenant, you're wasting your time."

The young officer straightened his shoulders. "I'll come right to the point, Corporal. You were a sergeant on your first tour, an advisor to the South Vietnamese marines. I'm curious about the details of your demotion."

"I believe that's all on the record, Lieutenant."

"Yes, that's right. But the record is halfway around the world. You give me your version."

"I punched a gook captain," Haney shrugged. "They busted me."

"You struck him only once?"

"No sir. I broke his jaw, smashed his nose and dislocated his shoulder."

"I see," the lieutenant replied, simmering slowly at Haney's subtle defiance. "Were you drunk?"

"No, Lieutenant. I never get drunk over here."

"Then just what the hell was the reason, Corporal?"

Haney glanced about the tent feeling a little helpless. Everywhere he turned he saw authority, drab green, suffocating, humiliating authority and this lieutenant, this college boy with six months' training and gold bars like jailers' keys, this sonuvabitch was going to rub his nose in it again. "Look Lieutenant, I don't want any more trouble with the Crotch. My wife is expecting a baby any day now. I just want to do my time and go home."

The young officer was not the vindictive sort. He was simply overeager to command the respect of his men, and a little intimidated by the experience of his NCOs. He started to relent then, realizing Haney was in a corner. "That's fair enough, Corporal. If you'll only tell me the details of the court martial, we'll start from square one."

Haney nodded. "We were working near the DMZ, route nine out of Dong Ha. Back and forth on sweeps, you know, to keep the road open. Every so often we'd come across these Montagnard tribes, pretty ragged groups, kicked off their mountain ranges by both sides and generally treated like shit." Haney's chest tightened and he clenched and unclenched his hands. ". . . so me and a couple of the guys, we'd take the orphans and fatten 'em up and pack them off to a Catholic orphanage in Hue—I'd made arrangements with a priest— but we could very seldom take the kids ourselves, we were so busy. And we'd turn the kids over to this Viet captain, and he was supposed to deliver the kids for us. Except the bastard was selling them on the slave market. Some rich family would want a servant to clean up their muck, and this captain was making beaucoup bucks, and I found out about it and busted him up. I'd do it again, except this time I'd cut the motherfucker's throat! This fucking war is supposed to have a meaning, Lieutenant! But any way you slice it, it comes out yellow pus and it stinks and there ain't no meaning except someone's profit. And I'm goddamned pissed that I've had any fuckingthing to do with it! Sir!" Haney lit another smoke to control his trembling and he glanced around the tent to avoid the officer's eyes. He did not like this stranger seeing weakness in him.

The lieutenant said nothing for long seconds. His own tough demeanor was a facade, and he knew that about himself, but the corporal before him was the real thing and the emotion that burst out — the glass-shard anger — had taken the lieutenant by surprise. "Well, I, uh, guess I got more than I asked for. You know, I'm only trying to get to know you men. And I know I'm a greenhorn. Well I, uh, can't learn anything unless I ask, eh?"

Haney half-smiled, suddenly embarrassed for the man. "That's right, sir. We all learn by asking."

The officer stood abruptly, self-consciouly, and offered Haney his hand. "We'll get along, Joe. I know you'll do your job."

"Yes sir."

"Let me know when your wife delivers. We'll get you to Danang and you can call home."

Outside, Haney squinted in the sunlight and returned to his men, sweating and cursing with the big rolls of wire, and the corporal threw in beside them. He took the sledgehammer from Burgess and began to drive stakes. It felt good to sweat and work, good to pound out the anger and forget the orphans, and try not to think of his own child who he would not be there to see, and he fell into a rhythm, the hammer arcing up and driving down. *God DAMN this fucking war! God DAMN this fucking war!* And the heads of the stakes became everything he hated and he beat them mercilessly into the ground.

They were two days clearing the bamboo and laying the wire, coils of concertina and tangle-foot set inches off the ground. And mines, of course, but not pressure type. The Claymores were set off by electric impulse and exploded outward, thousands of tiny shot that ripped flesh down to the bone. Six machine gun bunkers were built and manned continuously with smaller rifle pits every twenty yards around the circle. What had been a tranquil farming village became in forty-eight hours an armed camp with new tenants and a new routine. There was only one gate now, and it closed at dusk. No one went in or out after that. The marines quartered in one quadrant in squad tents — a sandbag wall four feet high around each tent with a bunker for shelter. There was a command bunker for the radio watch and maps and artillery co-ordination; and an area for light mortars, 60-mm, used mostly for night illumination; and two ordnance bunkers.

But they needed other things as well: an aid station with a wooden deck, a mess hall with tables and benches, a gravity shower. Li contracted to build them and the materials arrived by truck and the work began. Li paid good wages to his helpers and the marines began to spend their money and a little sphere of prosperity began to emerge. Shops were set up outside the camp and anyone with time off was allowed to frequent them.

But Madame Xiap had not yet arrived with her girls, and Vaseline was hard to come by.

They were waiting for Haney to return; Schrader and Burgess and Calderone sitting on the short sandbag wall that circled the tent, each of them eyeing the tub of beer and the precious ice, *nuoc da*, that melted more and more with every second. They couldn't really see the beer or the ice, both covered with sawdust, but it was there somewhere and that knowledge made them drool.

It was to be a private celebration, just the four of them, the old-timers of the squad who had swapped and finagled their way out of guard duty and had nothing to do the next day but drill the militia.

It wasn't much beer really, sixteen bottles of *Ba Muoi Ba*, but it was all they could scrounge and the lieutenant okayed the extra amount. The ration was two per man per day, if they could get it, but lately the asswipes down the line had been swilling more than their share and even Ahn Lac, the main village, was running short. American beer was out of the question. It was too watery anyway.

The rest of the squad had drunk their ration and were scattered about the camp or reading or writing letters. Work was done for the day, and the three fireteam leaders were sitting there drooling, only extreme loyalty keeping them from drinking the beer. It wasn't every day a man learned he had a son.

Calvin's radio was tuned to the armed forces station and he was crooning to the tune and snapping his fingers to the time. It was the Supremes; *oooohhh ohh ooohhh, baby love, my baby love* . . . He jumped down from the wall and began to move to the music.

"Oooeee!" Mingo hollered. "Step it out, momma!" and he jumped down too and did a respectable shuffle.

"C'mon, farmboy! Shake your ass!"

Schrader grinned. "I can't dance, Mingo."

"Bullshit! You square dance."

"Jesus," Calvin said. "You wanta be a white man all your life?"

They pulled him off the wall and put him between them and showed him a step or two, one direction and then another. "That's it man!" Mingo said. "You got it! Ain't we the Sleaso Sisters?"

"Do better with a few beers." Schrader was paying close attention to his feet.

"Man, you can't hold three beers. Who you kiddin', anyway?"

"I'm improving with practice."

"Sheeit! Two beers a day ain't practice—there you go bullshittin' again . . . Hey! Don't step on my shine . . ."

"Watch this, Chuck." Calvin heeled and toed sideways and spun around smoothly, the other two watching and stepping themselves and then Calvin stood stock still and Schrader looked up and there was Lieutenant King. They all stopped and saluted politely, not stiffly, because they were pretty salty after all.

"Evenin', Lieutenant."

"You fellas were looking pretty good. We'll have you put on a show sometime."

"Be glad to, sir," Mingo grinned. "Schrader got some lipstick hid away, some skirts too. He don't think we know it, Lieutenant, but he's kind of—"

"He's a lying sonuvabitch sir!" Schrader laughed and blushed, and looked at the ground.

The lieutenant was grinning. He'd begun to relax a little with the men. "Thought I'd tell you we got a message from Ahn Lac. Haney just passed thru. He'll be here in about fifteen minutes."

"Hot damn! Tired of waitin'. Thanks for the extra beer ration, sir."

"No problem, Calderone. I wish there were more. I trust you fellas wouldn't overdo it."

"No sir," Calvin told him. "Only Schrader. Two is overdoin' it."

"Afternoon, men."

They all saluted and the three of them relaxed, the officer gone.

"How far is Danang, anyway?" Schrader asked. The battallion had come up the coast on ship, bypassing that city.

"Seems about fifteen miles back to Highway One. Then maybe twenty miles south to the city."

"You ever been there?"

"Man, that's where we landed. But they whisked us outta there pretty damned quick."

"They shoulda copped a chopper for Joe, 'steada makin' him drive all the way."

"Who you kiddin', Mingo? What do they care if a corporal hits a mine?"

"Bite your tongue, man!"

"Bullshit. Joe's okay. He's almost here, ain't he?"

"Yeah. But maybe his luck's runnin' thin. He's been humpin' a long time."

Calvin spat. "Mingo, you are one superstitious mother."

"You don't believe in luck, *hombre*?"

"Sure I do, man. But it don't run thick or thin for no one. It's just *there*, the same everyday, and you either got the smarts to use it or you don't."

"Got it all figured out, eh?" Mingo smirked.

"What do you think, David?"

"I guess it's how you use it. Or how you plan for it. Like the weather. The odds are, it is or it isn't gonna rain at a certain time. You plant or side-dress or cultivate with that in mind."

"Like gettin' a broad pregnant," Mingo laughed. "The odds are this, or the odds are that, but it's really how you stir it around."

"Don't get me to thinkin' about pussy. When's that old Mama-san gettin' here anyway?"

"Soon enough for you," Schrader told him. "You were in and out of that last one fast enough."

"Man, that girl saw me coming," Burgess laughed, leaning on the sandbags. "She grabbed my hand and led me back saying 'Hurry up! Me go town,' then that little ass was goin' to town all right, ninety miles an hour . . ."

"She wanted your money quick."

"That's not what she got quick."

"Hey, David. You gonna get us some bargain pussy?"

"How the hell am I supposed to do that?"

"With the lingo, man. I see you sweet talkin' the whores in the lingo, I know you don't always pay."

"Ain't so, Mingo. I pay just like you." Schrader grinned.

"You lyin' cocksucker. You just don't want to cut your buddies in."

"Why should I muddy up my own water?"

"Some buddy! You come to San Antone someday, I'll return the favor."

"I wouldn't need your help in Texas, dumbass. They speak English."

"Not any English *you'd* understand."

"Listen to him bitch," Calvin said. "You'd think it broke his ass to spend the three bucks."

"Shit, you won't see any three-dollar pussy out here. You watch," Schrader told them, "five buck minimum, maybe seven-fifty."

"You're crazy as hell! What have you heard?"

"Haven't heard anything. I just know about commodities. And don't ask me what that is, you goddamned illiterate Mexican. When soybeans are short the price is high."

"Oh *Madre*," Mingo moaned, biting his finger. "There goes my savings. Listen David, if that's true you gotta help me out, tell the girls what *mucho hombre* I am."

Schrader winked at Burgess. "What do you got to trade?"

"Trade! I'm talking *favors*, you big ugly gringo. *Por favor, comprende*?"

"You know what my dad always told me—"

"Who gives a shit what your old man says!"

". . . he always said," Schrader went on with Midwestern persistence, "that anything worthwhile is gonna cost you a little."

"Hey, man. I got nothin' to trade. You and me got the same shit. The same lousy food and sweaty uniforms. The same stale cigarettes. What do you want, blood?"

"You could take some of my guard duty."

"*Cabrone*! See if I do you anymore favors."

"You never did me a favor."

"Yeah, but there was something special I was gonna do for you."

"What's that?"

"Never mind now, bastard. You just suffer."

"C'mon, Mingo, what was the favor?"

"I was gonna let you live."

Down the road that stretched away through the paddies a small billow of dust arose, and finally they saw the speck of a jeep.

"Here comes Joe."

"Yeah. I wish he hadn't split so quick. I woulda give him a PX list."

"He'll bring some stuff back."

"He won't bring no rubbers, though. The guy don't fool around."

"You'll have to ride bareback, brother."

"You got some stashed, Calvin?"

"You never plan ahead, Mingo."

"Jesus Christ! My buddies are screwin' me left and right! I'll prob'ly catch the clap and go home with my nose rotted and shame my family. Maybe they'll put me on the secret island they got for terminal cases, and I'll turn to puss while you two fuckers go Stateside. *Con amigos como ustedes, quien necesita enemigos!*"

"What did he say?" Schrader asked.

"Who knows. It's the English they speak in San Antonio!"

Haney pulled to stop before the squad tent, face caked with dust, but he was grinning pretty big. He held out a fistful of cigars. "Seven pounds, fourteen ounces of squalling fury."

"You heard him screamin', eh?" Mingo asked as he took the cigar.

"Yeah. Helen snatched the tit from his mouth and held the phone up to him. Sounds like me."

"How's the wife?"

Haney looked away. "She sounds fine. But she's lonely, I can tell. She wanted me to be there awful bad."

"You'll be there soon enough, Joe."

"Yeah, sure. It was great to hear her voice, and the little scamp's too."

"What'd you name him?"

"Sean Michael, after his grandfathers."

"Christ! Another Catholic Mick!"

"Let's drink to that!" Calvin said, eyeing the boxes in the back of the jeep. "What you got there?"

Haney shrugged. "Cases of Cokes, some pogey bait, soap and shit supplies. The usual stuff."

"And you didn't bring no booze?"

"Got guard duty. So do you, sucker."

"Oh man! We got us all off. Did some horse tradin'."

"Sorry, Calvin. I rushed out of here so quick, I didn't think anyone noticed I was gone."

"Well we're gonna' celebrate anyway. A little, that is." And he pointed to the tub of beer. "Compliments of the lieutenant."

"I'm ready."

"You're ready! We been starin' at it for two hours. The damn sun's almost set. What took you so long?"

Haney grinned, "I stumbled across an NCO club in the middle of nowhere."

"Bullshit! You drove to Red Beach."

Haney pulled a bottle from the tub and shook off the sawdust. "Had to celebrate right away. You understand." He popped the cap with the bayonet stub of his M-14 and took a long pull of the beer, and they all killed their first ones at once and tossed the bottles on the ground. It was the best time of day, the sun going down and the light slanting and throwing a yellow haze everywhere. The last of the farmers were coming through the gate, some of them leading buffalo, which plodded along, dropping their dung in great splashes wherever it suited them. The shopkeepers were hurrying inside as well, their trinkets and wares bundled or crated in chests and they walked loaded down or pulling carts. On the marine side of the compound it was rather drab. But in the old hamlet across the way there were trees and flowers and people congregating, and even with the hedge cut down there was color and contour enough to rest eyes. But out on the periphery it was half a mile to the nearest treeline, and the paddies and fields ran flat as a lake, with only the raised dikes to break the monotony. And to hide Charlie, if he wanted.

Haney stretched and reached between the sandbags and the tent and lifted up a gerry can. "I'm gonna douche. Open me a beer, David."

"You got it."

Haney stripped off his clothes and pried the helmet liner loose and filled his steel pot from the gerry can. He wet himself down and lathered with some soap lying there on the wall.

Mingo jumped up on the sandbags. "Here, Daddy. Let me help," and he tipped the water can over Haney's head so he could rinse. Then Haney sat bare ass on the wall and dripped and air-dried, and they finished their second beers just as the sun disappeared behind the mountains and the dusk turned orange-pink and began to fade to gray.

"They shouldn't've let you go alone, Joe. Dangerous for one man," Schrader said.

"Who else could they spare?"

"Me!" Mingo volunteered. "They can spare me anytime they want."

"No trouble on the road?"

"Naw—a lot of civilians past Ahn Lac. Then the regular traffic on Highway One."

"Still, they should've sent a chopper for you. Ten minutes after the mine-sweeper passes, Charlie could be out there packin' the potholes again."

"That's right," Mingo said, "or a small ambush or snipers. Come to think of it, it was pretty fuckin' dumb to send you by yourself."

Haney shook his head. "I've been thinking about those things, Mingo. About why we've been here a week now and nothin's happened but the incoming the first night."

"What's it add up to, Joe?" They all moved a little closer around him.

"Charlie ain't ready yet. Maybe we caught him off guard, moving in here so quick. The sweep was pretty well coordinated. So the gooks hold all their punches back until they've mustered some strength back in the mountains."

"Shit! And this was supposed to be easy duty! I thought the battalion was so shot up it needed a rest."

Haney laughed through his nose. "Rest! Goddamn Mingo, if they wanted to give us a rest, we'd be on perimeter guard outside Danang. But look where we are, out in the middle of Indian country, barely within range of the nearest firebase, the battalion strung out along fifteen miles and three-quarters of us are gooddamned replacements. Now wouldn't that seem inviting to you? If you were the gook commander?"

"What are you saying, man?"

"It's easy," Haney smirked. "The last time we were the

bulldogs, this time we're the bait. But I can't figure what we're the bait *for*."

"Wait a minute, Joe," Schrader protested. "The officer in those briefings was pretty specific about this duty. You know, the helping hand program and all. *Chieu hoi*."

"Sure, I remember. Something about rural pacification, a new direction in the fucking war. We are officially a combined action platoon within a combined action company, and on and fucking on—"

"You don't believe that?"

"Sure, I believe the words are real. They make up lots of words to describe what we're doing. Something for the newspapers, you know. Sounds very official. But none of it's got a damned thing to do with why we're really here. Something's going on that I can't nail down."

"So we're in for it again."

"That's my bet."

"Motherfucker!" Calvin spat. "And I wanted to coast along these last five months."

"Didn't we all," Haney replied. "But we can't slack up, and we keep on the men, you all understand that?"

"Sure Joe. That last patrol was pretty good, eh?"

"Yeah. Good and tight. I want to keep it that way. Is Krause gonna end up a shitbird, David?"

"Naw. He'll square away. He's got a pretty good beer gut, is all."

"He's gonna have to move faster."

"I'll kick his ass along."

"What about Summers, Mingo? He doesn't seem to pay good attention."

"Yeah. He's been moonin' about his girl. Thinks he knocked her up."

"You want me to talk to him?" Haney asked.

Mingo shook his head. "Let me do it. I'll give him the word."

Haney nodded. "Let's package it up real neat for ol' Davey boy here. Who I guess will be the next squad leader."

"Christ! What's the marines comin' to?" Mingo asked. "A corporal who can't even hold his booze."

"Or eat pussy."

Haney jumped off the sandbag wall and went in the tent. Night was falling, and a few candles were burning inside. They had no generator for electricity. The lieutenant had nixed lanterns as too bright, and since no one wanted to drop the sides of the tent in the heat, the candles were snuffed after dusk, unless you bought some screens from the vendors.

Haney came out with some trousers and slipped them on.

"Last beer, Joe."

"Let's have it."

"Damn, this is cold! Where the hell do they get the ice, anyway?"

"Who knows? Maybe it's trucked to Ahn Lac all the way from Danang. Then they cart it here packed in salt and sawdust, and it keeps pretty good down a deep well."

"Man, anything for a buck."

"That's right," Haney answered. "Just like home."

Schrader glanced across the compound to see figures coming toward them in the dusk. "Who's this?" and he squinted to make out the forms. "It's Mr. Li. Got a couple of his workmen behind him."

Haney instinctively moved closer to his rifle, but Schrader stepped out to meet him.

"Good evening, Lance Corporal."

"Hello, Mr. Li. Is there trouble?"

"Oh no. No trouble. I only wanted to come and congratulate your corporal. The lieutenant told me he has a son." Li looked behind and nodded and the workmen sat down a basket and hurried back across the compound. At night there was seldom traffic between the two areas, though not separated by two hundred feet.

Haney relaxed and walked forward with Calvin and Mingo. "What say, Mr. Li?"

"Good evening, sirs. Corporal? Congratulations."

"Thanks, Mr. Li. He's our first kid."

"May you have more. I was no longer a soldier when we had our first child, and so I was there when he was born. I hope you will be home when your next child comes."

"You can count on that."

"I've brought you a gift, perhaps to help you celebrate," and he stepped back and lifted the lid from the big basket, and it was full of beer. "It should be cold enough," Li told them.

"Damn, Mr. Li. That's nice of you," Haney said, perplexed. "Thank you very much."

Mingo was rubbing his hands together. "Let's drink it, man."

Li was stepping backwards, slightly bowing. "Once again, Corporal, congratulations."

"Wait a minute, Mr. Li. Stay and drink with us. Please. We would be honored."

"Well, of course."

Mingo was already opening the bottles. "When were you a soldier, Mr. Li?"

"Oh, a long time ago. From 1940 through 1954."

Schrader looked at him sharply. "You were in the Viet Minh."

"So you know about the Viet Minh, Lance Corporal?"

"Only a little, sir. You kicked out the French."

"Yes, as you say, we kicked out the *Phap*. But not just like that!" and Li snapped his fingers.

Haney handed Li a beer. "You must have been about Schrader's age in 1940."

"I was twenty years old, Corporal."

"Where were your folks?" Calvin asked.

"I was with my father and my uncle. We had lived almost ten years in Hong Kong. Our hamlet had been razed during a rebellion in 1931. The day this occurred, we were away on family business. We returned to find everything in ruin, my mother and my sister slain as well as my aunt and cousins . . ."

"The French?"

"Yes. The *Phap*."

"Which hamlet, Mr. Li?"

"Here, Ap Do."

"So they didn't kill everyone?"

"No. Some managed to escape or hide. They returned and rebuilt the village."

The four marines glanced at each other, Haney nodding his head knowingly.

"I have to say that for you Viets," Haney told him. "You always come back. It's been a long goddamned war for you."

"Yes. Too long. Maybe with American help we can end it soon."

Haney looked away. Even in the darkness, Li saw it. "You do not believe that either, Corporal?"

"No sir, I don't. The North Viets are tough, your own army has no morale."

Li shook his head and swallowed some beer. They all waited for him to reply. "After World War II, most of the able soldiers who were still alive were Communists. Many of them are still fighting. I believe they are the most experienced army in the world."

"They sure keep a step ahead of us."

"Oh?" Li arched his brow. "You mean the Viet Cong, do you not?"

"No sir," Mingo told him. "I mean the hard-ass regulars, under the North Vietnamese flag. A month ago, in the mountains west of Tam Ky."

"We heard rumors of a battle further south. I believe you hurt the Communists there."

"They didn't exactly throw us kisses, either."

"You fuckin' A they didn't."

" 'Nother beer, Mr. Li?"

"No. Thank you."

"So you learned to speak English in Hong Kong, no?"

"Yes, Mingo. In Hong Kong."

"Speaks it better than you, chile sauce," Calvin joked.

"Piss off! I'm improving!"

Mingo lit a smoke quickly and the glare of light showed his face and his cupid eyes half slitted. "What do you think the Cong is gonna do, Mr. Li?" he asked.

Li did not reply right away, but shrugged as though considering. Luc had not told the Americans of Li's secret meeting with Phan. He had thought it would only endanger Li's family.

"They will watch for awhile," Li told them. "The small strikes — the mortars and the mines — will soon enough begin to increase. Perhaps they will ambush your patrols, who knows? Your strengths are obvious. They will look for your weaknesses."

Calvin shifted nervously. "What about a ground attack on the hamlet? Much chance of that, Mr. Li?"

"If they are strong enough," Li said. "If they want you out here badly enough."

"Sonovabitch!" Calvin spat. "That's the same thing Joe was just saying."

Li raised his brows and glanced at Haney. A half moon had risen and the faces showed lean and brown as they stood in a circle. "You know something of the Communists, eh Corporal?"

"It's my second tour," Haney told him. "I was an advisor for awhile to your marines farther north of here. Then they sent me back to my own battalion."

Li nodded. "It shames me that you have to come and fight for us even once, much less twice! Our own young men could be much better soldiers, if they were inspired."

"Yeah, they could be, Mr. Li. We took a pretty sorry outfit and trained it into one of the best Vietnamese battalions in I Corps. And I'll tell you something, after all the crap we put those boys through—peasant boys, Mr. Li, you know, and poor city boys—after all the harassment and discipline and hard-assed training, all it really took was a simple change of attitude. They just needed to feel like real troopers. Hell, they were tough enough already. But they'd never had any confidence."

Schrader could see Li's eyes in the moonlight. He saw that Li was looking far off into the night sky. "I do not know what is to become of this young generation," Li told them. "It is not their fault that they have lost heart. We have become a broken nation, the bitterness runs deeply and for my own children it may even be worse." His voice trailed off into the croaking night sounds, and the marines stood silently for awhile, not knowing what to reply. They thought very little of what it was like for the Vietnamese. The peasants always seemed so accepting, as if it mattered little which way the country went, or to what end. But Li just then had sounded much like any of their own parents; and they all knew his son, Vo, bright and eager to help and listen, and when the marines left, that boy's life would go on to some end. And he wasn't just a background prop for their war, or for some picture to show Mom. But it was so damnably hard to think of peasants as having relevant lives, to appreciate anything but eating and sleeping and screwing.

"How about another beer, Mr. Li?" Schrader asked, to break the silence.

"No, thank you, Lance Corporal. I should return to my family. But I am happy to have stayed and talked. Congratulations again, Corporal Haney."

"Thanks, Mr. Li, and thanks for the beer."

"Goodnight, gentlemen." Li bowed politely and they watched his form dwindle in the distance, a militia man stepping from the moon-shadows to hail him, a dog barking quickly, and the four marines left smoking and drinking and pondering what Li had told them.

"That's a dude to take note of," Calvin said.

"Jesus, ain't he something? You ever know anyone like that, Joe?"

Haney shook his head. "No. Like he said, most of the old soldiers left in the Viet Minh were Reds. I've known some Viet majors and light colonels about Li's age. They must have been soldiers, too, back in the forties, but my guess is they were ass kissers and not much in a firefight."

"He'd have to know his shit," Mingo said, "to stay alive that long."

Calvin laughed and poked him. "You mean it wasn't blind luck?"

"*Cuidado, hombre!* Don't joke about luck. It's bad luck to joke about luck."

"Put your teeth back in, grandma," Calvin scoffed.

Mingo only closed his eyes and crossed his fingers behind his back.

Schrader finished his beer in a great gulp and stepped to the iced tub. They saw him stagger a little as he reached for the bottle.

"Oh, shit," Mingo laughed. "He's had his snout in the trough too long."

"Better shut him down, Joe."

"Fuck you two!"

"How many you had, David?" Haney asked.

"Five."

"You're a lying cocksucker!"

". . . six."

"What say you put a cork in it, killer?"

"I'm all right, Joe. I can do my job."

"One more beer and you couldn't."

"It's a goddamn conspiracy," Schrader complained, but he was grinning lamely and he dropped the beer back in the tub and it clinked another bottle and the sound carried across the mute camp. It was very still, the same as every night, hushed snoring from their own tent and a quiet game of poker two tents down, the men playing stud by candlelight with screens all around to keep the light in, the screens bought from the peddlers and the poker players sweating and bitching in low voices but there was nothing else to do. At midnight there would be another shift of the guard and the camp would bump and scuffle as men dropped tiredly into cots and the new guards worked the bolts on the machine guns, but then it would be quiet again. There was no earth berm to keep out flat sniper shots and cigarettes were lit quickly and smoked in a cupped hand.

Calvin stepped over to the tub. "Well, well — just three more beers," and leering at Schrader he opened them one by one and handed two to Mingo and Haney. "Sorry, kid. When you grow up you can drink with the adults."

"Screw you, Maggot. I'm hittin' the rack, anyway."

"Before the ground hits you in the face," Mingo said.

But Schrader ignored them and stepped into the dark tent, the air thick and warm and he stumbled to his cot there beside the entrance, one of the four choice spots next to the doorways. He heard his buddies laugh and mutter as he sat down heavily and fumbled with his boot laces. Stripping to his shorts, he took the rifle from his cot, already half asleep and the alcohol heavy on his eyelids and he dropped onto the cot and fell into a heavy sleep and he dreamt . . .

. . . he was moving toward the trees, but how? The trees were oaks and hickories, and that was wrong. He looked at his hands and they were gripping a hard black wheel, and when he looked around in his dream he was driving his father's tractor, disking, and the earth was tumbling and smelling rich. Schrader glanced over and there was Li, plowing with his buffalo, and the beast was crapping and the dung steamed, so it must have been a cool morning. Schrader stopped and let the tractor idle to stare at Li, and Li was beside him looking up, his buffalo gone, and Li wanted on the tractor. Schrader did not want to let him aboard, but suddenly Li was there

anyway and he firmly took the wheel from Schrader. But somehow the machine was no longer a tractor, but a long-snouted
and blackened .50 caliber in some kind of bunker and Li swung
it around menacingly. The bolt slamming home was the sound
of Schrader's own hollow death and he was on the outside
staring down the barrel, and Schrader knew in his dream that
he was going to die. But then Li was there on the tractor and
pulling Schrader aboard, and they were going along in the
field, the John Deere rumbling and they were cultivating soybeans, the plants strong and healthy green. Li was happy because it was his best crop. But when Schrader turned to look
behind, he saw the field all in ashes and smoldering and there
was so much despair in that smoking field.

Then the two explosions sounded, very real, not-in-the-
dream explosions, and Schrader was hurtled awake. He sat
bolt upright, very groggy, slow-witted, as the other men were
grabbing gear and charging out the tent, Schrader lagging
behind, fumbling for the rifle and cartridge belt and finally
running after the others, everyone to assembly points. A machine gun opened up heavily on the west end of the camp,
the post beyond the hamlet, and a hand flare whooshed and
the glare was harsh on Schrader's eyes.

"Brennan! Krause!" Schrader called out. "Murphy!"

"Yo! Up ahead!"

Schrader hurried up to his fireteam, huddled together low
on the ground. His head throbbed.

"Everyone got ammo?"

"Yeah."

"Watch the gooks on your left and right. They'll be nervous as shit." They hunched lower as another gun post opened
fire, on the north side, a hundred feet from them. "Murphy,
you haul ammo if we need any." Schrader was shouting over
the firing.

"Gotcha."

"Let's move it!" Schrader said, and they began to spring
low across the compound, fireteams all around doing the same,
everyone with a job and a specific place to go. No point running
blindly to the perimeter, there was already adequate guard
there to fend off a first attack. So they grouped first and counted
heads and got their bearings calmly.

Behind them the mortar crew began to shoot illumination

and the rockets burst brightly. It was a stark and dreary daylight that threw bizarre shadows as they hurried past the native huts to their posts, Schrader hanging back and spotting some militia men standing confused in the open. Haney was already on the perimeter with his grenadier. Schrader saw him dashing from the shadows, back and forth, dragging and pushing the militia men into their rifle pits, and Schrader ran to help him. "Goddamnit, Phuc! *Voi-vá, di!*" And he saw the little soldier gape at him wide-eyed and afraid and his knees buckled. When Schrader reached him, the militia man was gripping his carbine tightly but he could not get up. "Come on, Phuc! Goddamnit!" And Schrader jerked the man roughly to his feet. It was very bright in the flarelight, and the first line of barbed wire was only one hundred feet away. Schrader crouched low and began to drag the soldier along and then Haney ran up and together they snatched the man off his feet and dashed the fifty feet to a rifle pit and threw him in it. Then they fell flat on their bellies side by side.

The machine gun fire had ceased and all along the line rifle bolts were slamming home and the men were rustling in their pits.

"Where the fuck's your helmet and jacket?" Haney barked raspingly.

"Slow gettin' started, Joe. Sorry." Schrader was out of breath and his belly ached.

"You all right?"

"Yeah. Too much fuckin' beer. What were the explosions?" They were both straining their eyes, peering past the wire fifty feet ahead, the machine gun bunker to their right, and they were looking for movement out in the paddies. The flares were dropping low and dimming, but then three more mortars whooshed and the rockets burst like fireworks and it was day-bright again. But quiet.

"I don't know what the explosions were," Haney said. "Wasn't mortars or rockets. Didn't sound right."

"What the hell are the gunners shooting at?"

"Who knows," Haney replied. "Maybe spooks."

"Have you seen Luc?"

"Yeah. He was kickin' their asses in line on the south side. Most of them did okay, though. Maybe a third of them panicked."

"Mingo and Calvin on line?"

"Yeah."

"I'll hoof it over to my pit," and Schrader began to push himself up for a quick dash, but Haney pulled him down.

"Wait a minute, David. It's not right yet. Wait till the flares drop some more, then run like hell."

"Where you gonna be?"

"In the gun bunker a minute. Then I'll be in my pit."

Schrader nodded and lay on his belly and waited, his breath not so ragged then and his ears pricked for sounds. It was 3:30 in the morning and the half moon was a hand's breadth above the mountains and the crickets and frogs in the paddies were carolling in earnest and it seemed like just another tropical night—except for the man-made daylight and the rifle cradled hard and cold in his arms. No one had heard enemy rifle fire. *What were the gooks up to?*

The flares had drifted lower and Schrader could hear them hissing and it was growing dim. Haney said, "Go! Now!" and Schrader pushed himself up and sprinted the distance to his hole, past a gook, past Krause, past another gook and he leaped across the sandbags into the shallow pit just as three more flares burst on the night sky. He lay prone and propped the rifle in the gap between the sandbags. He was barefoot and in his scivvies and the cartridge belt dug into his waist. He squirmed around and pulled the belt off and took two magazines from pouches and propped them against a sandbag. He stared out across the paddies toward the hulking mountains and scratched the rash on his ass furiously. He could smell the cordite from the explosions, but he couldn't guess what they were . . . bigger than a hand grenade, duller sounding and heavier, not the crack of artillery or the sharp hammer thud of rockets or mortars. Even through his dream, Schrader could remember the sounds. Had two of the mines been set off?

He began to think it was a false alarm, the minutes dragged by and nothing moved outside the wire and he wanted to go back to sleep. He yawned deeply and slapped at a mosquito, and took the bottle of repellent from the kit of his belt. Someone was scurrying along the line and Schrader squinted and saw Haney coming his way. The corporal dove down beside him.

"What's the scoop, Joe?"

"Sappers," Haney told him. "They snuck up and threw a couple of charges, one pole charge at least, and maybe a satchel charge. Some of the wire on the other side of the bunker is blown."

"Did the gunner see anyone?"

"Shadows. Maybe he hit something, he ain't sure."

"Anybody hurt?"

Haney shook his head. "Stunned one of the guards. Lefever, from Carter's squad. Bloodied his nose."

"They'll keep us out here all fuckin' night." Schrader moaned.

"Looks that way."

"Will they let us sleep?"

"Maybe," Haney replied. "Just keep the regular guard posted."

"Plant a bug in the lieutenant's ear, will you Joe?"

"Larret will say something to him. I'm moving on," and Haney crawled away hurriedly and then began to crouch and run down the line.

Schrader rolled on his side. He still had questions. What was the gunner on the north side of camp shooting at? Why would Charlie risk two sappers if no attack was coming? And then he answered the last one aloud. "To keep you awake, sucker!" and he grunted and began to smear repellent wherever he could reach.

More flares erupted high above them and the flat, murky, water in the paddies reflected the light with a dirty glimmer. Shadows were jumping everywhere on the landscape, from the breeze that swayed the flares back and forth as they fell. But a man would not be a shadow out there. A man would have to stand from the muck of the paddies or show himself over a dike and then he would be dead and his shadow wouldn't matter then. Schrader ignored the shadows. He looked for little brown men.

In twenty minutes word to stand down was passed along; they could sleep in their pits. Schrader rolled on his back with the rifle stock comfortably beside his head and the sandy clay soil was cool on his skin. He watched the light change as the flares diminished and the stars shone stronger and he was asleep.

When he woke, it was gray dawn and he heard people

stirring about. He opened his eyes and there stood Calderone over him with his dick in his hands like he was going to piss. Schrader made a choking sound and tumbled out of the pit, jumping to his feet cursing.

Mingo grinned and the others standing around laughed.

"You'll lose that little thing of yours," Schrader warned, shaking his finger and reaching back into the pit for his rifle and cartridge belt.

"How come you couldn't move that quick last night, sucker?"

"I moved quick enough, just never you mind."

"Crap," Mingo told him. "I was on the perimeter before you were out of the tent."

"It wasn't that bad, man."

"Almost. You shoulda give that last beer you drank to me."

"You'll freeze right here on the equator before I ever leave beer for you." And he shook his rifle threateningly at his friend but the Chicano only laughed and flipped him the bird.

"I feel like kickin' some ass," Schrader growled. "Where's Phuc, that little bastard? He chickened out, last night. I thought I could make him a corporal, too."

"Man, they split before dawn. The ol' chief came around lookin' mean as hell—funny how a little *hombre* like that can suddenly look so mean and tough—he came around and got them out of their holes and marched 'em out the gate. I guess they're out searching the jungle. Ol' Luc's gonna bust their asses for sure."

"Maybe they'll find a body."

"Naw. That gunner didn't hit nothin'."

"How do you know?"

"It was Four-eyes Fletcher," Mingo smirked. "He can't shoot for shit."

Schrader glanced sidewise up the line, past the gun bunker with the stark and mean-looking barrel poking out, and he saw a line of infantry moving zig-zagged along the dikes.

"That's Carter's squad?" Schrader asked, as they turned to walk across the compound to their tent, the peasant girls giggling at Schrader in his scivvies.

"Yeah. Won't take 'em but an hour to circle the camp."

"Did you see where the wire was blown?"

"Yeah. Must've been a pole charge like Joe guessed. It blew about eight feet of wire clean across, neat as scissors."

"But what about the other explosion?" Schrader persisted. "A man couldn't get close enough to toss a satchel charge that would bloody Le Fever's nose. He'd have to throw it forty yards."

"Maybe it was a rifle grenade. You know, the old World War Two kind."

"Could be, Mingo. But you'd have heard it spit as it launched off the barrel."

"You got me, David. Coulda been half a dozen things."

"Who was on the gun on the north side?"

"Don't know yet. I wanta find out though. Funny, you know? Last night, Mr. Li told us this shit was about to start. And sure enough, here we go again."

They were walking along a row of huts, built closely side by side but with narrow and long yards behind, and Schrader took Mingo's arm and steered him between two houses.

"C'mon. I want to show you something."

"*Que paso?*"

Schrader didn't reply, but led him under the canopy of small trees that grew behind the house, past the gardens with peppers and yams and peanuts with their first yellow flowers and they came to a bamboo pen with a fat red sow stretched out on her side, and hungry piglets sucking greedily.

"She farrowed yesterday," Schrader told him. "Healthy little litter."

Mingo laughed and counted. "Eight of 'em. That's pretty good, eh?"

"Good for these scrub hogs," Schrader replied. "They're not the big hybrids like we got back home. Twelve or thirteen to a good litter. But these are handsome hogs, anyway."

A peasant woman stepped from the back of the house and saw them and stared. Schrader smiled and waved, and the woman smiled and went about her business, muttering something low and her husband poked his head out the door.

"*Xin loi,*" Schrader called out. Excuse us please, and they walked on past the yard to where the bamboo hedge had been and stepped across the stubble of the stalks. They were on the south perimeter then, and their tents were to the left and they walked toward them, along the line of neat little back yards on one side with wire and rifle pits on the other.

"You'll have to come visit me, Mingo. You'd like my folks."

"Do they dance and party, man?"

"Oh, hell yes. Dad gets out the Early Times to chase the beer, and Mom laughs a lot, you know, and has a good time. You'd like the place."

"I ain't no country boy, David. You won't find me ridin' no bulls."

"Hell, boy, you don't know what you're missing. I got two lined up special for you and Calvin!"

"Bullshit. I ain't livin' through this war just to get stomped by some bull. But I'll drink whiskey with your old man while you and Calvin get stomped."

They saw three men walking the perimeter toward them. It was lieutenant, with Sergeants Larret and Haney, and when they drew abreast Calderone saluted.

"Mornin', sir."

Schrader could not salute because he had no helmet or hat. Marines do not salute bareheaded like soldiers.

"Damnit, Schrader," the lieutenant snapped. "Where's your helmet and flak jacket?"

"In the tent, sir. I didn't grab 'em last night."

"You didn't get them? And you parade around the hamlet in your goddamned scivvies?" The lieutenant looked pained. "Did you get drunk last night?"

"No sir."

The officer glanced sideways at Haney.

"He was all right, Lieutenant," Haney said. "He helped me get the militia on line."

"You're not getting salty on me, are you, Schrader?"

"No sir."

"You think because you speak the lingo you're something special?"

"No sir."

"You're a goddamned fireteam leader, you know. You have to set an example."

"Yes sir. It won't happen again."

"All right, goddamnit. You men carry on." He returned Mingo's salute and the three of them walked on down the perimeter.

"This ain't gonna be my day," Schrader moaned.

Mingo laughed into his hand and poked Schrader in the ribs. "You think you're hot shit, Lance Corporal?" he mimicked. "Man, the lieutenant oughta put the lid on this salutin'. Some sniper's gonna pick his ass off."

"He's still a boot. What do you expect from a guy straight out of Rotcie?"

"What do I expect at all from this fuckin' Crotch," Mingo replied, looking around the camp disgustedly. "I'm about to eat another greasy damned breakfast from a little green can and at home *mi madre* is cooking *huevos con chorizo* for everybody. And good black coffee."

"Cut it out, Mingo."

"Oh *mi Dios*! What I wouldn't give to have some now."

"I think when the mess hall is finished, we'll have some peasant woman cooking for us."

Mingo shrugged. "That might be okay, but they'll just be fixin' the same stuff out of bigger cans. And you watch. I'll go home and Mama's good cooking will give me the shits. Man, they get you comin' and goin'."

Schrader chuckled. "You didn't expect to win anything from the Crotch, did you?"

"No, *amigo*. But I'd like to break even once in awhile."

"You'll be breaking even soon enough, Mingo. You'll damned well be winning."

"Yeah," Calderone grinned. "That's right. A hundred and forty-two blessed motherfuckin' days, and this cat is gone." And Schrader saw him tap the wood on his rifle stock, and he grinned privately at his friend, trying not to think of his own number of days remaining. It was far too depressing. To Schrader it seemed a long, long gray tunnel, and it went on forever.

It was a week later—a week full of routine days and nights broken by mortar fire and jumpy gunners on the line, a week of fuzzy sleep and bleary eyes greeting the dawn—that the whores arrived with the old crone they would come to call Madame Zap.

One morning a little blue bus came down the road, an hour after the mine sweep was complete and the big clanking tank had turned around to crawl back to Ahn Lac, a squad of marines riding it piggy back.

The bus driver stopped and looked around nervously. This was not his regular route and the old woman had paid him well to come this far inland, all the way to the end of the line.

Ahn Lac was as far as he had ever been, and he was wishing he had asked for more money as he stepped from the bus and viewed the nearby mountains glumly.

The old woman was right behind him, in black peasant pants and a pink top and she pointed her bony finger at the laden bus and ordered him to start unloading.

Haney's squad was drilling militiamen in the compound again, running them doggedly through fireteam tactics, making their tongues drag and sweating themselves, but when the bus stopped at the gate they took a break and oggled the women through the windows.

Luc, the chief, left the drill and strolled over to the bus, and Li stopped his work on the mess hall and walked over as well, leaving the work to his helpers.

Madame Xiap no sooner saw Li approach when her face reddened and her lips curled back from her black teeth. She angrily began to spit words, shaking her fist at Li and stamping one foot.

Schrader was standing beside Burgess, taking a drink from Calvin's canteen of Kool-Aid, and he could see that Li was greatly offended. He drew himself up and looked grimly at the skinny old woman who was still spitting words; but Luc, his friend, was trying hard not to laugh.

"Mr. Li's catching hell," Calvin chuckled, mopping his brow and leaning on his rifle.

"That old woman looks mean as a hornet."

"What's she saying, David?"

Schrader shook his head. "Too fast for me to follow. But I can guess. A couple of days ago, Li told me he was supposed to build the old gal's cathouse. But she didn't give him an advance like he wanted, and the lieutenant gave Li one to do our work, so he went ahead and started the work for us."

"Man, I'm glad too. That shower makes this place almost bearable." Behind them a hundred feet was a sturdy bamboo tower, intricately trussed, that held four big barrels of water. After hours, everyone showered in the water that had warmed all day in the sun and it had become the highlight of their day.

The old woman had about expended herself. She walked around joltingly in a little circle, one hand on her waist, the other pointed at the sky and the whores in the bus were clustered at the doorway in bright blouses and pants and they were giggling.

Li finally had a chance to speak. Schrader heard him begin to explain about the money the *Nguoi My* had paid him, but that only angered the woman again and her eyes bugged and she spat another emphatic sentence and struck a fist in a palm; once, twice, three times. She limped in another circle and snapped something to one of the whores sharply, and something was handed to the whore from behind and she ran a little folding stool to the old woman and placed it on the ground.

Madame Xiap sat down firmly, her little wrinkled turtle's face at once calm and business like, and she took a snuff tin from her black waistband and tucked a pinch behind her lip. "When can you start my work, Li?" Schrader distinctly heard her ask that.

"In three days."

"Bah! And where are my girls going to work? Out in the fields? They're not cows like your country girls."

Luc, the chief, stepped closer to the old woman. "There is no place for them to work, yet. But we have a house in the hamlet where they can live."

"I expect at least that," Madame Xiap told him. "To bring my girls this far out, and it's dangerous, I would expect that you at least house us. But who is going to feed them? Eh? It is expensive to feed these girls. I know you think I make a lot of money, but I am only an old woman trying to get by and—"

Luc held up his hands placatingly. "We will feed you and the girls, old woman. Do not worry. And they can help with the work."

Madame Xiap suddenly laughed and slapped her knees and showed her betel-stained teeth. "Hah! They will not like that much. But they will do as I tell them. Now you can get me some men to help with the unloading. The bus driver is about to piss from fear."

Luc nodded agreement and grinned sideways at Li, who bowed politely to the old woman who was still seated like a queen, and she nodded and Li turned and walked back to his work on the mess hall.

Luc took a few steps toward Haney and motioned with

his hand and Haney double-timed to the little chief. It was important that they treat Luc as one of their own officers. Haney, in turn, called to Schrader and motioned to Burgess and Calderone and they all trotted up and stood in a circle about Luc.

It was great for Luc's esteem in the hamlet to order the giant Americans about. But he was ever polite.

Luc turned to Schrader. *Toi thiet cac dan ong guip dan ba gia. Ong noi trung ta, moi.* I need some men to help the old woman. Please tell your squad leader.

Schrader translated to Haney.

"How many?" Joe asked.

"*Nhieu qua*, Ong Luc?"

"*Nam,*" Luc told him.

"Five, Joe."

Haney nodded at his team leaders. "Who's been workin' the hardest?" he asked.

"Thieu and Dien," Calderone said.

"Yeah, and Tran," Burgess spoke up, "and that little fella ah, Swan, or something like that?"

"Xuan," Schrader told him. "And Kong, too; he's really been bustin' ass."

"Okay. We'll let them take it easy and help the old she-bear over there. Goddamn, Mr. Luc. That's some tough old woman."

"*Nguoi dan-ba gia ran!*" Schrader told the chief, and Luc laughed and nodded at Haney and the four marines walked back to the militiamen who were scattered about the barren yard, dirty-faced and catching their breath, and Schrader mustered the five men who hurried toward the bus appreciatively. The marines got the others moving again.

The militia was divided into squads and fireteams as the marines were, and they were learning marine tactics and formations. They each had cards Schrader had printed for them, with the formations numbered one through six and the English and Vietnamese word was printed beside the number.

"Squads on line! Fireteam wedges!" Haney called out, and looked at his card. "Number three!" *So-muc ba! Di!*

At the command *Di!* everyone began to move, an American with each militia fireteam, pushing and directing and hurrying them along. After much flying feet and dust there were three militia squads abreast, the teams within the squads in four-man diamond shapes and the teams were scattered along the line like teeth in a saw.

Then the men began to charge forward, keeping in formation and growling like the marines had taught them, and when Haney shouted "Down!" they all hit the dirt and pretended they were firing. The American marines walked among them and gave a light boot to the slow ones and encouraged the quick ones, and then they were on their feet and charging again. And again, in various formations, up and down the bare yard between the two camps which had become the drill ground.

For an hour, they ran the militia steadily, then Sergeant Larret came from the command bunker and called it a morning. The sun was then too high and hot. In the afternoon they would train the militia on the machine guns. It was the easiest duty. But the next day they would be patrolling and there was nothing easy about that.

8

Madame Zap kept a radio tuned to the armed forces station, so when they stepped off the road and through the heavy beaded curtain, into the cooler interior with the Japanese card tables and folding chairs and souvenirs hanging from the ceiling, they were listening to Smoky and the Miracles. A little whore in a red and black dragon dress came and led them to a table, grabbing Mingo's crotch and giggling while she held Schrader's hand.

Ba bia lanh, co, Schrader told her. Three cold beers. They hung their rifles by slings on the nails driven into the posts and dropped their helmets and flak jackets on the dirt floor and flopped in chairs. They were dirty and sweaty and just off patrol. In pairs and trios, the rest of the squad was straggling in and the whores were greeting them and grabbing crotches and pouting their mouths like they wanted to be kissed. Except, they didn't kiss very good.

"Shit, I must've sweat five gallons," Burgess complained,

mopping his brow with his sleeve, wiping off the red dust so that he looked like a genuine black man instead of some exotic breed. "Bringin' up the rear is the hardest goddamned part of patrollin'. The fuckin' point man can't keep a steady pace, so we hump ass to keep up."

"*Chinga te, Cabrone!*" Mingo spat. "I keep a good pace. The hard part is on the point, you know. We take all the chances."

"I like it just fine in the middle," Schrader told them.

"Not me," Calvin said. "Too close to the radio man—that antennae is like a red flag."

The whore brought the beers and sat down on Calvin's lap.

"Buy me drink?"

"Maybe. If you good girl," and he gulped his beer and spilled it down his chin when she grabbed his dick.

"You think Joe's comin' by?"

"Naw," Mingo grinned. "He don't like the temptation. He didn't take R and R, you know. They wanted to save money for the kid."

"Man, he could have snuck off to Bangkok or something. The wife wouldn't have to find out."

Schrader looked offended. "He's a family man."

"Well no shit, Sherlock! But the man's under a lot of pressure and he needs to let off some steam. He could've met his old lady in Hawaii, sure and she'd've been five or six months pregnant and they'd had a great time, right? He'd have to stay sober and polite, and they could only screw dog-style and what he'd really need was to get crazy drunk and suck, fuck, donald duck with some knock-out whores for a week."

The young whore smiled big and squirmed on Calvin's lap. "Suck, fuck dona' duck. Me know."

"I pity your wife, man," Schrader told him, somewhat piously.

Calvin smirked. "You are such a fuckin' virgin, Schrader. Ain't you ever gonna leave the farm?"

"And what does that mean, asshole?"

"It means, you dumb chuck," and Calvin was leaning forward suddenly and the whore had wisely slipped from his lap, "it means that you got cowshit clogged in your ears and over your eyeballs and the real fuckin' world has passed you by!"

Schrader jumped to his feet. It was hot, and they had been tense even before they had sat down at the table. He had jumped up seeing red and ready to throttle and pummel and maim, but there on his feet suddenly, looking at the anger in Calvin and the surprise in Mingo and the others about the bar, the others who always poked Schrader for a laugh, always goaded a little extra because he took it and laughed it off, looking at them and then seeing what they expected, he felt strangely embarrassed and he didn't know quite what to do. He didn't want to hit Calvin and give them a show. He felt awkward and sat back down. He locked his gaze with Calvin's, not wanting the man to think he was afraid.

"We ain't supposed to brawl in here. The lieutenant will shut the place down." And indeed, Madame Xiap hurried in from the back to intervene, her little arms flailing and she wailed in her sing-song language. By the time she reached the table, Burgess had relented, and he was leaning back in his chair drinking his beer.

"No trouble, *Mama-san*," he said.

"Somebody hit somebody!" a voice called from another table and everyone laughed and the tension was instantly gone.

Calderone, who was sitting between the two larger men, pulled the old woman onto his lap and crooned. "Madame Zap, I love your ass. Will you give me a kiss?" And the old woman laughed raucously and covered her black-stained teeth with her bony blue-veined hand and she said something lecherous and made a lemon-sour face and everything was normal again. Something by the Mamas and Papas, *California Dreamin'*, came on the radio and Calvin bought the cute whore her drink. Saigon tea. A hundred and thirty dong.

"I could drink a bunch of this tonight," Mingo said.

"Guard duty, O-two hundred," Calvin reminded him.

"Ain't that a motherfucker?"

"You got a gun bunker tonight, Calvin?" Schrader asked.

"Yeah. West side."

"Who's on with you?"

"Matthews. From Harris's squad."

"He any good?"

Burgess shrugged.

"He's okay," Mingo said. "Seems to think quick enough. He can shoot, too."

"I'll be doin' the fuckin' shootin'," Calvin said. "If that boot can just link ammo and keep his head cool, that'll be good enough for me."

"I don't know, Calvin," Mingo said, shaking his head. "I think he shoots better than you."

"Kiss my ass, you half-breed Puerto Rican, you couldn't . . ."

"Hey, Cabrone! I ain't no Puerto Rican!"

It went on like that for another half an hour, through a third round of beers, with a pair of them alternately going at each other, or two of them against one, until the beers were done and they got up to leave. It was after 6:00 p.m. They wanted to make chow before it closed. The peasant women were cooking and the food was passable and there was fresh fruit. They wanted a shower before the water was gone, and their rifles needed attention and they had to sleep before guard duty. The whore wanted to make some money, and she went to each one looking forlorn and hugging and kissing but they all brushed her off. The have-to-have-it-now heat was gone. The place had been open for two weeks and the whole platoon had been sneaking in for ten minute quickies and the rush was passed. Business was good enough, at five bucks a throw, but there was no more hurry, and the three team leaders took their helmets and slung their rifles and gear and walked outside into the late afternoon heat. The gate was a hundred yards down the road, the sentry in the distance haggling with some kids, and the road was red dust and even the lizzards kicked up clouds.

It looked terribly familiar to Schrader. There in the distance were the ugly green squad tents caked with dust, near the more friendly native houses, some simple, some more elaborate, the touches of color and the animals and children everywhere. It even looked comfortable to Schrader for a moment, trudging down the road with his friends, looking like a nice place to ride out the war. A little incoming. So what? Sappers or a sniper. Easy enough to deal with. It was kind of nice to feel halfway safe. Yes, indeed. Kind of nice.

* * *

It was a moonless night and very dark, except for the starlight reflected from the paddies, and Burgess was standing guard. He sat like an ebony stone behind the machine gun and his eyes swept the paddies and fields west of the camp, and he was chewing gum and his mind was wandering to keep awake.

Across from him in the bunker, Matthews stirred and drank from his canteen. He was only a dark shadow. Neither of them spoke. The mosquitoes were ravenous, and three times Calvin smeared his face and arms with repellent.

Frogs and insects trilled sweetly, and Burgess shifted and stretched and the smell of gun oil and the feel of metal made him feel secure. He didn't mind guard duty. It was a quiet time. *It's safer like this, if anything pops. I'm awake and dressed and I got my rifle right here. Too many times I've woke up with shit comin in, and me fumbling for my boots and helmet and everything crazy and confused. But everything's crazy and confused anyway, even in the daytime when I'm hanging out and thinking everything's peaceful. It ain't. I guess it's just my mind curling around itself and saying; Hey man! Let's pretend it's cool for awhile!*

I'm lucky I can do that so easy. Always could, even when I was a kid. I didn't ask for this war and I ain't going home crazy like I see happening to some of these guys. Like Haney. Poor Haney. He's gonna have a rough time. It shows in his eyes sometimes and he knows it's there and he don't like it. But goddamn! How's a guy s'posed to get that kind of craziness out? This shit gets under your skin and you can't just wash it away. But it suits him now. Makes him hell on wheels. I always feel safe with that sonuvabitch running things . . . And that's part of the change in you, my man. You never trusted a chuck till you came over here. Maybe that's a weakness you picked up. Better watch it. Chucks are chucks, and they can't help what they are anymore than you can. They'll turn on you without knowing why. But so will your own. That's people, for you. Learn that, my man. Learn how to see into people and past their color, and you got an edge. You got the feel for it. And more than anything, don't show a man you're afraid. It's okay to show a woman. Women understand those things.

*But a man will smell it and try to take advantage of it just
'cause he's a man. Like those drill instructors. That's why they
fucked with you so much, 'cause you never rolled on your back
for them. They never got that power over you. Like the time
the three of them whipped your ass because you left formation
to help that poor kid, whatever his name was, him crying and
on his knees and gashing his wrists with seashells, and the DI's
laughing at him and poking him with their boots saying, "Hurry
up, private! Let's see some blood." So you went to him and
helped him to his feet, and they thumped you good for that.
And the time at the rifle range they made you dig a hole and
they buried you in it up to your neck and left you in the dark.
It was a fucking game and you knew it. What did they expect
you to do? Cry and beg? Those fools! One of them was a black
man, too. Sergeant Brown. Whitey Brown! You embarrassed
him in front of his buddies. He hated you for that. That's what
I mean by color. Brown wasn't your brother because he was
black. He was your tormenter because he was black, and
ashamed of it!*

*Well, don't grit your teeth and let your belly shake just
thinking about it. The past got no business controlling you.
But sometimes there's no stopping it. Now it's got me thinking
about that judge. That old bastard had too much power to put
me in the Crotch and here I sit now, wanting to be somewhere
else and not knowing if I'll ever get there. And for what? For
socking a cracker cop who was getting a feel of my girl. Didn't
matter there were four witnesses saw him put his hand between
her legs. Didn't matter I was on scholarship. Didn't matter I
had no police record and the cop was a troublemaker. Fuck
no! Nothing matters 'cept the judge's authority was threatened.
Listen here, nigger! A cop is the law and the law is my bread
and butter! He may as well have said that. He did say that,
only not in those words. And I was expected to thank the
motherfucker 'cause he didn't put me in jail! Sheeit! I never
understood why they expect you to thank them for the crap
they make you eat. I was so goddamned mad! That judge had
it all stacked and he sat there like King Shit and I couldn't do
nothin' but take it.*

*That's it, my man. Laugh at yourself some. That's good.
You get too worked up about it. It's just those motherfuckers
getting to you again. You ain't gonna be free 'til you put them*

*out of your head like they never existed. Your freedom is in
own mind. You can't stand up to them by yourself and take
away their power. Maybe all the niggers in the world can't do
that. And if we can't, then the only freedom left is what already
in us. We'll be free to die. Jesus, it seems so easy sometimes.
But they keep on throwing their shit at you and it smells so
bad you can't concentrate.*

*Goddamned mosquitoes! They must drink this repellent.
Maybe all I'm doing is putting flavor on their meat. If I had
a nickel for every drop of blood they sucked out of me, I'd go
home with a bundle. You must taste good, my man. Sweet
Mary thinks so. Can't fool a woman like her. Mmmm hmmm.
She's got the finest muscles in her ass, and that pussy is
sooo-oo soft. She just wraps her legs around and it's like moving
in and out of a cream machine.*

*Phew! Ain't no good getting worked up. Your hand's too
damned calloused anyway. Saturday I'm gonna have to make
it to that cathouse, for sure! You're falling in love with your
fingers. Oh sweet Mary! Who's with you now . . .*

Somebody's coming . . .

"Hey Joe! That time already?"

"Yeah, it's two o'clock. Kramer here'll take your place."

"That's fine with me. Give the mosquitoes some fresh
meat. You watch out now, Kramer. They're liable to grab you
by the ears and fly away. How would we explain that to your
mother?"

Chuckling to himself, Burgess left his post and went to
bed.

Before the Americans came to Ap Do and the other hamlets, the Communists went pretty much where they wanted
in the open countryside. The hamlets themselves were de-
fended by men like Luc and his militia. But when the peasants
went to the fields for their day's work, the Communists had
easy access to them. Either to talk politics or cajole or tax them
so much rice if they wanted to remain healthy. The militia was
no help to them then, bound to the hamlet like it was, and
with only one able leader; so Luc was the government terrier,
leashed to his house, and the Communists were the tom cats
dancing and spitting just outside his reach, with the whole yard
to run in.

These Communists were Viet Cong regulars. They were full-time soldiers though they sometimes dressed in peasant garb, and they were well-armed and smartly led. They're not to be confused with the Viet Cong irregulars, who were the farmer-guerrillas and not full-time soldiers at all. The irregulars held no sway around Ap Do. The peasants there were not sympathetic with the North so there were no farmers sneaking out at night to stir up mischief, or tunnels under the hamlet to store arms.

Li's old friend, Phan, led the third force to be considered, the North Vietnamese Army, and Phan's battalion had not yet shown itself, but they were out there on the slopes of the mountains, and they were pipelining supplies to the Viet Cong and urging them to more action. But the pesky marines were everywhere, patrolling, watching, turning every stone. And most threatening of all — the peasants were beginning to accept them.

Schrader jumped from the dike down to the edge of the bean field, only a three-foot jump but he landed hard and the walkie-talkie clipped to his flak jacket slapped his thigh and he rattled like an old can. Behind him a good thirty yards came Krause, stepping along the dikes and grinning at the peasant women who were working, and they would nod and grin back and quickly look away.

Schrader followed the edge of the field, next to the treeline, and he peered hard into the green shadows but it was too thick along there to see. It was the squad's day to patrol the fields, and because they were strung out so far, Haney and his team leaders each had a hand radio. All the work day they walked a long, irregular line about the fields, keeping hard to the treeline, circling the hamlet four or five times before coming in and escorting the merchants and whores inside and securing the gate.

The longer reconnaissance patrol, which was far more arduous, was usually complete by five o'clock and those men could then knock off.

Schrader glanced back at Krause again, to see if he was skylarking, and then Haney's voice squawked over the walkie-talkie, asking for reports.

"Okay here." Mingo's voice came across.

Schrader lifted the radio and pushed the key. "Okay here, Joe," he said and he dropped the box roughly and it swung by its clip and cord.

He heard Calvin check in. "Okay here. When's lunch, Joe?"

Ten minutes, was the metallic response.

Schrader peered ahead, across the flat plain, and the air shimmered in the heat. One of Li's fields was nearby, and he thought he saw the man working, or someone there at least, but he hoped that it was Li. The farmers irrigated from a small river that flowed from the mountains, with swift running water, and they robbed it with channels and wooden locks, and Li's best bean field lay along an irrigating channel ahead of Schrader perhaps a quarter mile.

The sun was high and hot and Schrader was ready for a break. One of his three canteens was Kool-Aid and he was saving it for lunch, for the C-ration chicken and noodles and a tin of peaches that he would mix with a tin of pound cake and maybe he would eat a tin of ham, too, and the last of the cookies his mom had sent. There would be ample time. Haney would give them three-quarters of an hour and Schrader could lean against a tree and shuck the sixty-odd pounds he carried and eat what seemed a proper meal.

He was reaching the furthermost point from the hamlet, and he glanced over his shoulder and saw it in the distance like an ants' nest, and he could see the tiny figures going in and out of the gate. Ahead of him and to the right lay the river, blue-green and cooled by the mountain slopes, but the patrol would turn and not reach it and Schrader could only imagine plunging into the water for a swim. Women would be doing laundry at the ford. Old Huong would be there, too, the man with the water contract and the bicycle-driven pump, and one of his sons would be pedaling furiously to fill the marines' mobile water tank. Schrader could picture the river clearly in his mind but it was off limits for recreation, and the thought of a swim was almost torturous so he shook the sweat from his face and paid attention to the patrol.

It was Li in the field all right, with his oldest son, and he waved as Schrader drew closer. They were hoeing beans, Li with his back straight and dipping with the hoe, letting his stomach and shoulders take the strain and saving his arms.

Little Vo was not so skilled, using his arms more and bending his back, and he stopped often for a rest.

Schrader no sooner leaped the irrigation channel when word was passed on the radio; break for lunch, and Schrader gave the sign to Krause behind, who passed it along to Brennan. Murphy was up ahead and Schrader whistled to get his attention, and all of them went to the shade of the trees, but they kept their distance from each other. Schrader found a spot where he could view the line of patrol, and see a ways into the brush as well, and he dropped his pack noisily and the cartridge belt and flak jacket and helmet all in a pile, and he leaned his rifle carefully against a tree.

He was soaked with sweat, so he took off his shirt and hung it on a branch and sat by his pack and rummaged inside for the tins.

Heat tablets are issued with C-rations, little blue squares that burn extremely hot and Schrader was heating his chicken and noodles with one when he saw Li and Vo take a rest, and he waved and called.

Li and his son walked to the shade with a water bottle and hunkered beside the American.

"How about some lunch, Mr. Li? I got some extra C-rations."

"No thank you, David. My wife will bring our meal, soon. But the boy needs a rest, if we are not disturbing you."

Schrader reached in his pack and took out the cookies wrapped in foil and offered some to the boy. *Cua toi me da bo lo nhung cai nay*, Vo. My mother baked these, Vo, Schrader told him.

The boy's eyes grew wide and he glanced secretively at his father, who nodded, and Vo reached out eagerly and took a cookie from the foil.

Schrader gestured. *Mot cai nua*, Have another.

Vo took one quickly in his other hand and munched them with delight. They were Mrs. Schrader's good peanut butter cookies, almost ovenfresh.

"He's a handsome boy, Mr. Li."

"He's my pride," Li said simply, and then glanced at the child affectionately. "I waited long to have a family. They mean much to me."

Schrader had started to eat his chow. He swallowed a

mouthful. "That sounds like something my father would say," he replied, wiping his fingers on his trousers.

"Does he have a big farm, David?"

"No sir. Not as American farms go. He owns three hundred acres, almost as much as lies around the hamlet. But he leases another six hundred acres."

Li had to think a minute to comprehend. He cocked his head and pulled at the stub of his ear. "That is *beaucoup* land for one man," he grinned, using the French word and shaking his head. "If we had only one little tractor here, think what we could do."

At the mention of a tractor, Schrader started and recalled his dream. He had no memory of it until then. He looked out across the fields with the fleeting thrill of *deja vu* and the beans in flower and the droning of the bees and the cast of the sunlight on the fields was something he had seen before. But it slipped away and he could not call it back, and he sat with his mouth open, full of half-chewed food.

Li had said something to him.

"What was that, Mr. Li?"

"This has all been done by hands and backs," Li nodded toward the fields. "The jungle cleared away and the dikes built. The water channels dug. When I was a boy, not so much land was used."

"How much less?" Schrader asked.

Li considered. "Half, at least," he replied. "Where we are talking now was once thick jungle. The water channels down the river were all the village had."

"It must have been pretty wild country," Schrader commented.

"Yes," Li replied. "When I was the same age as Vo, a tiger began to live and hunt, this side of the river. An old male. It ate some pigs and a buffalo, but the beast had to be endured because we could not have guns. Only the *Phap* and the guerillas and the bandits had guns. Then one day it killed a young woman and carried her off. All the men came together with what weapons they had, and some had only sharp hoes and cane knives, and a big hunt began."

Schrader was listening intently.

"I remember the men making great noises and singing and thrashing in the thick of the jungle to drive the tiger out.

I wanted to follow them, but my mother kept me back. Later, my uncle told me how brave my father was, so far forward. Two men were attacked before they drove the beast into a clearing. My father was the first man to shoot an arrow into the tiger, a good shot and it hurt the beast. Then other men shot it, too, and men with spears ran up, and that was the killing of the tiger . . ."

"I guess your father was some man. *Beaucoup homme*, eh?" Schrader remembered some of his school French. "What happened to him?" Schrader asked casually, then thought that he should not have, when he saw Li sigh deeply and look away.

"One night he went on a raid without me," Li began. "I had a fever, so he left me in the camp. When they returned, my father was not with them. He was wounded and captured. He died under torture. The *Phap* promised his life if he told them how to find the camp. But he would not. This I know because we had our people in the camp of the *Phap*, and I learned the way he died. They hung him upside down and cut his throat . . . This was during the brief rebellion of 1940. Many of the Nationalists had been armed by the Japanese, as a ploy to weaken and threaten the Vichy French. But we were betrayed by the Japanese, too. It ended in ruin."

Schrader heard no feeling in Li's voice, saw no anger in his eyes. But it was there in the man somewhere, as if the stoic response was his emotion turned inward, a sorrow only for his soul, the last of his family to remember. Schrader was only beginning to grasp the profoundness of family to the Vietnamese. He shivered in the heat of the day. There were ghosts all around. Li believed in them and when Schrader listened to the stories, times past and people who once lived were real to him, too.

"We had a civil war in America, you know," Schrader said, handing the canteen of Kool-aid to the boy and watching as he sniffed and drank and finally grinned.

"Yes," Li nodded. "Between the North and the South, to free the African slaves. It was over quick."

Schrader laughed. "Yeah. We don't like to drag our wars out."

"Drag them out?"

"Fight for very long, I mean."

Li nodded, as if he was tucking the phrase away.

Schrader stood up and walked a few steps out of the shade and looked up and down the line of patrol. He could see Krause and Murphy. Everything was okay. He sat down again to finish his meal, and then he threw the empty tins carelessly into the brush, looking dissatisfied.

"What I wouldn't give for some home cooking," he muttered, lighting a smoke to cut the taste of the grease.

"That is easy, David. I have been meaning to invite you."

"Sir?"

"To my home, for a supper my wife will cook. It seems that your sergeant and your lieutenant have been guests at Luc's house twice, but no one has yet invited the real fighting men to their home," and Li chuckled at that. "I will ask Mingo and Calvin as well, and your Corporal Haney if he will come."

"That sounds great, Mr. Li. Just let us know when."

"In a few days, David. If we can have the permission of your officer." Li stood up, and Schrader got to his feet. "We should return to our work."

"Okay, Mr. Li. See you later."

Li took his son's hand and they walked out into their field and took up their hoes, and Schrader leaned against the tree with his rifle beside him and he thought of home. Soon enough the radio was squawking, "saddle up!" and the lance corporal whistled the attention of his fireteam and they all clambered into their gear and continued their watch-dog circuit about the fields.

It was the next afternoon that Haney stood by the edge of the jungle and peered apprehensively at the hill and the wide, open plain his squad had to cross. The old woman's back was a long and narrow hill that cut the swaying grasslands like a fin in water, and its top was iron-red clay that looked like a wound, and Haney squinted to catch a hint of motion on the peak but he saw nothing. The hill stood apart from the higher mountains behind, like a child pushed from a crowd, and Haney was always nervous when they crossed that open ground.

But he was tense, anyway. It had been too quiet for too long, too itchingly, back-of-the-neck quiet, and the corporal knew it could not continue.

Calderone stood a little behind him, smoking, leaning his weight on his rifle.

Haney looked back down the trail at the men kneeling and sitting and looking wilted. He had not seen a smile or heard a joke cracked the whole morning. They were too hang-dogged to bitch.

"Do it quick, Mingo," Haney said. "We'll keep wide spaces, maybe twenty yards. Hold up when you reach the trees."

Calderone caught the man's edginess. Over the months he had learned to look for the signs, the darting eyes and the measured breathing through the nose. You could always tell with Haney. It would suddenly be like there was ice all around him, and those eyes moving and restless, trying to see it all.

Mingo nodded tersely and ground the butt under his foot. He rinsed his mouth from his canteen and hitched up his pants to ease the rash in his crotch. Then he stepped from the cover of the brush into the knee-high grass. It was taller in places, but thick and he had to look close. The gooks would lay stringers and there wasn't much warning when you popped one. There were trails worn by other patrols, but Mingo avoided all these and moved far to the right, closer to the hill. Its base rose from a sea of grass about four hundred yards away.

But he only glanced at it quickly. More important was where he put his feet. Mingo had a trick of moving his eyes in little half circles, back and forth and farther out, like the ripples of a pool. He would only look so far, then in those same rhythmic sweeps his eyes would come back to his feet. Out and back, a little bit at a time. His eyes were good and sharp and quick to see the slightest motion. They had to be. There were trip wires and punji sticks, spider holes and every conceivable type of mine. There were arrows and spears and swinging spikes and pitfalls.

But most of all there were snakes. Mingo was quick to admit it; what he looked for first, what he couldn't help but see first, were snakes.

It was hard, then, looking for all those things because Haney wanted it done quick and Mingo was gritting his teeth as the grass rolled at his feet. The faster he went, the closer in he had to keep his eyes. Mingo was seeing in twenty yard sections, out and back, and let the others worry about the rest of it.

He glanced behind and the motion threw sweat in his eyes. There were eight others in the open and Mingo was well into the grass. The squad would be strung three hundred yards before all of them were out of the brush.

Mingo's gaze jumped from a long brown stick to a glint of rock to a place where the grass was matted down. All of it went through his brain and was recognized and rejected and he went on looking about. A mongoose streaked across his path and he jumped.

Then the Viet Cong on the hill cut loose.

They waited until all the squad was in the open before their .50 caliber began to hammer.

Haney had kept a nervous eye on the hilltop, so he saw the flashes and was shouting a warning as the rounds thudded into the ground.

The gunners began at the end and worked up the line to the point.

Mingo heard an agonized scream as he dove on the ground and covered his head. The monster bullets kicked dirt around him, then the gunners worked back to the other end. His heart was in his mouth. He raised his head and saw flashes at the crest, looked down the line to see Burgess hustling his team back to the brush.

He jumped to his feet, screaming and waving to his team; "MOVE IT! GODDAMN IT! MOVE IT!"

They were scared but on their feet running forward, legs churning fifty, sixty yards. Then the guns swung their way and the men plowed into the ground.

The gunners worked them over good, chewing up the ground. But the deep grass was concealment and nobody was hit.

Schrader, in the middle, moved his team up. When the .50 swung to the middle, Mingo moved his team again. Haney hung back in some deeper grass, a wounded man there with the corpsman, and the radioman barking the coordinates into the mike.

Mingo got pinned down and Schrader moved his team again. The hilltop was barely within range of their rifles and Calderone lay flat with his eyes shut, his head spinning from the heat and his chest sucking air like a bellows.

He moved his team once more before the artillery came screeching in. The first spotter round landed jarringly close. Some seconds passed and the staccato of the .50 continued.

The next artillery round landed halfway up the slope, and the machine gun fell silent. The cannon-cockers had the range and began to walk the shells up the slope to the crest. They blew hell out of the hilltop for about ninety seconds, then everybody got on their feet and began to run like crazy. Haney left the tall grass and began to churn behind Schrader's team. Burgess and his men broke from the brush ahead of them all. It was a horse race, two-legged horses weighted with gear and tired before the start.

At the base of the hill the final rubber-legged, gut-busting assault began. They grunted and fell to their knees and cursed and choked and grunted some more.

Mingo lost his helmet and it bounced down the hill. His face was contorted and all he could see was the crest like something in a dream, distant and close both. He was snarling and he hated everything; the sun, the grass, the god-damnedmotherfucking-assbusting hill and the Marine Corps. He was just a spinal cord and a gun and he wanted to kill something.

But when he staggered to the top, firing blindly from the hip, there was nothing but smoking shell craters and empty brass casings. Around him there were cotton mouths and ragged faces and men dropping to their knees.

The wind moaned hollowly. They moved to the far slope and peered down. It ended in a tangle of jungle that swept unbroken to the barrier of mountains two miles away. There was no sign of anyone.

Mingo kicked a rock and started a tiny landslide. His chest ached too much to talk.

Haney walked the breadth of the hilltop. It was a finback, and as he looked over the waving grass a dizziness came to him and it seemed the fin was moving. He dropped to one knee until his head stopped spinning.

"What now, Joe?"

The voice was dim and distant, and for a moment Haney looked blankly at nothing. He knew that when they left the hill, Charlie could take it right back again.

"We go down. A chopper's coming for Harris."

"You want to leave a team up here?"

Haney shook his head. "No, we got to finish the patrol. If they want the bastard back they can have it."

"Until tomorrow."

"Yeah, until tomorrow."

Dragging their asses behind, the squad stumbled, limped and made it to the valley floor.

Market day was like a carnival.

It was exactly that to Schrader, walking along with the crowd, jostling between the stands, the mouse-like children dashing about, the smells of fried food and the sweet fruit and pastry, and the sing-song rhythm of a thousand voices.

The square in Ahn Lac was long and open, with rows of booths up the middle, back to back, and more stalls along the two long sides. Schrader was two heads taller than the people surging by him, but he was paid little mind as the peasants thronged around tending to the business of buying and selling, and the art of haggling and watching the haggle. Everywhere, people were pinching fruit and poking hens and fingering cloth, or putting a palm flat out at the refusal of an offered price. An old man was shopping for a suckling pig and he grabbed one squeeler up by the hind legs and pointed at the underside and shook his head disgustedly. The seller protested and reddened in the face, but the old man looked sour and walked on to another stall, and Schrader guessed the farmer had done a sloppy castration, or had not cut the hog at all.

He was walking alone, duty done for a time, having brought up the rear of the procession from Ap Do to the main village. It was about eight miles, but an easy hike on the road and they didn't have to lug their packs. Later in the afternoon, they would escort the peasants back, only one squad, but with the lieutenant and his driver in the jeep, zipping up and down the procession, and the corpsman riding too.

Schrader pushed his way gently through the crowd and walked out a side aisle to the one main street, and the small shop district. It was only one block long, the structures mixed, old French stucco buildings beside native shops of bamboo and thatching. The plaster was peeling from the buildings and the whitewash was fading, and Schrader had seen a hundred whistle-stops like this back home, little towns that once had the promise of prosperity.

Li had told Schrader of the logging trade that had gone on in the mountains, when there were coffee plantations, too, and a rail line to Ahn Lac. The line was rusted and grown over, east of the village, and now the mountains were inaccessible, unless you happened to have a reinforced battalion at hand.

Not that the peasants had benefitted when Ahn Lac was prosperous. Oh no. The logging and plantations were French enterprises and the businesses in Ahn Lac had been French owned, or owned by their Vietnamese lackeys, and the peasant's lot was a sorry one. In the 1920s and 1930s, the French were systematically robbing the Viets of their land—a people who for a thousand years had a land-owning farming class, and not a chattel peasantry at all. Schrader had learned this from Li, and discovered that the old mandarin system adopted by the ancient Viets was actually civil-service based. This came as a surprise to a kid who thought that Andrew Jackson had invented the civil service, and that all Orientals had been slaves to some Emperor.

It was quieter out on the street, away from the market square, but it was busy enough, nonetheless. Storefronts had been reopened and there was a barber shop and two new bars and new cafe. Ahn Lac was the biggest village clear to the coast, and battalion headquarters was there in a compound outside the village. A full rifle company was billeted at headquarters; three platoons and a heavy weapons' section. And a battery of 155 howitzers and a tank detachment, too. If the platoon in Ap Do ever needed reinforcements, it could only come from Ahn Lac. Marine units all over I Corps were spread thin, and lately a discernible pressure was being mounted by the Communists on the approaches to Danang, thirty miles southeast, and the ripples of that pressure would reach Ap Do soon enough. But Schrader had no knowledge of that, or care either, strolling along with the bright blue sky above and the afternoon free.

He meandered almost to the end of the village, down one side of the street, taking his time and staring about curiously, bumping into people and stone-walling vendors. He passed one of the new bars, dim inside and open, with some tables and chairs french-style on the sidewalk, and Schrader crossed the street there. But he turned at little feet padding behind him.

"Hey yoo! Yoo friends inside!" a wide-eyed and quick-footed urchin grabbed his shirt and gave it a tug. "Yoo friends there!" and he pointed at the bar. "Yoo come! Yes?"

Schrader patted his shoulder and followed along, and at a table in the recesses of the bar, in a corner, sat his three buddies. Half the tables were full of marines, but Schrader saw no one else from the squad.

"Hey, Joe! You gonna relax for a change?"

Haney shrugged. "Why not? Shuck your gear and sit down."

"Yeah, boot," Mingo told him. "Sit down and buy a round of beer."

Schrader dropped his gear heavily. "Classy place. Real floor. Tried the stuff yet, Calvin?"

"Not yet. Maybe later some better lookin' ones will come on."

"I don't know. These gals are pretty cute."

"Too skinny. Too something, but I don't know what. I want a change, man. These chicks all screw the same, like the action was tooled at the same factory, you know? Take a thousand little Toyotas or something and line 'em up and they all start the same and go the same and steer . . ." Calvin gestured grumpily, "These boom-boom girls are all alike, too. No imagination."

"Schrader don't require no imagination," Mingo said. "He just likes the woman to lay there."

Schrader thought of Becky Chaffee. You couldn't tie her down with a rope. "I know a gal who'd throw your skinny ass clean to Kansas, Calderone, and you'd crawl back and beg for more."

Mingo smacked his lips. "That will get me to Missouri! I promise you, man."

Haney was sitting quietly and half listening, the little urchin behind his chair against the wall, saying nothing, waiting for a handout or another errand to run. There were four girls working the club, busy with their regular customers, and Schrader had not gotten a beer. The boss was behind the bar, which was only a bamboo front with a plywood top, and he saw Schrader without a drink and he snapped at one of his girls. A slender young whore with almond eyes and nice teeth got up sulkily and moved toward their table. In two steps her mood had changed and she was smiling pouty-mouthed as she came up to them. She purred against Schrader and stroked his face.

"Wot want, honey?" she crooned. "You lonely? You think me prit-tee?"

Kha-Kha, Schrader shrugged. So so.

She pushed away roughly. "Hmph! You have no *con nguoi mat!*" No eyeballs.

Schrader laughed at her. *Mang lai bon bia lahn, co, va da phai, co la dep lam.* Bring us four cold beers, girl, and yes, you are very pretty.

Appeased, the little whore batted her lashes and went off to the bar.

"Uh-ohhh," Calvin told them. "Schrader's workin' on a freebie."

"The sonovabitch is a holdout," Mingo muttered, shaking his head at Schrader. "Why the hell didn't they send me to language school?"

"You started speaking it, Mingo, somebody'd shoot you for a gook."

"Bullshit! Mexicans don't look anything like gooks."

"From behind?"

"Well maybe from behind."

Haney laughed suddenly and they all looked at him. "Had a Japanese kid with us on my first tour. Born in Anaheim. Good trooper. That poor sucker caught more flak from MPs and CID or any other officer who didn't know him, thinking he was a gook in an American uniform, maybe a spy, you know. Let me see your ID, private, let me see your dog tags, what unit are you with? And he didn't look anything like a Viet." Haney laughed to himself, shaking his head, and his three buddies looked at one another and didn't say anything. Joe wasn't laughing much lately.

The girl came back with the beer and clumped them loudly on the table and looked at them saucily.

Nhieu qua? Schrader asked. How much?

Hai tram dong, she told him. Two hundred piastres. Two bucks.

Schrader paid, shaking his head. "This place ain't cheap."

"It's this real floor," Calvin told him, pointing down. "Gotta pay for the atmosphere."

"Buy me drink?" the girl chirped, rubbing against Schrader again. But he shook his head.

"You?" looking at Calvin.

"No, baby. Go away now. *Di di.*"

The whore looked at Haney, who was paying her no mind. "You?" she asked, and reached down quickly and grabbed at his crotch.

It was a common gesture. The girls did it to everyone. But Haney's hand moved like a snake to her wrist and the girl yelped in pain and dropped to her knees, her face contorted.

The club got suddenly quiet and the whore jumped to her feet just as the gray-haired boss hurried from behind the bar.

The girl screamed at Haney, "You Muthafuck!" and her boss grabbed her quickly and spun her around and pushed her toward the back. Then he waved his hands at them placatingly. "No trobble, okay? Eveyteng okay. Okay?"

Da phai, Haney told him. "No trouble." He took a hundred piastres note from his shirt pocket. "Here, give this to the girl," and the little man snatched the note quickly and grinned big and backed away, and the bar-noise started up again.

Haney glanced at his friends, red-faced. "She surprised me," he mumbled. Then he lifted the bottle and drank the beer in one chugging gulp, and abruptly stood up. "Thanks for the beer, David."

"Where you goin', man?"

Haney was putting on his cartridge belt. "Battalion head-quarters, to see the company clerk."

"Ain't Helen gettin' her money yet?"

"Not all that's due her," the corporal replied, the helmet on his head, slinging his rifle. "It's ten-thirty now. Be on the road at one-thirty. Have every swingin' dick there, and sober."

"Ain't that kind of early?" Mingo asked. "Nobody be leavin' till three, anyway."

"Lieutenant's orders. Do you know where your teams are now, by the way?"

The three of them exchanged glances. "Uh, yeah. I think so," Schrader mumbled. He really had no idea where his men were.

Calvin looked at the wall across the room.

Mingo stared at his nails. "They're somewhere close," he

mumbled. "What's the big deal, Joe? We don't have to hang around those boots."

Haney didn't answer. He just nodded and said, "See you later," and walked between the tables and out the bar.

"What does that mean?" Schrader asked. "Are we supposed to go find out teams or what?"

"It means take your own chances," Calvin told him. "Joe was telling us what he'd do."

"Well, I'm sittin' right here," Mingo announced, determined. "And I'm drinkin' this beer, and maybe I'll get me some of this sideways pussy, eh?"

"Any way does you. Up and down or diagonal and inside out."

Schrader was glancing around the barroom, the wall papered with American pinups, a loft in back in one corner over the makeshift bar. The club was just a large, high-ceilinged room and it showed no clue of what it had been before, when the French were there. Schrader had counted five buildings in the French style, not clustered but standing independently; three on one side of the street and two on the other. Perhaps old trading offices. Four of them were abandoned when the battalion had first arrived. And on the other side of the village, beyond the market square, was an old building, long and low, with the roof caved in, and Schrader thought it might once have been barracks or a hospital for French troops. But now the jungle was creeping in.

Schrader pointed at something on the ceiling. "What do you think those were?"

Calvin looked up. "You mean those outlet boxes?"

"That's what I think, too," Schrader said.

"So?"

"So they had electricity here once."

"Big deal," Mingo said. "That don't do us any good."

"I wonder where it came from," Schrader persisted. "You hear about the river being dammed anywhere?"

Calvin shook his head. "Maybe they had generators."

"We're s'posed to get one, ain't we?" Mingo asked. "I heard Doc Shelton bitchin' because we didn't have a refrigerator."

"That's right. His antibiotics spoil," Calvin replied. "But mostly, he wants ice cubes for his bourbon."

Mingo snapped his fingers. "That reminds me. I wanta take some booze back to camp."

"Why bother to carry it?" Schrader asked. "Old Houng can get you the same stuff."

"Yeah, but the last time I bought a bottle, the seal was broken. I think the old man waters it down."

Calvin laughed. "So let him make a little extra. Besides, man, it keeps you from gettin' drunk and losin' it."

Mingo paid him no mind. The urchin was still standing against the wall quietly and Mingo gestured to him. *Ven aca, muchacho,* and the kid stepped over eagerly, his eyes big.

"Wot want, you?"

"You know what whiskey is? A bottle of whiskey," said Mingo, holding his hands apart as though measuring a bottle.

"Sure. Me know," the kid said.

"Silver Fox, you know."

"Sure. Seelver Fox."

"A new bottle, kid. Tell him, David."

Cai chai moi. Khong mo. A new bottle, not opened, Schrader said.

"Okay." And the boy sped past the tables and out to the street.

Another whore came over to the table, taller than the first and moon-faced, her hair bobbed short.

"You drink?" she asked simply, not touching any of them and standing back a little. Haney had chilled the table.

"Three more beers," Calvin told her.

"Make it two," Schrader said. "I'm gonna finish this one and look around some."

Calvin gestured two and the girl walked off, and Schrader gulped his beer and stood and put on his gear.

"Watch where you put your feet," Calvin told him.

"Yeah," Mingo echoed. "Don't fall on any punji stick."

Schrader nodded. "You watch where you put your cock. Don't fall in a hole you can't climb out of."

Mingo grinned. "Calvin'll pull me up."

Schrader squinted in the afternoon light and glanced up and down the small block. First, he wanted to locate his men so he crossed the street, stopping for a peasant scurrying past with a pull cart, and then he spotted Krause in the barber shop, waiting for a turn.

Krause was baby-faced and still a little chubby, but they were sweating it off him quick enough.

"Hey Dave," the man said as Schrader walked in the open front, ducking beneath the thatched awning. The little barber looked up from the throat he was shaving and grinned.

"Where's Brennan and Murphy?"

"A couple of doors down, in the bar," Krause said. "They got a couple girls. They're still screwin'."

"Will you see them later?"

"Yeah. After I'm done here."

"We'll saddle up at one-thirty sharp. The lieutenant wants us on the road then. You tell the guys, huh?"

"Sure."

"And be sober."

"Sure," Krause grinned.

That wasn't good enough, Schrader knew, as he walked up the street to the edge of the village. He couldn't leave the responsibility with Krause. He would have to round them up himself, so he glanced at his watch and gave himself two hours before he needed to return.

Down the road, east of the village, he saw two camps dirty gray in the distance. One was theirs, and he could see the Stars and Stripes riffling lazily from a pole, and the snouts of the cannons. But across the road, in the middle of a plain was a billet for government soldiers, calling themselves Rangers, but Schrader had more faith in the militia at Ap Do. And thinking about the soldiers just then, it occurred to him that they might be patrolling. Schrader did not want to run across one of their patrols (as trigger-happy and jumpy as they were) and he eyed the land to the north. That was where the river lay, across a glistening green belt of paddies, and Schrader tried to count them, standing on the raised road but his perspective became too flat across the distance. He lost the last few paddies in a shimmering, narrow-visioned haze. It was perhaps three-quarters of a mile and he would have to zig-zag along the dikes. Either that, or turn west back through the village and walk north along the jungle that bordered the paddies. The village curved and bulged there as if to spill and overflow into the paddies, the last row of huts seeming to tilt outward a little, and Schrader shook his head and stared at the huts again but the illusion persisted. He was hearing the hum and buzz from the market square as he stepped off the road and down to a dike. The last hut was only a hundred feet away. It was a whorehouse, newly-built, with the thatching and bamboo still shiny and a wooden fence surrounding a small back yard. In the yard there were cubicles of bamboo and the marines would take the girls there and make their hurried, clutching love with only curtains between the couples.

Schrader heard laughter from the hut. Beer bottles slammed onto card tables. As he walked farther into the paddies the sounds abated and soon it was quite still, except for his own creaking and clattering. There he was, in the heat of midday, having hiked eight miles already, about to hike another eight, and he was walking around like a tourist, an armored tourist, with hand grenades and a great deal of ammunition and knives and a strangling wire he carried because he thought it looked evil, and he was only out for a friendly stroll. He did not notice the forty pounds of gear. Only the helmet bothered him. He took it off and hung its strap over a canteen that fitted aside his cartridge belt, and he put on his cap instead, pulling it from his shirt. *I'm a walking goddamned five and ten*, Schrader was thinking; *some hats for your kid, lady? some ammo, mister? some nuts and bolts? Sure, I'll shake 'em out of my head*. And he laughed to himself as he walked, and a flock of ducks quacked nervously as they poked and swam about an unplanted, flooded paddy. Schrader thought about that, wondering how late in the season they could still plant. *When's the first harvest? I'll have to ask Li.*

There were only a few peasants working that day, scattered about here and there, and one of them was ahead—an old greybeard, looking like a stick man in his black garb, and he grinned and waved at Schrader as he weeded and dug in the knee-deep muck.

Chao, ong. Schrader called. Hello sir. *Tai sao ong lam viec vao thoi-gia?* Schrader asked. Why are you working on market day?

The old man looked surprised and showed his blackened gums. He replied something quickly, too quickly, and Schrader only guessed at what the man said. Work never stops, he guessed.

Da phai. Nay la thuc, Schrader replied. Yes, this is true. and he walked on past the old man, who stared curiously at the American who spoke his language, wondering what he was doing hiking around alone.

Schrader was halfway across, and he began to step along quicker. He came upon one lone dike that ran straight toward the trees, with smaller dikes branching right and left, and he supposed there was a path at the end of it, into the jungle. He was a little nervous, coming upon the dim treeline all alone, an easy shot for a sniper. His rifle was slung over his shoulder, and he swung it niftily into his hands and carried the weapon at port, ready to jump left or right. Why the hell was he doing this anyway? And he harassed himself for stupidity, but soon he was among the cooling trees and nothing had happened and he relaxed.

There was a wide path through the jungle, marked by cart wheels, and Schrader walked along one side of it, then the other, crossing the path and eyeing ahead for any movement. He heard voices chatting, and laughing. Soon a group of women came into view, all of them young and slim except for one old bag-of-bones crone, who cackled as she told a story to the other women. The fresh-faced country girls were all giggling. They got quiet as Schrader came down the path, big and hulking, and he was not comfortable with their nervousness. He spoke as they passed, and the chatter broke out again; a few of the girls glancing back modestly. They were all carrying fresh laundry from the river. Schrader looked at his watch. Plenty of time.

He came upon a well-trod cross trail and he studied its direction. It appeared to curve back toward the south, where the village lay. Schrader thought he knew where the path came out on the road. He hiked on farther and there was the river, blue-green and glimmering. At Ap Do it was narrow and deep, but here the river broadened lazily, and peasants in the middle were only waist-deep in the water. There were women on the bank, kneeling and scrubbing clothes with soap and brushes. Schrader stepped from the jungle path onto a broad shelf of grass, with the water's edge a stone's throw away. He eyed the terrain. It all seemed peaceful enough. The Viets paid little mind to him as he walked to the water's edge and peered up and down the length of the river. He thought he might see an old foundation for a water turbine—the idea of electricity in Ahn Lac had intrigued him—but he spotted nothing. No concrete, no piers. The rough country on the opposite bank lay unbroken down to the water's edge; he saw no ripples in the current where a submerged foundation might lie. There was another group of women picking up laundry to carry to the village. Schrader hailed them and stepped close, speaking to the eldest—not an old crone, but a woman maybe in her forties, a bright orange sash about her waist.

"*Xin loi, ba,* excuse me, ma'am," Schrader began, "have you lived in Ahn Lac a long time?"

The woman looked at him curiously. "Yes, yes. All my life."

"And you were here when the French were here?"

The woman spat sideways and shaded her eyes with her hand, staring up at the big marine. "Yes," she replied.

The nao Phap da lam ra cua ho diem-khi, khong? Schrader asked. How did the Phap make their electricity?

The woman looked at him strangely, wondering of what importance was that. And Schrader thought she did not understand, so he repeated the question.

The woman gestured with her hand. *Toi hieu.* I understand. And she thought another moment. "They had machines on wheels. When we kicked them out, they took the machines away. To the north, I think."

Schrader nodded his understanding. *Cam on, ba.* Thank you ma'am. And he stepped back, bowing slightly.

"That's all you want?" the woman asked.

"Yes. That's all."

The woman walked away. Silly question, he heard one say. *Dien cuong,* another spoke. Crazy. And they all laughed. Not the maiden giggles of younger girls, but the raucous, deprecating laughter of salty married women, and Schrader felt himself blush.

He found some soft grass in the shade and he shucked his gear, and sat and watched the river, eddies swirling gently, the water pale green with a touch of blue, and Schrader had never seen water just that color. He had never seen anything anywhere that was quite like the things he was coming to know in this land. Oh, trees were trees the world 'round and hard work was the same everywhere, sure, and sadness was felt by all. But this land was touched by man in ways Schrader had never known, and to a depth that he could only guess. Not the surface scars of the war on the land, although that was part of it. But the thousand-year struggle to change it, to adapt it with only hands and backs, to grow with it until land and man became like siblings reflecting the same qualities. Schrader knew American history. He knew they had pounced on the American West and mauled it, broken it without knowing they did so, instead of approaching it quietly, and stroking it as one does a shy horse. The people back home did not reflect the land as did these Vietnamese. Schrader caught a glimmer of that and it made him sad, because to him, his farming brethren had always been the salt of the earth. But their earth, their land, reflected them and their works, and not vice versa. They had stamped it so heavily and so suddenly, that the qualities of earth that Schrader saw reflected in the peasants did not show so intensely in the folks back home, as if they were too proud to let the land touch them so deeply.

Yes, that's it, Schrader was thinking. *It's the difference in pride. Dad is proud, and Li is proud, too, but in different ways. Li would back down, I can tell, if it was the wisest thing to do. What's the word? Expedient. But Dad would never back down from anything. No. Not my Dad. He's too damned stubborn. Things have to give way before him.*

The river was swirling by and Schrader was caught by the murmur of it, and the blue sky seemed to merge with the water and the boy revelled in the peace of it all. He could not have articulated the things he felt, although he struggled to see these things clearly. Later, he felt, a long time later, after a life of adjustment and new strengths, he'd remember these rare moments in a strange place so akin to his home. This ancient land had touched him profoundly.

Mines explode in different patterns depending on how deeply they're placed and how level, and depending on the shape of the mine. This one puffed out like a cotton flower, and it was shallow because there was a lot of orange-gray at the center of the blast and not much earth tossed about. But the people were tossed.

Schrader saw the cotton flower suddenly erupt and then

he heard the blast, then he saw the bodies flying. One small body was lofted like a doll and a bigger body was thrown straight along the ground like a line drive, and a bigger body still, the marine, fell very hard as though poleaxed. Schrader was about three hundred feet behind, and he heard people screaming and he began to run up the road. He turned around and saw his team running up, and he waved them back and shouted.

"Keep back and spread out! Get off the goddamned road and stay put!"

Schrader saw that Mingo was already there. It was one of his boys who was down and Mingo was beside him. Schrader was sucking wind and he ran as fast as he could. The peasants strung along the road began to rush forward and there was a small crowd before Schrader got there.

Through a blur, he saw a young girl — Schrader found out later she was eleven — with her leg blown off. The stump dipped in a pool of blood, her body was twisted horribly, and she was quite dead. Schrader ran to the downed marine, Miller. He was bleeding heavily from his head but he was conscious.

"Gimme your kit!" Mingo blurted, pressing a gauze tightly against Miller's forehead, and Schrader dropped his belt to the ground and pulled the heavy compress from the first-aid kit and tore it from the wrapper. Mingo grabbed the compress and slapped it over the bloody gauze already used.

"Get his feet up, quick! Use the helmets."

Schrader propped the steep pots under Miller's ankles and then reached to undo the cartridge belt. "Where else is he hit, Mingo?"

"Nowhere, I don't think. But pull the belt off easy. Miller, you are one lucky sonuvabitch. You gonna get a month in Hawaii, hombre, or maybe Japan, before they ship your ass back here."

Miller groaned. His face and chest were streaked and splotched with blood. ". . . don' wanna come back . . ."

Another marine was there, from Mingo's team, the leading fireteam, with the entire squad spread half-a-mile along the road.

Mingo barked at him. "Henry! Get me Wilson's kit. Move your ass!"

"Where the fuck's the corpsman?" Schrader asked.

"The jeep went on ahead to the hamlet. Two miles, man. They'll be here quick enough."

Schrader glanced down the road to see if his men were in place. Haney was running toward them.

"Here comes Joe."

"He's been on the radio. You hear that, Miller? Big bird comin' for you, brother. Snatch a round eye for me." Round eyes were American girls.

Miller nodded slowly, ". . . you know it, Mingo . . ."

"Hey man, don't move your head! You turning black 'n blue already!"

Haney came puffing up, the radioman some steps behind him, and he pushed past peasants standing in his way. No one had time yet to look at the injured Vietnamese, but he was alive and a dozen of his neighbors were there to help him. The little girl was past help. They ignored her.

"Just the head wound?" Haney asked, kneeling there and touching Miller's shoulder.

"Yeah," Mingo told him. "Mighta gouged the bone some, too bloody to tell. But his brains ain't leakin' out."

Miller grinned like some grotesque movie monster. ". . . says I get a month off, Joe . . ."

"That much—easy. More if you get infected. Plus you get the holy purple one."

". . . big fuckin' shit!" Miller griped.

"Here comes the jeep," Schrader cut in. "Next thing you know you'll be between clean sheets."

Haney looked at Schrader. "They'll be flares in the jeep. Green smoke for the chopper. Signal up one of your men and be ready to clear the gooks off the road when the bird comes in."

"Calvin's comin' now."

"Okay. Use him."

The jeep roared to a stop, throwing dust, and Hennessey the corpsman was beside them in a wink, the lieutenant also, and Schrader stepped past them and took the smoke flares from the floor of the jeep. He walked a dozen paces down the road, past the body of the child and the heavy blood smell. The flies were thick in the red pool and covered the stump. He met Calvin running up the road.

"Who is it? Miller?" Calvin panted hoarsely.

"Yeah. He's okay, though. Head wound. But he's conscious."

Calvin's eyes strayed to the little girl. He had deep brown eyes that showed strongly against the whites, and they softened and Schrader saw them moisten. He looked away quickly and turned away from Schrader.

"Joe wants us to clear the road for the chopper."

"Sure," Calvin said, still turned away.

"Your boys in place?" Schrader asked, just to banter — just to give Calvin a little time.

"Sure. Everything's set. Everything's perfect."

"Here's a flare."

Calvin reached for it.

"Rotten goddamned thing!" Schrader muttered.

"Yeah. Pretty rotten." Calvin turned away again, staring across the grassland to the jungle. "You know how many times I've seen this shit, man?"

"Lotta times, Calvin."

"That's right. Lotta times." Schrader could see his jaw muscles working and he gripped the flare tightly, his rifle hanging in his left hand. "Chopper be here soon," Calvin said. "Folks bunchin' up."

"Yeah. We better clear a zone. Help me move the little girl."

Calvin froze. "It ain't a little girl anymore," he said harshly. "I don't want to touch it."

Schrader said nothing. He'd seen Burgess stack bodies and never flinch. Yet Calvin stood there while Schrader took the girl's arms and pulled her gently to the side of the road, and the whole time he stared at the corpse as if in a struggle to look away, but his eyes would not allow it.

By then the corpsman was with the wounded peasant and the crowd on the road was growing, and the two grunts began politely to move the people off the road. It was then that two Vietnamese came running frantically from the direction of the village, a woman and a man and the woman was in the lead. As she drew close and saw the little girl she began to scream. The scream rose in crescendo; it went through Schrader like a knife of ice. Burgess winced and closed his eyes tightly.

He shuddered and turned away. The woman was screaming and the man weeping pathetically and Schrader could feel that his friend wanted to run.

"I better check on my team," Burgess tossed hurriedly over his shoulder.

Schrader ran up to him. "Hey, Calvin, the chopper will be in."

"Look, man—" Burgess stopped and turned on him. "—I ain't listening to this shit again! I've heard it enough. Here's the smoke. Get the driver to help you with the chopper." Schrader took the flare and Burgess hurried down the road as though the screaming was a swarm of hornets.

In a few minutes the chopper appeared low in the distance, *whop whop whopping*. Schrader hailed the private who drove the jeep and they tossed out the flares; Haney and the lieutenant motioning the peasants away, and the helicopter came drifting in. The engines drowned out the parents' agony —thundered over it dispassionately as if the war had no time for grief.

And the rotors blew the flies from the blood.

9

"What the hell are you doing, man?" Mingo said. "Hey, Calvin, look at this!"

"Damn! The boy thinks he's Sea School."

Schrader was shining his jungle boots, something no one ever bothered to do.

"He wants those stripes bad."

"Eat it, asswipe. I just thought I'd spiff up for dinner; somebody's gotta represent the Marine Corps."

Calvin and Mingo looked at each other and laughed.

"You just the one to do it, brother. Me'n Calvin go on home so's you can represent all three of us."

"Did old Houng bring the booze, David?"

"It isn't just booze. Cognac is special."

"Special! Smell me!"

"You will in a minute," Schrader told him, taking some cologne from his foot locker and splashing it all over his chest.

"Hey, gimme some." Mingo grabbed the bottle and doused himself. "I got a carton of Salems. Li likes 'em." Each of them had ordered something special from the weekly PX run. Calvin had a carton of tea bags and Haney had purchased a small case of instant coffee. They were gifts for Li and his wife.

Haney stepped into the tent with a towel around his waist, his hair dripping.

"Could you hurry it up, Joe? Don't want to be late."

"For chrissake, David! You said he didn't tell you a definite time."

"No, just after the evening's work was done. That's all he told me."

"Relax then. The gates aren't even shut yet."

"The boy's hungry," Calvin said. "He don't want his supper gettin' cold."

"Man, I'm hungry too," Mingo added, rubbing his belly. "I hope Mrs. Li can cook."

Calvin was dubious. "What can we expect, Joe?"

"For a formal dinner like this? Should be a real treat. Relax, Calvin. You won't be disappointed."

"As long as it ain't dog meat," Calvin muttered. "I ain't eatin' a goddamned puppy, no matter how good it's cooked."

Schrader poked him. "What you gonna do, ask what everything is before you eat it?"

Calvin shook his head. "I guess not. You see any dog meat, just let me know."

"How the hell we s'posed to know that?" Mingo asked. "You think it's gonna sit up and beg?"

Haney laughed at them. "This won't be like the roadside vendors, all duck eggs and fish sauce. Wait and see."

Schrader was wiping the dust from the bottle of cognac. As he looked up, Mingo was taking a shirt from his locker, the brightest, most flower-patterned shirt Schrader had ever seen.

"God Almighty! Run it up the flagpole!"

"Flagpole your ass!" Mingo scoffed. "This is my Big Kahuna shirt. Show some respect."

"Hey!" Calvin chuckled. "You gonna wear that?"

"You know it!" Mingo replied, but he looked a question at Haney.

"Fine with me," Joe shrugged. "But Sergeant Larret might not like it much."

"Hymnnn . . ." Schrader sang flatly, and the others took it up in chorus. ". . . Hymnnn! Fuck hymnnn!"

"What about all this gear?" Calvin bitched. "We got to lug it too?"

"Not the cartridge belts," Haney replied. "Just stick a couple of magazines in your pockets."

"Helmets and jackets?"

"Yep."

"Goddamned, Joe."

Haney cut them off. "Hey! We're only going down the street. It ain't R and R. We can leave all the gear outside. Except the rifles. We take those in the house."

Calderone looked sad. "Man, am I gonna look dumb! A sweaty goddamned flak jacket over my beautiful shirt."

"Beautiful shirt!" Schrader laughed. "That thing would start a fire just layin' in a barn."

"That's right," Mingo said proudly. "Heat and sex go together. This shirt is all sex."

"To a honeybee maybe."

When they were cleanly dressed and smelling good (they'd all used Schrader's cologne) they took their gifts and gear and walked across the compound. Mingo was carrying his flak jacket in his hand, and the westerly sun gleamed off his shirt, and he was a tropical garden in yellow and turquoise and magenta, helmet on his head, rifle over his shoulder, the fruit punch man gone to war.

Li met them at the top of the steps. He was dressed in a long black coat fitting snugly at the neck and ending just below his knees. His white trousers were neatly pressed and he did not look at all like the peasant farmer they knew.

Behind him there was giggling and three little heads poked around the doorway, until a sharp word came from inside and the heads vanished, *Pop*! like that.

"*Chao*, Li."

"Good evening." Li bowed as they came up the steps, the bamboo popping and groaning beneath their weight.

"Are we late?" Scharader asked.

"Oh no. In Vietnam one is seldom late. But Americans like to be prompt, so all is ready. Please come in."

They set their jackets and helmets in piles on the narrow porch. Haney looked apologetic. "We have to keep the rifles handy."

"Of course, Corporal," and Li motioned them inside.

None of them had been in Li's home before. It was the only pole house in the hamlet, and the hardwood floor, deeply polished, surprised Schrader. He thought it was mahogany with its red tint. The inside walls were covered with tapestries, and a breeze came through the open windows.

A low table was set in the front room they first stepped into. The house was perhaps twenty by thirty feet, and there were four rooms in all, each with a low ceiling only inches above Schrader's head.

Mrs. Li was standing beside the table, dressed in a pale yellow tunic. Her handsome face was composed and turned slightly down.

Chao ba Li, Schrader spoke. Hello, Mrs. Li.

She smiled and showed good teeth, but she looked apprehensively at the rifles. Schrader quickly leaned his in a corner, and the others did the same, barrels clattering one against the other. There was no sign of the children.

They sat on the floor, on mats grouped around the short-legged table. Li's wife began pouring tea from a porcelain service.

"This is *che-kho*," Li told them.

The marines kept their gifts beside them. Li was extremely polite and had not glanced at them. Calvin placed his on the table. "Here's some American tea, Mr. Li. I hope you like it."

"Very much, Calvin. Thank you," and he smiled and his wife beamed as she poured. She indeed liked the orange pekoe.

One by one they presented their gifts, awkwardly, and the host and hostess gratefully accepted. But still, Mrs. Li did not sit with them.

Li hefted the cognac and eyed it in the light streaming through the window. The cognac glowed a deep amber. "Even when I was fighting the *Phap*, I coveted their brandy. I would like to drink it now." He opened the bottle; Mrs. Li left the room and reappeared carrying a tray with five slim cups. The cups looked like ivory, all etched with blue figures. Li poured for them. "I admit to hearing of this cognac," Li told them. "My friend Huong had to send to Danang."

"That old man can get anything," Mingo said. "I got an uncle like that."

"Huong has nine children," Li commented, sipping his cognac. "He must be resourceful to feed them all."

"He was never a soldier, was he?" Haney asked abruptly, leaning forward with a certain intenseness.

"Why, no."

"Did it bother you when you came home after the war, to see all the men who didn't fight?"

"Perhaps, Corporal. But I had no idle time to dwell on it. Men have different passions, you know. Most men have no politics at all."

"I got politics," Schrader announced. "I'm a Republican."

"Jesus, I should've known it!" Burgess scoffed, shaking his head.

"You see," Li told them, "in America you can joke about your differences. But in Vietnam we seldom joke about politics. It is safer to keep quiet."

"I don't know," Schrader replied, shaking his head. "It gets pretty serious when my dad starts talking about F.D.R. He thinks Roosevelt sold the country down the river."

"And my mom loved him," Calvin said. "She thinks the sun rose on that man."

Li laughed and poured more cognac for Haney and Calderone. "And here you both are, in the same house together. It does not seem that you have to live your politics in America. Or am I wrong?"

"No, sir. You're not wrong," Haney told him. "In America, you live the easiest way you can. That's what everybody wants. The easiest way."

"Nothin' wrong with that," Mingo objected.

"No indeed," Li said. "I would gladly trade my bull for a tractor."

"But you wouldn't trade what you believe in for a tractor, Mr. Li. You wouldn't forget there are things worth fighting for."

"Amen, brother," Calvin said.

Haney looked across the table at him. "We're not thinking the same things, Calvin."

"But I can dig it," Burgess told him. "You want to believe in this stinkin' war, Joe—excuse me Mr. Li, no offense to you—but for me this war stinks. A judge *made* me join the marines. I would *never* have volunteered for this! Never! Joe here wants to believe the war is a good thing 'cause he could die anytime and he don't want it to be for nothin'."

Li glanced at Haney as he poured more cognac. From the beginning the Viet had been curious: why had they volunteered to come halfway around the world? They had everything in America. Youth, homes, freedom.

"Calvin," Li began, "neither would I have been a soldier, had not fate forced it upon me. I would have stayed here in Ap Do and had as many children as Huong. I am sympathetic with you, and I am sorry that you are forced to be here now. But, my young friends, I would like to thank you all for being here. That is why I have invited you. To thank you." And he raised his cup in the European fashion, and the three of them grinned uncomfortably. Haney did not grin. He stared at Li until Li cocked his head as if to ask was anything wrong. Then Haney smiled.

"No one ever said that to me," Haney told him. "I've been here almost two years. Nobody's ever thanked me."

"They are all afraid of you, Corporal. It is difficult to be grateful to someone you fear. And yet look at our new prosperity, eh? And the Communists leave us alone and we feel safe in our fields . . ."

"And the Cong plant mines to get us, and kill a little girl instead," Calvin said bitterly.

"Yes, a terrible thing. Unforgivable. But there would still be killing if you were not here. Understand that. My neighbors will never thank you. And they will make jokes behind your back. Yet they want you to remain. But for me, it is different. I was a soldier once. I hope that each of you is someday an old soldier like me."

"I'll drink to that," Haney said.

Schrader's stomach growled loudly.

"I think I hear the call to dinner," Li joked and he glanced through the doorway to his left and his wife appeared quietly, removing the large tea service from the table but leaving the brandy cups and bottle. All through the conversation, wonderful aromas had been drifting their way. Even Burgess was eager to eat, his visions of a plump puppy on a tray with a mango in its mouth dispelled.

Outside, the sun was below the level of the windows and the light filtering in was rose-colored and soft, and they could hear the banter of Li's neighbors, and the quick, high, squeal of a hog. In the mountains six miles away it was already dark on the east slopes, under the forest mantle. Soon the people would lower their shutters and light lamps or candles. The hamlet would fold up like a curled and sleeping hound, with one ear pricked for the fox.

Schrader was thinking it was barely a hundred feet to the first line of bunkers and rifle pits, behind Li's small yard, and another fifty feet to the first line of wire. And they were sitting and talking perched six feet off the ground with nothing to stop incoming but thatching and bamboo. But he didn't like thinking that. He wanted to relax and enjoy himself.

In a moment, Mrs. Li had returned bearing a tray with bowls of soup, steaming hot, and rice cakes and fish sauce. The soup was thick with noodles and chunks of meat, and Burgess began to eat with relish, dunking his rice cake into his soup and not caring a damn what the meat was. But he hoped it was pork.

After they had eaten a while in silence, Li looked proudly at his guests. Mrs. Li returned again with a laden tray; this time she carried a large bowl of rice and two roasted chickens.

Madre! Mingo said low, his eyes big and round, and Li broke the chickens apart with his fingers and they were stuffed with herbs and peanuts swelled soft and juicy.

"This is great," someone croaked around a mouthful.

"No kiddin'. Your wife is a fine cook, Mr. Li."

"She does credit to her mother," Li replied. "There were other young women I might have chosen, but none better."

"Is her family in Ap Do?"

"No, but they do not live far. When I first returned home—almost twelve years ago—her father came to me knowing I would want a wife. He had known my father and thought that I, too, would be an honorable man. So it was arranged."

"What were your father's politics?" Haney asked.

"He was a vague Nationalist," Li answered with a low chuckle. "We were small landowners in an era when most peasants had lost their land. Times were bad, but we prospered through luck and honest labor. To own land remained paramount to us. For that reason Communism remained unattractive. Later though, after the 1940 rebellion was crushed—and if you wanted to kill *Phap*—the Vietminh Communists had the best machine."

"What were some of the other parties?" Burgess asked.

"My goodness there were many, Calvin. Mostly forgotten now. The *Viet Nam Quoc Dan Dang*—VNQDD—was the party my father and uncle favored. When we returned here in 1940, we were technically beneath the banner of the *Quang Phuc Hoi*, a party destroyed when the insurrection failed. There was the *Cao Dai* and *Hoa Hao*, but they were religious zealots who opposed not only the French, but other Nationalists, too. There was the *Phuc Quoc* and the *Dai Viet* and the Nationalist Party of Tong King. There was quite a jumble of patriots when you Americans first arrived."

"To fight the Japs?" Schrader put in.

"The Japanese, yes. But also the Vichy French. Remember, the Vichy had sided with the Facists, and all French troops in Indochina began to work for the Japanese. It was the American OSS officers who first contacted the Viet Minh and they began to supply us with weapons and equipment, and they lived and fought with the Viet Minh."

The sun had fallen behind the mountains and dusk was graying, and the hamlet was settling into quiet. Li stood, then stepped to the window and dropped the hanging shutter, leaving just a gap for air. He did the same at the other window and pulled a curtain across the door. Mrs. Li came in the room with lighted candles.

Burgess and Schrader were still eating, and Calderone was smoking, and Li offered more cognac all around.

"Funny," Haney mused, "you don't think of Americans fighting here before us."

"Not nearly so many of you as now, Corporal. There were just a handful, but they brought with them much that we needed, and it seemed that they were glad to have us for allies. But when the war ended, everything changed, of course."

"How do you mean?" Burgess prodded.

"Well, the Viet Minh again became the enemy. Because it was largely Communist, you see. British forces came and accepted the surrender of the Japanese. It was the Allies' plan to give the country back to the *Phap*. But before the French could arrive in force, the English needed someone to police the countryside, so they rearmed the Japanese soldiers and our former invaders were then our policemen."

"Christ," Haney muttered, "how long did that last?"

"Only a few months, until the *Phap* were again here in strength."

"Did the Viet Minh and the British get into a scrap?"

"A scrap?" Li asked.

"A battle, I mean," Mingo said.

"Briefly. But many of us were just waiting, thinking we would be rewarded at least with our own provisional government, for fighting against the Japanese. We did not know that the Communists were striking their own bargain with the *Phap*."

They were all absorbed in the tale. It was a history none of them knew. "What do you mean — 'bargain'? " Burgess asked. "What were they up to?"

Li sipped his cognac before he answered, swirling it about in his mouth. It was such a complicated story. "First I must tell you that there was another army in Vietnam after the war, an army of Nationalist Chinese who had been pressing the Japanese from the north. Mao Tse Tsung had not yet defeated Chiang Kai Chek; China was not yet Communist. Some of the smaller parties within the Viet Minh turned to these Nationalist Chinese for protection from the Communists, who were trying to wipe them out. The French feared Chinese influence — as did the Communists — and they began to betray the other Nationalists to the *Phap*, a group at a time, or a man at a time, and soon there were only Communists and French."

"Butt-fucking each other," Haney said with a trace of disgust.

"Don't sound real smart," Mingo put in, "zapping your own allies."

"Perhaps not," Li replied. "But it seems to have worked. That is, the Communists achieved what they wanted: a single-minded politic behind a unified campaign, and with that they defeated the *Phap*."

"You say 'they defeated,' Mr. Li. But you were still fighting, too. Were you a Communist for a time?" It was Haney asking.

Li pulled at the stub of ear thoughtfully, and shook his head. "No. I was never a Communist. But neither was I anything else. There were many different camps I was with, at one time or another, the politics mattering little to me. You see, my friends, I could never forget how the *Phap* dishonored my mother, because of course they raped her before they shot her and we found her and my sister shamefully nude and my father entreated only one thing to me after that. Kill Frenchmen. And it was in the Communists' strategy to kill many *Phap*, of course, so I was tolerated. There were others like me who stayed and fought until the *Phap* were gone. But my uncle talked politics loudly and did not like the Communists. He often loudly declared that a man should be able to own as much land as he wanted. So they killed him."

"Jesus Christ," Schrader said, shaking his head, "it sounds like a goddamned free-for-all."

"Free-for-all? What is that?" Li asked.

"It's a game we play in the States. Everybody stands in a big circle and tries to throw the others out. The last one in the circle is the winner . . ."

Li nodded understandingly. "Yes. That's what we have had in my country. A free-for-all. And the Communists have thrown everyone else out of the circle."

"But they ain't thrown us out," Mingo muttered fiercely.

"That's right," Schrader agreed.

But Li only sipped his brandy, and Haney and Burgess looked at each other doubtfully and the room fell into a lull. In the shadow-flickering candlelight, with the chirping night sounds overlaying their quiet, the darkness outside seemed to press menacingly on the little house. The hamlet was very still. Every night for a long time these people had lived with the tensions brought on by the war. Schrader was just getting a glimpse at the extent of those tensions, and the extent of their adaptation, so easily written off as merely Oriental acceptance. It seemed to Schrader that Li had lived a horror story; mother and sister raped and murdered, father killed like a butchered animal, uncle assassinated and friends tortured left and right. And Li could sit calmly and tell of these things. But it wasn't because he had accepted any of it, in any way. He could not change it, so he lived with it. *But that's not the same thing as accepting.*

Mrs. Li came into the room to clear the table. Quietly, she stepped around the marines and smiled as she worked. Haney offered Li a cigarette and they smoked and drank the last of the cognac, and Li told them stories of his boyhood: the stories that Schrader already knew about the tiger hunt and the viper bite that cost Li his ear, and the wild elephants that used to come down from the mountains. There was more sugar cane grown then, he told them. The elephants could ravage a field in an hour, and it was dangerous work to drive them away.

They began to drink *ruoi nep*, the native rice wine, sour-like *saki* but not so heavy, and after a cup or two you didn't notice the taste anyway. And the room shrank and the faces grew more intent as they listened to Li's stories, eyes straining in the dim, smoky room to catch every nuance in his face. And the time slipped through another bottle of wine, the room growing even smaller, and then the sharp, wracking sound of a machine gun bolt carried across the air, signalling midnight and the changing of the guard, and they called it an evening; all of them thick-tongued, even Haney.

Li came down the steps with them, Schrader clumsily tripping and clattering as he fell and they all laughed a bellyfull, the noise breaking the night like glass and setting the dogs barking, but none of them cared. Tomorrow they might pay. But there were a lot of tomorrows.

A few days later their easy war turned nasty. The Communists controlled most of the countryside throughout Vietnam, with freedom to move at will and shift forces where they wanted, and the Marine commanders could only parry thrust for thrust, and they had to hold the cities. To the southeast lay Danang, a very important place, and the Communists were beginning to reach for it.

It got them all awake at once, the hollow *whooshing* in the distance, Haney shouting "Incoming!" and the whole squad churning into motion, grabbing gear and diving from the tent as the explosions hammered around them. Big damned explo-

sions. ". . . fuckin' rockets!" Mingo screamed hoarsely and ate
dirt as he pushed his face into the ground.

They scurried for the sandbagged shelter beside the tent,
fine protection from mortars but these were big 122s and the
bunker seemed pretty flimsy as the earth shook and trembled
and sand dripped down their necks. They were tumbled pell-
mell atop each other, Mingo down in one corner with bodies
piled all around and he fingered his rosary and bit a hole in
his lip. You could hear the motherfuckers coming like a freight-
train and you sucked your asshole up to your throat until it
exploded and rattled your teeth, but you were okay if you
heard the explosion.

Mingo heard the one that was going to get him. He knew
it was the one when his ears picked it up still far away, and
the sound came to him like a finger pointed and he flinched
in that half-instant before explosion when there is no sound at
all, and all of them in the bunker were rocked like rag dolls
and Schrader got a rifle in the face as the earth seemed to tilt
and shift and he was thrown out the doorway of the bunker,
bloody-nosed and stunned, his ears ringing. But it was not a
direct hit. In the darkness Schrader glanced a huge crater
beside the bunker, smoking and smelling of cordite, and he
felt the heat on his face but he was too stunned to move.
Someone was grabbing his leg and pulling him back in the
bunker, the bunker half caved-in and seemingly useless but it
was blessed shelter nonetheless.

"Okay David?" someone was shouting over the tumult. It
was Mingo, peering at him closely, tangled in a melee of bodies
and rifles but his arms were free to pull his buddy inside.

Before Schrader could respond, the rocket attack ended
with the ominous silence that always hit them like a fist, and
Haney crawled outside and began to tug out the others.

"C'mon! Quick! Everybody out!" And Schrader crawled
foggily, Mingo pushing him from the rear.

"Where's my rifle?"

"I don't know, man, here! Is this yours?"

"Gimme . . ."

Haney was still yanking them out of the bunker, some of
them shaken like Schrader, none of them badly hurt.

"Prep your teams and hurry it up!" Haney was rasping at
them. "Get your ammo together and get the militia on line!

Something's fuckin' coming; I can feel it!" He pulled Greenlee, his grenadier, to his feet and they dashed out toward the line. But they only ran a few steps when the shooting started, first a solitary rifle barking sharply, then a machine gun firing a quick staccato, then the whole west side opening up in a cracking and thunderous eruption of fire, and it was mostly coming in.

"Oh, Jesus . . ." someone moaned.

The perimeter lit up in flare light, two, three handflares and the south machine gun opened up heavily. Men began scrambling for ammo cans and the rest of them formed in teams and ran like hell to the perimeter. But they were on their bellies crawling after ten steps because the fire was so heavy, and they could see in flarelight little men coming across the paddies and bunching up on the wire. Little men, not in black pajamas, but in regular army uniforms.

There was no time to muster the militia, to even glance and see where they were, belly-crawling desperately, bloodying elbows and knees, gasping, and a pole charge exploded sharply and barbed wire was blown apart and someone was shouting hoarsely: "They're coming through!"

All of them, including Schrader, lurched to their feet and sprinted for their pits, firing as they ran, and diving headlong behind their sandbags. Schrader grunted in pain and began to fire blindly, pulling the trigger even before his head was up and the rifle stock was in his shoulder. Grenades exploded and there were screams behind him in the hamlet. Mortar flares boomed and flashed overhead and lit the landscape fiercely and Schrader could see the little bastards plainly, coming up in a ragged, charging line and laying down a very heavy fire. *Steady now. STEADY!* And he began to aim deliberately, the battle noises receding, the pounding of his rifle fading, the trembling in his groin forgotten as he saw men dropping in his gunsights, dying or kicking in pain. The barrel kept moving as if of its own accord, and the finger touched the trigger and the rifle was a living thing. Every instant seemed a lifetime all its own, void of past or future, void of remembrance, a bittersweet, aching instant of lifetime, filled only with the fear and thrill of death. Schrader was growling and spittle dripped from his chin. He repeatedly fed the rifle what it wanted, what it *needed,* to sustain that awesome and terrifying thrill.

He was shouting, not that he could hear himself, but shouting nevertheless. "THE CLAYMORES!! GODDAMNIT! FIRE THE FUCKING MINES!"

Soon enough an explosion burst fifty feet in front, earth erupted in a stabbing flash and the hot balls of steel tore outward. Bodies dropped heavily, flesh and cloth torn from them to splash on the ground under the bright burning flarelight like paint on a canvas.

Another mine exploded, set off by the gunner's helper in the big bunker, six Claymores running out from there in a fan shape and attached by buried wire. Schrader was reloading, his head tucked behind sandbags expecting the sharp bark of another mine when he heard a sudden *whoosh* over the crack and whine of bullets and the machine gun bunker bucked and seemed to fly apart. Schrader watched the machine gun tossed high in the air with a helmet and parts of bodies and he stared openmouthed a few seconds as the debris settled and *thunked* around him. Then he began firing again, a little rattled, his side of the line now minus a gun.

He knew it was a RPG rocket-propelled grenade, smaller than a bazooka but as deadly. But the knowledge flicked through him unimportantly until he saw the backblast from another RPG, saw the projectile lance across his left front to bounce off the top of another bunker like a flat stone skipping water and he heard the rocket explode way off behind him. And it was when he swung his rifle far left to cover that dike, trying to stop another rocket, it was then that he first noticed the militiaman there in his pit, firing away bravely, maybe a little too quickly, maybe not aiming like he should, but there nonetheless and standing his ground. Schrader fired half a magazine at the dike to his left and saw tracers from other rifles kicking dirt there. He swung back to his front, deaf by then from all the noise. He saw a militiaman to his right as well. The big carbine jarred the little man's shoulder and Schrader saw his whole trunk bouncing, too nervous to hold the rifle down tight as he had been taught to do, but he was sure enough in a firefight.

The next bunker south fired three mines at once and a line of soldiers shredded — eight or ten men — and in the shadows beyond the flarelight Schrader could see others coming over the dikes a hundred yards away, not charging in a line but tumbling cautiously over. He fired out into the dimness at them, his heart pounding, but the shadows from the flares were tricky and sighting was not easy. There was no enemy closer than that. Suddenly, their front had become eerily quiet and the marines' fire stuttered and weakened and staccatoed to a stop. All along the south and west lines it fell silent. Schrader's ears rang painfully. He heard voices crying, "Corpsman!" glimpsed houses burning behind and heard wails of pain.

The next wave of enemy was down behind the dikes and the seconds lurched, then stretched thinly forever and ever. *Amen, sweet Jesus*, and Schrader was slurping nervously from his canteen when they came again. An awful damned lot of them, welling up over the dikes in a mass and shouting and the din of battle shook the air and Schrader went back to work not as scared this time, shooting carefully through the slot in the sandbags and wincing at the hail of bullets whip-cracking around, but he laid down a steady fire. The bunker to the south took a rocket. There was a great flash; earth and debris flew everywhere and Schrader felt a little panicked, *oh mama pray for me*, thinking the other gun was gone, too. In a few seconds the M-60 began to hammer furiously again. The little men were dropping in front of it and Schrader wanted to cheer. There was no time. Much of the barbed wire was blown apart, not slowing the soldiers one whit. Some of them got as close as a pitcher and his batter before they were shot down.

Schrader's rifle clicked empty and he ducked down to reload, pulling the rifle in and fumbling to fix his bayonet, fingers like noodles, hands shaking, finally locking the blade in place but when he looked again there was something flying at him and he cringed as the grenade exploded near his pit. The explosion jarred him and his nosebleed started and the rifle was up and there was a little bastard almost on him, and in bug-eyed reflex he shot the soldier down and the man screamed and kicked, and Schrader stuck him hard with the bayonet and shot him three more times and he smelled the flesh burn.

. . . *oh mama I'm tryin'* . . . He thought how desperate she would be if he was killed, and he saw his own funeral and the picture made him crazy and he began screaming; "*NO! GODDAMNIT! NO-O!*" And he pulled the rifle tightly into his shoulder as though it was the golden key to his whole life and he used the weapon in a maddened rage, shooting and shooting and shouting hoarsely and shooting and it seemed to go on and on, one limping, crawling second after another and his mind went blank in those frozen moments and he did not know how long had passed when the Cobras came darting overhead, guns blazing, rockets flashing, the whole landscape seeming to erupt and the rotor wash blowing dust in Schrader's face.

His body just seemed to collapse and he went limp and let go the rifle, laying down on his side and resting his neck, breathing hard, cotton-mouthed and shaking and drenched with sweat.

He knew the gunships, the Hueys, could blow them to hell and back. He lay there washed-out and limp, too tired to flinch at the debris dropping around, and when he glanced out once he saw on the edges of the flarelight—like something glimpsed in a daze—the shadowed dash and tumble of little figures footing for the treeline and the flash and smoke of the choppers and then he lay back down half-collapsed.

It was over—at least for the time. Schrader was coming awake with the ridiculous notion that he was alive. He grinned to himself, even laughed a little, choking on his dirt-caked tongue, and then he gulped a canteen of water and tasted the blood from his nose. *Jesus in heaven, I'm still here!*

His empty magazines were scattered about where he'd tossed them, and he reached and stretched and scooped them back to the pit. There were three full magazines left him, sixty rounds, and maybe ten in the rifle. He had fired over two hundred rounds and the barrel was searing hot and he'd burned his arm here and there. Kong, the little militiaman, was grinning at him, peering over the top of his hole, and Schrader waved him down but the marine was grinning too. It was starkly bright from the flarelight, and the battle was retreating toward the treeline—it was a quarter mile away then, still crashing loudly, but on the perimeter nothing stirred and there was a razor-cut sharpness to the tenseness.

Tracer rounds were stabbing upwards at the Hueys—the gunships with their searchlights ablaze were darting and dancing in support of each other—and they seemed impervious to the ground fire.

Where the hell did the flyboys come from? Some passing

night patrol? There were only four ships. God bless their sweet-smelling asses!

The Cobras had chased the enemy pell-mell back to the treeline, out of the flarelight, but Schrader saw the rockets exploding on the ground and then abruptly, one by one, the helicopters disengaged and re-formed in a group high in the air.

In a second it came to Schrader that the ships were out of ammunition. He knew that it was time for him to move, time to check on his team, but goddamn it was still awful bright. The gooks would not come immediately back, he knew that. In a minute the artillery would be on them, there was too much open ground . . . Yes. Time to check on his men . . .

Schrader rolled quickly from his pit, grunting at the pain in his elbows and knees; he began to crawl up the line. *Damned if I'll crouch . . . I'll take my fucking time.* All the while he glanced nervously to his right at the ominously quiet paddies and the twitching shadows. He crawled past a militiaman and slapped him encouragingly on the foot, and the fellow nodded big-eyed at Schrader and glanced quickly back at the fields. Brennan was next, slouched back and smoking, giving the thumbs up. His helmet was off and Schrader pointed. Brennan plopped it on his head. Schrader crawled on, past the militiaman Phuc, who only glanced at Schrader. After fifteen seconds of bruising belly-crawling Schrader came to Krause, who was stone dead. Schrader peered into the pit and saw the purple welted hole in the top of Krause's head. He saw blood had burst from his eyeballs.

Schrader squeezed his cold hand gently, then unconsciously and soundlessly crawled on. The next militiaman was wounded and unconscious; a bullet seemed to have smashed his shoulder and the wound was seeping blood.

"Corpsman!" Schrader hollered, crouching on his knees over the pit. He laid the little Viet out straight and took off his gear. "Corpsman!" *Christ, were the corpsmen even alive?*

"Murphy! You okay down there?" Schrader called and he saw the man poke his head up.

"Yeah! Okay. Is the kid hurt?"

"He's shot but he's alive. Krause bought it, man . . ."

". . . poor sucker . . ."

"I'm going back to my hole, Murph. You keep hollerin' for the Doc, but keep your head down." By then, Schrader lay flat again; he'd done what he could for the militiaman. "Someone be comin' with ammo!"

"It's a good thing! I'm almost bust . . ."

"How much you got?"

"Two magazines!"

"You'll make out." And Schrader started to turn away when he peered down the line, maybe forty yards, and there was Mingo doing the same thing, and he flashed his buddy the okay. It was good to see Mingo alive. It made Schrader swell a little inside, for just a second, and then he was crawling back to his rifle pit and peering with concern at the open fields. He was almost there when the American artillery began to shrill overhead and explode in the trees way across the paddies.

Schrader slouched in his pit and sucked greedily on a cigarette; he relaxed and wondered where Haney was. *He should be here by now*. His rifle pit was farther to the left in Mingo's sector but Joe was a floater in the defense scheme and he might have been anywhere, helping fill a gap or taking over a machine gun.

Young hard-nosed Xuan came hurrying down the line with the ammo boxes. They'd made him a militia corporal. It was a good choice. He was lugging bullets for his own men— the .30 caliber M-1 ammo did not chamber in the Marines' M-14s—and he was tossing pouches in every other hole and moving on.

"*Ong Luc dao*?" Schrader called to him. Where's Luc?

The Viet pointed to the other side of the compound, but he did not stay to talk. Schrader's eyes swept the breadth of the hamlet. Three huts were burning and men were working hard to pull the thatching down to keep the fires from spreading. Li's pole house was intact, but his neighbor's hut was afire and Schrader could see Li and others with ropes and poles, pulling and pushing over the hut to beat out the flames. Overhead, the artillery was still shrieking and when Schrader peered over his shoulder he saw the shells bursting in the trees half a mile away.

In a few seconds two men hurried along the perimeter.

It was the lieutenant and his driver and they were hauling ammunition. Both of them dropped beside Schrader, breathing hard.

"How's it on the other side, sir?"

"Quiet as a damned nursery. You fellows caught it all over here. Here's another hundred rounds, Schrader. Make it stretch."

"No sweat, Lieutenant."

"You got casualties?"

"Krause is dead. One militiaman wounded. I think the Doc's with him now."

The lieutenant bit his lip and wiped sweat from his brow. "How about the other teams?"

"I don't know, sir. I ain't been that far down the line. Mingo's okay, though. I saw him in the distance."

"Didn't Sergeant Larret find you, Schrader? Didn't he give you the word?"

"No sir. What word?"

"Joe Haney is hit pretty bad. You're taking over the squad."

Schrader felt suddenly cold and hollow. He bolted from his pit and crouched beside the lieutenant. "Where is he?"

"Easy Schrader. You can't do him any good."

"I asked you a fucking question, Lieutenant! Where's Joe?" Schrader had grabbed the smaller officer roughly by the arm, not thinking of consequences, and his face was grim enough to make the lieutenant back up.

"Settle down, Schrader. He'll live. His kneecap is shot away, hurts like a mother, but Joe will be okay. He's over by the command bunker. Choppers coming soon."

"I'm going to him—" Schrader rasped, but it was the lieutenant's turn to grab him.

"Don't you think you should check on your squad, Corporal?"

"I ain't the one, sir. Mingo and Calvin are first in line."

The lieutenant shook his head. "They're going home in four months. I don't want to change squad leaders again."

"Then court-martial my ass," Schrader said quietly and he pulled away from the lieutenant roughly and began to sprint across the compound. He did not give a damn then for corporal's stripes, he did not worry about the brig. He only wanted to see his friend.

They had begun to gather wounded near the command bunker. The men were laid out in a row, with two corpsmen there to attend them. He found Haney looking pale and waxen, one trouser leg cut off and a heavy wrap around his leg. Schrader winced at the thought of a knee wound.

Haney was conscious but glassy-eyed from morphine. His skin looked damp. Schrader knelt by him. "Zigged when you should have zagged, eh?" he joked lightly.

"Million dollar wound, kid . . . gonna be a gimp now."

"Bullshit, Joe. Plastic knees are better, ain't you heard?"

". . . sure."

"The chopper will be here soon. You hug that baby for me. I'm expecting some of Helen's cobbler. You tell her that."

". . . you come anytime, David, understand? Any god-damned time. You get my stuff together, eh? Mail it home."

"First thing, Joe." Schrader was holding his hand. He took out his filthy handkerchief and mopped Haney's brow.

". . . better get back now, kid . . . might start again."

"I'll put you on the chopper. Thing's are quiet. Arty's givin' the gooks hell."

"How's Mingo? Calvin?"

"They're okay."

". . . casualties?"

"None, Joe. Everybody's fine. You taught us good."

". . . you got the squad . . ."

"I know."

". . . gotta be meaner, kid — can't be pals all the time . . ."

"I'll be mean, Joe. I'll ream their green asses out."

"Sure you will . . . creampuff." Haney was fading from the morphine. Schrader watched him struggle to keep his eyes open and in the distance he could hear the approaching helicopters.

"Taxi's coming, Joe. Gimme a kiss bye-bye."

". . . you ugly sucker . . ."

Burgess and Calderone came tearing across the compound then, feet pounding, rifles held high. They had heard the choppers, too. Schrader stood aside while they knelt by Haney. One of the corpsmen motioned him aside. It was old Doc Shelton, maybe a little grayer now.

"You three stick around and help me load," Shelton told him.

"Sure, Doc. Glad to see you with us."

"Kid, I am too old for this shit. And after tonight, I am too goddamned scared."

"Last hitch, ain't it?"

"Hmph! If I make it. You got a smoke?"

"Here. How's Joe gonna be?"

Shelton shook his head. "Stiff-legged all his life. Bad arthritis when he's old. But maybe he's a lucky hand at that . . ."

"He got enough morphine in him?"

"Plenty, Schrader. He won't wake up till he's halfway to Japan. Then they'll give him another shot. Knock him out again."

The artillery from Ahn Lac had ceased to fire, clearing airspace for the helicopters. It became quiet around the compound, except for the crackling and popping of the fires and the orders shouted here and there. The last of the flares dropped to the ground—the phosphorus sizzling—the shadows swelled and lost their shapes. They would evacuate in the dark, by the lights of the choppers.

Then Calvin and Mingo were standing with them.

"He's out," Mingo said, nodding at the open-mouthed and unconscious Haney.

"We'll put him in the second load," the Doc told them. "Got others worse hurt—here." He dug into his leg-pockets and took out two flashlights, handing one each to Burgess and Schrader. "In case you need more light—here's Henessey now. Remember! Only six to a load!"

And a third corpsman came on the run as the helicopters drew nearer, *Whop, whop, whop*, and the flares settled to earth and sputtered and dimmed and it was suddenly night— deep velvety black, and none of them could see a goddamned thing. They blinked and rubbed their eyes, and the three corpsmen were talking with their heads together. Schrader laid his rifle on the ground and shined the flashlight on Haney's face.

Mingo drew them aside. "Screw the Doc! Let's put Joe on the first load."

"You got it," Calvin replied. "Count the places on the chopper. Last one is for Joe, no matter what."

Schrader nodded in the dark. "Who'd you lose, Mingo?" and in the growing dimness he could discern the man look away.

"Lost Henry. Nice kid, too. And one militia. Can't think of his name."

"Calvin?"

"Hoffman's wounded. He's here in line."

"The new kid?"

"Yeah."

"You're lucky, Calvin."

"No I ain't. Soames is laying out there cold. He got no face anymore."

"Who were the poor bastards in the bunker?" Mingo asked.

"Harris was one of them," Schrader told him.

Burgess shook his head. "That kid could shoot after all; he was flat layin' 'em down."

"Lieutenant said you lost Krause."

"Yeah. Head shot. I don't guess the bodies go out till morning."

By then they could all see a little and the corpsmen were easing men onto stretchers and the choppers were coming in.

"Let's go!" Shelton hollered at them, and the lieutenant came up on the double and someone tossed green flares onto the drill ground, pocked here and there by craters that would hide a fireteam. The helicopters drifted in slowly, running lights killed, a spotlight shining directly below. In a few seconds the first ship touched down. All hands began to scurry with the stretchers, or ran beside them to hold plasma; but the three marines kept their eyes on the empty stretchers. One of them was for Joe.

Schrader was with the corpsmen, rear-ending a stretcher up the ramp, hurrying, hurrying, and he saw his buddies slap a stretcher down beside Haney and quickly, furtively, slide the corporal onto it. Doc Shelton pointed to a man, number three, and they grabbed him and hustled him onto the chopper. Schrader came off the ramp and the rotors were blowing up a storm, deafening them all, and it was dark in the periphery of the ship's lights. Schrader hung back a second, eyes on Haney there in the shadows, the wind from the copter blades blowing against him. A corpsman and the lieutenant hurried on number four—fourth of the eight marines wounded—and Shelton pointed to number five, and a corpsman and Mingo, who was counting and saw what was coming down, hurried off the ramp to load the stretcher. Quickly, Schrader and Burgess picked up Haney's stretcher and stepped along behind them. Doc Shelton looked around nervously, not able to hear mortars over the rotor noise, and they were up the ramp with Haney before the Doc noticed.

"THAT'S NUMBER SIX!" Mingo shouted hoarsely, and Doc Shelton looked around quickly and started to wave NO! but another corpsman had heard Mingo's shout and he signaled to the radioman who told the pilot bye-bye, and the ramp was up and the chopper lifting before Shelton could say a word.

By then, the other ship was coming down and there was no time for redress. They were all getting nervous. This was taking too long.

The lieutenant called some men from the command bunker, and he signaled to the three team leaders in the dim lights of the green flares and burning huts. "Back on line, you three! We got enough help." And Calderone and Burgess hoofed it away, but the lieutenant held Schrader by the arm.

"You steadied down, Schrader?" he shouted over the whine of the engines.

Schrader nodded tersely.

"There's ammo cans over there! See 'em? Your boys might need it!"

He pushed Schrader away as the second chopper landed, Schrader's insubordination forgotten, and then the kid was beating feet toward the perimeter with the heavy cans, relieved that Joe was safely away.

Schrader gasped, and lunged into his rifle pit, lingering there to catch his breath. He would not move until the choppers lifted. If they were mortared there would be no warning sound because of the noise. He peered through a slot in the sandbags at the dark, star-lit, rice paddies, his rifle still warm, the stock hard and reassuring against his chest. He'd always figured Haney to make it home clean. Just like he'd always figured that for himself. *Funny*, he thought, *nothing ever works out like you figure it will.*

The three medical evacuation ships got safely away, taking militia and injured civilians as well.

Schrader couldn't figure it. A major assault such as that should have mortars hidden *somewhere* for support. Yet the helicopters drew no fire. Schrader crouched through the long

morning hours trying to reason it out. The gunships had caught
the gooks flat-footed, he knew that. And thinking back, trying
to recall the numbers of soldiers he'd seen, Schrader doubted
the marines could have held the line. They would have needed
the men from the other side of the compound to fill the gaps.
A separate assault on the north and east sides might have
collapsed the camp like an accordian.

That the North Vietnamese did not immediately re-group,
Schrader could only credit to the cannon-cockers. Their fire
must have caught a lot of soldiers amongst the trees, and maybe
their mortar crews too, as the element of surprise turned totally
around for them.

Shit-house luck, he thought, and he yawned long and
hard, jaw popping, wishing they'd go on yellow alert so a few
of them could sleep.

The 155s from Ahn Lac were bursting flares high over the
camp. A wind was tossing them pretty good and the landscape
seemed to ripple from the constant motion of shadows. It played
tricks on the eyes. For long moments, Schrader had stared as
a soldier's body sprawled coldly across a dike, swearing the
man had moved but he knew he had not. There were bodies
strung on the wire, flaunting gravity like puppets, and they
would move too. Except Schrader knew they didn't. The lieutenant had ordered them to put bullets in all the corpses.

There were forty-two bodies out there that they could see.
What lay beyond the dikes was anyone's guess. In the morning,
they would go and have a look.

At 3:30 the lieutenant came around, and again at 4:30. At
dawn they could relax some. Help would be coming from Ahn
Lac, maybe some permanent reinforcements. They'd known
from the beginning that there were too few of them: only sixty-
five men, including corpsmen, radiomen, mortarmen, and
machine gunners. Their casualties from the rocket barrage and
assault were five killed and eight wounded; almost a quarter
of their strength.

At a little past 5:00, dawn began to break and the last
flares drifted down and sputtered and burned out. The morning
showed faintly rose in the east, a soft light, easy on the eyes,
not glaring bright like the flarelight, and as troopers have always done, they took heart at the dawn. The column would
be starting out from Ahn Lac with the mine sweep, or maybe

they would be flown in. There would be air support to work
the jungles and maybe an extra platoon to sweep the treeline
all around.

Schrader was feeling pretty good. The morning was a misty
light gray and steadily brightening and he wanted to stand up
and stretch. Folks were moving around back in the hamlet,
he could hear them talking. A baby was crying. The mortars
went off, far to the south, like any other sound in an average
morning and after the hollow *whumphh*! there was a lag of
silence, then the ripping of the air like the tearing of a sheet
as the mortar rounds arced downward and exploded. Schrader
was comfortable in his pit. There was even time to pull a few
sandbags over on himself, and he pushed his nose as low as
he could and rode it out. The ground bucked and the noise
was terrific but he wasn't afraid. Fear seemed to have been
squeezed from him, like a spent quota, and he lay there half-
amused and feeling strangely immune. And sure enough, after
a time the last round exploded and the new stillness ran away
in the distance like a chased deer and then the real sounds of
people hurrying came to him and he stood and dusted himself
off.

He stepped from the pit, rifle slung, and began to trot
down the line to check on the squad. They were all staring
down the line at something. Schrader could not make it out
but he began to run faster, seeing a stain on the ground, a big
stain or some kind of splash and Mingo was suddenly in front
of him, racing ahead, and they got there and saw the big gory
stain — the splash on the ground that had once been Calvin
Burgess.

A mortar round had exploded squarely on his back and
he was twisted wretchedly, half out of his pit, and his innards
were scattered.

Schrader smelled the flesh burning and he gagged but his
stomach was empty. Mingo turned quickly away, his face hard
stone and he shouted pathetically, "PONCHO! Somebody bring
a poncho!" and a marine came running with one and Mingo
shook it out. He stepped to Calvin quickly and took his arms.

"David!" he snapped.

And Schrader shook himself and walked to the pit and
took Calvin by the boots. As they lifted him, the skin that was
still attached began to stretch horribly and Schrader feared

that the body would break in half. The spine was already snapped like a stick. They smeared a red stain to the poncho and then wrapped their friend up.

They looked at each other, horrified, but there was nothing to say. In the distance they could hear the helicopters . . .

The ships brought a relief platoon and the clean-up began in earnest. Grimly, the bodies of the dead marines were loaded, and flown out, Schrader and Calderone watching the chopper lift off, and that was all there was to Calvin Burgess. Except what they kept very privately inside themselves. There would be a body bag for him at graves' registration, and an impersonal tag, and some grief in a city apartment that would not be much noticed. But that was out of sight of the two survivors and they struggled to keep it out of mind.

They were kept busy. There was wire to patch and re-string, new Claymores to set, bunkers to rebuild. The relief platoon swept the paddies around the west and south lines and gathered and stacked the bodies — sixty-eight of them — and the lingering wounded were shot out of hand. Two booby traps blew up — two marines wounded — but to Schrader, still numbed, it seemed inconsequential compared to the slaughter of the night. And the militiamen, who had fought so well, seemed more like comrades to the Ap Do marines than did the unknown men of their relief platoon.

Luc was proud — as proud as a man can be in the face of near disaster — for he had known all along that his men had mettle. He and Li had sought out the two marines and very earnestly expressed their sorrow, Luc standing stiffly while Li translated, and then the little chief marched off to the business of rebuilding his hamlet.

Li lingered a moment, smoking with them. "Calvin was a fine man," he told them, but there was not much else to say and Li sensed that silence was best.

The villagers already were setting corner poles to rebuild the burned houses. A buffalo that was killed was being hurriedly dressed out. Muffled wails of mourning still carried across the air to where they stood, attesting to the peasants killed in the attack.

Li shook their hands very formally and bowed, and returned to his work. Calderone and Schrader stood there a time,

both of them empty of feeling; looking around the hamlet as
if they had just then seen it for the first time. Something was
different. Something intangible. Schrader struggled to voice it
but the words would not come. Calderone *felt* the difference
and accepted it and did not try to put it into words.

These people had been pushed around for years upon
years. They had rolled with it and taken their licks in silence.
But then one night they fought back, and they won. That was
the difference.

But the two marines could not see it, then. What lingered
in both their minds was the sight of Calvin, twisted and man-
gled, and there was little other vision left to them that morning.

Soon enough it would be business as usual around the
hamlet; soon enough the peddlers would be shoving wares
under their noses and the whores would be grabbing and rubbing up against them and Madame Zap would be raising the
price of her beer. That was the Orient they had come to know.
They did not expect to see anything new or different.

"That doesn't make any sense!" Schrader told the other
marine, but the man only shrugged. He was a grunt from the
relief platoon. They were eating lunch.

"Hey, I'm only tellin' you what I heard," the guy said.
"But he's the C.O.'s driver; usually knows the score."

Calderone and Schrader shook their heads. They had
been told that some of the hamlets were to be abandoned.
Battalion was sending two companies, half their strength, south
to Danang.

"And we hold just Ahn Lac? That's all?" Mingo asked.

The guy was wolfing his beans. "That's the skinny," he
mumbled. And he motioned toward the mountains where all
through the morning, jets had been shrieking and bombing.
"Lotta gooks out there," the guy cautioned. "Don't make sense
to try to hold this little place."

Schrader kind of resented that, the implication that they
could *not* hold. But he finished his cold meal in silence while
Mingo pumped the newcomer.

Which companies were going south? The kid didn't know.
Would it be a permanent move? He didn't know that either.
He didn't seem to know much, except that they were mounting
out.

"Bullshit!" Mingo spat.

"Wait and see," the newcomer grinned. "You hicks don't know shit from shinola out here. This place is the end of the line," and the guy took his mess gear and walked away to rejoin his buddies.

"Couldn't be," Schrader muttered, looking to his buddy for encouragement. "It would leave these folks in a bad way."

"What do they care about that?" Mingo replied, smashing his ration tins. "You think Bobby fuckin' McNamara gives a shit about Ap Do? Or some nigger boy, Calvin Burgess, who just got wasted? I mean, if we're gonna split, we shoulda done it before last night!" And he threw the smashed tins angrily and glared around for something to hit but there was only Schrader. Not Schrader and Calvin. Not Schrader and Calvin and Joe. Just Schrader there, staring back gloomily.

Mingo softened and swallowed his anger and stared away at the mountains, trying to shut it all from his mind, and he put his hands over his ears to drown the noise of jets in the distance, thinking, *one step at a time, hombre. There's still another night. Yes, always another night to survive.*

10

The captain was new to them, not swaggering like some, but tightly professional and to the point. He was older than most captains . . . graying. Maybe he was a mustanger from the ranks.

Schrader was not liking what he was hearing:

". . . trouble around Danang, large enemy forces have been spotted near the approaches to the city and the Danang defenses need reinforcements. At 1400 hours today you men will be flown to a new camp where you will rejoin your company." The captain glanced at his watch. "That gives us time to break camp and pack; leaves room for one last chore." The officer paused again. "The indigents of this hamlet are to be evacuated and resettled. This entire sector west of Ahn Lac

has been declared a free fire zone, due to its present unten-
ability. This is a new policy, men, unfortunate I admit. But
we must deny the enemy the resources and shelter to be found
here. I believe that's all, Lieutenant."

The lieutenant snapped to attention. "Sergeant Larret,
dismiss the troops!"

And Larret snapped to and saluted the lieutenant.
"PLATOON!" he called. "TEN HUT! Dis-MISSED!"

Such is the nature of command.

The trucks that ground down the road toward the hamlet
were not for the marines. By that time the camp was broken
and the relief platoon had rounded up the peasants. They were
gathered in a field beside the gate, surrounded by the Americans and their own militia, looking very much like prisoners
when the big trucks pulled up, a dozen of them, with a unit
of South Vietnamese soldiers aboard.

By direct order, the Ap Do platoon was confined to their
sector, and they could only watch from a distance. It rested
sourly with a lot of them. The captain knew that they had friends
among the villagers. He did not want any wavering of duty.

It was ugly at first. There was some shoving and head-
knocking; a lot of angry words. No one understood what re-
settlement meant. Where would they be taken? What of their
animals and belongings? But no one had answers for them and
even Luc was in the dark. He was the one who eventually
calmed them down, speaking to the crowd very earnestly and
as honestly as he could. They were a hard working and patriotic
hamlet, were they not? They made money and paid taxes.
Surely these disruptions would be temporary. Surely the government would not punish loyalty.

But who will take care of the animals, someone wanted
to know? Luc could only shake his head and look away, and
the anger might have erupted again but the trucks arrived with
the government soldiers and by then there were far too many
rifles to go against. Some of them might have thought that the
marines would not really shoot them, but the government
soldiers would shoot them dead. And the Vietnamese captain
looked like he meant business.

The Saigon troops jumped from the trucks with all the
discipline of a gang of bandits, and the Viet captain strutted

like a peacock. He stepped over to Luc and touched the brim of his cap with a swagger stick in a token salute. Luc returned the salute formally. Even from a distance of two hundred feet, Schrader could tell that Luc did not like the man. They spoke with their heads together, for a brief time, then Luc abruptly turned his back and strode away, calling his militia to him harshly and ordering them to fall in. The militia jumped in response to the order, and fell in smartly, dressing right as the marines had taught them, looking professional, and suddenly the Ap Do platoon was clapping and cheering them, stomping their feet and whistling. Those are our boys, goddamnit! But the cheering died away shame-faced as the Saigon troops formed in line and with the relief platoon helping, began to edge the farmers toward the trucks.

The Ap Do marines got very quiet then, and there was much lighting of cigarettes and looking away, but Schrader did not look away.

Earlier, he could have easily gone and spoken with Li, but he had been too ashamed. And in his young mind burned so many things he might have said, but it all went unspoken.

He watched Li approach a truck with his family, and lift the children aboard and hand them the large bundles they were carrying. Other farmers were pushing up alongside. Li's wife climbed aboard and he handed her two still larger bundles, and then Li handed her the precious tool bag: a long rough canvas bag with straps and heavy wood handles; everything he would need to build a new home. And then Li glanced across the span toward the camp, and Schrader half-raised his hand, but Li turned his head and climbed on the truck and sat with his back to the platoon.

It was the last sight that Calderone and Schrader ever had of him. And the last knowledge.

It took half an hour for the marines to cram three hundred and fifty civilians with the belongings they could carry and forty militia men onto ten large transport trucks. Then the Saigon soldiers went in one truck and the relief platoon began to load onto another.

The graying marine captain walked toward them with the lieutenant. Sergeant Larret stood up and ground a butt under his foot.

"Fall in, men," he called wearily, and the platoon fell in

smartly enough, Haney's squad forming the shortest line, Schrader there at the head now.

They watched as the captain and the lieutenant parted, the captain double-timing back toward the trucks as the convoy started to grind gears and move slowly away.

"At ease, men," the lieutenant told them. He had become a much improved officer, able to relax with the men and take advice, too. And there was the matter of Schrader's insubordination which went unreported. "In a short while, the choppers will be here for us," the lieutenant began, "and in the meantime there are some things that were left for us to do. We will of course carry out our orders to the letter. Corporal Carter, when the platoon's dismissed you will deploy your squad about the perimeter. You are to stand guard and you will be the last squad to enplane."

"Aye aye, sir!"

"You mortarmen and gunners are to stand by your equipment and you will enplane first. Petty Officer Shelton, your men can stand down and not participate, but they will enplane one corpsman per squad."

"Aye aye, sir," the Doc sounded tired.

"And now we have this last thing, men. We can't leave this village and the livestock for the enemy. You understand that, I know."

As he was talking, they began to hear the droning of planes in the distance, not jets, but prop jobs. And they sounded like they were flying low. Some eyeballs flicked that way but nothing could be seen yet.

"— you mind paying attention, Hansen?"

"No sir."

"So we have to burn the houses and kill the stock," the lieutenant continued. "But I want it done smartly, with no goddamned skylarking, and I want the animals killed efficiently and with as little pain as possible . . ."

The planes were droning nearer.

"Corporal James!"

"Sir!"

"Your squad is to begin setting the houses on fire."

"Aye aye, sir!"

"Lance Corporal Schrader."

"Sir!"

"I know you're a farmboy, Schrader, I know you can do this right. You and Calderone take your men and begin shooting the animals. Show them how you want it done. I'll be along to help you shortly."

"Aye aye, sir."

"Sergeant Larret, you can dismiss the platoon."

They broke ranks just as the planes flew into sight over the horizon, three of them, old DC-6s and they were flying low. There were pods attached, not bombs, and the planes fanned out and began to spray the fields and jungle around the hamlet. One of the planes flashed over the camp as the squads were double-timing, and the stuff was oily and smelled pungent.

Calderone wiped it off his face. "What the fuck is that?" he asked.

Schrader sniffed it. "Brush killer," he said. "We use it on the farm," but he was too preoccupied to give it much thought. He was trying to rationalize what he was about to do, but none of his rationales worked right. Like his granddad used to say: *that dog don't hunt, son.*

The squad was gathered around Schrader and he had to talk loud over the drone of the planes. "The bulls and cows first," he told them, "and any calves. They'll be staked. Come up and try to give them a quick shot behind the ear. If they're facing you, shoot 'em in the forehead, about two inches above the eyes." His voice quaked a little and he cleared his throat. He noticed that his hands were shaking. "If a bull smells blood and breaks loose, never mind trying a head shot. Drop 'em high behind the shoulder, in the heart, and then finish him quick through the head. I guess the hogs are next. They'll smell the blood and start squealing and running in circles in the pens. Shoot down on them, through the heart. Any chickens or ducks?"

"They took 'em all, Dave."

"Any dogs left?"

"A few."

"Leave 'em be," Schrader told them. "They'll make out. Let's go do it. Team up in pairs. Mingo, you come with me," and he stepped off hurriedly toward Li's house, his stomach beginning to flutter, seeing someone on Li's porch building a fire against the thatching. Li's bull was a well-groomed giant, massively chested and heavy horned and gentle. He knew Schrader's smell, knew it sometimes came with his master's, and he did not shy when the farmboy stepped up and stroked his nose and scratched the beast between the ears. Then Schrader stepped back and blew a hole in the buffalo's head and it dropped heavily straight down, and the cows jerked at the ropes in a panic and Mingo shot down one of them. The other cow reared her head and snapped the picket rope, an action that put her on her rear legs and Schrader shot her then and she crashed into the thatched shelter and through the hog pen, and the old sow was on her feet squealing, busting out and Schrader made a bad gut shot and the hog rolled over in pain and Mingo finished her off.

Other shots were ringing through the hamlet and animals were lowing and squealing and the fires were beginning to burn. They began to shoot the piglets and the boars and the planes were spraying all around them, and the helicopters were whopping into sight. Schrader was shaking with rage and shooting and smelling the blood and the animals shitting in fear. His hands were white and bloodless on the rifle and the animals kept dropping and the fires burning stronger, and Schrader was shaking badly, very, very badly, and he wanted to cry.

End of Part One
June, 1966
Thua Thien Province
Republic of South Vietnam

> *The private wound is deepest.*
> WILLIAM SHAKESPEARE
> *Two Gentlemen of Verona*

11

Six years later, Florida

It seemed a bigger place at first: the long neat lawn that stretched toward the palms, the towering hedges, the tennis courts. Then the people began to arrive in long, rag tag processions, shrinking the place; and after a few days the park was a hobo's blend of odd tents, strange shelters, and sleeping bags with crumpled bodies cringing from the morning sun which, in July, was hot by ten o'clock.

Schrader stood in the shade of the hedge, beside one of the gates. Radio chatter squawked from his handset. All the posts were checking in, a dozen of them there and about the campsite. Everything was quiet. Locals were coming hesitantly through the gates, into their own park, to gawk at the out-of-towners.

It was the summer of 1972 and the Democrats were holding their National Convention in Miami Beach. All the grand hotels were full, there and in Miami. The dissentient Left Wing was digging in. For the purpose of appeasement, and nervous from the pall of the Chicago convention, the Democrats struck a deal with Miami Beach: give the dissenters a place of their own, and the Democrats would clean up the mess.

There was a budget. Civil Defense arrived. There were first aid supplies and johnny pots and water tanks. There was a charter. It was granted to the Student Mobilization Committee, SMC, and the other groups came together beneath their banner. There was a staff for liaison with the city. There was radio equipment so the Left Wing could secure itself.

And there was a chief of police trying to put on a good face. He wanted to know how they would police themselves. He wanted to know who would—

Schrader felt a tug on his sleeve and he turned to see an old woman, barely five feet tall and brightly dressed, staring up at him with intense eyes.

"You're one of the veterans, aren't you, young man?"

"Yes ma'am." He was dressed in a jungle jacket with cut off trousers, and jungle boots, and around the hair that fell to his shoulders was a bandanna of camouflaging. He wore a button that read: *Vietnam Veterans Against the War*.

"I've brought you boys some groceries," and she took his arm with strong bony fingers and pulled him to a cart standing just inside the gate. There were three sacks of groceries in it.

Schrader looked closely at her, saw her clothes slightly worn and mended, saw the tiny blue veins beneath the stretched skin of her neck. She could not have weighed ninety pounds.

"We can't take your food, ma'am."

"Nonsense! I heard some of you boys were selling your blood to buy groceries. You'll be too weak to fight the cops!" She said this with such unexpected fierceness that Schrader had to choke down a laugh.

"We really don't want a fight with the cops."

"Of course you don't. We never did either, back in the old days. But there always seemed to be some dumb cop face poking its nose into our business. Never leave you alone, do they? Working folks try to organize, try to better their lives, and the company men call city hall and here come the coppers!"

"So you're an old union hand, eh?"

"You betcha, young man. Flora Minsky is my name. I've been a member of the International Ladies Garment Workers since 1925, since before Dubinsky took over. The Companies always had a hatful of dirty tricks. Used every one before the NLRA was passed in 'thirty-seven. But you probably don't know any of that history."

"I know a little of it, Mrs. Minsky. I know people have forgotten how rough it was back then."

"Rough!" The old woman's face turned to an angular smirk, and her eyes blazed. "Why these youngsters nowadays wouldn't have cut the mustard back then. What with mean cops and goon squads and vigilantes. Even judges on the take! Why a trip to the pokey for unlawful gathering might mean weeks out of your life—weren't many liberal lawyers come galloping to get you out." She shaded her eyes with her hand and stared at the crowd milling about the park. But for her delicate coloring, she might have been a tough old Vietnamese. "But that's all past now. You young folks have your own struggle. I think it's terrible that the government doesn't listen to you boys. Who else knows the war better?"

"No one in this country."

"It seems to say a lot, when our own fighting men throw their medals away."

Schrader smiled sadly. "Sure. It says we're traitors and crybabies . . ."

"Now, don't you be discouraged. We'll stop this war, you'll see. You boys will get proper credit. Keep on struggling. Never give up. If we'd given up in the nineteen twenties and nineteen thirties, America would be a fascist state today. You listen to me. I'm not just rattling memories in a coffee can. Now you take these groceries and pass them out to the other veterans. Several of us pitched in to bake those loaves — Don't look at me like you're going to argue!"

"Yes, ma'am. We're glad to have the food."

"And it's just for you veterans. Not the barefoot riffraff."

"We're obligated to share, Mrs. Minsky. I'm sure you understand."

"Oh, very well, But not the bread. That's just for you boys."

Schrader stooped down beside her. "Do you see that big green tent out there? That's the first aid and communications center. If you need help while you're in the park, go there. And thanks. You're a jewel."

He wrapped his arms about the sacks, winked at the old woman, and began to tread through the crowd, weaving around the prone bodies and disorderly camps with an arrogant stride, in many ways still the poster marine.

"Hey man! Is that food?"

"Sure. How many of you? Three? Take a little. Not the bread, please."

"Hey! The dude's got some food!"

People gathered round and hands reached out. Apples and cans of tuna disappeared. A great bunch of bananas vanished into the crowd. Schrader set the sacks on the ground. He took the four loaves of bread and stuffed the tuna that remained into his jungle jacket, grabbed three jars of peanut butter, and left the remainder on the ground.

"Help yourselves, folks . . ."

First aid was an old G.I. squad tent, where the red cross flag there hung limply. Two vets, Rosen and Sugarbear, were rolling up the sides of the tent.

"Got some chow, grunts. Home baked bread."

"Too bad you won't have time to eat any," Rosen told him. "Mingo needs you for a powwow, other side of the park, the picnic area past the swimming pool."

Schrader set the food on a folding table, emptying his pockets. "When?"

"ASAP, brother. And take your radio. Mingo's went on the blink."

"Is there trouble?"

Rosen shrugged. He was dark-bearded and handsome, as Schrader imagined an old Jew from the Bible to be. "Who knows, around this zoo."

Vaguely disturbed, Schrader began his walk across the grounds, his mind flicking back over the weeks and months. He had come to Florida on impulse, thinking the convention a place to make known his views on the war. But first one task then another had been thrust on him until he began to feel smothered by responsibilities: breaking up fights, enforcing rules, evicting drunkards from the park, returning children to mothers who were sometimes too drugged to notice them missing. There was no time to express himself. But no one wanted his opinions. At college, he scoffed at the ROTC types who buttressed the Right Wing. He wanted to be taken in by the Left. He agreed with them. The war was rotten. Yet he found the Left disdainful and rude. Schrader had the trappings of a fascist, he was a baby killer. His humor was off-color and his politics naive. He could not speak of the war even remotely without feeling their resentment.

At the veterans' clubs it was no different. He was too vocal about popular politicians, too angry at the military high command, too irksome and altogether too skeptical about America. And his stories of war spawned their resentment, as well, or winks and grins behind glasses of beer, to tolerate this kid from the hippies' war.

He turned his back on all of them.

One day he had received a letter from some one named Adelita Garcia, in response to letters he had written to Mingo at an old address, letters that were never answered. He'd had an urge to see Mingo again, to joke and carry on in the old way, to have a friend he could trust beyond any doubt.

When Schrader came home from the war, Mingo had been at El Toro to meet him. They were stationed near one another at Camp Pendleton. There were good times for a few months until Mingo was shipped out again, to the 5th Marines, and finally to the city of Hue during the Tet offensive. A few weeks after Mingo left, Schrader got orders for the 26th Marines at Dong Ha, and finally Khe Sahn. In the late spring of 1968,

Calderone and Schrader shipped back to the States, only days apart, each of them hollow-eyed and dispirited, and full of grief at the slaughter.

Calderone was discharged and back in Texas before Schrader could locate him. In Hue, Mingo had a squad of replacements killed around him. For weeks, he ate and slept amidst the stench of corpses. He killed civilians. He came home a junkie — smoking it at first, so fine and pure, hitting it later, smuggling half a kilo when he came home. He never answered Schrader's letters. The junk had formed an inner circle even David could not enter. But within a year it was gone: both the drug and the money it brought him, and Mingo tumbled for a year, in and out of rehab, American street junk never filling the hole in his heart like the god-touched heroin of Vietnam.

In the fall of 1970, Schrader received the letter from the Chicana . . . Mingo is in trouble . . . Please, will you come . . . He'd read the letter one dismal day as he leaned on a rail fence in the barnyard, over his ankles in mud, his father muttering angrily at a penny decline in the market price of hogs. Schrader had been living at home, commuting to college, working hard on the farm but not — in his father's eyes — hard enough. Two days after the letter arrived, Schrader was on his way to Texas.

"David! Over here!"

Schrader turned to see Mingo trotting his way, dressed much the same as he, mustachioed, more heavily muscled than he had been in Vietnam, his hair thick and black and tumbling down his back. Seeing him, Schrader's mood began to lighten.

Calderone faked some punches at him, posturing. "We got a meet with the chief, boot. Big doings."

"What's up?"

"Man, you look awful. Ever hear of sleep?"

"Never mind that. Is there trouble?"

"Don't hardass me. After we meet with Blackie, you catch some sacktime."

Mingo was gripping Schrader's arm and shaking him roughly, threateningly, and Schrader was starting to grin.

"I couldn't sleep, Mingo. I took an extra shift."

"Your head on straight?"

"More or less."

"Dreams coming '

"Dreams can't hurt you."

"Right, boot. They can't hurt you. They only cost you a little sleep, maybe a little self-respect, because they put you back in a place that terrified you. They put you back in a place that hated you and wanted to see you dead. But that can't hurt a man, can it?"

"Lay off!"

"Why don't you talk it out with some of the guys? Tell 'em about the kid, David. Get it off your chest . . ."

"I'm okay, Mingo. You copy? We've all got things that are choking us. Some of us open up, some of us don't. It's enough just to have the brothers around me. It's enough. Everyone's hurting."

They had walked beyond the swimming pool, the late morning sun bearing down, sweating them, and they stopped a moment in the shade of some live oaks.

Calderone grimaced in exasperation, put his hands on hips, stepped around muttering in Spanish. Finally: "Don't crash and burn on me, *hombre.* I need you. You run things here a few more days, then you go to Tallahassee to help out a few days, then you go to Texas. You decided that, no? You'll help us organize, no? So don't fall out with your ass frazzled when I need you the most—" He stopped pacing and flashed his white teeth, *por favor.*

Schrader said nothing. He sat down abruptly in the grass, cross-legged, jaw muscles working, his pent-up anger churning to the surface. "Sure. I'll come to Texas to help out. I'll be okay for that. But I don't want to stay here and eat any more of this. The park's filled up with street freaks and derelicts. I hear cat calls from the local toughs: 'piggy piggy!' People bitch to me when the Hare Krishnas dance through their camps. And when I put a stop to it, other people call me a fascist and some one bounces a rock off my shoulder. Christ! It might have been a knife! And another one of the drunks I tossed out threatened to shoot me." He was breaking a stick into little pieces and his voice trailed away lamely. Mingo was watching, measuring him. Things were changing between them. Calderone was taking the lead and Schrader was leaning, depending, his life and values seeming to fall in flakes and chips around him. A part of Mingo was ashes, where David had not yet burned. What rose from those ashes was desperate for direction; Mingo plunged heart and soul into stopping the war, and it sustained him. But Schrader was not so resolute. His mind was awash with images of violence — a tide that would swell to prominence and then recede, swell and recede in kaleidoscopic rhythm — for a moment as sharply etched as bodies tumbling in the flarelight, and another moment as blurred and indistinct as grief could color it. As though seen through eyes half-turned away in shame. He tried very hard to keep his politics foremost — to work for his convictions — but the images kept hammering him, draining him.

"You got to stick it out, *hombre*. I'm very late getting home. There's a mountain of work waiting for me. If we both split now, there's no one else who knows the whole scheme of the park."

Schrader looked away, scowling to hide his emotions. "I, uh . . . I worry a little about your being — well, about me being on my own."

"You think first chance, I'm gonna stick a needle in my arm?"

"It's not that. You don't need a babysitter anymore. You've been clean a year. It's me. I don't want to be the boss. I don't like giving orders. I'm a good second stringer, Mingo. That's what's left in me. No more charging in the front ranks."

Mingo sat down beside him. "C'mon, David. You're discouraged, that's all. None of us expected to be cops down here. But it's a good thing it turned out this way. That's right! A good thing! Otherwise, there'd have been a real mess. Another farce for the Democrats."

"So what the hell do we owe them!"

"They say they'll bring our brothers home. They'll end the war."

"That's all rhetoric —"

Mingo shrugged. "If it's only rhetoric, then we've been shafted again, but we can't just sit around with our hands in our pockets during an election year. Time to get off the ropes. Time to counterpunch, man. If we can augment the Democratic campaign, and pull some votes from Nixon, I say right on! And if we can keep the peace here in the park, so the Democrats smell a little sweeter, right on! That doesn't mean, brother, that we can expect to have lunch with the Speaker of the House. We're an embarrassment to all of them."

Schrader could only mutter with disgust, his anger spent. He was being pointed like a weapon, used like a weapon. Mingo held the trigger, and that was all right. He trusted Mingo. But sometimes he gave not a damn for the tenets of the Revolution: civil rights and free all political prisoners and freedom of speech and on and on in one garbled cacophony, muttered from a million mouths he did not know or care for. But at any time, on any day, he could close his eyes and be back in the jungle — he could smell it, and feel it brushing his skin — and American boys were still there, his brothers everyone, and that was bitter gall to him.

Of a sudden, the forgotten handset clipped to Schrader's belt squawked mechanically: *Security one, this is Central, over.*

Schrader handed the set to Mingo, who was eyeing him curiously.

"What's it going to be, David?"

"Let's go back to work, eh?"

"*Muy bien.* Now you're talkin'!" He keyed the set. "Central, this is Security one. Go ahead, over."

The reply came: The chief of police has left his office. Be informed, he is on his way. Over.

"Roger that. Security two is with me. We're checking out for thirty. That's three oh. Security one, out."

Mingo handed back the radio and they stood up, walking slowly to the meeting place.

"The Yippies are making trouble," Mingo told him. "That's what this meeting with Blackie is about. They're going to have a smoke-in on the amphitheater stage."

"A what?"

"They're going to smoke pot. In public. To incite and inspire the crowd."

Schrader scratched his head in perplexion. "What for?"

"Big politics. Pivotal point for the Movement. The Yippies want to show the world where the heart of the Revolution lies."

"Christ! That will bring the cops into the park, riot gear and all — when does this happen?"

"This afternoon," Mingo told him.

"You know Blackie's boys are itching to come in here and knock heads. And that's what the Yippies want."

"Sure. Confrontation politics. With press coverage, of

course. The Yippies start it, then run to the rear and throw bottles."

Something occurred to Schrader and he stopped in his tracks, grabbing Mingo's arm. "Say, what's this meeting all about?"

Mingo grinned. "So? Has a light come on in your head? Are you guessing what I'm guessing?"

"Oh no, *amigo*. The chief can't dump it in our laps."

"You don't think so? What are his options? To have his boys busting heads and his town smeared by riot on the six o'clock news? Or to have the news show a hundred freaks puffing *ganja* in a local park? Great for the hometown image, no?" Mingo pulled him along. "C'mon. We're gonna be late."

At the far end of the park, across another expanse of lawn, were tables and benches set out neatly in the shade. As they neared the spot they saw a car, marked Chief of Police, pulling up at the curb. Traffic on the nearby avenue was light. The man who stepped from the car and walked to the shade to greet them was well-dressed, of medium height but sturdy, and his handshake was solid.

"How are you men doing?"

"I'm okay, Chief."

"Hey, Blackie! You keeping the lid on?"

"I was about to ask you the same, Mingo."

"Sure," Calderone grinned. "The lid is on till tomorrow. After that, it's no concern to me."

The chief looked at Schrader. "And you're letting him run out on you?"

"He's pussywhipped," Schrader quipped. "There's no stopping a man with *'tang* fever."

"*Cabrone!*"

They were walking to a table, the chief between them, laughing at the crack, slapping Mingo on the back. When they sat down, the chief got to business:

"George will be here soon. We can talk this over in the meantime. What the hell are the Yippies trying to pull? Everything's been going along great."

"How did you hear about it, Chief?"

"They announced it to the press, of all things. Why they want to make trouble is beyond me. I'll tell you straight—I don't want to bring my men into the park."

"We believe you, Blackie. But some of your men feel different."

"Ah, their blood is up, that's all. Half the freaks in the park give the finger to my boys every time they cruise past. But your people have had things their own way all week. They won't settle for less now. If I muscle my officers into the park, there will be a riot before they could ever reach the stage, to arrest the Yippies. Our own townsfolk will be mixed up in the crowd. Not a pretty thought. This is a quiet little city. And we owe you vets thanks for the money and effort you've saved us. It's a damned shame if all your good work goes up in pot smoke." He gave them a certain look, and Schrader glanced Mingo smiling slyly.

They sat quietly, waiting, while the chief lit a cigarette. He looked at them squarely, his eyes friendly. "I was wondering if, uh— Well, it occurred to me that some, uh, positive action from within your own ranks would save us all some headaches."

"Amen," Mingo muttered.

"Can you stop them?" The chief was showing a poker face, but his question was edged with apprehension.

Mingo tried to look bored. "I don't know, Blackie. We're not supposed to do anything without approval of the Committee."

Automatically, Schrader took the cue. "That's right, Chief. We've had differences with some of the other groups in the past. We'll all be working together until the election. We'd better not bruise any egos."

The chief put up his hands. "Look fellas, you both know what will happen if you put it before your committee. They'll talk it to death. And in the end, the Yippies will do as they please."

"More than likely," Mingo agreed.

"So why let them spoil it for everyone?"

"Why don't you let them smoke their weed, Chief? Let the reporters get their pictures, and by tomorrow it will be old news."

"I can't do that. This isn't Berkeley."

"How many of your men will it take, Blackie?"

"Phew! I don't want to think about that. As soon as we saw you vets could handle the crowd, we kept a normal routine about the park . . . But I have to have your answer this morning. Otherwise, I put my men on alert."

"Did the Yippies announce a time to the press?" Schrader asked.

"Four o'clock." The chief looked glum.

A new resolve had been building in Schrader since Mingo's pep talk. He began to think of Mrs. Minsky, tiny and frail and good-hearted. If the crowd turned ugly, any elderly folk in the park would be in danger.

"Let's do it!" he blurted, grinning and rubbing his hands together. "Damnit! Let's do it!"

Mingo glanced at him sidewise. "If there's any backlash, you'll be the one to catch it."

"Sticks and stones," he shrugged, feeling better than he had in days.

"That's great!" the chief slapped a beefy hand on the table top. "If you want, I'll slip some plainclothesmen into the park to—"

"No thanks, chief. We know you have a few men seeded here and there, but anything more would be out and out collusion. We'll do it alone."

"Okay. You've got it. Say, here comes George. Let's hear what the boss has to say."

George Rodney was a distinguished looking man, graying, with an affability that had embraced all the vets from the very first. He was the Director of Civil Service for the entire United States. They shook hands all around.

"Well, gentlemen, I had an interesting phone conversation this morning," Rodney began, and he motioned them to seats. "It was from a man on the Democratic National Committee. Shouldn't say whom, I suppose. He was congratulating us for keeping the peace here in the park. They're very pleased, really, that no Chicago-type incidents have errupted. And he happened to mention a tidbit he'd heard about the Yippies. Something the Yippies are plotting? Is that what you were discussing? Good. This gentleman was concerned that their actions might turn the situation sour, so to speak. Any danger of that?" Rodney looked them over pleasantly. Here was a man who dealt with disaster on a national scale. Earthquakes, floods and hurricanes and thousands of the homeless were his forte. Schrader looked down, smiling, thinking all that the Yippies could muster would not put a hair out of place on this man's head.

"These men think they can handle it, George." The chief smiled hugely.

"That's wonderful! Er, by *handle*, I suppose you mean prevent?"

"Yes sir," Schrader heard himself say. "We can prevent it."

"That takes a burden from my shoulders, my young friends. I can tell you that. I'm a civil servant. Party politics are not my line of work. Politicians make me uneasy."

"Government makes me uneasy," Mingo retorted, and they all laughed.

"Mingo, I hear you're leaving us. Is that true?"

"Yes sir. I have to help organize more chapters around the state. And there's work needs doing in the Chicano community."

"Are you returning next month to help us with the Republicans?"

"No sir. Not a chance."

"You've done a fine job. We'll miss you."

Mingo shrugged it off. "There's a lot of good vets around, sir. We've already agreed to run your security next month. But it will be a different crew."

"Because we've all crashed and burned," Schrader put in.

Rodney smiled paternally. "I heard about your run-in with the Krishnas, David. I'm glad you weren't hurt."

"It was nothing. A brief scuffle."

"You're looking thin. Getting enough to eat?"

"Sure. The local folks are great. They help out."

Rodney took a twenty dollar bill from his wallet and stuffed it in Schrader's pocket. "Some beer money for the boys."

"We don't need your—"

"Now, now. It's nothing. I wish it was more. Do you have a list for me?"

"Yes sir." Mingo took a slip and handed it over. "Mostly first aid supplies. The radio batteries are important, and a half dozen new flashlights. Oh yeah, the crappers ain't being washed out. There's been complaints."

"I'll have it taken care of. There's one other thing, please.

When you're evicting undesirables from the park, I'd like you to be sure to call police assistance. Hold the offenders at one of the gates until some of Blackie's men show up. What's this about a drunk going to his car to fetch a pistol?"

"We took it away from him, boss. He was three sheets to the wind. Couldn't have shot himself in the foot."

"Maybe, and maybe not. No more risks like that, please."

"Okay."

"I'll be around the park most of the day, with a radio. Keep your eyes and ears on the Yippies. They're liable to become suddenly clever." Rodney shook his head. "I'm beginning to think there's nothing worse than a hoodlum with a college education."

They joked about it afterwards, and called it the Battle of Flamingo Park.

It was late afternoon when they found a quiet spot on the beach, a few blocks from the campsite. Mingo was swimming in the surf and Schrader was watchdogging, stretched out on the warm sand. Eddie Malone had scooped a hole for himself, and he lay face up, bad leg raised on a cushion of sand, his eyes red-rimmed and sleepless. He was dark featured and good looking in a hard way. Leo Marconi was prone on a towel, dressed in trousers because he was embarrassed by a skin rash doctors could not explain. Leo was as thick-trunked as two men, burly and red-bearded, and he was joking about the rumble. They were east coast boys, both of them First Air Cavalry.

". . . it's true!" Leo was laughing. "Sugarbear threw the punk twenty feet off the stage and he hit the ground runnin'; scooted off like one of them toy moto' cars!"

Eddie Malone looked sour. "Typical jody windbags. Squeeze 'em and they fizzle."

Somehow the Yippies heard of what the vets were planning. Two hours before their announced time, nearly a hundred of them took the stage and began rolling and smoking joints, inciting the crowd with a loudspeaker:

> *The Revolution can't wait*
> *Smoke pot and smash the State!*
> *Grind the pigs to fish bait!*

The Revolution can't wait
Smoke pot and smash the State!

When thirty or so veterans charged onto the stage, though, the gang of Yippies scattered. There was time for most of the vets to grab a neck and wring it a bit, then *poof*, the hoopla was over. The Yippies took to their heels, the crowd had a good laugh, and the crisis that never really was, never really became.

Schrader sat up abruptly, eyeing the flat plane of ocean. He had lost sight of Mingo among the waves, and then he spotted him, bobbing and cavorting.

"Take it easy, David."

"That's right, man. Relax."

He lay back on his side, head propped on an arm. Before him stretched a long white beach fused to a green ocean, overlaid by blue sky like a silk sheet flowing to the horizon, where a ribbon of orange haze was growing. All the world seemed color to him. He was sand on the beach. Ancient.

"You coming on to that stuff, brother?"

Schrader smiled. The salt breeze told him secrets, whispering.

"Mushrooms are really something," Eddie grinned, tilting his head back to chug at a beer.

David stirred. He opened his mouth but nothing came. He tried again, heard words. "You could have eaten it yourself." Was that his own voice?

"Naw. My way to thank you for standing my watch last night. Besides, you looked like you needed a recon through your head."

Eddie's leg had been too swollen for him to walk, so Schrader had taken his shift. He glanced at the leg then, propped on the sand, badly scarred: a welt ran from shin, across the knee, to his lower thigh. Stitched by an AK-47, one dark night on a mountainside claimed by the N.V.A.

Through the morning and early afternoon, before the Yippie debacle, Eddie had limped the streets of Miami Beach, passing out leaflets, trying to cajole passersby to join a demand for troop withdrawal. When he returned to the park, he had a pint of whiskey. In the first aid tent, sharing a swallow, Schrader watched him drink it down. A month's supply of painkillers would last two weeks, then he would begin to booze it earnest. When word came about the Yippies, they rushed from the tent toward the stage, Eddie limping badly but somehow keeping up. Schrader remembered the grim set to his face. All over the park, in twos and threes, veterans were hurriedly diverging on the stage. Somehow, by chance, they had reached it en masse, the crowd shouting, eager for a show. While Schrader was wrestling a man to the ground, out of the corner of his eye he saw Eddie flip two others with his cane, *trip, trap*! so very neatly, so ruthlessly. He had wanted to hurt them. Schrader saw that—his own foe face down and helpless, yelling—but Schrader paid him no mind as he watched that deadly light in Eddie's face. But then those two broke away and ran from the stage, and Malone limped to David and together they tossed the other one into the crowd.

Laying on the beach, warm in the sand, Schrader thought of Joe Haney whose own leg was shattered, going home angry and in pain. They were all the same. That was the wisdom the breeze whispered in his ear. They were the same flesh and blood and dreams, all of them melted and mingled and re-cast by the one fire. Schrader felt safe with his friends, but safe from what, he could not say.

The orange haze of sunset crept skyward. The crisp blue turned steely gray and the water darkened, no longer green. Mingo came in from the surf, hung all over with seaweed, arms out, stiff-legged, hamming it up. He dripped among them, kicking sand. "Igor want *cerveza*?" he moaned.

Eddie laughed. "Save us! A chile ghoul!"

Mingo cocked his head. "Say, man, is that chilly or *chile*?"

"Don't answer that!" Leo put in. "Here grunt, have a beer."

Mingo hunkered, beer spraying when he popped the tab. He eyed Eddie closely. "How's the leg, airborne?"

"I'll skip the next jump, thanks."

"There's a store down the block. You want some ice for a pack?"

Eddie waved it off. "Ice is seventy-five cents. That buys a quart of brew. Besides, I hate ice packs. They don't do me any good."

"You went at it too hard today."

"Ahhh, I'm gettin' too wound up. And for what? None of

this is doing any damned good. Everyone knows how he's going
to vote. And most of them Republican. I tell you, the man in
the street associates the Democrats with freaks and radicals. I
talked myself blue in the face all day, and didn't change one
person's mind. Come November, Nixon and his gang are gonna
roll up a big score, I guarantee! Christ, Leo, toss me a beer.
I need to get down."

"I got a bag of smoke," Leo winked. "Been saving it till
dark."

"How'd you get smoke if you're broke?"

"I took it off one of the Yippies. He was too busy to notice."

"Break it out. I got a pipe."

They drew in a tighter circle about Eddie, who packed
the pipe. Dusk was deepening, the glare of street lights throwing shadows, the surf breaking to catch the light in foam and
cast it back. Salt wind mingled with the scent of hemp. Seeds
popped and sparked.

Schrader listened to the talk and watched the faces fade
in the shadows, taking his turn at the pipe which somehow
seemed to extend the sensation of the muchroom. He was cozy
inside himself. Or, inside the *inside* of himself, a layer deeper
than he could plunge on his own. Something was there, something coldly perceived and fearful. Schrader could make it
whimper; he could make it flee to the darkest recess and remain, trembling. That was good. It had no business running
freely in his mind, spilling its terror. He would kill it if he
could: break it and rend it. But the thing was a part of himself.
He could only struggle half-blind until those rare moments
when he could see the creature and chase it to its cage. Only
then did David feel free.

Mingo nudged him. "How's the trip?"

It was a voice from outside. Schrader refocused. He was
on the outside. *Flick!* Inside. *Flick!* Outside. They were staring
at him.

"Still rushing?"

"I guess so. It's mellow." There passed what seemed a
long pause. They were still looking at him, faces made old and
gaunt by shadow, eyes made wise and deep. "I shouldn't have
done it. Something might go wrong at the park."

"Forget it, man." It was Leo, always first with a good
word. "Rosen can handle anything that comes down. You just

sit back and let it take you." He shoved a beer into Schrader's hand. "Besides, if you had to react, you'd do fine."

"Sure, David. Even a firefight. You'd get right into it."

"No way, Eddie. Not drugged." He looked to Mingo for support.

"It was different for us," Mingo told them. "We didn't do drugs first time around. We'd hear talk of it, you know. There were always a few guys who sneaked it, sure, but we didn't billet like the Army. When you guys finished a search and destroy, you'd go home to a big basecamp. There were places it was safe, where it was okay to smoke. But in the Marines, we were mostly small units out in the middle of some jungle, a platoon or company at the biggest. Maybe you could throw a rock clear across the camp. There was no place an NCO or an officer couldn't find you. Unless you were on patrol. And only a damned fool would get stoned on patrol, right?"

"You got that right!"

"So it never caught on," Mingo continued. "Besides, we had a squad leader who would hang your ass out to dry if he caught you."

Mingo laughed at that suddenly, and David took it up, remembering Joe. Their laughter carried down the sand, across the water, back to them on the wind. The surf laughed with them. It gurgled and guffawed. Schrader turned his head to hear it better, but the ocean swallowed it.

"Tet changed everything," Mingo said woodenly.

"Amen, brother." Leo replied, shaking his head. "Tet changed the whole world."

They grew silent. The night had dampened. It was full upon them but impure, spoiled by city lights, marred by mists that hid the stars. Mingo stood to brush himself. He picked off the last of the seaweed and put on his shirt. "How 'bout a change of scenery? We're out of *cerveza*."

"I'm for that. What's say we make the party I told you about?"

"Party? You mean noise and bright lights and strangers in my face? Not me, Eddie. I've had that all week."

"This is different, Mingo. It's across the line in Miami. Be some rich liberal broads there. They don't care how we look. We're colorful. Their token gimps and heroes."

Mingo shook his head.

"David? What do you say? A couple of war stories might get you a comfortable sack for the night."

Schrader had a vivid image of a monstrous grocery sack with a brass bed and goose down mattress. He was laying in the bed wearing his jungle boots, a naked and lovely woman curled by his side. "Vote for McGovern" was tattooed on her ass.

"David! Hey boy!"

"What? Oh. No thanks, Eddie. I'd end up standing in a corner with my mouth open. Hey. You're broke. Here's a few of the bucks old Rodney gave me."

Eddie reached for the money, but David handed it deliberately to Leo.

"So you won't drink up your bus fare."

"Piss on you, Jarhead." But Eddie was grinning wryly.

They got to their feet and dressed, and passed the pipe around. Marconi took their cans and litter to a barrel. Then he stuffed a few buds in Mingo's pocket.

"Keep the wild man out of trouble, Leo."

"See you guys." They split up as they walked from the beach to the broad city avenue. It was brightly lit. Schrader paused to take some deep breaths, as though preparing, but there were only evening strollers and flashing tavern signs. He'd worn trousers and a sports shirt, but enough uniform in his boots and bandanna to feel comfortable. And of course, his pin: V.V.A.W.

They found a liquor store soon enough.

"Get a couple quarts, man."

"I'll wait out here, Mingo. You get it."

"*Me dare dinero, hombre.*" He held out his hand.

A few minutes later they ducked through an alley and were back on the beach. There were grand plans to be made. V.V.A.W. was an organization finally coming into its own: the media was beginning to pay them mind, the public was becoming sympathetic. Through the spring and early summer, as the Texas chapters grew stronger, there would be interviews on radio and television. There were already requests for speakers. The first donations were trickling in.

The schemes that David and Mingo hatched, as they walked for hours up and down the shore, were not unrealistic. Speaking engagements could be scheduled, fund raising benefits

could be arranged. Guerilla theatre was planned. The link with
returning GIs at Fort Hood was to be strengthened. Already
in Austin there were crash pads for these newest veterans, to
help ease them back into the world. The head of the Texas
delegation, John Kniffin, was in Tallahassee. Schrader was to
meet with him. They would return to Texas together, and the
work could begin. They were confident and excited. Finally,
people were going to listen.

A pale, sickle moon was late rising, a bare glimmer on the
water, as they drank their last beers. From tinfoil and a can
Mingo fashioned a pipe, and they smoked Leo's buds, Schrader
past the drug rush, feeling the introspective glow of coming
down. Walking back to the park, they left a trail through the
wet sand.

"You going to keep mum, David, or let loose to some of
the brothers?"

"And tell them what? That I have bad dreams? Maybe I
should ask some one to hold my little hand."

Mingo was unperturbed. "The pressure will out, one way
or another. You can go back to the VA shrinks."

"Right. For the standard Freudian line and maybe! Just
maybe! If I act strange enough, they'll give me a big bottle of
thorazine. Wow! Then I can walk around like a class-three
turnip, and not bother a soul."

"Or, thick head, you can rap it out with the only men in
the galaxy who understand." He paused in his Latin way. "Or,
at some time *en su vida*, you can slip over that edge we're all
so secretly afraid of."

"Crap. If I flake a little, I'll get over it. Look around you,
Mingo. Look at some of the other brothers. Eddie hurts everyday. Ron's in a goddamned wheelchair for Christ's sake! Leo
has something mysterious wrong with his body. Alton and
Gunny are all shot up and scarred. I'm the goddamned lucky
one! So I'm not putting my trip on their heads, and that's all
there is to it."

"Okay. Okay. I shouldn't have brought it up again."

"No kidding! Since when is your life so sunny? You're
about to screw up the best thing that ever happened to you."

"Me and Adelita are none of your business."

"Hoop de dooh! None of my business, eh? You pepper
brain! For six months I watched her pull you out of every

gutter in Austin. How many times did we lock you in a room, me watching her flinch at every filthy thing you said to her through the door. Marrying the woman doesn't seem like such a big deal. You love her. You won't ever have a better woman."

"If you're so hot on the idea, then you marry her."

"Kiss my ass if I shouldn't try!"

"You wouldn't stand a chance."

"Sure. I don't have your goddamned Mexican charisma. Too bad you can't see past your nose, though."

"That's exactly it, man. I can't see past my nose. I can see the war. It's a big mural painted on the wall and I'm standing right up against it. My future is somewhere in that picture, but it's too close and the colors are too bright, and I can't sort my future out. What's to be for me, David? Eh? You tell me. I'm a junkie—"

"Cut it out, Mingo! Don't think of yourself like that."

"I'm a fuckin' junkie! You understand? Ain't no way to pretty it up. What kind of future can Adelita have with me? I can't even think of anything I want to do, or anything I want to be. It scares me, man. I'm not sure I can get into a normal life. I don't even remember what a normal life is like!"

"Then hold onto Adelita, and be good to her. She'll show you."

They had ceased to walk, standing tensely by the dark water, waves tumbling near their feet. Tight-lipped, Mingo kicked a hole in the sand.

"I don't want to hurt her anymore than I have," he muttered.

"Then don't! That's easy enough."

"Easy enough to say."

"So practice. Use your pepper brain to think of new ways to be nice. Maybe you should think a little less about the revolution. Maybe we all should."

"It fills a hole, brother. For the time being, I have to fill it with something."

"Yeah. Sure. I can dig that. But something with substance, you know. Not hot air and cardboard. Isn't all this getting a little heavy, Mingo? We're putting ourselves through something weird again, something we only partly understand. You'd think we'd have had enough of that. We could be in the mountains, Mingo, a thousand miles from all this noise. We could be deep in the woods. We could be anywhere but here."

Calderone put his arm around him and pulled him close. "People need to know the truth, David. That's a simple fact. I can live my life around that fact for a while. It's real enough to hold me up. Words like duty, man, those are clumsy words. Duty got us all neck deep in crap. But that's kind of what we feel, no? But it's not enough to keep you together, then back away. Don't let me talk you into anything. Maybe I've been wrong to drag you into this. It's been because I needed to lean on you. But you have to go your own way, *hombre*. It's only going to get heavier."

"You didn't drag me into anything."

"You know what I mean. You could be back home in Missouri, milking cows or whatever. You came to Texas to help me out. It put you on a different road."

Schrader thought of his mother, graying, lines of work deep in her lovely face, eyes going far away sometimes; to what, Schrader could not guess. It was six months since he called her. It hurt to see her aging so young. He had put that hurt aside, that consideration, for an altogether fiercer hurt, and his family was dim to him: a father whose understanding was gone, brothers and sisters he hardly knew.

There was no where else for Schrader to go. His only friends were around him.

"It's three o'clock, David. I need to pack a few things before I split."

They were near the edge of the park. They could see the tall lights beside the tennis courts.

"You waiting for the sun to come up?"

"*Porque*? I can be across the causeway and maybe through Miami by then."

"Just be careful. Those cops aren't as nice as Blackie's boys. They'll be headhunting for freaks out alone on the streets."

"Sure. I'll be nice and meek. Yes sir, no sir . . . works every time."

"And tuck your hair up under a goddamned hat! What kind of a Marine are you, anyway? We're you drafted?"

"You mean shafted?"

The ocean laughed and sighed behind them.

* * *

The chimes toned off-key, flatly, slapping the mute walls
like dough, falling flabbily, hollow machine voice saying: Passengers for Winona, Jackson, Baton Rouge and New Orleans,
may now board, gate seven. All aboard please.

He shifted, hard-backed bench digging at his shoulders,
butt and numb thighs. The lights were glaring, his eyes wanted
sleep, and he began to nod. Someone who kicked his foot,
mumbling *Sorry*, dragged two children who looked back curiously, runny-nosed, as lost as Schrader.

"Got a cigarette, bub?"

He shook his head.

"Spare change?"

"I'm broke, pop. I got enough for a couple of meals."

The old panhandler shuffled away, sour smelling, teeth
gone.

Schrader's clothes were still wet from the rain. He dug
in his pack for dry socks, took off his boots and changed socks,
all the while glancing about the station, seeing the two police,
the exits, wondering where the stairway led. They told him to
lay low. Okay. He would treat life as ambush, as they should
have done all along.

In Florida, everything had come apart. A Federal grand
jury, convened in Tallahassee by the Justice Department, had
indicted six members of V.V.A.W. for conspiracy. A conspiracy
of violence and terrorism, a picture of veterans wreaking havoc
in Miami Beach to disrupt the GOP Convention.

Now, in the press, they were anarchists. They were ter-
rorists. And they were backpedalling in frustration.

John Kniffin was arrested, a three tour combat Marine,
wounded for his country, decorated for bravery. Scott Camil
was under arrest, another Marine, head of the Florida delegation. Bill Patterson was arrested, Peter Mahoney, Alton Foss,
Don Perdue. All of them combat veterans. All of them friends
of Schrader and Calderone. Each of them had voluntarily sur-
rendered to the police, after the indictments were handed
down.

The vets had always been too trusting. Their organization
had become infiltrated with government provocateurs. The
charges, in fact, were lodged by paid informers of the FBI,
men who had lied about being veterans, men who were ex-

pected to produce for their silver. Locked in secrecy with the grand jury, these men spun fantastic tales.

The chimes toned again. People turned their heads, jerked their children's arms for silence. Schrader closed his eyes and stretched his legs. There was an hour before the Dallas bus. Hamburgers sizzled at the snack bar. His stomach rumbled.

Get out of the state, his friends told him. The grapevine carried ill winds: Schrader's name was before the grand jury. The possible charge was conspiracy to murder a police officer. The news stunned him. The friends had hurried him out the door, driven him from Tallahassee, pointed him to Atlanta. He had other friends there who hid him, who scraped up some cash, who got him a lift to Memphis with a trucker, who had dropped him off in Tennessee rain.

He sat on the bench until his bones and muscles ached, and the wet clothes leeched the feeling from his skin. He could not fathom the malice. He wanted his mind blanked; to fold himself again and again until he vanished. Across the country, members of Vietnam Veterans Against the War were being punished. Their phones were tapped, their reputations smeared. Agents went to employers and jobs were lost. Medical records disappeared, and disability payments stopped. Their homes were searched. They were arrested, thrown in jail without hearings, threatened with violence, blackmailed. The conspiracy charges had become an indictment against all of them. Apparently it would not do, to have public confidence in them grow.

Outside it was raining again, wind buffeted the windows, and people rushed in ruffling like hens. It was a very black night. The depot was empty except for those driven inside by the storm. In his wallet, Schrader had seven dollars and a bus ticket. In his pockets he found two quarters and a dime. He bought a candy bar and chewed it slowly, wondering where he would go, what he would do. From Dallas he could ride his thumb to Austin, find where Mingo was laying low, and go there. Mingo would figure. Schrader would go along. He was only a second stringer, after all.

He lifted his pack and stepped wearily to the bathroom, to wash and change clothes. The room stank. There was a turd in one of the urinals. Schrader moved to the sink at the far end and propped his pack against the dingy wall.

He turned on the tap and stared hard into the mirror, at his own haggard face and into his own eyes as if he'd never seen them. He stared deeper and he saw a man, alone, lost, having left his values behind. He stared even deeper and he saw the stranger.

And isn't it a frightening thing—when a man sees this stranger for the first time, and sees his future a gray blur, and his past denied . . . and his present in a filthy men's room in Memphis?

> *In shame there is no comfort,*
> *but to be beyond all bounds of shame.*
> SIR PHILIP SYDNEY
> *Arcadia*

12

Austin, Texas 1979

In his dream the sand was very white, like sugar, but for the stains around the piss tubes. He could smell the urine but there was something else, too. Yes! The blood. He could smell the blood. It was all white sand in his vision, all white sand except those sour yellow stains. But when he turned his head in his dream he saw the boy, very tiny, very bloody, looking at him. *Looking at him!* And he was terrified because he knew what came next. Oh yes, he knew.

The tinny old alarm went *clang! clang! clang!* He sat straight up, wrapped in the sheet and stupid with fear. Spittle drooled from his mouth. Dim room with shades drawn, blank nougat walls, the clock choking on its last *clang*, wheezing dead tin: that was his wake-up world.

He sat there not knowing where he was or when he was. His neighbors brought it all back. He heard a screen door slam like a shot. A woman's voice shouted in Spanish *No te vallas corriendo, diablito! Se lo voy a decir a tu Papa!* The crack of her voice jarred him. Little feet footed down the driveway. Quick little feet, too fast for pregnant mama. There was the clatter of kickstand, wheels bouncing, the fantastic getaway of Joey Mendoza heard through drawn shades tossed lightly by breeze, the only life in the house.

He found the shower, tripping over shoes with his heart still racing: *thumpa thump! thumpa thump!* The water on his head, in his ears made the sound of heart in throat an undersea engine, gurgled and muted. The shower made him human.

David was drying when a knock came; he slipped on blue-jeans and a shirt and opened the door. There stood Adelita, looking smart, low heels and hose, tailored maternity suit.

"Hey, good-looking—" He tried to smile but the sunshine was too much.

"David, you look awful," and she stepped past him purposely and walked into the kitchen, her softly done blue-black hair shining. She was beautifully boned, confident in her pregnancy that she looked better than ever.

"What? No hug and kiss?"

"*Es broma, no?* You look like the leavings for the cat."

"I went a little overboard after work."

"Cuddling with the waitresses, eh?" Her eyes cut into him.

He put out his hands. "Now wait a minute. Did Jessie tell—"

"Jessie and I didn't talk about you," she cut in primly. "But I know you too well. I can tell when you're about to screw up."

"Look, honey, if you came to give me hell about—"

"No, no," she protested. "I just came for a friendly visit, seeing how you're too far out in left field to visit us. If you want to mess up the good thing you have with Jessie, that's your dumb business." She sat daintily at the kitchen table.

"Hmmm. This is all shooting by me like a comet. You want some coffee?"

She patted her bulge. "I shouldn't drink coffee. You have any juice?"

"Frozen. I'll make—"

Zip! She popped out of her chair, put her gentle hands

on his chest: "Sit down before you fall." And she busied herself making the juice, which involved the blender, which played the devil with his ears.

"So you saw Jessie today?" he asked.

"I stopped by the club this morning. She was setting up the bar. Let me tell you right now, if you break up with Jessie, she's still going to be my friend!"

"Whoa. No one's said anything about that."

"I'm just giving you warning. Don't expect Mingo and I to cut her out of our lives."

"Adelita, please. Let's start over again. What's got you so riled?"

She poured two glasses of juice and sat down. Her eyes sparked a little. "We haven't seen you in two weeks."

"I'm sorry."

"What was the last thing we talked about?"

He looked at the dirty floor. "You asked me to stand for godfather."

"And you think that's not so important?" she snapped. "You think we were asking for a damned football score?"

"I know it's important, honey. My head's been—"

"Don't honey me, David Schrader. I don't want to hear the shape your head is in. Mingo is hurt! His best friend can't give him a straight answer. Is that any way to treat Mingo?"

"No. It's a rotten way to treat him."

"Are you afraid to talk to the priest? Is that it? Just because you had a chaplain once who told you to kill gooks for God. That must be it. Now you can't even talk to fat old Father Benito who never hurt a soul in his life! Please don't give me that old story, David." She was wound up and cutting deep. He could see that he had hurt her.

"I'd be proud to be your child's godfather, Adelita."

"Oh, would you?" she sniffed. "We hurt my brother's feelings, just to ask you instead."

"Ramon is a fine man. A much better choice."

"It's too late now. No one likes to be second best."

He took her hand. "I'm very sorry. The time got away from me. Please forgive me."

She looked away from him, "Of course I forgive you. But I want you to come after work tonight, to talk to Mingo."

"I'll be there. Will you make some—*migas*?"

"Maybe. David, I'm sorry if I made light of your troubles."

"Forget it, kid. Why should a grown man be scared of his dreams?" Schrader drummed his fingers on the table top. He could hear street noises, children playing. "I thought I was over them, Adelita. But here they come again. Glorious technicolor."

"Oh, David. Maybe it's the crazy life you lead. Maybe you should quit working in a damned topless bar, and come out in the light of day sometimes."

He tried to shrug it off.

"I fibbed," she admitted. "Jessie and I did talk a little about you. She told me about the last night you stayed with her."

"That I woke up screaming?"

"No. That you woke up with a scream. That's different. She thought you had shouted some one's name. You were sweaty and shaking, she said. Big deal. So why stop seeing her?"

"That's easy to understand. I don't want her to see me like that, scared out of my senses. It takes away a man's dignity."

"And that's so important?"

"If you're a man." He nodded.

"*Madre*! I'll never understand how thick-boned a Marine skull can be."

"A little less dense than a Mexican marine's, I'd guess."

"Oh, do I ever hope for a girl!" She seemed to glow, lighting the dreary kitchen.

"What does the doctor tell you?"

"I'm in great shape!" she talked with her hands, much like Mingo. "My weight is perfect. My blood pressure is perfect. The baby is turned just like she should be. Feet here, butt like so . . ." Adelita's hands danced about. ". . . and her little head is right here. Oh yes! Her heartrate is a hundred and forty beats a minute."

"And the doctor isn't concerned about the miscarriage?"

"Oh no, David. Not at all. That was four years ago. I was working too hard; I wasn't taking care of myself very well. And I got sick, remember?"

"Sure I remember."

"But I'm fine now, David. You don't need to worry."

"Then I won't."

"You'll come tonight for sure?"

"Promise."

"Then I'd better go. I have a list of errands that drags on the ground."

"I thought when you quit work, you'd have some spare time."

She laughed prettily. "This is my spare time. See you tonight!" With a light kiss she was up and gone, door shutting quietly, fading steps, the slam of a car door. Of a sudden, his tiny cottage seemed to close on him. For about five minutes he thought about getting up. Then he did get up, and paced the house opening all the doors and windows. It was near noon on an Indian Summer's day in October.

He turned on the radio and took his time making brunch. He ate slowly, while he read the paper. The house had a fenced back yard, some nice trees. He lay in the sun a while to pass the time. Then he showered again and dressed. Schrader worked down town, north of the river. It was a pleasant wait for the bus, there by the little stone church, the air very autumny, the passersby friendly, elms and crepe myrtles yellow and red. Then the bus came to carry him to work.

The Red Duke was a deep and narrow club, a few blocks from the pink granite capitol that seems to crown the city. The bus let him off in the light and warmth, but the club seemed a cave—a den from Dante: dimly lit with red lights, smoke-filled, noisy with the jabber of voices and wild laughter. And it was cold; the air conditioner pumped hard filtering the sweat-sour smoke. Mostly, it made his nose run.

If you stepped off the street into the club, a scantily dressed waitress would greet you. If you were a member or looked like you had money, she would welcome you fondly. Otherwise, you got a chilly reception. Inside there was a circular stage with mirrors and colored lights, and on the stage a woman danced topless. There was a small bar in the back, and behind that another mirror that reflected it all back at you. The music was too loud, and you paid too much for your drinks. Lots of men did.

That day he stood just inside the door and let his pupils adjust to the dimness. A heavy tune was playing: bluesy, whining, the rhythm reaching out and the sound shooting through him like radium. The stale smoke hit him in the face, lapping around him, dirty water on a wharf.

A slim girl was dancing; pretty breasts but she was no dancer. She was stiff and too self-conscious. You could always tell when they only did it for the money. They steeled themselves and performed because the tips were good. Most of the daytime girls were like that. The night crew was something else again. Those girls loved it. Nights were wilder and the girls were pretty salty — good, gritty dancers, dirty dancers if need be, down-in-the-dirt, dog-scrogging dancers, and the men loved it. They went wild over it. He had seen respected men, legislators, churchgoers with spittle running down their chins, eyes bulging at these women and their faces red with whiskey fever and lust.

The night girls were not on yet. Happy hour was just beginning and when the song ended he walked through the narrow club, past the tables, past the stage to the bar.

A cluster of businessmen gathered there, slouching, leaning on the bar, touching and teasing the waitresses as they carried trays of cocktails. Jessie moved breezily behind the polished counter. She was tall and trim, with an easy humor that kept her wisecracking customers at bay. They were regulars, big daytime spenders but Schrader seldom saw them at night.

"Cool it boys, here comes the sheriff."

Schrader grimaced as he ducked beneath the counter. He tried to smile at the banker who made the crack. "That's Sergeant Sheriff to the likes of you."

The banker guffawed, his face crimsoned by the red light, his laughter void of humor.

"Take it easy on my boy, Mr. Neville," Jessie told the man, winking slyly at David. "Good help is hard to keep."

All the men laughed, Schrader the butt of their joke, but when Jessie stepped close to kiss him full on the mouth David could see the envy in their faces. That set it straight.

"Scotch water, scotch rocks, beer with a neat bourbon!" A waitress clattered dirty glasses onto the bar.

"You want me to get them, baby?"

"Oh no," she told him. "You wash the glasses and clean the bar. I'll make the drinks."

Moving apart, her hand lingered across his chest, along his arm, locked briefly with his fingers. He longed to be alone with her. He wanted a normal life, instead of hurried hours between their shifts. But he didn't know how to ask, how to admit he cared that much. And now the nightmares were knocking his life akilter.

"Wash the dishes, son. Look snappy now!" It was Neville again, the banker.

Schrader tore his eyes from Jessie and gave a mock salute. "I'm still dazed from the kiss," he grinned, filling the sink and gathering the glasses.

"A kiss! God Almighty!" Neville complained. "I've tipped that gal about a thousand dollars this year, and she patted my cheek once. What the hell does a kiss cost around here?"

"That's nothing, shithead," one of Neville's buddies said to him. "I've tipped her that much at least, and offered her a trip to Puerto Rico."

"You were taking your wife on that trip."

"So? There's two sides to an island, ain't there?"

Jessie was calmly mixing drinks, paying them no mind.

"Schrader, you understand about business, don't you?"

"Sure, Mr. Neville, I understand about business. It's like terrorism. The ends justify the means."

Neville looked blankly at his buddy the broker.

"He's saying anything goes, shithead. Same thing you're about to say."

"My point exactly," Neville continued, raising his voice to cue his friends. "Anything goes in real business, right boys? And love is a little like business, isn't it Schrader?"

"I suppose . . . if you're making love to your secretary."

The broker, a little drunk, shook his finger in the air. "Shithead doesn't do that anymore. His second wife caught him humping his secretary—and after much headache and very great expense, that secretary is now his third wife! She makes sure Neville's got the ugliest office help of any bank president in this goddamned town."

"The point that I'm about to make," the banker continued, undaunted, angling to draw a crowd, "is that love and business are very much the same." And with a showy flair he reached for his wallet.

Jessie was busy with still more drinks when another waitress called: "Three beers, three flaming fuzzy fuckers!"

As Jessie placed a special tray on the counter, for the flaming cocktails, Neville pulled a crisp thousand dollar bill from his wallet and shook it near her face. Schrader stiffened, saw instant red, then relaxed. Jessie only smiled demurely and built the drinks: tequilla in small snifters, galliano floated on top.

"A year's tips for one night, Jessie girl. What do you say?" And Neville laid the bill on the bar beside the tray.

Some of the men snickered, glanced at Schrader, grinned expectantly. At one time or another, Jessie had rebuffed each of them.

Expertly, she built the cocktails, took the high proofed rum and began to top the drinks. Neville glanced around, the center of attention, and only Schrader saw her slop the rum on the tray, on the bar, on the thousand dollar bill.

"You're very sweet to ask, Mr. Neville. But I only mix drinks for a living. Drinks like these —" And with that, Jessie struck a match and touched it to the 151 proof rum and the cocktails flared into blue flame that trailed neat as a cat's track to the bill, which began to burn merrily.

"Drinks up, Heather." When the waitress took the flaming tray away the banker noticed the other small fire.

"Jesus Christ!" he screamed, real terror in his voice as he slapped at the bar, the others not comprehending until Neville began to huff and puff as he flapped the charred greenback in the air. "My money's burning!" he screamed again. Some one tossed the contents of a scotch and water, poorly aimed, and it slopped Neville's sleeve, dripped down his arm and sputtered the tiny fire out. Even in the dim red light, they could all see the banker was ghostly pale.

David felt a friendly poke across the bar.

"It wasn't even shithead's money," the broker giggled. "If it was, I guarantee the sonuvabitch would've dirtied his drawers."

The businessmen roared with laughter. Jessie stepped to the register to clear a tab, her chin turned up with satisfaction, a knowing smile on her lips. Schrader sidled up to her. Some one punched a song on the juke box and the air began to vibrate to bass guitar.

"Score one for the working girls," Schrader spoke in her ear, and she tossed her head and leaned into him as he nuzzled the soft flesh of her neck.

"I'm sorry about the mess I left last night, kid. I had the bar all cleaned, just before closing, then the girls wanted to have a party and Christ! Half the regulars stayed after hours . . ."

Jessie closed the cash register drawer. "Did you enjoy yourself?"

"Hell, no. It was all the same fools I see every night. I don't know why I let them talk me into it." But he did know why — he was afraid to go home and sleep.

"You don't look very rested," she said, her hands busy with the bottles and glasses and ice, her eyes intent on her work.

"Same old thing," he replied.

"You could come see me, you know, if you wanted to talk. The middle of the night is a lousy time to be scared."

"It goes away quick enough. But thanks, honey."

She smiled and held his eyes. They had been friends a long while, before they were lovers. Both had been hesitant to ruin a good thing.

"We've some business to discuss, away from the girls. Let's go in back," and she gestured toward the front to one of the waitresses. "Heather! Come tend the bar, honey."

He watched her leg muscles tense as she bent neatly to come under the bar. She was tall and trim, and he wanted her right then. He followed her down the dim hallway to the office, watching her.

The room was small and crowded with two desks and a couch. She sat on the edge of a desk and showed him lots of leg. He shut the door and she heard the lock click. He looked at her and then at the couch and smiled.

"Don't do that now, David."

"Okay. Let's talk business." But he stepped up to her and pulled her close and she came pliantly enough. She was so soft and warm. He kissed her deeply. He liked the taste of her mouth and the quick jabbing of her tongue. Her back arched like a cat's beneath his hand, and she moved the point of her knee so slowly up his thigh that he wanted to whimper at the touch.

Then something of her good sense returned. She held him in check. *She doesn't want a tumble in the office, to lay there with her skirt around her neck while I go to work,* he thought.

He nodded in understanding, and took a step back.

"How long is this, this *retreat* of yours supposed to last?" There was exasperation in her voice. Her expression betrayed that she still did not understand.

He thought that she deserved a straight answer. "The longest a cycle ever lasted was about three months. Sometimes they're gone in a couple of weeks."

Jessie bit her lip and looked away. "I wish I could help, David. But you won't let me. Every relationship seems to reach a point where, either it has the momentum to get up the hills, or it doesn't. And if it doesn't — I'm afraid we're losing steam, you know what I mean, David? If you won't share this with me — " but the words trailed off and she smiled at him weakly.

He saw so much in that trembling smile. *We're both too old for these moonlight romances,* he thought, *too shakey on our feet.*

"Just give me some time, Jessie. Please?"

"I hate being alone at night. So do you."

"It's rotten."

She straightened up and tossed her head primly. There was business. She was the boss.

"Lieutenant Logan paid us a visit today," she began.

"Logan? He's not on vice, is he?"

Jessie shook her head. "Narcotics."

Schrader raised his brows. "Is there some trouble?"

"Two things, David. First, the lieutenant wanted to pass a tip along to Connors from the boys on the vice squad. April Mae has been soliciting downtown."

"Christ!"

"She drives around in that big Chrysler and does business through the window. The other day, she propositioned a man just as his wife was coming from a store. The woman copied the license and called the cops."

"Did they haul her in?"

"No. But she's on their list. If she tries to turn a trick in here, they'll come down on us hard."

"Connors will want to fire her," Schrader said. He thought

about Connors, the owner, who had once thrown a football for The University of Texas and had won a lot of games. He had a lot of buddies on the force and among the alumni.

"Connors blows hot and cold," Jessie replied. "April Mae has some solid call customers here, and that's money in Connors's pocket."

"So what are we supposed to do? How can we tell if she's setting up a trick or not?"

"I'll talk to her, David. I know she wants to keep this job. But that wasn't the main thing on the lieutenant's mind."

"Then what was?"

"Our lovely Rita. Logan is convinced she's dealing from the club."

"Dealing what?" Schrader frowned.

"A little bit of everything: qualudes, amphetamine, cocaine. But even that isn't what he's after. At least, I don't think so. It seems he wants to nail Rita for something else, but he wouldn't say what. Where do you know the lieutenant from, David?"

"Me?" he laughed. "I don't hang around with cops. I've talked to him a few times here in the club, that's all."

"That's funny," Jessie frowned. "He told me that I should be sure *you* know about Rita, so you could keep an eye on her. But he doesn't want Connors to know anything about it. Connors is his buddy, but he shows you preference."

"That's just smart," Schrader said. "Connors has a big mouth. Loose lips sink ships."

"It's not just that. The lieutenant speaks kind of, well, familiarly about you. As though he knew you from somewhere."

David shook his head, trying to recall. "I never met him before here. I'm sure."

"It must be my imagination, then. Damn Rita! I don't care what she does on her own time. But I can't have her dealing from the club. I have my reputation as a manager to protect."

Schrader kissed her mouth lightly. "I'll keep an eye on her, Jessie. And if I see anything suspicious, I'll fire her."

"Good. And right away, too. Don't wait until the end of the shift."

"I guess I'd better go up front," he told her reluctantly, wanting to stay and hold her close. "Do you have my starting bank?"

"It's in the drawer below the register."

"After work, I'm going to see Mingo and Adelita. You want to come?"

She shook her head. "I just saw Adelita today."

He turned to go.

"David—try and get some rest, okay?"

When he closed the door on her then, it was like turning out a light.

By ten o'clock Schrader wanted a drink. It wasn't the shaking cravings or anything like that. But he was outside when everyone else was drinking and dull-witted, and there he stood, the smug teetotaler. Everyone hates a smug bastard, so he had a bourbon.

The place was in the yahoo stage. That's when some wobbly-legged senator or banker would stand on his chair and holler "YAHOO," as in his humble country boyhood. Even if he was raised in River Oaks.

"Three scotch waters, bourbon coke!"

"Vodka martini up, Margarita rocks!"

"Four flaming fuzzy fuckers!"

He was busy enough. The whiskeys went to Lilah, sweet, lithe, black Lilah. Schrader stirred the martini and poured it out, then shook the Margarita. April Mae took them away, her short blonde hair matted with sweat, portrait of the hard-working girl. The flaming fuzzy fuckers were for Rita. She slouched sexily across the bar, her proud lovely breasts a magnet for one's eyes, her dark eyes half-closed and dreamy. When Schrader lit the rum, the flames jumped and writhed in Rita's black eyes. She hoisted the tray and wove through the tables, and he thought of Salome with John the Baptist's head on a tray. Rita had that dark, hard beauty.

A relative quiet came between songs, but the voices droned on and on. He felt saturated with smoke and his nose was beginning to run from the air conditioned cold. And he was irritable.

Another waitress came to the bar. Holly was slender and poised, with the big-eyed prettiness that stares at you from magazines.

"David, can I have two blended daiquiris?"

"The blender is broke. I'll shake two."

"It's not broken," she challenged. "I saw Jessie use—"

He cut her off rudely. "This is a bar, Holly, not an ice cream parlor. Tell your customers I'll shake two."

"Crap! You just don't want to clean the damned blender!"

When Christian came to the bar, Holly was looking at him angrily, knowing he'd have his way. She was working hard that night, selling a lot of drinks, but Schrader was feeling sort of mean. When Christian called out "Scotch soda and two martinis," he looked at Holly.

"What's it gonna be?"

"Oh, just a minute you bastard. I'll go see what they want." And she stepped back to her table.

"Kind of slow for a Friday," Christian began to chatter as he made her drinks. She was a tall, auburn-haired Oklahoma girl, with a band of freckles across her nose. A curl fell across her eyes and sweat trickled down her neck. "I wanted to make a hundred bucks tonight, but it don't look like I will. Got a dentist bill, David, that you wouldn't believe."

Schrader grunted, trying to ignore her.

". . . that sucker had to give me *five* hits of gas before I'd let him touch my mouth. Lord, do I hate those drills! Hey boy, are you listening to me?"

"Are you *saying* anything?"

Holly stepped back up to the bar then. "They'll have two tequila sunrises, instead."

"What are they, faggots?" he sneered.

The women looked at each other. "What's eating him, tonight?"

"I don't know. Maybe he's constipated."

They had a great laugh over that, but Schrader got more surly.

Christian took her drinks and left, but all the others came to the bar at once.

"Bourbon water, and a beer!"

"Two Margarita rocks!"

"Scotch mist, whiskey sour, martini rocks!"

Suddenly he was surrounded by women demanding things of him. Schrader felt he had to take control.

"Whose turn is it to dance?" he snapped, not moving on the drinks, making them wait.

"Mine." Holly spoke up.

"We thought we'd take two rest songs in between," Lilah said. "Everyone's feet hurt."

"Sorry. One rest song. Get their blood up and they'll drink more."

"Easy for you to say!"

"Yes. Disgustingly easy. Now dance, Holly!"

"Ooooeee! Listen to that boy!"

"Hardass!"

"Maybe he's not gettin' any."

There was some more grumbling, but Holly danced and Schrader made all the drinks and the bar was clean again. He liked it that way when he was mad. Usually the women ran over him, anyway.

He drew himself a beer and about that time the owner came in and sat at the bar. Connors's hair was mussed and there was lipstick on his face. Even in the dim light Schrader could see it.

"New shade, sweetheart?"

Connors grinned hugely and wiped his mouth. "Whew! My eyeballs are steaming!"

"I thought your girlfriend was out of town?"

"Hell, she is!" Connors laughed. "My ex-wife flew in from New Orleans today, got my boy with her." He winked. "She's gonna do a number on me."

"Trying to get back together?" asked Schrader, pouring him a heavy bourbon.

"Naw. She's got a couple boyfriends. Sweet Barbara wants more alimony, that's what. So she's going to screw my brains out and we'll sashay round with the kid just like old times."

"Will you give her more alimony?"

"Shit no! But I'll take what she's handing out." He winked and they both laughed lecherous laughs. "You know, she's got one honey who's a banker and another who's a big cheese with an oil company. I send her $1750 bucks each month and she don't work a lick and gets taken out all the time. What the hell does she need more money for?"

Schrader didn't know Connors's wife. He knew she had been a cheerleader in the days Connors was a big jock beating Oklahoma.

"Give me another bourbon, David. Slow Friday, ain't it?"

There were perhaps thirty men in the club. Usually on a Friday there were twice that.

Some drinks were called and Schrader set them out. At the front of the club a loud group came in, pulled together two tables and hooted and shouted. Middle-aged, prosperous.

Black Lilah came to the bar and called some drinks. She had a heavy voice that dripped sweet as syrup.

"Hey baby!"

"Hello, Connors. Look like you havin' a little action tonight."

"Just warmin' up, sugar. C'mere. Got something to ask you."

Lilah looked at him suspiciously, then kind of glided over. Connors put an arm around her waist and pulled her close.

"How would you like to work a little extra tomorrow?"

"What do you mean? The club ain't open on the weekend."

"Not here, baby. Down in San Marcos." Connors had another place, not a private club, but topless, the Honky Moon.

Lilah tossed her head and laughed. "You mean work around those *crackers*! What you tryin' to do, Connors? Get me mauled?"

"Aw baby, you can handle those boys! You'll knock their eyes out."

"Un hunh. Them cowboys are too rough."

"You can do it, baby."

"No way. Besides, I ain't got a car and I can't get down there."

"We'll get you there. Bring you home, too. Give you fifty bucks plus your regular time, and then there's your tips."

Lilah smirked. "Crackers don't tip."

"Well, they ain't seen nothin' like you, honey. You got ways about you. Skin those boys right down."

"An extra fifty? In cash, that night?"

"Yep."

"All right, Connors. What time you pick me up?"

"Seven o'clock," he said, trying to put his hand on her butt.

She nodded and pulled free and carried her drinks away.

"Nothing works like money," Connors said to Schrader.

"You think it always works?"

"In one way or another."

Schrader knew what was coming and he waited.

"Listen, old buddy. This is kind of an experiment with Lilah. I've been thinking about spicing things up down there, you know? Them cowgirls I got working are okay, but they don't shake it up like these gals. And they don't push drinks. I could sell a lot more liquor down there with some classier waitresses. Trouble is, I'm all set to begin this weekend and my ex-wife pops up. I feel kind of obligated to spend time with her, if you know what I mean." He winked again at Schrader.

"I think I know what you mean."

"Yeah. So I was wondering if you'd take Lilah to San Marcos and kind of run things for me. Maybe give a hand if the bar gets too busy. Bank the money for me."

"Where you going to be?"

"We're driving to Dallas. Old times, you know."

"My weekends mean a lot to me, Connors."

"Sure. I'll give you the Cadillac till Monday, drop it by tomorrow morning with a full tank of gas."

"And what are you going to drive to Dallas?"

He looked kind of embarrassed. "Well, I'm trying out a new Buick."

"What else are you offering?"

"Fifty bucks plus your time."

Schrader shook his head. "Not enough."

"Aw David!"

"I had other plans—if you know what I mean," and he winked.

"Sixty."

"Seventy-five."

"Christ! It's just an experiment."

"It's my Saturday night."

"Sixty-five."

"Would you like another bourbon, Connors? Maybe clear your head?"

"Okay. Seventy-five. You are one tight bastard, David."

"I'll just draw it out of the night's take. Lilah's too."

"Leave a little for me, will ya?" Connors moaned.

Schrader poured them each a bourbon. "Your buddy Logan came in today."

"Any news?"

Schrader nodded. "April Mae is turning tricks downtown. Logan just warned us."

"Damn! Couldn't she be more careful?"

"She's pretty brassy."

"Should I fire her?"

Schrader shook his head. "Let's just make sure she doesn't hustle in the club."

"Man, I don't want to get shut down."

Schrader shrugged. "If you're really worried, then can her."

"How much would I lose?"

"Hard to say, lot of fellows come in here just to see April Mae. They drink a lot."

"You know she's fucking all of 'em."

"Sure. But no money's passing hands in here. We're safe on that."

"Just watch her close, David." Connors talked sometimes like Schrader was his platoon sergeant, but he ignored it. Connors had beat the draft with a trick knee.

It was one o'clock. In another hour Schrader could close and count the take, and get the hell out. *It will be good to see my friends*, he was thinking. *But better to see Jessie. Sure. I could go spend the night—and then have a dream that would frighten the wits out of me. Maybe I would wet the bed right beside her. Maybe I would flail about and break her jaw. That would be peachy!*

Schrader muttered to himself.

Connors saw his lips move. "What'd you say?"

Schrader shook his head tersely.

"David, you ain't been yourself lately."

"You mean I've been trying to get more money out of you?"

"And a tight-lipped bastard to boot. You gotta talk to the customers, boy. You gotta keep their throats dry."

"The turkeys don't come to talk to me. I'm the chrome fixture that pours the drinks."

"Then pour me another, boy! And try to look like you enjoy your work!"

Schrader filled his glass and looked at him blandly. "Connors, I just figured out something about you."

"What's that, son?"

"You never left the football field. You have Texas Stadium in your head somewhere, with crowds and the cheering and everything. You're still calling signals."

He slapped the bar. "David, you're absolutely right! I never thought about it. I guess that's why I'm a success, while those other clucks I played with are coaching high school ball!"

"You got something nice to say about everyone, don't you?"

"Hell, yes!" he grinned. "Daddy taught me never to smirk when I'm holding the cards."

He's holding cards all right. His clubs are making a bundle for him, thought Schrader. *Connors is a small town boy made good: football famous, man about town, successful entrepreneur. Opportunity drops at his feet. Start with closet lust and liquor license, push drinks across bar, drop coins into purse. Clink. Clink. When the purse gets too heavy, buy a Buick. It lightens the load.*

The men keep coming and drinking and Connors keeps stumbling along on golden feet — the whole machinery clicking along on the sweat and effluvia of women.

I only ride shotgun.

At a quarter to closing all the girls climbed up on the tables and shook it up. Connors turned the music louder and the customers jumped to their feet and shouted.

Rita straddled one man's shoulders — backwards — and choked off his yahoo with a grinding thrust, while he danced crotch-blind and Rita draped her great, lovely breasts over his sweating bald head.

Connors glanced at Schrader nervously. He had that look. Could Schrader spot any vice cops?

Rita was bobbing around the club with her crotch in the bald man's face, and the other girls formed a line behind him. Soon there was a reeling, twisting line, weaving among the tables, chairs kicked aside, drinks splashing, hands groping sweaty flesh.

Connors hurried to the front to lock the door.

When the record ended, no one would stop. They booed and stomped and kept weaving around. Schrader stepped from behind the bar and pushed another number on the jukebox. The great snake came alive again.

Every night is Mardi Gras, thought Schrader. The noise was terrific.

The bald man tired and Rita was hoisted to other shoulders. Someone handed her a drink. She tossed her head and whirled around. In the red light Schrader thought she looked beautifully wicked. She was young and hard-edged, and in a few years these nights would spoil her beauty. She knew, and didn't give a damn. Knowing her was to almost gape at her drive for self destruction and gratiation both. The real hard cases, the bitter beauties that thrive on thrills and pain, are really very rare, and Rita was one of them. The other women did not mess with her. Between her and black Lilah, though, it was a stand-off.

A couple of drunks climbed on the stage and were stripping; jackets and shirts flying; ties stuffed in glasses of scotch. A shoe bounced off the mirror behind Schrader and knocked a quart to the floor.

He made a move to come from behind the bar, but Connors waved him back. Fine with Schrader. Connors was better at it.

Connors pushed his way to the stage and grabbed one drunk by the belt and neck and yanked him to a chair and stuffed him in it. Schrader always thought Connors was fun to watch. He fooled lots of people with his pot belly and balding head.

He snatched the other drunk, like one grabs a naughty child, and carried him to the bar. The fellow weighed about a hundred and sixty pounds and Connors carried him at arm's length up off the ground and never showed a strain.

"You broke my Wild Turkey, Niederwald, and you cracked my mirror." Connors was holding Niederwald chest high so he could see the broken mash. Then he propped him on a bar stool.

"You're a good customer, Freddie, and decent enough when you're sober but you gotta pay. You know you gotta pay, don't you?"

Niederwald blinked like an owl. "Sright Connors—gottapay—Good fella Connors. Dontakenoshit."

"Fifteen bucks for the whiskey; two hundred for the mirror. Two hundred, fifteen bucks. You got that much?"

Niederwald grinned stupidly and fell off the stool. "Gotta-bundle," he mumbled from the floor.

Connors stepped to the jukebox and punched the reject button. The music stopped abruptly and Connors paid no mind to the boos and hoots of protest.

"You girls put on your tops and clear the tables. Drink up, sports. That's all for tonight."

Schrader leaned against the wall, watching. Connors was seldom around for closing, and Schrader was weary of all the accompanying gripes. He knew Connors was staying late to draw some cash from the till, so he turned up the lights and ran the tabs through the register, took in money and credit cards and handed out change.

Niederwald was still stretched out on the floor. He'd had a dozen drinks and bought another twenty for the girls. His tab was a hundred and twelve dollars.

Connors picked him up and stretched him out on the bar. Niederwald woke up and peered around wide-eyed and Christian came over and put a plastic rose on his chest.

"You look so cute, Freddie!"

"Lesh doit onnabar!"

"Oh Freddie. You're so *short!*"

"Hey Doc! Come over here." Connors was calling to one of the customers seated in a corner. Through all the ruckus and hoopla he had remained seated, drinking deliberately, paying little mind to the zoo. His name was Richmond and he was a pathologist. Everybody trusted the Doc. He held money and was an accepted dispute settler. Most week nights he was in the Red Duke.

The doctor walked to the bar looking neat and cool — in contrast to the midnight slobs and sweaty women. He looked closely at Niederwald stretched out on the bar.

"All the signs of a sclerotic liver and a weak mind. Do you want to operate?"

"Yeah. Let's open up his wallet." Connors dug into Freddie's pocket and handed the billfold to the doctor.

"Count it out, Doc, so Freddie won't think we rolled him when he sobers up."

"What is his tab?"

"A hundred and twelve bucks for the drinks, and I'll throw

in the mash he broke. But the cracked mirror is another two hundred."

The Doc took a thick wad of bills from the wallet. "What do you have to say about all this, Fred?"

The drunk shook his finger in the air. "Gottapay you know — Connors bustmyass."

The money exchanged hands.

April Mae and Christian came over. "What about our tip? Freddie always tips good. Isn't that so, Freddie?"

But Freddie had bitten the dust.

Christian poked at him. "Out cold."

"Well ladies, ten percent seems adequate."

"Listen to that!" April Mae barked. "This ain't no greasy spoon, Doc. Twenty percent or you don't get through the door." She reached over and neatly snatched the wallet and removed a twenty and a ten. "Besides, we had to listen to those *awful* stories about his ex-wife again! Counselling don't come cheap, you know."

"Been thinking of switching to psychiatry, myself."

"We could set up shop, Doc," April Mae teased, putting her arm through his. "You heal 'em and I'll peel 'em."

"Then you'll have to heal 'em again," Connors guffawed, making a stabbing motion, as if he were giving a shot.

April Mae scowled at him. "Button your lip, you big creep!"

Connors only grinned into his bourbon. Any of the girls could back him down.

When Schrader finished counting the take, Connors stepped behind the bar. "Goddamned slow!" he moaned, taking two hundred and stuffing it in his pocket.

"Give me a receipt."

"Remind me Monday."

"Come on, fat cat," Schrader said, grabbing his arm. "If I let you pull that again, Jessie will have my ass."

"You afraid of that gal?"

"Why don't I just give her a call now?"

"All right, goddamnit." Connors scrawled a receipt.

"What about the two hundred for the mirror?"

Connors touched his fingers to his lips. The mirror would not be replaced anytime soon. "You want me to stay and help?" he asked.

"Go on home. I'll lock up and make a deposit."

"I'll drop the Caddy off in the morning." Connors left and took the last lingering customers with him. When the girls finished changing, Schrader walked them to the front to let them out. Assorted boyfriends were waiting outside.

"Let's have another party!" Christian blurted.

"Not tonight," David nixed.

He locked the door behind them and turned off the air conditioner. Then he bagged the deposit slip and money, and poured himself one last drink. Staring into the angled mirrors behind the stage he saw himself fractionalized and older, and the mirrors within mirrors showed him older into infinity, and more broken. Staring harder he tried to find the whole man, but he was not there. Or, just ahead of Schrader's sight, he spiralled inward, downward to a mere point, and disappeared.

13

Schrader stepped into the street and felt the wind blowing cleanly from the Colorado River. The wide avenue was deserted; the city seemed empty as he walked with the fat money pouch to the corner bank. He felt smoke-filled and stale.

This bank, thought Schrader, *is a pee-colored brick monster with metal maws, and it eats the money pouch: Clankety-click.*

He began to walk toward the east side, to see Mingo and Adelita. The night streets suited him; the shadows and wind-driven noises were like a hymn to his own introspection. He was pushing drinks. Drinking drinks. Laughing too hard at bad jokes. Shaking his head at the bony old men wanting women sent to their rooms. *No sir, I'm no pimp . . . But why not?*

He passed beneath the large neon sign advertising the VFW. Schrader remembered the World War II veteran who'd boasted to him about how they'd *won* their war. *And who the hell are losers like us*, thought Schrader, *to besmirch the image of American veterans, with our long hair and guilty consciences dragging behind us?*

At Eleventh Street he crossed the bridge. Austin is a divided city, sliced neatly north and south by a freeway — whites in the west, in the scenic hills; browns and blacks in the east, in the old flood plains of the river.

On the eastside streets that night were lots of folk: cigarette-lit faces and knowing laughter from dim corners, families on their porches, fat mamas with voices like trumpets and children who pretended not to hear.

The only life Schrader believed he ever saw in American streets was in its working class neighborhoods. He looked around him and saw the families of his brothers. These were the folk who sent their sons to the infantry. They were not sophisticated enough to question, and they were far too patriotic to refuse.

Turning a corner Schrader saw Mingo's house. They had remodeled it together when Mingo and Adelita were first married. They had added rooms and a front porch, built the cabinets and did the trim. Schrader smiled, and thought it looked like a window-lit Jack o'lantern, the crooked grin shadow cast by the porch lopsided, like Mingo's.

Mingo was holding two jobs; they were always up late. He heard Schrader's steps on the porch and came to the door.

"David! Hey! Where the hell have you been?"

Schrader only shrugged. There was a dead silence and Mingo must have read something in his face, because he hugged him close.

"Things spinning around, David?"

"More or less," he mumbled. "You been all right?"

"Sure, brother. We've missed you. We stop by; you're never home. We leave notes; you don't answer. When the hell you gonna get a phone?" In a crew shirt, with a gold chain around his neck, Mingo looked sleek as a panther.

"You just in from night work?"

He nodded. "I gave 'em notice tonight. Two more weeks."

"Joe's giving you a raise when you get your license, right?"

Mingo grinned. Joe Garcia was Adelita's father. He owned an electrical contracting company. "We worked out a deal, but first I gotta pass that damned test."

"You'll do okay." Looking at Mingo, sometimes, took Schrader a long way back. He was remembering the quick-footed kid who faced any danger. He was remembering the junkie who could not face himself. Mingo had come a hard road to get what he had.

"I'm sorry I haven't given you an answer about standing for godfather."

"Aww, it's nothin'," Mingo waved his hand. "I know you got things in your head now." *Mingo is always smoothing things over for me,* thought Schrader. *Somehow, I've come to depend on it.*

"I'd be proud to do it, Mingo. I should have told you so right away."

"You don't mind talking to the priest?"

Schrader shrugged. "I just don't want to lie to him about what I believe in."

Mingo laughed. "Oh yeah? Since when did you figure out what you believe in?"

Adelita walked in from the kitchen, wearing slacks and a flowered maternity blouse, and she gave Schrader a hug. She had a long wooden spoon in her hand.

"Suddenly, you're a housewife," said Schrader. Adelita had always been a working wife. "That's hard for me to get used to."

Mingo put a finger to his lips. "Shh, *hombre*, don't start a fight!"

"Two children, that's all," she smiled. "Then I'm going back to school to get my master's. *Es correcto, no?*"

"*Oh, si, despues dos jovenos.*" But Mingo glanced at Schrader to wink. Adelita raised her hand. "I'll smack you with this spoon, Mingo, if you make jokes about it!"

Her eyes went wide and she drew breath sharply.

"Here, David. Quick!" She took Schrader's hand and placed it beneath her blouse, low on the warm flesh. Feeling a certain shyness, he tried to pull away.

"Stop that! There."

He felt a distinct ripple in the drum-tight flesh, and then a sharp kick against his palm. "Damn, girl. Doesn't that hurt?"

"You have to be tough to be a woman, David."

"I always knew that. Hey, what do I smell cooking?"

"You should ask, you big stiff. I think there's enough for you."

Mingo pushed Schrader ahead of him, and they walked

into the kitchen. It was a pleasant room, with the signs of constant use that all good kitchens have. Schrader saw *chorizo* with the eggs, and tortillas and re-fried beans. There was pastry from Cisco's and good black coffee.

They were at the table, and Schrader was helping himself to the *huevos con chorizo*. "You'll never guess who I got a letter from last week."

"Hoos thot?" Mingo's mouth was stuffed.

"Eddie Malone." Schrader watched Adelita. Her eyes dropped to her plate and her mouth grimaced.

"Hot damn! Eddie Malone!" Mingo croaked happily. "How the hell's he doing?"

"Okay, it seems. He's coming through Austin sometime soon. Or so he said in the letter."

"What for?" Adelita's tone was wary.

"Who cares what for?" Mingo told her. "It will be good to see him, right David?"

"Sure. It's always good to see a brother."

"How long has it been? Four or five years?"

"Something like that."

"You think the VA ever fixed his leg?"

Schrader shook his head. "He was too badly shot up, Mingo. He'll always limp. The best the surgeons could hope to do was get all the metal out."

"Man, do you remember the time—" and Mingo retold a story they all knew, a story about the old days, the political days in the streets. Schrader laughed as Mingo talked, but he saw chagrin growing in Adelita.

". . . he'll bring us some East coast news," Mingo finished. "Be nice to hear about the old gang."

"Just as long as he doesn't bring trouble," Adelita said, pushing her plate away. "You two be careful. Don't get involved in any of his schemes."

"Give him a break, honey. Poor Eddie has had—"

"Never mind getting all soapy, Mingo. I know the trouble he's had. And I can remember how he used that to his advantage. You other vets were always ready to make excuses for him. So many times, when we really needed Eddie, he'd be drunk or downed out."

"Hell yes, woman! He had five operations on his leg. Five times the butchers cut on him! I've seen Eddie hurting pretty bad!" Mingo looked at Schrader for support, but David was quiet.

With a deliberate calmness, Adelita held a bowl out. *"Mas huevos*, David?"

"I'm sorry I shouted," Mingo finally said. "No need to shout at you, baby."

Schrader took some eggs and glanced between them. Adelita was the thread that bound Mingo's life together. Mingo could tell the world to go squat, but he could not stay mad at his woman.

"I just don't trust him, Mingo. I'm sorry, but that's how I feel."

Mingo retreated. "Can I at least have him over for dinner?"

She laughed brightly. *"Por supuesto. Sabes que yo lo daré la bienvenida."* Of course. You know I'll make him welcome.

"Sure, baby. You're nice to all my hairy friends. Even David, here. Who you didn't like so much either, once upon a time."

Adelita looked at Schrader in a certain way. "That was before I knew him."

What she shared with Schrader was this: together, they had pulled the monkey from Mingo's back. It had been a hard fight. *I was stronger then*, mused Schrader.

"Give me the last of those *huevos*," Mingo growled. "Schrader, you dirty *perro*, why didn't you speak up and help me out?"

"Don't answer that, David. We don't want him to know whose friend you really are."

"Cabrone! And after all these years!" Mingo swallowed his food and shook his fork. "If my baby comes out with blue eyes, you're going to think Khe Sanh was a hippie picnic!"

"Here David, have some more coffee."

They ate the mountain of pastry on the plate, every crumb, as Adelita slowly grew quiet and began to yawn.

"Don't stay up for me, kid."

"Oh *gracias*, David. I *am* tired."

"Yeah, honey. You go on to bed. I'll clean up here."

Schrader looked at Mingo and raised his eyebrows.

"Part of the two-kid deal," Mingo shrugged apologetically. "Once in awhile, I get mess duty."

She stood up and leaned over to kiss Schrader. Her *largesse* collided softly with the table. "Don't be a stranger, *Forastero*." Already, her lids were heavy.

Forastero means outsider. A long time past, Adelita had joked and called them that. *Los forasteros.*

Mingo walked with her back to the bedroom, and Schrader cleaned up the table.

"I got the dishes soaking," Schrader told him, after a time, when Mingo came back.

"*Bueno.* Leave the damned things for now. Let's grab a *cerveza* and go outside."

They went through the house to the porch, and then out to the street to sit on the curb. The streets were empty by then, and the neighborhood was quiet. They each had a beer.

"You think Eddie will really come through Austin?"

"Who knows, Mingo? My letter was a xeroxed copy. He might have sent twenty copies just to cover all his routes."

"Is he dealing?"

"That's my guess."

"Adelita was hard on him."

"Maybe not. She might remember better than us. And she had her own politics before she met you. She had her own way of doing things."

Mingo nodded, sipping his beer. "It's been a tight squeeze for me, *amigo.* Fighting in a racist war and being brown-skinned, too. Seeing things two ways, trying to sort out what's really me. Eddie never cared much about the Vietnamese, like you and me. He didn't care if they bombed Hanoi for Christmas. But he always looked out for his brothers. That's good enough for me."

"Sure, Mingo. It's good enough for me, too."

They sat quietly, listening to the faint city noises. Away on the freeway, a semi wailed into the distance.

"Do you ever think about Mr. Li, anymore?"

"Sometimes." Mingo nodded.

"I dreamed about him the other night. I guess it was two nights ago, maybe three."

Mingo looked at his friend, his head cocked.

"Do you remember the drill ground, there between the hamlet and the tents? Remember how hot and dusty it was?"

"Sure, I remember."

"Well, we were back there. No one else, just you and me. And we were staring around, because we knew we didn't belong there. I mean, it wasn't during the war or anything. At least, it didn't *feel* like that. And then Li came stepping across the ground toward us. His feet were kicking up dust. I could taste the dust in my mouth."

"What happened?"

"Nothing, really. I can't remember."

"Bullshit! Tell me about the rest of the dream."

"Well. Li stepped up to us. There was sweat running down his face. Then suddenly he had a rifle — from nowhere, you know how dreams are — and he, uh, he shot you, Mingo. He shot you dead and I saw your blood splash all over the dust but I couldn't do anything. I couldn't scream or run or stop him. Then Li pointed the rifle at my face and I saw a flash and felt the burns — and then I woke up."

"Jesus Christ," Mingo muttered.

"Nice, eh? I tell myself that they're only dreams, that I shouldn't be frightened. But they scare me more than the real thing ever did. It's the helplessness, you know? In the nightmares, I never have any control of events. I can't choke down the fear and it runs away with me. You know me, Mingo. I was always scared in a firefight, but I could control it."

Mingo was frowning. Schrader could see his face shadowed in the streetlights. "*El temor.*" He rolled the Spanish slowly off his tongue. "Fear is the pits, David. The absolute pits when it gets the best of you. I wish I could help, brother."

Schrader might have said more, but something held him back. He couldn't confess a weakness to Mingo, just then. He couldn't tell him his guts were gone, even though Schrader felt it to be true. There was a growing brusqueness in Mingo, a confidence that he had his life in hand and could overcome any obstacle. He was showing a certain resiliency that Schrader felt he lacked, and sometimes it vexed him.

"I'd better be going, Mingo. It's a long walk."

"Have another *cerveza*, man. I'll loan you the truck, you can drive home."

"No, thanks. Maybe the walk will tire me out."

"It's a nice night for it." He stood and stretched on the curb. It was then that they noticed the police car that had pulled to a stop around the corner.

"Ahh, *chinga!*" Mingo spat.

"*Que paso?*"

He motioned at the squad car. "We got a new cop on the East side, a guy named Manley. He's been hasslin' me. He's stopped me three times while I'm walkin' home from the night job. Shook me down once—spread-eagled—the whole thing. He's asked around about me, too. I don't know why."

"You think it's official harassment?"

"No. Why should city hall bother with me? He's just a hyped-up cop making himself known. Like a dog pissing on a fire hydrant."

Mingo and Schrader had been cops in Vietnam. They had stopped citizens and demanded their papers; told them where they could go and when; spied on them at night in their villages.

The squad car slowly rounded the corner and came toward them. Schrader got to his feet and stood beside Mingo.

"Let's be polite, David. Adelita doesn't know this cop's been bugging me. I don't want her to worry."

"Sure."

The car stopped twenty feet away and they stepped out one at a time: the shotgun cop using the car as a shield, the driver blinding first Schrader, then Mingo with his light.

"Kind of late to be on the street, Mr. Calderone."

"Not if you work nights, Officer Manley."

"This is your house?"

"Yes it is."

"Been living here long?" The cop kept sweeping his eyes around, as if he expected an ambush.

"Four years."

"Does your wife still live here with you, Mr. Calderone?"

"Of course she does. My *pregnant* wife is sound asleep right now."

"Mmmm hmmmm. And who are you?"

"David Schrader is my name."

"Let me see some identification," he snapped out his hand impatiently.

"I haven't any on me," Schrader lied.

"No driver's license?"

"I don't have a car."

"Credit card, voter registration card?"

"I don't have any credit and I don't vote."

"Social security card?"

"Somewhere at home."

"Where do you live, Mr. Schrader?"

"South of the river, on Elizabeth street." He told him the address. He was annoyed.

"Why are you out so late?"

"I'm the bartender at the Red Duke. I closed up at two o'clock and walked over here to see my friend Mingo."

He looks like he's about to eat a canary, thought Schrader.

"Mr. Schrader, with no way to verify your identity, we might have to take you in."

"Oh really?"

"That's right. We've had several crimes tonight, and it's our job to check any likely suspects. Unless there's some way to prove who you are." He spoke as if he knew Schrader was lying about his identification.

"You might ask Hank Logan," Schrader told him. "That's Lieutenant Hank Logan. He's a buddy of mine. He'll tell you I'm me." Schrader was bluffing.

"I expect the Lieutenant is off duty."

Schrader shrugged. "Have your dispatcher wake him up. He owes me a favor." It was a lie.

That stopped the cop for a second. "So Lieutenant Logan is a friend of yours?"

"Yes he is."

"And does he know that friends of his chum around with junkies?"

Schrader looked at Mingo and shook his head.

"Ohhh, so *that's* what it is," Mingo said. "You found out that I was on the stuff once, and now you're just doing your duty." And then he laughed at the cop.

Manley stiffened. "Everything I do in this uniform is my duty, Calderone. Including checking up on junkies."

"It's *Mister* Calderone, officer. We're in front of my house and I'm a taxpayer and a voting Democrat, and you can call me Mister."

"Well, Mr. Calderone, we like having you on the right side of the law. I'm just here to remind you to stay there."

"Well, thank you very much."

Manley was thick-necked and burly and Schrader could see the muscles in his jaw work. He watched his gun hand.

The other cop had not moved. He seemed to Schrader sort of dumpy in the dimness.

"Mr. Schrader, I'm going to believe you're who you say you are. And if you've fooled me, don't think you're getting away with anything. I'm likely to turn up anywhere." He shook his flashlight at David.

"I know. I see you everywhere."

They went and sat on Mingo's porch and waited for the police to leave. "Weren't we gems? Thank you very much officer."

"It's nothing, David. There's plenty over here to keep them busy. After a couple of weeks, Manley will forget all about me."

"Who the hell would have told them about the junk?"

Mingo shrugged. "A lot of people know me. Some of them don't like me much."

"Who's his partner?"

"His name is Quigley. Kind of pasty looking. Lets Manley do all the talking."

"Piggly Quigley," laughed Schrader.

"Yeah. That's the joke on the street. Somebody will paint it on the side of Safeway. Let's have that beer."

"No Mingo. I have a long walk."

"I'll drive you home."

"What! You'll leave Manley and Piggly Quigley to protect your wife? You must be crazy."

"Then we'll see you soon. What do you say?"

"Okay."

"And don't brood about those cops."

"Goodnight, Mingo."

Schrader brooded about the cops right away. He muttered to himself for two blocks. *Mingo is no felon. He's been clean a long time, and I cannot understand this suddenly cropping up from nowhere.* Still muttering, he glanced over his shoulder and saw the same squad car nose around a corner. *They're watching me. What do they think? That I have a pocketful of white powder?* He cursed and kicked at a can, set some dogs barking, stepping along faster. For a couple of blocks he did not glance behind him. But when he did, there was the squad car again, with only its parking lights on, cruising slowly two blocks away.

Schrader didn't really know what happened next, or why he did what he did. Maybe an old rusty switch closed, a long-dormant neuron synapsing with a jolt of mischief, little boy snooping and pooping through the night. Suddenly, it seemed great fun to run them a race. More than great fun! It was the paramount thing to do. *RUN!* some one shouted in his ear. Children laughed!

So he ran. It was a narrow-laned, dimly lit neighborhood that he knew fairly well, and it had a maze of alleys behind neat little yards held back by fences. When the flashing lights came on, dazzling the dark street, he began to hoof it in earnest. But the car roared up quickly and he had to plunge sideways into an alley just ahead of them, the squeal of brakes stuffing his heart into his mouth. He tore through the alley and into another street, running left, dodging back right into another alley. Schrader was afraid one of them would leave the car, but when he remembered Piggly Quigley he knew the one in shape was the one driving. So he slowed up to listen and heard the car roaring a street away, saw the glare of the lights as they rounded another corner. He ran back the way he had come, through the same alley, and ran in the opposite direction from the squad car. They might have called another car. He had to decide where to go.

There were only three passes under the freeway near enough to do him any good. Eleventh Street was too far north, the police station was at Seventh Street, and First Street was where they would expect a man who lived in South Austin to go. And then there was the river bank, dark and secret, littered with derelicts and worse. He grimaced at what was his best prospect, suddenly sobering to the fun he was having.

Schrader was only walking fast by then, trying to placate neighborhood dogs, heading east and away from the freeway. After he turned south he had to hide from the patrol car a couple of times, but finally he reached First Street and turned west, keeping to the shadows. A police car was parked at the intersection under the freeway, perhaps routinely, but he kept to the shadows across Holly Street and dashed to the river, cursing his stupidity. *Why did I run? You can't toy with the police, fool. They have all the power. You had all the power once, remember? You, alone with your rifle were a sudden power. But behind you stacked up that awesome power of tanks*

*and artillery, the planes and bombs and missiles, the Pentagon
and the CIA and God . . . and now you begrudge these nice
police their little bit of power. Shame on you.* He was footsore
and tired and he laughed out loud, the sound bouncing off the
darkness like a flat rock. *Some warrior,* he thought, *limping
down here with the winos and muggers; sneaking home. Some
home, cluttered and dingy, hardly worth sneaking to. Some
sneaking, stumbling along like a recruit and laughing like an
idiot.* He shook his head. *Some idiot to get yourself in this
mess.*

The dark bulwark of the bridge loomed in the night, a
black ribbon of river lapping beneath. Passing under, he hurried along the bank to the next bridge and passed under that
too. At the third bridge he walked up to street level, looking
around for the police. Schrader was hoping the cops had kept
his antics to themselves. Maybe they knew he was goofing
them. There was little point to continuing the game. Manley
knew where he lived and worked, and fleeing from a cop was
grounds for a warrant. *If they wanted me, I would be easy to
catch,* Schrader figured.

Soon he was in his own neighborhood: one much like
Mingo's with small, working family homes, yards full of live
oak and pecan. Only in south Austin, there were more whites
to mix in the brown and black stew.

It was half past three when he rounded the corner of his
block. Right away he saw Jessie's Fiat parked in front of the
house. She had a key.

Quietly, he let himself in and slipped off his shoes. Jessie
was stretched out on the bed, the streetlight shining through
the window accenting the line of sheet across her breast and
down her side, one trim calf carelessly off the edge. Her hair
was tumbled. He stood in the dark and watched the rising
swell of her breasts. He had a certain feeling for the woman
that he could not give a name. There was a calmness about
her, and a sense of order that drew his tangled nature.

Schrader had been brooding, mind churning. But watching her, it was all forgotten. His resolve was forgotten. He
thought to himself about his resolve. *My stupid, chicken trick
of pushing her away—what was the use of that?*

When he slid beneath the sheet she started in waking;

but at his touch she purred throatily and curled into him. There was a current. He felt bumps rise on his skin.

"Mmmmmm. Sorry to see me, David?"

"No, baby." He kissed the very tip of a nipple and she gasped, then her mouth was all over his, and he lost himself in the taste of her. They made love very softly, silently, her skin tone changing from shadow to light as they rolled about. He could not hold her close enough.

At some point they fell asleep. But well into his slumber, Schrader felt the nearness of her. The yeasty tang of their lovemaking stayed with him. He must have slept very unconcerned for awhile.

Then the thing began to creep all around him. It was a shapeless thing that somehow had body, a silent thing that somehow made sound and it always portended his dreams: the shadow noise creature most of us first meet as children.

Schrader found himself standing in an encampment— white sand everywhere—an edge of desperation to the activity around him. There was the smell of urine. Cries of pain. *Corpsman! Corpsman!* Blood smell. He tried to see, but everything was so dim, there was just the sand. He tried to touch, but the blur of figures around him kept from reach. When he called out, no sound came from him. Schrader looked and saw the little boy at his feet, and when he groaned in his dream, the sound was real. He knew where he was. He knew what he would do to the child.

Schrader knelt slowly by the boy, his gut quaking. The small boy was staring at him. He could hear him moan.

Something in Schrader whimpered.

Then there was an intrusion. In a dream where no one would touch him, Schrader suddenly felt a touch. There was a different voice, not frantic, coming from half a world away.

"David. Are you all right?"

The dream began to fragment, the camp was gone, sand slipped away, blood smell lingering when he awoke.

"Wake up, honey." Jessie was sitting up, looking at him.

Embarrassed, his hands floundered about the damp sheets. But it was only sweat.

"You're shaking! Oh, I'm so sorry . . ."

But when she reached to touch him, he turned to ice. He

was encased in a glacier and he did not want her touch. He
didn't want anyone near him, for the shame.

She drew back. "What did I do, David?"

"Nothing."

"Oh no, boy. Don't close up on me now." She began to
stroke his chest and face, and then she pulled him to her.
Absent was the ponderous dread, the degradation, that seemed
to linger after his dreams, like a bad taste. Finally, there was
some company. He fell asleep on her breasts.

14

Connors woke David and Jessie late in the morning: honk-
ing the horn on his big white Caddy, singing as he walked to
the porch, pounding on the door.

"Connors, you jackass!" Jessie shouted through the window.

"Jessie? Sweet Jessie! Is that you behind those curtains?
Honey, you can't give that boy a little leg and expect to be his
boss, too! Next thing you know he'll want to be on top!"

"It gets lonely on top, Connors. Haven't you heard?"

"C'mon, Davey boy. Wipe your face and come to the door.
I got some fine stuff waitin' on me in the Buick."

They parted the curtains to see a hot red Buick pulled up
behind the Caddy. The engine was running, windows up, with
bleached blond behind the wheel. A ten-year-old with big ears
was peering out the passenger side.

"It's sixty degrees out, Connors. Can't she cut the engine
and turn off the AC?"

"Are you kiddin'? Lorri Beth can't breathe reg'lar air like
you and me. Says it takes the peach out of her skin. Don't
know what difference that makes. Most the time, she's flat on
her back under the sheets in the dark."

Schrader put on some pants and went to the door. He
made a horrid face at the sunlight assaulting him. Connors
dropped the keys in his hand.

"The tank's full, boy. Don't leave no funny stuff in my ashtray."

"Doesn't matter in a Cadillac. Cops only check the ashtrays in old Fords. So that's your ex-wife, eh? Nice looking lady."

He poked Schrader in the ribs. "Remind me to tell you sometime what she did to me after a certain Baylor game. God, that woman used to have an imagination!" The horn honked loudly, the ex-cheerleader waved. "I gotta run, man. Don't go flat on me, now! Pick up Lilah and do the gig straight, okay? No closin' early, no droppin' her at the club and then splittin'!"

"Don't worry, Connors."

"And don't let Lilah put her hands on your body! That leads to miscegenation, son."

"You know that word?"

"What you mean? That's a fine old Southern word. See ya Monday, hyah?"

Back in the bedroom, Jessie raised her eyebrows. "Miscegenation, eh?"

"Sure. Rhymes with copulation, integration, sensation and sweeping the nation!"

"Umm hmmm. Also castration and ruined relation!" she teased, grabbing a part of him she should not have, unless she was serious. Which she was.

When it was well into the afternoon, and they'd showered again, Jessie dressed and prepared to go.

"Will you miss me?"

"Christ. You'll be back before I notice you're gone."

She yanked at his ear. "Be nice. Tell me you'll miss me."

He pulled her close. "I'll miss you passionately! I'll count every moment!"

"Don't overdo it. Just kiss me."

"Say hello to your folks for me, eh?"

"Bye."

Schrader slept for an hour after she left, her fragrance heavy in the bedding, easing his sleep. Then he dressed for work and locked the house.

The Cadillac sat gleaming on the curb, reeking affluence, representing so many things for which he might have reached. *When we were still green, the war new to us and the rhetoric*

*real, the Cadillac was what it was all about. Democracy. And
we were all going to have just such a chariot. We were going
to come home and dive into life with all the energy of men who
know the real value of living. Sure.*

Lilah had an apartment near the river, east of Schrader's
house. She met him at the door dressed in bra and panties.
"Hel-lo, David. Come in. I'll only be a minute."

"You have a beer?"

"In the ice box, honey."

Two chocolate boys sat at the kitchen table, big-eyed and
handsome, staring at him shyly. They had the hopefully cautious air of youngsters with no fathers.

"Hello, boys."

They squirmed and grinned.

"What are you eating?"

"Hot dogs," one of them ventured, meeting Schrader's
eyes.

"You got enough for me?"

"No sir. We got none left." They were maybe six and
eight, and they giggled suddenly and poked at each other.
"Henry ate four! He took mine and ate it too!" Henry was the
youngest one.

"Goodness!" Schrader teased. "Henry, let me see that
belly." He reached out and thumped the boy's tummy. "Looks
like you're about to pop!"

Little Henry screwed up his face and made a muscle.

"He wants to be a football player," the older boy said.
"Watches the Cowboys all the time."

"What's your name, son?"

"Charles Lee."

"You want to be a football player, too?"

"No sir! I want to be a basketball player!" And with that,
he leaped from his chair and fetched a ball lying in the corner,
little Henry on his heels, and they tumbled about, bouncing
the ball from the walls.

Schrader drank his beer and watched them.

*Everytime I'm with a child, I remember the children of
Vietnam. Always they would come and take your hands, pull
your shirt, surround you in knots and touch you gently. All
of them talking in their lilted accents and begging and laughing
when you gave them rations or gum. Or sometimes we tromped*

into their villages and took away their uncles or burned their
homes and they would huddle together, and there wouldn't be
much laughter or any chewing gum either . . .

"You boys stop bouncing that ball! I told you about that!"
Lilah came from the bedroom, dressed and looking sassy.

"I didn't know you had kids."

Lilah smiled ruefully. "Had Charles Lee when I was sixteen. Henry got a different daddy—my momma keeps them
most times."

"They're handsome boys."

"My sweethearts." They were huddled about her legs and
she patted their heads absently. "Ain't easy sometimes, David.
I'm a young woman and I like to have my fun. I don't get a
penny from their daddies."

Schrader knew Lilah turned some tricks; she was not the
only girl in the club who did.

"You have a nice place. You dress well. You're doing okay."

"I guess. One boyfriend pays my rent. Men buy me clothes.
But I won't be young and pretty forever."

He was uncomfortable with this talk before the children,
but the boys did not seem to notice. *They must be used to*
seeing strange men with their mother, he thought.

"I want to travel awhile," Lilah went on, "want to see
some things. I'm trying to talk momma into keeping the boys
a year or two. She tells me I'm crazy! Asks me what kind of
mother could leave her children? Hmph! I was a fifteen year
old child when that smooth-talking nigger came along. Things
been downhill ever since. Should I wear a wig, David?"

She had a short, soft Afro that framed her face nicely.
"No, you look fine without one."

"You gonna protect me tonight?" she smiled slyly.

"I was hoping *you* were going to protect me."

"Got a piece here," she said, showing him a little .32 in
her purse.

"You ever shoot a cracker?"

"No. I drew down on a buck or two, though, I can tell
you that! I'm tired of black men. They always jivin', promising
big things that never amount to nothing. White men treat me
better. Old fella pays this rent is a white man, don't expect
much. He won't marry me, though. All you white boys get to
shamefacing when it comes to marrying."

"None of us are any good, white or black. You ought to know you can't trust a man, Lilah."

"Lord, don't I know! You seem different though. You're a gentleman."

Schrader said nothing.

"All the girls feel safe with you. Somebody gets nasty, go tell David. He'll throw the bums out. No matter what, you always take our side."

"It's only my job. Now come on, we'd better go. Where do you drop off the boys?"

"No where. They're staying here tonight. Charles Lee is my big boy, ain't you honey? He'll take care of things."

"Yes, Momma."

"You know where everything is honey, if you get hungry again."

"Yes, Momma."

They were really very handsome boys, he thought.

"Give me kisses. Mmmm."

"Goodbye boys."

"Will you come play with us sometime?"

"Sure," Schrader lied. "And don't open this door for anyone but your momma."

"Yes sir . . . no sir."

They weren't three steps out the door when the ball was bouncing off the walls again.

"Ooooeeee! I forgot you had the big Cadillac. Connors must trust you."

"I'm his personal boy. The Cadillac is just a crumb to keep me around."

"Some crumb, honey."

"Well, I do everything but shine the man's shoes."

"I wonder what he would do without you and Jessie."

He shrugged. "I'd be easy enough to replace. But Jessie would be—something else again." Schrader opened her door and she smiled demurely. Then he got in the car.

"Jessie is some lady," Lilah said as they drove away.

"You're buddies, huhn?"

"Yeah. She's helped me out. You two would make a very nice looking couple."

"You think so?"

"How many gals we seen you go through now, Mr. David? How many does Jessie make?"

"None of it has been serious, Lilah. I'm not telling any lies or breaking any hearts."

"You can lie to a woman just looking at her a certain way. Don't take words to lie."

Schrader snorted. "What kind of romantic crap is that? There's not a woman working these joints that doesn't know her way around. This heartbreak stuff is for teenagers." Lilah was quiet for a time while they were driving south on the freeway.

"I didn't mean to get personal, David. I just thought you and Jessie would, you know, be nice together. I'm sorry."

"Don't apologize. I've been touchy. We're all lonely. You, me, Jessie, Connors. We all think it's terrible, but we don't do anything about it. So we must secretly like it, eh?"

"Don't know about liking it," she replied. "Lonely is the easiest thing to be. Guess it's about the hardest to do anything about."

Schrader glanced over and did not see the hard-nosed whore he knew Lilah to be. She is someone else entirely.

In Hong Kong he had kept a whore for a week, a young girl, always smiling. But sometimes he had caught the hopelessness in her eyes, and the fright. She had taken him to her family once, deep within the off-limits part of the city. The crush of humans was a nightmare, a veritable cage of people. He had thought that she knew she would never get out of that forsaken place, and her solace was the honor and well-being of her family. They fed him well, and treated him with courtesy and respect. There had been perhaps fifteen of them crammed into one tiny room, and he had sat there like some monarch and had eaten enough for the half of them. And all of them who could, worked, but this very young girl with the sometimes sad eyes. She made the most money of all, and they are proud of her. Proud.

San Marcos was half an hour's drive across the prairies and hills south of Austin, and the sun was setting behind those hills when they arrived at the bar. The Honky Moon sat right off the freeway and the garish neon sign had just began to sputter and blink. Lilah was touching up her face. She pursed her lips and flashed her eyes.

"I'm ready," she told him saucily.

They drew some stares and hard looks. It was a big place and half full and it quieted down some when they walked in. Schrader took Lilah straight to Connors's office to change. A lot of eyes followed them.

Schrader returned as many glances as he could, walking to the bar. *It's always best to smile*, he thought.

The woman behind the bar said, "I've been expecting you, David."

"Hello, Leslie." He stepped behind the bar and drew a beer he did not particularly want. It was to lend himself a certain legitimacy. The noise picked up again, and men turned back to their business. It was a long bar, and Schrader walked to the other end to speak with the woman. "Did Connors discuss this with you?"

"About bringing the colored girl down here?" she asked.

"Yeah."

She looked away. "Yes, he did. I told him it was a bad idea, David. He just laughed at me. Said it would be a nice change for the boys."

"He's as thick as a brick wall."

"Well, I made him promise to show up, too. These fellas don't get nasty when Connors is around."

Schrader shook his head. "Connors is with his ex-wife in his new Buick up in Dallas."

"Goddamn him!" Leslie was a buxomy, long-legged cowgirl and the sparks jumped from her violet eyes. "He's the lyingest sonuvabitch I know! Excuse my language."

He laughed and patted her hand. "We'll just have to break out the shootin' irons."

"That's no joke," she said sternly.

"Sorry. How are these other girls doing?"

"Only fair. They're not real enthused about their dancing. Mostly they sit with their boyfriends when they're not waiting tables."

"At the Duke the girls sit with the customers."

"I know. But they work for big tips. These cowboys don't tip."

"These yahoos aren't cowboys."

"A few of them are. The others sure like to think so."

"You watch Lilah shake things up."

It was about then that Lilah walked from the office. She wore bikini bottoms, a negligee bra and cape, and high-heeled shoes. All in red. It was not much less a costume than the other girls', but it looked like a lot less.

"Godddddamnnn!" someone said.

She walked back to the bar. Everyone was looking at her, and she loved it.

"Leslie, this is Lilah."

"Hi honey."

"Here's a tray for you, Lilah. You can work any tables you want."

"Looks pretty dead in here."

"Pool is the big attraction," Leslie told them. "Sit and have a drink before you start."

"Thanks. A daiquiri on the rocks."

"Connors had some idea about me helping out at the bar."

Leslie shrugged. "Beer crowd tonight, David. You can bank the money, though. Connors usually does that."

One of the waitresses played a song on the jukebox and began to dance. The Honky Moon was built on two levels, and the small stage was below, near the dance floor. A few tables were filled there, but most of the men sat higher up, near the pool tables. The girl aroused little interest.

Lilah finished her drink. "Think I'll go to work," she said, and slinked into the crowd. They were waiting for her to dance. Lilah served half a dozen tables, carrying on with the men, before she went to the jukebox and chose some songs.

The first was a bluesy country number. With the opening chords of the song she captured everyone's attention, and the tables on the dance floor suddenly began to fill.

Sometimes it was unpleasant for Schrader to see the lust in men's faces. They were mostly decent men, certainly, but there were the others. The ones who somehow never spoke well of women. In their faces Schrader thought he could sometimes see a great dislike for women, but the lust was there too and it was an angry lust. *How the moods of love and hate can be so entangled is beyond me. I have come across Vietnamese women beaten and stabbed and shot and raped. How can we call ourselves civilized when our sons do that?*

The first song ended and the response was wild. They clapped and whistled and stomped their feet. Lilah took off her bra and cape for the next song and the air grew heavier. She was selling a lot of beer.

A couple of men were still shooting pool and they had a small crowd with them. Some mean remarks filtered Schrader's way. He asked Leslie who they were.

"The Harvey brothers. Bad news."

"Why is that?"

"They fight dirty. Stompers, you know."

Schrader watched them over the rim of his mug. They did not like a girl of color in their midst. "What do you have there, behind the bar?"

"Billy club is all. What good is that against a pool cue?"

"Not a hell of a lot."

The dance ended to more raucous applause and Lilah was again at the bar taking drinks. Her caramel skin was flushed and there was a slight smile on her lips.

"Nice job."

"Putty in my hands."

The evening wore on, Lilah dancing every half hour, the other girls working a little harder because of her.

"Drink sales have picked up," Leslie commented after a time.

Schrader was bored, and he did not care to drink. For an hour he read magazines in the office, or tried to nap, but there was no sleeping over the heavy base thump of the jukebox. Nothing about the job was fun to him any more.

He went and sat at the bar again. A party near the pool tables left, and he went to clear the table to give the girls a hand.

"Why did you bring that nigger whore here, mister? You oughta get her out of here."

The older Harvey brother leaned on his pool cue, looking at Schrader. Both brothers were hairy and mean-looking.

Schrader groaned. *What is it to me what he calls her? If he was raised stupid and rude, why does it fall on me to teach him better?* He turned away to ignore the remark, and he looked straight into Lilah's eyes. *What was it she had said? All the girls feel safe with you, David.*

The brothers were standing on either side of the table. Schrader sighed. *One of the rules is: try to split the enemy forces.* He stepped toward the younger one, who was smirking. Their small crowd of buddies was grinning—smelling a fight.

"Put your drinks down, the both of you, and clear the hell out. I won't have you talking to my girls that way."

They both laughed. "You hear what the pimp said?"

Stepping up to the younger one, Schrader spoke across the table: "And take this ugly baboon with you. I can smell him from here."

It never takes much to start a bar fight. With a snarl, the younger one lunged at Schrader, who snatched up the cue ball and laid it across his temple. He was out on his feet but his momentum carried him into Schrader and he staggered under the weight.

The big brother leaped over the table, quicker than Schrader thought he could move. David put a left and a right in his face but it barely slowed him down. He hit him once more before he was on Schrader with his big meaty arms squeezing him like a cushion. Schrader tried to knee him; he only grunted. Schrader stomped the man's foot pretty good but he roared like an ape and picked Schrader up and slammed him into the wall. Schrader's head hit something hard and blood ran down his face. For David, things were slowing down and getting dim. The faces all around became distorted and he knew in a sickening moment that he was about to be stomped. *There's no one to help*, he thought. *They'll all stand around and watch because I'm only the pimp who came in with the nigger whore.*

Somewhere in the dimness he saw something dark move, caught the motion of a silvery gold arc and heard the crunch of something heavy striking bone. Schrader was splattered and thought it was his own blood, but the grip around his chest loosened and he sensed his antagonist dropping to the ground.

Lilah was standing over Schrader, the primeval savage, the handle of a shattered beer mug still in her grip.

Hands were on Schrader, lifting him up, putting him in a chair.

"Nice job fella . . ."

". . . wouldn't want to mess with those two."

Schrader's vision cleared. The two Harveys were crumpled on the floor. Leslie went over with a towel. "I called the cops, David—here, let me do that. Mmm. You might need stitches."

He looked at Lilah and winked.

The police came quickly enough. They took the brothers outside and asked if they wanted to press charges? No, they did not. "Just warn them not to come in here again." The police looked relieved. Schrader was relieved just to look.

After the bar closed his head cleared and he was driving Lilah home. It was almost three o'clock, and there was little traffic. They drove some miles in silence before Lilah moved over close to him. She stroked his hair softly, probed her fingers around the gash on his forehead.

"Does that hurt?"

"Not too bad."

"I think you need some stitches."

"No. I'll heal fine."

"They say not to sleep too soon after a knock on the head."

"I won't."

She was quiet for some time, and then: "David, I'm so embarrassed. One of my boyfriends is waiting for me at home, so I can't ask you in to, you know, say thank you and I thought we could just pull over somewhere and I could show you."

"Lilah, listen, you don't owe me anything. You don't have—"

"Well, I do, David. I do. I—"

"No really, you—"

"No one ever fights for a whore, David. You listen to me! No one ever fights for a whore except to *have* her. I only know one way to really thank you . . ."

Schrader took her hand. "I, uh, I almost turned away from it. What the hell did it matter to me what he called you? I didn't want to fight those brutes."

"I know. I saw. But you did it anyway."

"It was more for myself. If I back down just once, I don't think I'll ever stop running."

"We all got to back down sometimes. Don't you know that? Like right now. You got to back down from me. You pull this car over, David. Jessie doesn't have to know. You can't leave your friends owing you like that."

There was, after all, not a lot more to say. It was a long empty road and a big car and he later recalled the gash opening and the blood running down his face into their mouths, and the taste of it made them wilder and they steamed up that big

car. She was wonderfully foreign to him. It was quite fine there
for awhile, in the restricted space, an occasional semi rumbling
past and just Lilah's soft wetness to hold him.

Later in the wee morning, alone in his kitchen, Schrader
drank bourbon from the bottle and stared at the smudged walls.
He remembered Calvin Burgess. His throat grew tight and he
gulped the liquor fiercely, but the hot rush in his chest only
made the image of Calvin more vivid. He might have had sons
like Lilah's: handsome and full of promise. He might have had
a fine life.

Calvin had been a window for Schrader, a glimpse at a
new world, a sight quickly shuttered when he had come home.
Stateside, the world was the same—Chucks and Splibs. The
Brothers had known that. Schrader recalled their faces—
Calvin's and Willie's and Jackson's—when the white boys would
talk about how they would all get together after the war. Sure,
those silent black faces would say. Sure.

Schrader drank until the pain in his head went away. And
when the pain was gone, he drank until Calvin's face blurred
to indistinctness among the smudges on the wall. Then Schrader
passed out on the floor.

Sweet dreams, Marine.

15

Schrader had always thought there was a promise in war,
a vision fashioned from youth and near-death that shows things
fine and noble. It is a promise that if you can only *live*, this
aura of nobility will remain.

But in fact it only diminishes, as something once seen in
a very bright light, later dimming.

When Schrader first met Eddie Malone they were still
basking in the light of the war. The promise of fineness was
fading, but they could not let it go. The more of them who
kept together, the longer this light seemed to glow. It was the
binding glue of Vietnam Veterans Against the War.

Monday, Schrader was dressing, looking ruefully at his bruised forehead, remembering those days and Eddie and the others. It had all come apart, the promise forgotten, all of them wearing down in the light of an everyday world. One day he had awakened and realized it was gone. It was the sound of a car trailing away on an empty road, and Schrader was thirty-five. The war was over. But still he had not forgotten.

He was ready for work and locking the house, when Eddie Malone pulled up in a rental truck, shouting his name, wheels running up on the curb. He grinned at Schrader from the cab, his dark Irish eyes roguish.

"You get my letter, grunt?"

"Only a mimeographed copy, you bum! Climb out of that cab. Let me have a look at you!"

"I'm just passing through, David. I can't stay long."

Malone looked great, lean and tanned. He had seen Eddie go to drink pretty badly. There was a time he seemed to waste away. Eddie pointed to the gash on Schrader's head. "You're not slowing down, are you?"

"A couple of rednecks feeling froggy, is all. I took out one. A friend of mine took out the other. Not much else to tell. You're the one who should be talkin'. What's all this about, anyway? You in the interstate moving business?"

Eddie glanced about and did not answer. Schrader gestured toward the house.

"Come on in."

"You were on your way out?"

"I'm tending bar downtown, Eddie. I can be late."

Eddie followed him into the house, limping only slightly. He had no cane.

"Still pouring drinks, eh? That surprises me."

"It's a job." Schrader shrugged.

"Writing anything?"

Schrader shook his head. "Never mind about me. Tell me where you're going in such a rush?"

Eddie laughed and stretched. "I've got four hundred kilos of pot packed away in the truck. I left San Antone about an hour and a half ago, on my way back East. Thought I'd stop by to say hello."

"Just like that, eh?"

"I'll be back."

"So will Halley's Comet."

"Not as quick as me, sarge." He saluted. .

Same old animated Eddie, thought Schrader.

"No one's as quick as the frenetic medic."

"Or as mean as the green marine, eh? You old grunt! You look like you could still take a couple hills."

"I feel like a couple hills fell on me," Schrader groaned. "You hungry?"

"As a matter of fact, I could eat a sandwich. And my thermos is empty. You got some joe?"

"I'll make a pot. Help yourself to some chow. There's bread and fixin's in the reefer. You're really leaving soon?"

"Right off. But the quicker I get back, the quicker I can turn another truckload."

"Sounds like they're hot for the stuff."

"It's already sold, David. Sweet deal. A little piece of it is mine, but the next trip I'll have a bigger piece."

"Are you packing?"

Eddie grinned. "Little ol' .45 in the truck, nothing heavy. Just for Jody and the roadsigns."

"Make yourself a couple sandwiches for the road. Saw Mingo and Adelita the other day. She's out to here with a baby."

"Yeah, I heard. She'll raise a spitfire. Mingo must be busting his britches."

"You know it. If he grins any bigger he'll swallow his ears."

Eddie sat and ate his sandwich and it was like there were three other people in the room. He seemed in motion even when he was sitting still. He had always been that way, Schrader thought. Only booze or a stiff downer snuffed him out.

They swapped stories for awhile. "Say, did you hear"— or "let me tell you about—" They had a lot of friends in common. It was like gossiping with the mailman and they were laughing, but suddenly Eddie looked away and when he looked back at Schrader he was different.

"Leo Marconi died," he said quietly.

It took some moments to comprehend. "What do you— what do you mean? Was he killed?"

"Not that you could prove."

"What the hell happened, Eddie?"

"I wasn't around when he died. Hadn't seen Leo in two

years. But his brother talked to me about it after the funeral. Those funny things that were happening to Leo just never stopped. The skin rash never went away for very long, and he had a lot of nausea. About the last year he was alive, he began to have some kind of seizures. His brother says they were scary as hell. His family thought it might be epilepsy but, get this, three goddamned specialists ruled that out. They didn't know what the problem was. Leo kept getting worse, and when he died, was all used up. Wasted away, man. Leo Marconi."

"What did the autopsy prove?"

Eddie shook his head. "Neural deterioration of some sort. Said they couldn't pinpoint it."

Schrader slammed a fist onto the table. "In a pig's ass they couldn't pinpoint it! You were in Miami Beach the night we talked about the defoliants!"

"I was there," Eddie nodded. "I remember his story pretty damned good. We were just then learning about the toxins in the damned stuff."

"Remember how Leo talked about being sprayed for three days running? They'd bivouac somewhere different each night, and get sprayed the next day."

"Yeah," Eddie nodded. "It was in his food, his water, all his clothes. Were you ever sprayed that bad?"

"No. When did he die, Eddie? I never heard a word."

"It wasn't ten days ago. The funeral was last week. I took a train to Philadelphia and sat with the family. A lot of the East coast guys were there."

Schrader bit his knuckle until he tasted blood. He wanted to break something.

"It happened too fast to get word to everyone," Eddie said. "Don't feel bad you weren't at the funeral."

"He married a little gal, didn't he?"

"Yeah. Nice kid. It's a good thing they didn't have any children."

Schrader laughed harshly. "A good thing, all right. He loved kids but I guess it's a good thing. Goddamn, that sounds perverse!"

"You'll tell Mingo, eh?"

"Sure. I'll tell him. He's worried about those sprayings. All this talk about genetic defects passed on to babies."

Eddie reached across the table and took one of Schrader's hands and squeezed it hard. "The war ain't over, is it? You and me, we try to go about our business, do this, do that, close our eyes against the pictures in our minds but the pictures don't go away. Someone like Leo dies and we can look at each other and know privately that the war ain't over yet!"

Schrader wrapped his arms tightly about himself, in reflex to the spasm of grief that suddenly shook him. He didn't want any of this. Not the knowledge, not the grief, not any of those pictures that would not go away.

Eddie was looking through him.

"It's over," Schrader told him. "The war is a long time over, Eddie, and nobody thinks of it anymore. You and I are just sentimental slobs and who cares about a guy called Leo Marconi, anyway?"

"Sure, brother."

Schrader groped for something to say. "Can I—can I do anything? Does his wife need money? Can I help with the family?"

"There's plenty help up there, believe me. Grodecki and some of the old gang are around. Everybody took it hard."

"Jesus, I hate to tell Mingo."

"I'd hang around myself but I'm obliged to haul this stuff north."

"You really coming back?" asked Schrader.

"You watch me. I'm riding a lucky streak."

"You're not drinking?"

Eddie shook his head. "No booze, no downers. I'm a born again dope runner, brother. Clear-eyed and sharp-witted. See how short my hair, how white my smile? Who could suspect an all-American boy like me?"

David tried to laugh but it came out flat. He was thinking of Leo, seeing him in a hundred personal ways, funny and sad. He was a trooper in the First Air Cavalry, and now he was a casualty of the war. But since there was no war in anyone's remembrance, how could it have killed him?

We must have made it all up, thought Schrader. *They must have put us somewhere with the whackos and when we got out again, it was with these wild imaginings of a place*

*called Vietnam. Whoever heard of such a place? And we've
wandered around ever since like asylum escapees. I mean, a
war that never was can't kill you ten years after! Any fool
knows that!*

Eddie was watching him closely.

"I'll be all right," said Schrader.

"Then I'll head on my way. Sorry if I've made you late."

"It's nothing. I know you're on a tight schedule. Thanks
for taking the time."

"You want a lift to work?"

"No. Don't mix in the downtown traffic."

Eddie looked at his watch. "Little Rock by midnight, a
couple hours sleep, then on through Nashville."

They walked outside and Eddie climbed into the truck.
It rumbled to life and Eddie drove off. Schrader stood staring
at the space where the truck had been. Then he walked to the
corner and caught a bus, and it moved him from a space he
had been to a space he would be. It seemed to Schrader that
all reality was only a continuum of moving spaces accenting
the two dimensional lines of their lives. And between the spaces
and the lines, Leo Marconi had been a flicker that had caught
his eye. He wondered, *were any of us more than that?*

Schrader was late for work.

The day shift was done and his girls were working the
floor when he walked into the club. The noise and smoke
overwhelmed him at once. The darkness was oppressive, and
he wanted to turn and leave the damned place. But Jessie was
there.

She was alone behind the bar. When she saw the purple
gash on his forehead, she winced painfully. "You poor thing!
Oh, it looks awful!" She gave him a soft kiss across the bar and
held his hands. "Lilah told me all about it, David. Are you
feeling all right?"

"Sure. I'm okay."

"Damn Connors! It's all his fault! If he did his own dirty
work, this wouldn't have happened to you."

He squeezed her hands. "I don't want to talk about that.
How are you, baby?"

She smiled secretively. "I missed you, you big dumb marine. But it seems I can't trust you when I'm gone."

How much had Lilah told her?

"You go and get your body busted up, and what good are you to me then? Now I ask you?"

His guilty conscience slipped away. Schrader could only stare at Jessie in appreciation. She looked so fetching, he wanted to nuzzle up to her.

"How were things in Marble Falls?"

"Relaxing. Smoke free. The folks are fine. I saw Nellie. I'd like you to know her better. Old friends are wonderful, aren't they?"

"It breaks your heart when they die, Jessie."

She looked at him strangely.

"Two scotch waters, Jessie. And a vodka martini, up."

"Hi Christian."

"Oh, David, we're all sorry 'bout your pumpkin head. Here, mmmmmm, give us a kiss. Lilah told us all what a hero you were!"

Schrader winced. Suddenly he wanted something to do. "Here, Jessie, let me make those. You come around here and sit down."

He felt better then. He could keep busy and talk with Jessie, and the girls could coo over him now and again. He wouldn't have to think about how he was going to tell Mingo.

Jessie watched him make the drinks. "I've cleared the register for you. There are only two carryover tabs."

"Which tables?"

"Table three, with old Senator Miles and the bankers. And number six, with those three lawyers."

As Schrader poured out the martini, he watched Senator Miles's distinguished elbow lurch off the table. The Senator was in his cups. His home district was conservative, and very Baptist. The old senator was seated next to Rita (who was talking with one of the bankers). Schrader wondered if he was getting a clandestine hand job; Rita's hands were under the tablecloth to the elbows. Some of the girls could pull it off with remarkable composure. It was always the men who gave it away.

"Can I make you something, Jessie?"

She shook her head. "I feel all grimey. I want to go and shower, and put my feet up."

Schrader busied himself with some glasses, trying not to show disappointment. It was between songs, and not too noisy.

She leaned across the bar. "Whose place tonight? Yours or mine?"

"Yours, of course. You always have clean sheets."

"I'll pick you up at closing," she winked and blew him a kiss. He watched her stepping nimbly around the drunks and waving to the regulars as she left.

"One Manhattan, neat, and two Margarita rocks! I'm sorry about your head, David."

"So am I, Holly. You want to trade heads?"

"No thanks. I don't pick fights I can't win."

"With my head doing the thinking, you would."

She laughed. "Pretty soon you can start telling people you got the scar in the war."

"Are you kidding? That's what I'm telling them now!"

He served her drinks just as April Mae stepped onto the stage. She spun around gracefully as she slipped off her bra to a rock and roll tune. They were lovely breasts. April Mae told Schrader once they'd cost her fifteen hundred dollars. They were a commodity that she parleyed as well as any broker in the club.

"Hey, David! We're out of peanuts!"

"Bourbon water, two cuba libres! And turn up the juke box, honey!"

Long John ambled back to the bar and handed Schrader his glass of scotch. "Put some water in this, will ya?"

"No stomach for it tonight?"

"No stomach at all, anymore. You watch yourself, kid, or you'll end up like me." Long John was in his late forties. He was in the club most nights, and Schrader could always depend on his help if there was trouble. "Where's Connors tonight?"

Schrader shrugged. "I had his Caddy all weekend. He came and got it this morning. He looked pretty down in the mouth."

Long John raised his brows and leaned closer, smelling some gossip. "What happened? Wouldn't his ex-wife come across?"

"I think she took one look at all the money he was flashing and demanded more alimony. He told me she's putting a lawyer on it."

Long John threw his head back and laughed. "What a damned cluck! He thought if he was nice, she'd ask for less!"

He walked back to his table, shoulders shaking, and in a minute Schrader could see Doc Richmond laughing about it, too. He knew they were each two or three times divorced.

"Double scotch, straight up, two Margaritas sour and a Courvoisier!"

"Bourbon water, bourbon coke, salty dog!"

"Gin tonic and one gimlet!"

When Mondays were good, the joke went, it was because Sundays with the little lady were so bad.

"David honey! Go up front and help Rita with those college boys."

"She can handle them, Christian. What do you want?"

"Bloody Mary and a vodka martini. She told them three times they can't come in without a membership!"

"I don't feel like rousting some kids. There, you see? They're leaving."

When Rita came to the bar, she was short-tempered. Schrader guessed she was getting strung out. "Scotch'n soda and a double Jack rocks. Those damned punks! I almost called for you, David. They ruined the bar scene in Texas when they lowered the drinking age!"

"What the hell, Rita. In six months they might be in uniform, fighting in the Mideast."

She tossed her head defiantly. "That wouldn't be any skin off my nose, baby."

"I don't suppose it would."

"David! Reject that song, will you please?"

"Sure, Lilah."

She chose another song and whirled her caramel body onto the stage. There was some table pounding, but by and large the crowd was subdued. *Blue Monday*, thought Schrader.

"David! That fella said this was the worst Old Fashioned he's ever had!"

"It's not an Old Fashioned, April Mae. It's a Manhattan straight up. That's what you called. Check his ticket."

"Gee, I'm sorry."

"How many has he had now?"

"Uhhh, six."

"Let me see, hon . . . Jesus! He's had a daiquiri, a Margarita, a Tom Collins, Black Russian, a Rusty Nail and now this one. Is he trying all the flavors?"

She shrugged. "Maybe he's rating bartenders for *Texas Monthly.*"

"If he pukes, you'll have to clean it up."

"Not me, sugar. I'm a high-class dame!"

One by one, the hours slowly passed, and Schrader busied himself needlessly when the bar drew slack. He restocked the display and washed a shipment of glasses. The floor behind the bar needed mopping; there was a new keg to tap. Schrader didn't want to get the blues about Leo Marconi. He had his own problems. But little things about him kept coming to the surface — the good times and serious times, the laughs.

It could be a very serious thing to Mingo, Schrader knew. The brush killer called agent orange had been sprayed all over I Corps. They had friends with genetically malformed children. It was not a thing the government could have gotten away with, had they sprayed twenty million World War II vets.

"Two whiskey sours and a beer!"

By closing, the crowd had thinned to the hard drinkers, and the girls were all yawning. Jessie strolled in as Schrader punched the tabs through the register. She came behind the bar and stood beside him.

"Want me to count the cash?"

"Please. You look swell."

"Thank you. I took a long nap."

"This damned liquor key keeps sticking! You think between the Cadillacs and the Buicks, we could get a new register?"

Jessie shook her head and diligently paid attention to her count. "There! Eight hundred, thirty-seven dollars and seventy-five cents. Less a hundred dollar bank; that's a good Monday night. Just think, David. With a thousand-dollar Friday, Connors can add a Mercedes to his fleet."

When the last of the grumbling customers was gone, and the girls had changed their clothes, Schrader let them out the front door and locked it. Back at the bar, Jessie was counting out her next day's bank.

He hugged her from behind and watched their reflection in the mirror. It seemed he looked much older than she did.

"Would you mind driving over to Mingo's for awhile? There's something I need to tell him."

"No, I don't mind. Anything important?"

Schrader saw his reflection shake a haggard head. "I don't guess you could call it important."

"Why don't you take this deposit to the corner, and I'll call Adelita. Meet you outside?"

It was a chilly evening. The air was damp and threatening a cold rain; the harsh concrete echoes were muted. Schrader hurried to the corner and back. Jessie was starting her old, battered Fiat, and he clambered stiffly inside. The car had some pep. In no time, they were around the corner on Eleventh Street and headed across the bridge. There was no one on the streets that night, and without the people, the old neighborhoods seemed to sag and show their age.

It was just as quiet on Mingo's street.

Adelita met them at the door and hugged Jessie, then she winced when she saw Schrader's forehead. "You've been in another fight!"

Before he could defend himself, Jessie laughed: "But it wasn't his fault, Adelita," and she explained some of the tale.

He stood there fidgeting while Jessie talked. He'd lost the damned fight. The sooner it was forgotten, the better.

"Here," he interrupted, "let me take your coat."

Adelita laughed. "Stop blushing, David. It's not everyday you get to slay a dragon for a fair maiden."

"Hmph! Lilah's hardly a maiden."

"Shame on you," Jessie told him, "every girl is a maiden when a man fights for her."

"That's right, *hombre*. Don't be a grump about it."

"Oh, fine. It's my head that got busted, but I shouldn't be a grump! I'm too damned old to be throwing hands in a barroom. I should have kept my mouth shut and let those goons have their laughs."

"But you never could do that," Adelita said.

"He learned to charge in the Marines," Jessie teased.

Adelita cocked her head. "Maybe. Mingo says he just instinctively leads with his chin."

"Piss on Mingo," Schrader grinned. "When's he going to be here, anyway?"

"Anytime now. I told him to take the truck to work. I thought it might rain. But you know how Mingo likes to walk the streets. Do you want some coffee? Come on in the kitchen."

They sat at the table and talked, and Jessie and Schrader drank coffee. Still Mingo had not come. He saw Adelita glance at the clock and frown.

"He's still with his girlfriend," Schrader joked.

"Oh, hush."

Adelita rolled her eyes. "He wouldn't dare."

"Show me those new clothes you bought?"

"Okay. Come on in the bedroom."

The women walked to the back of the house, and Schrader took his coffee and sat in the front room. It was quiet and he was thinking of Leo Marconi. Then he heard something thump heavily on the porch. It was an odd sound. He was getting up to look when the door opened.

There stood Mingo. He leaned forward and fell into the room, his face a bloody lump and his clothes torn. He curled into an agonized ball to clutch his ribs, sucking air through a mashed mouth.

Schrader got beside him, on his knees. "My God, Mingo!"

Mingo grabbed at Schrader's arm. It seemed all Mingo could do to breathe. "Hey *hombre!*" he wheezed. It was like the rasping of a squashed frog, and Schrader was suddenly afraid.

With his sleeves, he wiped blood from Mingo's face and head. "Lay still, Mingo. I'll be right back."

The women had heard nothing from the bedroom. Schrader took Adelita by the arms.

"Mingo is hurt," he told her. She saw the blood on his sleeves and tried to pull away, but he held her. "Think of your baby, and keep yourself calm. Jessie, would you soak some towels in hot water—now come on!"

Adelita twisted free and ran ahead, and there beside him she made a sound like a frightened lamb. Mingo painfully straightened his legs and pulled his wife to him. Blood was dripping on the carpet from a couple of cuts on his head, and Schrader could see he wanted to curl up in a ball again.

"Not on his chest, Adelita. Don't put weight on his chest." Gently, he tugged her away. Jessie rushed in with the towels. Schrader leaned over close and whispered in her ear.

"Hold Adelita, Jessie. Put your arms around her and hug her. I don't think it's as bad as it looks." He was hoping desperately it was not a car. If he had been hit by a car, he'd be all busted up inside.

". . . 'm okay babe . . . punks . . . some punks jumped me . . . be okay."

Schrader undid his coat and shirt and felt his ribs. They were bruised and Mingo winced at the touch.

"I'll call an ambulance," Jessie said, and got to her feet.

"No! uhhh . . . no doctor!" Mingo half rose but collapsed again. "Be okay—"

"Yes, Mingo! You need a doctor!" Adelita cried.

"Please baby, give a few minutes. Just sore, little bloody. Ain't that bad."

"You're crazy!" But she kissed his face and tears fell into his cuts.

Jessie looked at Schrader questioningly.

"Wait a bit," he said. "You can get some blankets."

They covered Mingo and let him lie on the floor, and they all sat around him. He began to rest easier. The bleeding ceased from three or four gashes and his face was cleaned, but his whole head was puffed and discolored. Schrader was more concerned about Mingo's insides.

"You feel something sharp inside? Maybe a busted rib?"

"Don't think so—could be cracked, though."

"You seen these punks before?"

"No. Never seen 'em." But his eyes slid away from Schrader's and he had an inkling that he was lying.

Schrader took his handkerchief from his pocket. "Here Mingo, spit in this. Cough it up, a big wad . . . There's no blood. You hear a ringing in your head?"

"No man. A herd of cattle."

"That's normal enough."

"Just like old times, eh?" Mingo managed to laugh. Schrader remembered a bunker once that had been blown apart by a rocket. They had both spit blood for a week.

"If you two start joking, my blood pressure is going to climb!" Adelita told them sharply.

" 'kay, baby. No jokes."

"Where did it happen, Mingo?" asked Schrader.

"Few blocks away. Laid in an alley awhile. Couldn't move."

"How's the *cojones*?"

"You know me. Those are the last things they'd get. I want to sit on the couch."

"Not yet. Wait a few minutes."

"I'm going to call an ambulance," Adelita said.

Mingo took her hand. "In the morning, first thing, we'll see Doc Mirandez. I promise."

"*Tu eres un cabesiduro!*"

"*No es nada, mi amor solo. Unos machucones* . . . A few bruises."

"Would you like something to drink?" Jessie asked.

"Ahhh, lovely senorita. A *cerveza, por favor*. And now I'm going to sit on the couch . . . *Estoy aqui tirado como un hombre viejo.*"

Schrader helped him to his feet and he sucked wind sharply. He was still not steady. "There!" he said. "Now I'm master in my house again."

"Oh Mingo! You could be lying out there still!"

"Don't cry, baby. Hey—" He looked at Schrader. "You ever see her cry? I've seen her cry once."

David shook his head. "It's good for her now."

"Ahhh. *Mi cerveza. Gracias*, Jessie." It hurt Mingo to raise his arm.

Adelita was looking pale. "I think I'll lie down for awhile," she said. "Will you come with me Jessie?"

Mingo looked at her with concern, and laid a hand on her stomach. "Are you all right? Do you feel any contractions?"

"No. I'm just a little shaky."

"Are you sure, baby? I don't want nothin' to happen to you."

"I'll be fine after I lay down," she said, and Jessie helped her along.

When the men were alone Mingo motioned to Schrader, and when he came close Mingo gripped his forearm. Mingo's strength was returning. "You should tell me what happened, when you left here Friday, amigo."

Schrader's mind was blank for a moment, and then it came to him who had beaten his friend. "Manley!" he blurted.

"You got it," Mingo replied.

Schrader told him then of the chase he had led the cops, and what a game he had thought it was.

"So that's it," Mingo said. "It's foggy, but I remember when the cops left they said something about telling Schrader not to fool around anymore."

David was stunned. "Tell me how it happened, Mingo."

"You know they'd stopped me a few times," Mingo began, holding a towel to his face. "Tonight when they pulled over I wasn't in the mood for any crap. When they got out of the car, I couldn't see anyone on the street. I asked them what they wanted, and didn't lose my temper, but they started with some shuck'n jive and I started away from them. Arrest me! I told them, if you got charges, arrest me! Next thing I knew, my skull was laid open and I was on the ground. They both worked me over then."

It's like a bad dream. Schrader stared into Mingo's mashed face, his insides still soft from the news about Leo. *We are a world apart, Leo in his cold grave, but we are all linked and it is one picture.* Schrader looked at his friend.

"What are you going to do, Mingo?"

His jaw muscles worked. "I'm going to have *la venganza* for this."

Schrader did not have to ask what he meant. "Count me in," he said.

"*Bueno* . . . now help me up. I want to sit with Adelita." Mingo grimaced when he moved and grabbed Schrader's arm again. "God forbid, if anything should happen to the baby because of this, if Adelita is so upset that she miscarries, there will be a killing for a killing. You understand?"

Schrader nodded brusquely, but inside he went cold.

"You don't have to come on this, David. It's my vendetta."

"I said count me in," Schrader growled, trying to sound fierce, but his stomach was tight. *Hell to me is prison,* thought Schrader.

"*Muy bueno. Tu siempre has sido mi hermano.*"

Yes, I've always been your brother. But I'm ashamed now.

"Tomorrow we'll talk some more," Mingo said. "Help me along, now. *El viejo* needs a cane, eh?" And he laughed almost pleasantly, as though nothing at all had happened. It made Schrader shiver, to hear the laugh and smell the blood still fresh on Mingo. He knew then that in Mingo's mind the matter was settled. Mingo would have his revenge.

* * *

The afternoon was clear and bright and the first threat of winter had bolted like a white-tailed deer. A breeze was chopping up the lake and it lapped on the sand at their feet. Mingo had wanted to take a ride, and Schrader had Jessie's car. The stretch of beach was deserted. The blue of the sky and the green of the hills danced a colored waltz on the water, but it lent Schrader no calm.

"It's just another search and destroy," Mingo shrugged. "Except I only work him over. Manley is the one. When Piggly Quigley sees him, he'll piss his pants."

"It will take you some time to heal," Schrader said. Mingo really looked bad. The doctor had taped his ribs and when he moved, it made Schrader hurt just to see it.

"I need the time to plan," Mingo answered. "Time to scope out his routines. Where he lives, what he does. I still have friends on the streets."

Mingo and Adelita had a lot of friends. Their house was usually open to the down and out, and Mingo always had spare change. The men hadn't talked much, and now Mingo cocked his head toward Schrader, as if to study his thoughts.

"You think I should forget this," Mingo said. "You think I have everything to lose, that I should just *me traque mi orgullo*, swallow my pride."

"Part of me thinks that way."

"You're afraid?"

"Of course. Wasn't I always afraid? But didn't I always come through?"

"This time I know you're afraid for more than yourself," Mingo said.

"You know the tenets of your life better than I," Schrader told him. "If you want to risk what you've built for yourself, I'll go along. We owe each other. Besides, it's not just your pride, I know."

Mingo shook his head. "No, it's not just my pride. They thought they were thumping on some nobody greaser. But they threatened the well-being of my wife and my baby. They don't have the right to toy with lives like that."

"Then there's something else you should know," Schrader said. "Eddie Malone came through town yesterday."

"Goddamn! Why didn't he call me?"

"He was carrying a big load of weed, only had a little time."

Mingo grinned and shook his head. "That sonuvagun. Will he be back?"

"He said very soon. He told me something else, Mingo. Leo Marconi is dead." He told Mingo all that he knew. Mingo's swollen face stayed the same, but his eyes changed imperceptibly as he turned away. The narrow beach and flat expanse of lake seemed to stretch forever. The wind beating around them whistled tauntingly at the fragile moments that were their lives.

After a silence that tugged at Schrader's heart, Mingo turned and said: "Then Manley will be paying for a lot of things."

Yes indeed, Schrader thought to himself. *For all of the times we were pushed but did not shove back, Manley will pay.*

We must take what small victories we can.

16

A week passed while Mingo healed. Business at the Red Duke was brisk, and Schrader's nights were a blur. His mornings he spent comfortably with Jessie. She picked him up at work, or he kept her car and let himself in with her key.

It was not the usual rush of romance for Schrader, not the white hot flare of passion that comes to nothing in the end. That was the way he had known women for years, and he had fed like a starving man. Jessie, somehow, did not lend herself to that. Beside her, he slept easier. There was little terror in his nights.

Still, there was absurdity beyond measure. The crew at the Red Duke—the regulars and the girls—showed less constraint each night, working themselves into a pre-holiday abandon, testing the fevers that would soon be lofting them through the biggest paydays of all, the wildest times, the most resounding crashes on the second day of the New Year. And in his smugness, Schrader thought there was nothing they could do that would surprise him.

It was a slow, rainy, Wednesday; the regulars sat about dejectedly, and even the jukebox was still. Schrader wiped glasses dry, and watched the clock.

"Where the hell did everybody go?" Connors leaned heavily on the bar, slopping his fourth bourbon.

"Prayer meeting," cracked Schrader.

"Hell, I need their tithe right here!"

"Amen to that, brother. You've got some expensive tastes."

"Comes from bein' a poor boy, David."

"Crap! Everyone in here tells me what poor boys they were."

Connors looked offended. "Well, I'm the genuine article son. I was picking cotton when I was five. Daddy had the whole family in the field."

That line has become a standard Southern homily, so Schrader ignored it. He wearied of the Texas elite magically sprung from dirt farmers and cowhands. Though in Connors's case, it might have been true.

There were barely a dozen customers. Schrader's glasses were dried and display racks cleaned and he yawned against the cash register.

"Two scotch waters," Christian said. "And stop yawning."

"Heard any new jokes?"

"There ain't any, honey. I've heard them all."

Long John and the Doc went to the bar. Then little Freddie Niederwald.

"Did you hear what April Mae said she could do?" Freddie laughed. "Damnedest thing!"

"What's that?"

"She told me she could smoke a cigarette with her twat." They all had a good laugh.

"That's anatomically impossible," the doctor said assuredly. "The musculature isn't suited for inhaling, Freddie."

Connors perked up his ears. "You say it's impossible, Doc?"

"Absolutely."

"Y'all wait here," and he sat with April Mae, their heads together over a table. Schrader saw what was coming.

"My gal here says she can do it," Connors announced.

"That's right," April Mae said, and Connors lifted her easily onto the bar.

Doc and Long John and Freddie looked at one another. As if by signal, they all reached for their wallets. Connors rubbed his hands together. "I'll lock the doors, Davey boy. You count out the money in the register."

In a few moments, everyone in the club was gathered about the bar.

"How much we got in the kitty, David?"

"Three hundred twenty and some change."

"Goddamn! Is that all?"

"Your voucher is good, Connors. If you got the balls."

He reddened and took another two hundred from his pocket. "There's five twenty. I'll cover everything over that."

Greenbacks rained onto the bar. No one was betting with April Mae.

"David, you want a piece of this?"

"I never bet against a lady."

April Mae smiled demurely. "Your momma raised you right, honey."

"I'm betting *your* momma raised you wrong!" he told her. Connors was starting to look worried. There was almost two thousand dollars to cover.

"Lilah! Come help me. Stand back, you warthogs!" April Mae held her legs out straight while Lilah pulled off her panties. There were some parched mouths and wide eyeballs then. April Mae was a real blonde.

Schrader was standing behind her, trying to keep aloof. The men were in a half circle before the bar, and the girls were clustered together on the side. Someone lit a cigarette and handed it to April Mae. From behind, Schrader saw her reach down between her legs.

"Well, at least she can hold it there," the doctor said. "That's really quite good, my dear."

"Yeah, but it ain't smokin'!" someone said.

"Quiet, goddamnit!" Connors barked, sweat beading on his forehead. "Let the girl concentrate."

She sat up straight and placed her hands behind her head and began to writhe. Her muscles rippled.

"Ohhh Jesus!" Long John moaned.

April Mae went on like that for some time, but nothing happened.

"What's the matter, baby? What's the matter?" Connors was really sweating.

She took the cigarette and looked at it with disgust. "A goddamned Winston! Somebody give me a Marlboro!"

In an instant another was lit, and they all leaned forward like the Dutch Masters, their unisoned breathing warming the air behind the bar.

April Mae began to writhe and grind again. And then like a desperate signal from the guard, a white puff of smoke billowed out to hang proudly in the air.

"YAAHOOO!" Connors whooped.

"Amazing!" the doctor said to no one in particular, in the uproar that followed. "I really should write a paper on it."

Long John looked disgusted. "Impossible, you told me! You sonuvabitch, you're buying my drinks the rest of the year!"

"A round on me!" Connors laughed, scooping up the money.

"One round! You cheap bastard!"

April Mae neatly snatched the wad of bills from Connors grip. "Twenty percent, remember, sugar?" And she counted her cut before she put on her panties.

The next day Schrader saw Mingo. He was healing quickly. His swollen head seemed human again and he could move without pain. They were sitting on his porch in the morning sun. Adelita was away.

"You've missed some work. Do you need some bucks?"

Mingo shook his head. "Naw. If it gets tight, old Joe will help us out. He and Adelita's mother came over last night, brought some groceries. But we have good savings."

"Did you quit the night job?"

"Yeah. I take my test in a couple of days, anyway. Then I'll start at full wage with Joe." He looked at Schrader closely. "Do you still feel all right about this?"

"Sure. I've made up my mind to do it. But I've been in the dark awhile. You'd better fill me in."

"Okay," he began, "for six nights now, they've eaten supper at only two places. The Round Up near the edge of town, and that Dixie Diner off east Seventh."

"I know both places. Who's scouting?"

"Ricky Lopez and Jesus Martine are the two you know."
He gestured with his hand. "Five brothers, all told."

"Big number."

"We'll need some help to pull it off," Mingo said. "Watchers and signallers. You and me do the heavy stuff, though. There aren't many times Manley is away from his partner, but it happens sometimes. I think I've figured a way to get to him alone."

"Wait a minute, Mingo," Schrader said, something dawning. "You mean you want to do this when he's on duty? And armed?" He couldn't believe the cheek of it.

"You know it, man! Just once I want to rub their noses in it." And Mingo went on then, almost breathless, to describe his plan. Schrader listened at first with reserve, but as his plot unravelled he saw the old knowledge re-revealed. Mingo was Schrader's cat man on ambush, his point man on a hundred patrols. *This is a good plan. With some daring and luck it would work.* Schrader was taken with enthusiasm and they traded ideas through the morning, slowly working the plan to a military fineness.

By the time Adelita returned from shopping they had taken the idea as far as they could. They needed more details, some reconnaissance, a system of signals and a tight timetable. But it could be done.

Old training dies hard.

A couple days later, Lieutenant Hank Logan paid Schrader a visit.

He'd been neglecting his house, surrendering it to legions of roaches while he slept in comfort at Jessie's. But Friday he passed the morning hours cleaning.

When he answered the knock at his door, there stood the lieutenant. He was a graying man about the age of Schrader's father, tall and fit.

"Sorry to bother you at home, David." Logan was always polite. Schrader guessed it was his way of putting you off guard.

"Come in, Lieutenant. How the devil did you find me?"

"Jessie gave me your address. I spoke with her just awhile ago."

"How about some coffee?"

"Fresh pot?"

"Yep."

"Good and black, then."

They sat at the kitchen table and Logan came right to the point. "That woman Rita Darnell, I think she's been dealing pretty heavy. Her name's been coming to my attention too much lately. I'd like to ask you some questions."

Schrader studied him for a moment. Logan seemed too open to be a cop. "Why do you trust me, anyway? Who's to say I'm not as involved as her?"

The lieutenant smiled slightly. "Trust me to do my homework, David. I've checked you out; you're a pretty good kid. Good war record. You may have smoked a little pot, but you're not the type to deal hard drugs."

"Ten years ago, you wouldn't have thought so well of me."

"Times change, son." He shrugged, waiting for Schrader's reply.

"How can I help, Lieutenant?"

Logan took an envelope from his coat and produced a stack of pictures. Some were mugshots, and some were obviously taken from a concealed camera. "You can tell me if you've ever seen any of these men in the club?"

"Tell me first what she's dealing. It sort of ruffles me to be a fink."

"Uppers, downers, cocaine," he replied. "Anything she can make a buck on. But I'm certain she's turning to heroin. And I can smell a big junk deal."

"You think she can put together the money for something like that? Seems unlikely to me."

"Some of your customers are pretty wealthy; you know that. I'm digging to see if one of them is involved. But it doesn't have to be one of them. Any one of the local biker clubs could come up with a quarter million in no time. Rita doesn't need to have money; she only needs to know where to get it."

Schrader looked through the pictures slowly. Yes, there was a face he knew. "This man was in the club last week. Rita sat with him alone."

Logan looked at David sharply. "You're sure?"

"Yes. Usually she's crawling all over her customers, but this guy she kept her distance from. He had a couple drinks and left."

"What night was that?"

Schrader thought back. "Tuesday."

"And you haven't seen him since then?"

"No. Look, Lieutenant, I'm going to fire that girl. If she's not around, I won't be a fink and the club won't get a bad name."

"I'd appreciate it if you didn't," the lieutenant said. "I know we were rough on some of you fellows years ago, and I guess it galls you to cooperate with us. But if we can lock up a big time pusher, don't you think we should?"

"That's nifty to put it on a moral footing. Since you've checked me out, you think I have morals."

"That's right."

"There must be half a million square miles in Texas. Why would they do a deal in a crowded bar?"

"Sometimes it can be the safest place. Everybody drinking, eyeballing the women. A couple brief cases in the hands of respectably dressed men. A trip to the bathroom and the deal is completed."

"So Rita is getting together the junk man and the money man?" I asked.

"That's what I think," Logan replied. "She takes her cut in greenbacks or heroin."

"Are you going to put surveillance on the club?" Schrader casually asked, knowing that could scotch Mingo's plan.

"Don't have the manpower right now," Logan said, "and I'm kind of working on this thing alone. Besides, the man in the picture has left the state. Probably nothing will happen till he comes back."

Schrader chuckled. "You're a trusting soul, Lieutenant. I haven't had a good thought about cops in years."

"Hell, David, we're just two marines passing the time of day."

"You?"

"That's right. Mortars. Saipan and Okinawa." He finished his coffee and got up to leave. Schrader walked him to the door. "And keep mum about this to Connors," Logan told him, "that boy gets to drinking, he talks too much. Fancies himself a drinker and a brawler like his daddy, but he couldn't hold a candle to old Pete."

"I'll keep it to myself."

"And if you spot the fella in the photo before we do, give me a call."

"Don't worry, Lieutenant. Good-bye."

After Logan left, Schrader sat down and thought furiously. He had been puzzled about the lieutenant for the year he had known him. Logan might have lied to him about the surveillance on the club. *He might only half trust me*, thought Schrader, *be playing me to see if I was involved.*

For Mingo's plan to work, Schrader had to slip from the club unnoticed. It happened often enough that he needed fresh fruit or change for the register, and then Christian would tend bar. Ten minutes or forty in a night club is hard to recall. If there was surveillance, though, Schrader's absent minutes would be logged.

He walked to the corner store to use the phone. In a short while, Mingo drove up to the house.

Mingo listened quietly to the whole tale, while he and Schrader were sitting in the back yard.

"You mentioned you did Logan a favor once," Mingo said. "What was it?"

Schrader laughed. "His nephew was pretty drunk one night in the club. Tried to start a couple fights. I sobered him up in the office and drove him home. Didn't think much of it, but Logan's wife was very appreciative. Favorite nephew it seemed. And a theology student, too."

"So there's a good chance the lieutenant was straight with you. As far as he's concerned, you're okay."

"I guess so."

"Then he was probably telling the truth about the surveillance, at least for the time being. This might make things better for you, David. If you're aiding in a drug investigation, you're a little less likely a suspect for assault on a cop."

"Manley must have a lot of enemies," Schrader said. "They'll be checking out more suspects than us."

"That's my guess, too. But we can't count on it."

"We need to move on this soon, Mingo. Before this mystery junk man returns. Are you feeling strong?"

"Yeah. The ribs are a little sore, still. But I work out on the heavy bag okay. I'll have a talk with the others tonight. Did you get the ski masks?"

"Yes. And some oversized coveralls for us both. How about the weapon?"

"I have it. Sawed-off, double-barreled twelve guage. Cut-down stock. Looks mean as hell. You put it under his nose, he'll freeze all right. He'll feel like someone shoved an icicle up his ass."

"I'd better have a look at the bathroom windows in both places."

"Sure," Mingo said. "We can go this afternoon. I'll buy you a beer."

Schrader was feeling good. Logan's unexpected appearance had threatened to thwart their plan, but it seemed then, they might even turn it to suit them.

"It was strange today," Schrader said, "drinking coffee with Logan, all the while scheming to beat hell out of another cop."

"Maybe Logan's okay," Mingo replied. "We've both known some good cops."

"I'd like to think he is. He was in 81s on Saipan and Okinawa."

"No kidding! There you have it, brother. He trusts you 'cause he's an old grunt. You can't get any thicker than that."

Schrader shook his head. "Still, Mingo, he wants me to aid and abet a policeman."

"Big deal! Help put a couple pushers in jail. Lock the sons of bitches up, that's what I'd do!"

"That's pretty cold, coming from an ex-junkie."

"All the more reason to hate a pusher."

"Just the same, don't tell any of the guys."

Mingo laughed. "Pssst! Hey fellas!" he joked from the side of his mouth. "Did you hear Schrader is a pig?"

Schrader winced. "Remember how we played cop?" he asked Mingo. "Tell some poor farmer where he could go, what he could do. How must I have appeared to them? Big, hulking white man with enough bullets and grenades to wipe out a village all by myself."

"What must they have thought of *me*?" Mingo asked in turn. "In a peasant's hat I looked like one of them. You Anglos at least appeared just like they expected. But I was their cousin. I was the traitor, not you."

Schrader slapped him on the shoulder and tried to make a joke. "They were killing each other all the time. One more brown-skinned runt didn't make much difference."

"Didn't it?" Mingo eyed him and scoffed. "Gee, you make my life much easier."

Schrader knew Mingo had gunned down some peasants in Hue. How could he have known? The Communists regulars were all dressing like civilians in some of the heaviest fighting of the war. Mingo once confessed that if he had only held off the trigger two seconds longer, those people might still be alive. *But two seconds is a lifetime in a firefight.*

"I'm sorry," Schrader told him. "It was a bad joke."

Mingo smiled wanly, "C'mon, let's have a look at those windows." And he started toward the backyard gate, whistling the Marine Corps hymn. *He's covering up.* Schrader knew. And he shuffled along in Mingo's wake.

It was early one shift and Schrader was cursing, muscling a keg beneath the bar. In the middle of happy hour he'd run out of beer, and he was behind on drinks.

Above him he heard someone rap on the bar: "Hey mister! My scotch has a cockroach in it!"

Schrader muttered angrily, banging his head on the bar as he looked up crossly. But there was Eddie Malone.

"You made it, you sonovagun!"

"Not a hitch, David. I even stopped in Virginia, to help a State Trooper with a flat tire."

"You're crazy!"

"Couldn't have worked out better," Eddie laughed. "The trooper escorted me all the way to the Shenandoah turn-off." Eddie was sharply dressed. Schrader thought he'd made a bundle.

"Is that a silk shirt?"

"Don't drool on it, sarge."

Two girls came to the bar.

"Where's my martini, honey?"

"C'mon David! Two bourbons 'n cokes and a rum soda. I'm gettin' behind, babe."

"Okay ladies. This is my buddy, Eddie Malone. Eddie, this is Lilah and Christian."

Malone didn't waste a second stepping over to them. Eddie was always quick with the ladies, and Lilah smiled and gave him a knowing glance. Christian looked him over unabashedly.

Schrader busied himself serving up the drinks, and when he set them out, Christian said to him: "Nice to see you have some classy friends."

Eddie and Schrader had a good laugh. They'd been in rags together.

"What are you drinking, Eddie?" Schrader asked him.

"Some soda water, with a lime."

"How long you staying this time?"

"Same deal. They're dragging their feet in San Antone, though. I might have to stay a couple days."

"You can use my place, Eddie. I'm not in it much now."

"Got a steady woman, David?"

"Sort of."

'Don't tell me the old sarge is going down for the count?"

"It doesn't hurt so bad," Schrader laughed. "If only I'm house-broke enough to get away with it."

Eddie shook his head. "Man, with all the stuff flouncing around in this place, you must really have it bad."

"This place is a mirage," Schrader told him. "All those customers are dying of thirst. But what we serve them here disappears when they walk out the door. Give me a good, solid woman anytime."

"Me. I like my mirages," Eddie replied. "That way, when I walk out the door it's a whole new world."

"Have you seen Mingo yet?" Schrader asked.

"No. Thought we might get together when you're off work."

"Sure. I'll call him later and set it up. He quit his night job. Got his master electrician's license last week."

"Adelita sure changed that boy around."

His tone made Schrader bristle in a funny way.

"Excuse me, Eddie. I'm short some bottles here." And Schrader slipped under the bar and went to the storeroom, found the bourbon and the tequila. What the hell, he was thinking. Adelita never liked Eddie. Turnabout is fair enough.

Back at the bar, he found that Rita had discovered his old friend. She was almost throbbing under Eddie's gaze, and they leaned and touched like old friends sharing a private remark. Rita could lay it out before a man with those dark eyes, and Schrader knew she was the kind of woman Eddie preferred. Eddie was a take it and run soul, too. And it surprised Schrader then how much alike they seemed.

Christian came back to the bar. "Scotch Mist and an Old Fashioned. Rita, you got some men on seven."

"Mind your business, sweetie," Rita warned.

"You mind yours, Rita," Schrader cut in and pointed. "Table seven."

She eyed him sharply and squeezed Eddie's arm. " 'scuse me, baby."

"Sorry to break that up, Eddie," Schrader said. "Business, you know."

Malone shrugged it off. "Hey, it's your show. Still a sergeant, I see."

"Everyone finds his level. Let me make these drinks."

Eddie watched him quietly as he handled a rush of orders. And when he finished:

"Pretty smooth," Eddie said "But you ought to own the damned place instead of being the flunkie."

"If I owned it, I'd be chained to it. Who needs the headache?"

"Still man, you've got too much on the ball to be taking orders. You need to get yourself something."

"Like you, Eddie? You mean I could live my life on the edge of a dope deal?"

Malone grinned and winked. "This is only temporary. But the money will get me something better."

It was Schrader's turn to grin. "You'll spend every dime of it on a good time. It's the lifestyle that comes with the work."

"I hear you, brother. But don't count me out. Just kick me in the ass if you see it coming."

Then Rita went back to the bar. "Scotch water, JD rocks, Manhattan rocks."

Eddie sidled over and stroked her hair. "Don't let my mean friend bother you. Inside he's butter."

"David?" she raised her eyebrows. "David is our daddy. Just last month he threw out a cracker who hurt my arm. We all *love* David." And she smiled and turned her head just so, but the barbs were in her eyes.

Eddie laughed. "Still throwing hands, you old Jarhead!" And he nudged Rita. "That's what he likes best about the place, never mind the tits and asses. Your head's healed pretty good, though. Ready for the next round now."

Eddie doesn't know how close to the mark he is, thought Schrader.

They passed an hour trading stories: Grodecki is okay,

Kane is doing such, and Gunny such. Leo Marconi's family was taking his death very hard. There was talk of pressing a lawsuit, but the whole thing looked hopeless. Who do you sue? The government? The chemical companies? How does a working class family get a Congressman to notice them?

"Gloomy, ain't it?" Eddie remarked.

"You'd think that between us, we'd have more good news."

Eddie turned and eyed the club. "Hey David, if you don't mind, I'm going to take one of Rita's empty tables. Get a little closer to those hot pants. I'm chilly."

What can I say? thought Schrader. He thought to warn him about Lieutenant Logan. *No, Eddie would tip Rita off. I know that for certain.* Schrader knew Eddie had no use at all for cops. *And that will ruin my connections with the lieutenant. Eddie's dealing pot and Rita might prove dangerous to him. What to do?* Schrader reasoned that Malone was leaving town soon enough, so he pushed a card and a pen toward him.

"Just fill this out, Eddie. Private club laws, you know?"

"Sure." He scrawled it out quickly.

When Schrader glanced at the card, he saw it was a phony occupation and name. "Still covering your tracks, eh?"

"Old habit," Eddie laughed. "Learned it the same place you did." Malone got up and walked to a corner table and took a seat.

Rita was at his table quickly, sitting beside him, touching again. Schrader shivered. It wasn't the air conditioning.

It was 2 A.M., and Mingo was yawning and Adelita, bleary-eyed, was holding her head.

"I can't wait up anymore," she said. "I'm going to bed . . ."

Mingo kissed her. "G'night baby."

"Say hello to Eddie for me, if he shows up." There was I-told-you-so in her voice.

Mingo got up and closed the kitchen door behind her. "What time did Eddie leave with that broad?" he asked Schrader.

"About ten. I wasn't sure he'd make it out the door with his pants on."

"Are you going to warn him about the broad being cased?"

David shook his head. "I can't. I know he'll tell her. And if I really have Logan's confidence, I'd like to keep it."

"But we don't want Eddie to go down," Mingo objected. "We gotta be careful about him."

"I agree. If he's not gone in a couple of days, I'll tell him about the lieutenant. We've got that much time, at least. Now what about Manley?"

"Are you ready to go?" Mingo asked.

Schrader felt his pulse quicken. "Whenever you say. It's your ambush."

Mingo nodded. "I like the lay-out at the Round Up," he began. "Manley and Quigley like the Monday-Wednesday-Friday specials. Manley gets the enchiladas, and Quigley likes the pork chops picado."

Schrader burst out laughing.

"Shhh! I swear it's true! I've had my men in there the last three times. They always get the same thing. And you say the window in that place is easier?"

"That's right," Schrader answered. "Just an old double-hung, nailed down. They're counting on the bars and the alarm for security. And the bars unbolt from the inside."

"And since the place will be open for business," Mingo continued, "the alarm will be shut off."

Schrader's coat was hanging from the chair. He took some things from the pocket. "See here. I've cut the nail heads off, left a half inch shank. The same with these hex head bolts. Tomorrow morning I'll go to the Round Up for breakfast, pull the real nails from the window and slip these heads in. I'll have to pry the window some to loosen it up."

"I don't think I want you seen in the place recently," Mingo objected.

Schrader shrugged. "You can get someone else to do it, but I eat there often enough."

"Let's get Jesus to unjimmy the window," Mingo told me. "Then Wednesday morning, Ricky Lopez can replace the bolts on the bars. Looks like just enough shank here to hold the bars in place."

"Yeah. A good push from the outside and they'll come off the casing."

"All right!" Mingo said, rubbing his hands. "We'll try it Wednesday night, and if there's a hitch, we'll try again Friday." They proceeded to finely tune their plans. Manley by then had been shorn of his humanity; he was the faceless enemy.

Schrader did not want to know, say, if he had a wife and child. Because he did not want to care. It was easy in the war if you could keep from caring. Schrader had found he could not. So in his mind, Manley had no face.

They never saw Eddie that night, and Tuesday night Rita wasn't at the club. The time dragged by and Schrader was edgy.

Wednesday he went to an all-night market and bought limes and lemons, and checked the receipt carefully. The date was marked, but not the time of day. Then he drove to work. He was keeping Jessie's car.

Rita had returned to work. She was quick to tell Schrader about Eddie. "We were in San Antonio," she began, "checking things out, you know. Eddie got his truckload quicker than he thought—smooth fella, that friend of yours—he's gone now, left this morning. Probably past Little Rock."

"Did he say when he's coming back?" He was serving her drinks, not liking the second-hand information.

"Eddie said he was going to hurry back, and not just for the weed! I think he likes me."

"That's nice. Here are your Margaritas."

"But you don't like me much, do you?" Rita put up one hand and smoothed her hair.

Schrader thought he'd better be careful. Soon enough he might depend on her good will. "I, uh, never thought *you* liked me. You're always so, uh, abrupt, Rita."

"That's just my manner, honey. Don't you think we ought to be friends? I really like Eddie. He's so strong. That's the kind of a man I need. You won't say anything to louse it up, will you?"

"No, Rita. Honest. It's none of my concern." He gritted his teeth and said it. "I like you all right. You're a good kid."

She smiled a genuine smile. Then she took up her drinks and turned away, back to whatever it was she did. *Yes Rita,* he thought, *you could fall for Eddie Malone while you screwed one john and jacked off another.*

It was almost nine when the phone rang. When Schrader answered it, Mingo was curt. "They've pulled into the parking lot. Are you ready?"

"Ready," Schrader said. Mingo hung up.

Schrader was in luck. Business was just brisk enough to distract the girls. He called for Christian.

"What you need, baby?"

"I'm out of fruit. You mind handling the bar awhile? I might have to shop around to find some decent lemons."

"Whew! Be a relief. Bunch of stiffs tonight."

The Fiat was in back in the alley. In the shadows he kicked off his shoes, took the coveralls and sweatshirt and put them over his clothes, slipped tennis shoes on his feet and fumbled the laces thinking, *time, TIME!* The ski mask was in the seat with a pair of gloves. He raced the engine and drove from the alley looking everywhere for police, ran a light on Congress and cursed his stupidity. *Easy now! Don't get stopped!*

It was a tense drive. Every car was too slow, every light too long; the second hand on his watch kept sweeping around until he wanted to tear it from his wrist.

He parked the car in the shadows down from the cafe. The parking lot was full, and loud *conjunto* music carried down the street. The jagged rhythm of the accordian matched his racing pulse, and he walked casually, looked around and ducked quickly to the rear. A thick hedge of some kind grew close to the wall. Schrader pushed through, and there was Mingo kneeling beneath the sill. The window was already cracked open.

Mingo put his finger to his lips. Schrader understood. Someone was on the toilet. A hundred feet away, he saw Ricky Lopez in his old Ford. Lopez was part of the signal relay: two men outside, two men inside, and Mingo and Schrader in the back.

They heard the rusty squeak of a paper holder, and then the can was being flushed and someone left the stall to wash his hands. Then he was gone.

Mingo glanced at his watch, then took it off and put it in his pocket. "Pretty good time," he whispered.

"What's going on?"

"They've ordered dinner. We wait."

Each of them put on his ski mask, and Mingo handed Schrader the sawed-off shotgun. He broke the chamber. The gun was empty. *At least we aren't going to risk a murder,* thought David.

He worked the window up and down. It was stiff. There

was a bar of wax in Schrader's pocket and he rubbed some in the runners. Then he eased the window down. The music from the jukebox was pretty loud.

Someone came into the bathroom and Schrader ducked from the sill. Mingo glanced at Ricky Lopez. A signal was arranged for each cop. They didn't think they'd come in together.

Minutes passed. Schrader's hands were sweating in the gloves; the ski mask made his head itch. *What if someone was in the john the same time as Manley? I don't want to hurt anyone else.* They were counting on the bluff of the empty shotgun.

Lopez signalled quickly with a flashlight. One long blink for Quigley. As tense as they were, they couldn't resist the urge to peek. Quigley went about his business in the urinal, then washed his hands. He preened in the mirror, sucked in his stomach and swelled his chest.

When he left, Mingo looked at Schrader and nodded, and Schrader pushed the window all the way up. *Manley will be coming soon, or he'll wait until after his meal.* Schrader had his hands on the bars.

When the two short flashes of light came, he shoved hard on the bars. They wrenched free from the wood casing with a snapping sound, and he dropped them into the stall. Figuring maybe ten seconds, Schrader dove through the window, caught the top of the stall and pulled his feet inside. The bars were in the way, blocking the stall door. He yanked them savagely into the cramped corner and took the shotgun from Mingo just as Manley turned the knob.

Quiet then. Schrader squatted with his feet on the bowl, shotgun tightly in his grip, his blood pounded the old rushing sound in his ears. *Will he notice the bars off the window? Will he go for his pistol?*

Schrader heard the door close. Manley stepped to the urinal. The jukebox was making plenty of noise, and Schrader burst from the stall with all the anger and malice he could muster.

Those are awfully big holes at the end of a twelve gauge. Schrader put them right under Manley's nose, hammers back, and the cop gaped in disbelief and his eyes grew wide with fear. Schrader uttered no word, and the very silence was part of another psychological fear. Manley's hands flew up involuntarily.

Mingo leaped through the window like some leopard. Once in, he stepped around Schrader, lifted Manley's pistol, and tossed it into the commode. Schrader motioned Manley against the wall. Mingo ducked between them and locked the door. Then Mingo went right to work.

Two quick punches to the gut and Manley was doubled over. He was heavily muscled, but after he lost his wind he was helpless. Mingo hit him on the side of the head and then he was on the floor bleeding a little; bleeding a lot when Mingo broke his nose. *Splat! Splat!* Manley's eyes swelled like balloons. *Splat! Splat!* his mouth was a bloody hole, and his head was bouncing off the tile. *Splat! Splat! Don't kill him*, Schrader thought! *Splat! Splat! Splat!*

Mingo stood up and kicked him hard in the ribs. He looked a question at Schrader. *Again*. He nodded. *Thunk*. Manley was unconscious, but he moaned.

It was enough. Mingo motioned Schrader toward the window. He clambered out and pulled at Mingo, to help him. They took off their masks; Mingo took the shotgun, and never having said a thing they went their separate ways.

Schrader stayed in the shadows on the way to the car, and when he got behind the wheel, he was shaking and fumbling for the keys. He saw Ricky Lopez pull quietly from the lot. Mingo was in the back seat.

The Fiat started and Schrader turned around in the street, still shaking, and gripping the wheel hard. He missed a gear. At a stoplight, watching a car in the mirror, he clutched too quickly and the car jumped and died.

Steady. Don't muff it now!

He drove away. *Slow, go slowly*. He went straight to the club. The wind through the car window was fine, and blew the smell of sweat and fear away. The alley was dark behind the Red Duke. He stripped the coveralls and sweat shirt, rolled them up with the mask and tennis shoes, took a bag and stuffed them in it. A half block away he knew there was a dumpster. He hurried through the alley, tossed the bag inside and walked back. It was quiet, and he saw no one.

The music blared when Schrader unlocked the back door,

carrying the fruit, and trying his best to look bored. He had been gone forty minutes.

"Long line," he remarked to Christian, who was busy making drinks.

She shrugged. "Didn't even miss you. I like tending bar."

Schrader glanced at the sink. "Now I have to wash your glasses."

"Couldn't keep up with those, too," she giggled. "I've been drinking my mistakes."

Good, he thought, that's perfect. "I'll take over, honey. Thank you." And he went to work as calmly as he could, realizing gleefully that Christian was true to form. She was young and carefree and she never glanced at the clock. Ten minutes or forty was all the same to her. The others would be hazy about his absence; they were busy on the floor.

Schrader turned around, rang open the register, put the receipt for fruit in the till, and drew out four dollars and twenty-eight cents. *So let them prove it*, he thought.

There was nothing more to do but wait for the heat they knew would come.

17

The lights flickered dimly, constantly, as if with calculated meanness, bouncing the glare from the smudged walls with a flatness that wearied the eyes. The corridor was like a tomb. The man across from Schrader stared heavily at the flyspeck next to his head, or perhaps it was a spot of blood from some unknown turmoil. The walls knew the story but they were mute.

Beside Schrader, a down-and-out kid with the soles taped to his shoes tried hard to keep awake. Finally he curled up pathetically on the bench, his feet brushing David's trousers. He mumbled something.

Jail is a rotten place.

Not that he was locked away. Schrader had been questioned by two detectives for an hour, and then told to wait in the hall. If he glanced to his left he saw the bars. No, he wasn't locked up, but it was jail enough.

He'd seen or heard nothing of Mingo.

A uniformed sergeant shuffled slowly down the hall. His stomach spilled over his belt and his shoes were scruffy.

"Schrader!"

"That's me."

"Come with me, mister." At the desk he returned Schrader's wallet, belt, keys and pocketknife. "Sign this," the sergeant told him.

First Schrader counted the bills in his wallet, then he signed his chit. In the front of the police station there was more light and cleaner air, there were busy, righteous workers and proper secretaries doing respectable jobs. He was not one of them and they looked at him warily.

He was going out the door when someone called to him. It was Lieutenant Logan. The lieutenant walked up and took Schrader familiarly by the arm. "What the hell's going on, son?"

"That's what I'd like to know, Lieutenant." Schrader decided to play it to the hilt. "I was walking into the club when they arrested me. I wasn't booked or charged or given a phone call. I'm goddamned mad!"

"Everyone's uptight about the Manley case," Logan shrugged. "We're just taking care of our own. Nothing personal."

"Are you working on the case?"

"No. Not my department. I know they've hauled in a bunch of suspects though. You just got caught up in a general dragnet."

Schrader did not believe it was as casual a thing as that. Manley or Quigley had certainly said something about them. They were definitely suspects.

"Come on into the office," Lieutenant Logan said, smiling.

Schrader pulled his arm free. "Not on your life. I'm not going back in there. And you can grin this away if you want, but I'm thinking about getting my lawyer."

"Who's that?"

"Brady Coleman," said Schrader, off the cuff.

Logan chuckled like Santa Claus. "Birds of a feather, all right."

"Go ahead and laugh. Brady will take my false arrest case for *migas* down at Cisco's!"

"Take it easy, David. I know Brady. He's a good ol' boy, and I know about Mingo Calderone and John Kniffin and a lot of you fellas. You've all been active for a long time. You're no strangers to me even if I've only met a few of you."

"We *were* active, Lieutenant. We haven't ruffled anyone in a long time. All I know about Manley is that he questioned me and Mingo one night. And he wasn't very polite, either!"

Logan wagged a finger. "You shouldn't admit a motive to a police officer."

"Cut out the good guy, bad guy stuff. Your two buddies in back were comic book hard-cases, and now here you are like Captain Kangaroo."

Logan laughed at that. He was a good-natured sort. "Will you at least talk to me out on the street?"

Schrader relaxed. "Sure," he replied, and followed Logan outside, knowing he had something Logan wanted. They walked up the street toward the flea markets.

"Have you seen our junk man again?" Logan asked.

Schrader looked at the lieutenant from the sides of his eyes. If Logan was stringing him along, why not return the measure?

"You don't expect me to help you now," Schrader answered.

"David, it was only a general dragnet," Logan told him again, looking exasperated. "You'd had some contact with Manley recently, so they hauled you in. That's how we catch our crooks sometimes. Think of your job and Connors—"

"I'm giving Connors two weeks notice," Schrader cut in. "I don't give a damn about his club or your drug bust."

"At least help me put away a couple of junk dealers. I know you care about youngsters on the street."

"Junk dealers!" Schrader spat, stopping on the corner and turning on him. "Why don't you check out your own goddamn cops!"

Logan eyed him closely. "What do you mean, son?"

"I mean, Mingo Calderone is a damned hero! That's what I mean! He was fighting for his country when Manley was playing circle jerk in junior high. He was strung out for a little while, but he hasn't touched the stuff in years. So why is Manley throwing it in his face now? Eh? After all that time, why is Manley—who has enough to do—why is he suddenly harrassing Mingo about heroin?"

The lieutenant arched his brows. "Why do *you* think?"

"I think he's shaking down small time pushers, that's what I think. And hookers and anyone else. I think he and Quigley are stopping high school kids for booze and pot, and letting them go for whatever is in their pockets. I've heard some street talk. I think he's a bad cop who gives you *all* a black eye." It was a mouthful, and Schrader had gotten angry again. He jammed his hands in his pockets and glared at the street.

Logan said nothing for a moment. Schrader had raised his voice and passersby looked at them oddly. Finally, the lieutenant said: "You help me out with this, I'll see what I can do. Maybe they'll lay off you and Mingo."

"Oh yeah? I thought you weren't on the case."

"I'm not. But I'm the senior lieutenant on the force. Now will you help me out? You might keep some kid off the junk. Your buddy Mingo would help."

Schrader looked at him, but couldn't make him out. *Was he sincere? How do I know that he isn't also investigating the Manley case? That he won't take my help with one hand and lock me away with the other?*

"All right," Schrader said. "I'll help if I can. But it better come to fruit quickly."

"So you haven't seen the junk man?" Logan asked again.

"No."

"What about Rita? Has she done anything unusual?"

"Not that I can tell."

"Wasn't she gone Tuesday night?" Logan asked.

"She told me she was sick," he answered, trying to hide his surprise. *Were they watching the club after all?*

"Do you have any ideas where she was, or who she was with?"

"No, I sure don't, Lieutenant," he replied, thinking *Damn you Eddie Malone!*

"Just keep a sharp eye for me, David. That's all I ask. This Darnell woman is only one little punk, but she might be in a position to put a lot of junk on our streets."

"Okay, Lieutenant. Sorry I blew off steam." They shook hands. "How's the wife, anyway?"

"She's fine. I'll tell her you asked. That nephew of ours has straightened out. Gave up on the clergy and joined the Navy. You call me now, eh?"

"Yes sir. Take it easy."

Logan walked back to the station, and Schrader looked around for a cab, caught one on the run and gave the address.

When the cabbie pulled to a stop and he paid him off, he could hear them arguing from the street. Rather, he could hear Adelita. This was the hardest part for Mingo, he knew. He walked across the porch and let himself in.

"You!" Adelita yelled, pointing at Schrader sharply. "I don't know what to say to you! Doing a thing like that without a word to me! As if I didn't matter! You think I could trust one of you!"

Schrader saw she'd been crying, but she was too angry for that then. Her eyes flashed with betrayal.

"Baby, don't get all worked up again," Mingo said, his hands raised in defense. "The thing is done; there's no backing out; now we just sit cool and—"

"Sit cool! You crazy Mexican! I'm having a baby in eight weeks and instead of enjoying my pregnancy, I'll be worrying about her dumb father going to jail because he had to play marine again! Sit cool, you say! *Te sentaras tranquilo en prision por un largo tiempo!*"

"No one's going to prison," Mingo said. "And we weren't playing marine. It was serious business, Adelita. They can't push us around like we were nothing!"

"Listen, you two," Schrader cut in, "at least keep your voices down. You don't know who—"

"Shut up!" Adelita snapped. "You just stand there and keep quiet! I know about Mingo and his anarchistic sense of justice. You, at least, should have steered him right!"

Schrader shut his mouth quickly enough, but looked nervously past the curtains to the street. The effect of that made Adelita lower her voice, but her scorn was heavy.

"Oh great! Now we're peeking out the windows like the old days. Maybe we can join hands and sing a song."

"You wouldn't remember any of the words," Mingo told her.

"Oh I wouldn't, eh?" It stung her. "I'm just a pregnant, middle-class wife now, right? I don't understand my revolutionary husband. Just excuse her, boys, that's what happens to women! Damn you, Mingo Calderone! Did you ever see me flinch? Did I ever run away? Just who was it who kicked that deputy in Killeen, anyway? You all had your damned hands in your pockets, and I stood up for myself!"

"Then you understand, baby—" Mingo began.

"I understand all right," Adelita continued, taking a deep breath to still her trembling. "I understand that I'm a different woman now, older, and I'm going to be a mother. You're different, too, Mingo. We're not fighting the war against the system anymore. How could you not think of the baby?" And with that her arms dropped to her sides and she sagged, anger spent, her fright showing as the color left her face.

Mingo stepped to her quickly and she let him hold her.

"It was for the baby," he said gently. "I don't know how to make you understand. But it was for the baby. And you. And the other children we'll have. They'll learn to be proud and unafraid."

"You can't fight them, Mingo! Oh honey, don't you know we can't fight them. We have to compromise everyday. In spite of all your passion, the world will stay the same."

"Then we'll keep our own fences around us. Strong fences. Maybe the bastards will keep out. That's all I want! Leave us the hell alone!"

She sighed, and with her head on Mingo's shoulder she looked at Schrader and asked: "What are we going to do now, David?"

He could only shrug. "Wait it out, like Mingo says. My story must have held up, or they wouldn't have let me go. How about yours?"

"They kept me an hour or so, talked to Adelita here at the house."

"You know what he did?" Adelita asked, punching him only partly in play. "You know what he did?" She twisted his ear hard. "He came in last night and sits down in front of me—very seriously, get this—he says, 'Me and David just beat up a cop and you gotta tell 'em I've been with you all night!'" She was laughing by then. Schrader was laughing too.

"So I couldn't sleep," she continued, "dozed off about four-thirty and at seven they were knocking on the door. 'Mrs. Calderone, we'd like to talk to your husband.' "

"They must not have known you were at Jessie's," Mingo said. "Otherwise they'd have picked you up earlier. It was on all the local news last night. An on-the-spot report right there at the cafe."

"Logan told me they've hauled in a lot of suspects."

"You saw him?"

"Yeah. He still wants me to help him. And he's acting like it doesn't mean much that we were hauled in."

"What's all this?" Adelita asked.

"You can tell her, Mingo. I'd better call Jessie at the club." Schrader walked to the kitchen and used the phone. Jessie was working the bar for him. She told him what she could over the noise of the jukebox. When he returned to the living room, they were sitting on the couch. "Jessie said the police questioned each of the girls. They took the receipt for lemon and limes; they'll talk to the clerk at the grocers."

"That could be a weak spot," Mingo said.

"I doubt it. It was busy that afternoon. I picked a new cashier that looked pretty flustered. If he remembers my face, he won't remember the time of day."

"Are you going to tell Jessie the truth?" Adelita asked.

"I don't know what to do," Schrader admitted. "It's probably best that she not know."

"You're right," Mingo said. "The fewer who know, the better."

"Wait a minute!" Adelita objected. "You mean, you used her car and slept in her bed and you're still going to lie to her?"

Schrader was reminded then of a talk he'd had with Jessie about Leo Marconi. They hadn't told Adelita about his death. Mingo wanted to wait until after the baby came. *What is it we're protecting these women from, anyway? Themselves?*

He felt a little ashamed. "I'll tell her Adelita. I promise. But now for another problem."

"What's that?" Mingo asked.

Schrader looked at Adelita questioningly.

"Oh no, you two! No more secrets from me!"

He nodded. "It's about Eddie and Rita. I had to lie to the lieutenant today, to cover for Eddie. That dog won't hurt very long."

"No kidding! He'll have to keep his dick in his pants."

"Who? Eddie Malone?" Adelita scoffed. "That boy thinks with his glands."

"Next time he's in town, I'll have to tell him about Rita."

"Yeah," Mingo shook his head, "and there goes Logan's drug bust and his good will, too. That could have been important to you."

"That's dumb," Adelita told them. "If he's going to run and tell that woman she's under surveillance, then don't tell Eddie."

"And if the cops get a fix on his truckloads of weed, what then?" Schrader asked. "What if he's busted?"

"Wait a minute," Mingo said. "Hear me out. Let's just go to Eddie and lay out this thing about Manley. Let him know we're in a pickle, tell him that Logan's connection is important to us. He won't say anything to the broad."

Adelita looked at Schrader doubtfully.

"Like you said, Mingo. The fewer who know, the better."

"Oh come on, David. This is Eddie Malone we're talking about. Sure he likes the ladies, but we're more important to him than some chippie out of a bar."

"You say she's good-looking?" Adelita asked.

Schrader nodded glumly. "She's pretty hot stuff."

"Then I wouldn't risk it," Adelita told him.

Mingo looked at them both as if they were crazy. In his mind, every brother was trustworthy.

"I'm sorry, Mingo, I'm more vulnerable to her than you. If Eddie breathed a word about Manley, she'd have something on me. That wouldn't be comfortable. I trust Eddie's good heart, but not his mouth."

"All right," Mingo gave in. "We won't say anything to him. But because you're being paranoid, you're going to lose a valuable contact with Logan."

"You're both making a mistake," Adelita said. "But maybe it's academic. Maybe you'll get the goods on this woman before Eddie returns from Washington."

Mingo laughed. "Or maybe Eddie will find something he likes better in San Antone."

Schrader didn't see the humor. Eddie was his brother, all right. But he did not like his fate dangling from Malone's libido. He didn't like that at all.

Jessie went home worried—another visit by police had given her the jumps. Now that she knew the truth, it became aiding and abetting. For a few days the paper ran pictures of Manley's swollen and bloody face—successively farther from front page—hinting once that the job was mob work.

The pictures of the cop were not pleasant, and for a few days Schrader let Jessie be. She had seen a new side of him, a frightening side. But, before she left that afternoon, the bar quiet, with happy hour just begun, her face brightened, and she kissed him with a sudden warmth.

"Do you want to see me tonight, David?"

"Just say the word."

She smiled secretively. "Hurry home, then. Take a taxi. I'll be at your place."

"If I can't get a cab I'll run all the way."

"Don't wear yourself out."

He was whistling after she left, wiping the bartop.

"My, my. Look how happy this boy be!"

"Hey, Lilah! Give us a smile, Black Beauty."

"Sure. And you give me two martinis, straight up, very dry."

"You got it. Say, push these clowns into their second drinks, eh? I don't want a rush at the end of happy hour."

"Okay; pour that extra on the side. I'll take it to them."

"Big tippers?"

"They got the look, honey. By the way, you heard about the detectives coming back here?"

"Jessie mentioned it. She's worried they'll make trouble for me. But they got nothing to go on, Lilah."

"Sure, David. They got nothing 'cause you wouldn't do a thing like that. But I think we should have a talk just the same."

He put the martinis on her tray. "When?"

"Let me handle these drinks. Then we can go to the office."

When he called Christian to tend the bar, she put her freckled face close and straightened his collar, smoothed his shirt. "We're watching out for you, David."

Schrader bent over, ducked under the bar to the other side, and followed Lilah down the hallway, trying to be a good sport, trying not to leer as she swayed. She sat on the couch in the office and crossed her legs. He leaned against the wall.

"Don't think I'm being nosy, David. None of us believe this stuff about the cop. These detectives just trying to flush a rabbit out of the brush!"

"Yeah. Sure."

"But loose talk could hurt a man, right?"

"I suppose. Loose talk to the wrong people."

"You watch out for Rita. You hear me? Be specially nice to her. Don't let any slips out your mouth. Last couple days, in the dressing room, she's been flappin' her gums. Asking too many questions about the night the cop was hit. Asking like she's telling, you know? Like she doesn't really care about the answers. But she cares. Don't let her get something on you!"

"I've got nothing to hide," he shrugged.

"Okay, sugar. That's fine. That's your business. Me and Christian and Holly and April Mae just keep our mouths hushed. We want you to know that."

"Thanks for worrying," he winked, trying to grin it away.

Lilah preened and stretched, not to tease, just the unconscious gesture of a working girl. "You and Jessie okay again?"

"We were always okay."

"Mmm hmmm. If you say so. You know, a gal like Jessie might be nervous 'bout a man who could hurt some one like the cop was hit. She's worked the bars a long time, sure, but she never sold herself to it. She ain't as thick-skinned as the rest of us, honey."

"Can I go now, teacher?"

She laughed musically. "After you write on the board, fifty times, don't trust Rita! Don't trust Rita!"

He reached and she took his hand and he pulled her to her feet.

She flashed her strong white teeth and tossed her head, the sleek filly of a roadside-tumble friend. He watched her ripple down the hall and tried to think of Jessie.

It was a great day to picnic: days before, a Caribbean storm had brought warm rain and balmy weather, taunting November. Mingo's car was packed. The trunk seemed to bulge

with opulence, enough food and drink for a squad. There was
the last minute disorder common among humans.

"Who's driving?" Mingo hollered.

The women looked up, then back at each other. "Do you
want to sit in front or in back?"

"Let's sit in back. We can talk."

"You drive, Mingo. Don't speed on those curves."

"Can you fit in back, mama?"

Adelita groaned getting in. Schrader held her hand to ease
her back as, crayfishing, she squeezed in place.

"You're getting huge," he said innocently, and saw her
blush. "I mean your stomach, honey, your—whatever it is.
Not the rest of you! Honest!"

"I'm a sow!" she blurted.

"No you're not. You look great, kid. I only meant the baby
was getting big—help me out, Jessie."

"Oh no. I do my own hoof from mouth extractions."

Mingo grinned, turning around in the seat, all of them in
the car. "Don't lay that trip on us, Adelita. I watched you eat
two pastries at breakfast."

"Oh hush! We'll never get there if you keep yakking."

They lost Austin quickly, driving west. Few cities disappear so fast—around a couple curves, over a few hills and
it is gone. But the suburbs have sprawled in ranchy Texas
fashion, landscaped just so, bringing shopping centers where
Comanches once roamed.

Soon enough they had driven beyond the suburban jumble, the hillsides free of houses and thick with wild Texas brush.
Adelita's *abuelo* owned a small ranch on the Pedernales River.
He was a fine old man, still spry at seventy, and the son of a
rebel Villa rider—or so they said—a man who had liked the
loot in Texas so much, he had brought his whole family.

They were driving the rim of a great basin, an expanse of
Hill Country that seemed to range forever; warm wind came
through the open windows; Mingo and Schrader drank beer.
Mingo was quiet. It suited David. The girls were laughing,
Adelita too hard, each of them aware of the underlying strain.

They had not guessed the extent of the pressure. Surely
a session or two with detectives would be the end of it. Their
alibis were solid. They knew Manley had enemies. Most of all,
they thought they had a hidden ace: lack of motive. Manley

and Quigley knew they had beaten Mingo senseless, but who could they tell? Mingo's and Schrader's motive remained obscure. Yet they were generally suspect. Adelita heard talk from the neighbors about quizzical police. Curious merchants pried her. The padre stopped for a visit, and her mother wanted to know what to tell the family. That was the pressure that made Mingo squirm—the little ripples he had not foreseen. Still, he was a man who seldom voiced regrets.

"Oh look!" A herd of deer poised by the roadside suddenly burst into motion, the buck shaking his horns; they ran, and disappeared over a ridge.

"Be a late rut," Mingo told Schrader. "The weather's too warm for the bucks to get their blood up." He began to slow the car, finally turning left onto a narrow dirt lane cut through a scruboak flat, the brush very dense. Now and again the bottom dragged and the car lurched and bounced. Adelita hugged herself and leaned into Jessie, who put her arm around her.

"Ugh! How much farther?"

"The next cattle guard."

They came suddenly to rough open pasture dotted with oaks and elms. As they crossed the last cattle guard they could see the broken range ending at a chasm, where it disappeared, and then the taller bluffs showed on the other side of the river.

"This is gorgeous!" Jessie exclaimed.

"The old man has three hundred acres," Mingo told her. "Maybe a half mile of it runs along the Pedernales. The cattle aren't his, though. The place is a family campground now."

When all the leaves have dropped along the Missouri River, autumn has just come to the Hill Country. Elm, blackjack, and sumac gleamed a tangled riot of colors. The wine-colored fruit of prickly pear cactus shone like rubies. Once out of the car, they could almost feel the land yawn and stretch into slumber, the diffused light of fall casting a sleepy haze.

"Mmmm. Smell the juniper?"

The four of them walked to the rim of the valley and watched the river, perhaps a quarter mile below. It shone blue-green, a mix of cedar and sky, darkening from current to pool, rippling white over short rapids. It curved away, cutting steeper bluffs opposite them, as much canyon as valley—gentler slopes here, limestone cliffs there.

They had the picnic beneath a cluster of elms and cotton-woods, at the very rim, on a carpet of yellow leaves. It was already past noon. When the wine was opened the afternoon began to flow like the eddies in the river: rapids of laughter, pools of thought, long tumbling stretches of talk.

"No more wine, David. Just one glass to relax."

"Nice to see you being careful, Adelita."

"Why take a chance with the baby?"

"You're so right," Jessie told her. "A friend of mine drank carelessly all through her pregnancy. Her baby was born lame and deaf in one ear."

Adelita shuddered. "How could a mother forgive herself?"

"Some don't know any better."

"Nonsense. There's common sense, you know."

Schrader was staring down the valley, remembering the woman they had seen miscarry in some hamlet west of Danang. Her pregnancy was quite advanced and the corpsman was working madly to induce the fetus to pass, to save the woman. She was screaming and she was very afraid. They had a patrol to tend. Mingo left one of his riflemen with the corpsman, and they had moved on. Later, the headman told them the woman had come from farther inland, from a hamlet recently sprayed with defoliants.

"Common sense doesn't do much good," Schrader scoffed, "when you're up against something unnatural. Modern poisons are—"

He saw them staring at him, puzzled. The conversation had moved on while he was lost in thought.

"What's that?"

Am I crazy, he thought, *bringing this up to Adelita?* "It's nothing, really. Hunger is making me senile."

Mingo slapped his belly. "*Sí! Mi barriga* is talking to me!"

"Then let's eat!"

There was a bustle as they hurried to lay out the picnic. It was a small feast. The outdoors keened their tastes. They sat there, closet Neanderthals, gorging themselves. Only Adelita showed restraint, still smarting from the crack about two pastries. When they finished and had packed the remains, the sun lay a handsbreadth above the hills. To the north they could discern the line of a cold front, deeper blue and domed, coming to them on the wind.

"It's getting chilly," Adelita said, putting on her sweater. "I love this time of year. Maybe we can have a fire? *Que pensas, caballeros?*"

"Sure, baby. In a jiffy."

Fallen wood lay all around the pasture. Mingo and Schrader began to shuttle armloads, ranging farther and farther from the camp, building a huge pile. Cattle nosed about curiously, eyeing them while keeping distance, calves running quickly to their mothers showing sidewise whites of wild eyes.

Mingo whistled Schrader's attention. "Come over here!" he called.

Schrader kicked disgustedly at a cedar stump too tenacious to uproot, breathing hard, feeling his face flush.

As he approached, Mingo said: "There's oak layin' everywhere, man."

"Cedar makes a sweet fire."

"When you throw up your lunch, will that be sweet enough?"

"Hell, we got plenty wood already."

"Come look at this." Mingo pointed behind a cluster of prickly pear.

There lay a big pile of cow pies, dry but still dark with humus, and they were crowned with bronze-capped mushrooms, ivory edged, reflecting the slanting sunlight like tiny faerie shields.

"The right stuff, no?" Mingo asked.

"*Si! Es cierto!* I haven't seen any of these in years! You know, if it was early in the day and I hadn't just stuffed my gut, I'd eat one right now."

Mingo shrugged. "Pick 'em and let 'em dry. Save them for another time."

"You want some, don't you?"

"Naw. I better not." Mingo looked at them wistfully. "If I pull anymore stunts, Adelita might throw me out in the street."

After the fire was going strong, while the sun was setting, Jessie and Schrader slipped and scrambled down the valley slope to the river. There, it was more deeply dusk and cooler, and the water tumbled musically. The hills and ridges were purpling with shadow on one side, shining a last caliche glimmer on the other.

They left Adelita and Mingo cuddling by the fire. Sometimes Schrader could watch them and it all seemed so easy: the love, the hope, the life they planned together. Solitude seems to feed itself, though, and lonely men build pride beyond measure. It keeps the finest things at bay.

"Wouldn't it be great to have some land like this?" Jessie asked, breaking the easy silence. "To have a little cottage and a garden, that sort of thing?"

David smiled at her, his thoughts going to home. His father and brother would be tucking in the farm for winter. Winter graze would be ankle high, the only green in a somber landscape of stubbled fields and barren hardwoods. The ponds would be freezing over and the echoes from the rolling hills would ring sharply on the crisp air. "Sure, Jessie. I'd like to have some land like this."

"I'll bet it could be farmed if some one knew how."

"Naw! This is ranch country."

"But you've said yourself that these bottomlands could be row cropped."

David chuckled kindly. "You mean tomatoes and leeks for the Austin organic set?"

Jessie poked him. "Don't tease me. Couldn't you be a farmer again?"

"It takes a lot of money to get started."

"That's not answering the question."

"Maybe you'd like to come home with me, Jessie. You can meet my mother and see for yourself the kind of commitment it takes. It can be a good life, but it takes everything you've got."

"So you could never farm again? Is that what you're so evasively saying?"

Schrader remembered the sleek stock and high yielding fields that were his father's pride. American farmers fed the world, he would boast. And David remembered Li's great bull shuddering spastically when he shot it; and he remembered the shameful waste at Ap Do, and the farmers they had ruined. Runty little shit farmers slopping in the mud.

Schrader nodded. "That's what I'm saying, kid. I don't have the heart for it anymore."

Knowing what had passed at Ap Do, Jessie could only smile sadly. Once again, the war seemed to steal a chance from them. As the path widened she measured her stride to his, taking David's arm as they stepped along a broad grassy bank. The river sighed a tumbling song. "Will you really take me home?" she finally asked.

"Of course, I will . . . My mother will be beside herself. I've never brought a girl home before . . . I had a halfway sweetheart when I was in Nam, a girl named Becky Chaffee, but she was married before I got out of the Corps. I lived at home for awhile after that, while I tried my luck at college, but I couldn't get on with the local girls anymore . . . One of the little nits actually asked me how many Commies I killed. Shouldn't blame her though, should I? The hype was everywhere. Everybody knew all about the war, second hand . . . Anyway, that's how come you'll be the first girl I ever brought home."

"I'm thirty-two, David. I've worked the bars for ten years and I can't remember some of the men I've slept with. I may not be quite the girl your mother's been expecting."

"She'll love you," Schrader replied. "You'll have the old man in the palm of your hand, no time flat . . . Something tells me, with you around, he and I will get along better."

"Do you fight?"

"No. We grumble. Mom's in the middle, don't you know; and if it gets unbearable, one of us finds something to do elsewhere . . . It's time for that to change, Jessie. Christ! I haven't been home in three years."

"Oh, David," she laughed, half-sadly, "you're a wreck. A two hundred pound chunk of bone and muscle careening around through life, with no plan and no ties and that's fine if that's how you really want to live. But don't you think all this effort should have some reward?"

"Like a little security?"

"If that's not too middle-classed a word for you," Jessie told him. "I guess keeping up with your family is too heavy a responsibility."

"You have a mother's sensitivity."

"Shouldn't I have?"

"Like I said," Schrader grinned. "Mom will love you."

"And while I'm bitching," Jessie teased, shaking her finger, "don't be condescending when I talk about selling leeks and tomatoes! Adelita and I have some ideas, and you can be a part of them or not. So there."

"So she's told you about the old man giving her a piece of this land, when the baby is born. That will be great for them."

"Unless your recent antics squelched it."

"Not much chance, knowing the old Senor. Adelita is his favorite grandchild. Mingo is all aces with him. The old man himself was pretty outspoken when he was younger. He grew up in the days when cops did what they wanted to Mexicans. I don't think he'd be alarmed 'cause Mingo put a cop in the hospital. Hell, he didn't kill the sucker."

"Is that the line you draw, David?"

"No. Honestly it's not, honey. Violence is a poor response. Hell, the war taught us that. But sometimes it's the only response that gets attention . . . It felt so good! I have to tell you it felt *good*!"

She glanced at him pensively. "A last hurrah, I hope?"

"That's right. I'm losing my running buddy to a wee little tot."

"Oh, David, why didn't you stop him? I haven't rebuked you, and I don't mean to now, but surely you could have stopped Mingo from risking all this?"

"How?"

"By refusing to help."

Schrader shook his head. "He has other buddies. Mingo would have cut me out of it, and done it anyway. And I'm the one who knows him best. Nobody could have backed him up as well."

"You might have told Adelita. That would have stopped it."

"I couldn't do that. Mingo trusts me."

"The cheek of it amazes me. The arrogance, really."

"I thought we could get away with it, Jessie. Damn, we are getting away with it! This will blow over soon enough. There were no witnesses, no proof. Worse crimes than that go unsolved all the time."

She sighed and leaned into him, as they paused on the river bank. "I want things back to normal, please. You'll go along with that, won't you?"

He nodded and kissed her, and they turned to walk back.

Sunset was barely a glow. The worn path seemed to blend with the river bank as the light failed. A gust of wind whistled and moaned down the valley, an owl swooped from a cotton-wood. Around a bend they saw the flicker of fire at the crest of the slope, and Jessie found the goat trail that led to the top. With a scurrying effort, and pulling and laughing, they reached the top.

"Oh, when I can do that again!" Adelita wailed.

"Phew!"

Jessie sat by the fire and rubbed her arms. The wind had taken a chill. Schrader wrapped a blanket about her and knelt and stroked her hair. It felt good to have her near, with the flames and the velvet darkness. They spent the pile of wood and let the fire burn down to embers, huddling in blankets against the cold that blew so cleanly. It seemed to blow through the heart of him. Staring at the fire he could feel no heat inside, only the warmth of the woman beside him, and he pulled her closer as if to trade some of that warmth for his burden.

It's such an unfair trade that women make.

It was late one evening at the Red Duke when the phone rang.

". . . can't hear. Who's this?"

The music was blaring. Connors had turned it up again.

"WHO? EDDIE! HOLD ON, MAN." Schrader reached beneath the bar and reduced the volume, waving impatiently at Connors's drunken objections.

"Hey, Eddie! Nice to hear from you. You had good luck, eh . . . Don't Eddie, don't talk over this line . . . Yeah, that's right. You never know . . . Sure, Mingo's fine. Yeah, there's been some trouble. How did you hear about that? Rita? Yeah, she's here. When you coming back? I got something to tell you. It's important, Eddie . . . Oh yeah? For Chrissake, see Mingo this time . . . Okay, I'll get her for you. Hold on a sec."

Rita had her tongue in a senator's mouth. Schrader thought he was copping a feel, but his view was blocked. He called to her.

"Oh honey!" she squealed into the phone, and Schrader moved to the other end of the bar. Connors told him a sorry racist joke; then a pretty good sodomy joke, about the man who came to inseminate the old farmer's cow. Schrader had heard it told better and Connors muffed the punch line, but David laughed with him just the same. Connors was feeling low because his ex-wife's lawyer was dragging him over the coals.

"Ooooeee!" Rita whooped as she hung up the phone. "Guess what, David honey?"

A warning began to sound dully in his head. "What?"

"Eddie's flying me to Philly for the weekend. Friday night flight." She tickled Connors under the chin. "I'll need to get off work early, okay? But I'll be on time Monday night. Promise."

Connors leered a half smile at her. "Rub some sweat on me, baby . . ."

She slinked behind and put her arms around him, rubbed her breasts against his back, licked his ear. Connors eyes began to glaze. When she reached down below the bar level Connors stiffened suddenly and then relaxed, his lips going flaccid.

Schrader was drying glasses, trying to ignore them.

"Well boss, what do you say?" he heard Rita whisper throatily.

It took Connors a couple of heartbeats to find his voice. "You be here Monday night, hyah? Or it will take more than a little rubbin' to keep your job."

"You're a peach," she laughed as her eyes bit into him, and she pinched a welt on his cheek. Then she looked at Schrader.

"You'll have a great time, Rita. Philly's a good town."

"That's what I hear, lover. Eddie's flying back with me, you know."

"Oh? What's up?"

"Business," she winked, and turned jauntily back to her work.

Whose business, he wondered? His? Or theirs? What he had feared from the first time he had seen them together no longer seemed unlikely. It was snowballing. Standing behind the bar, watching Rita laugh and move her body from hands to hands, he began to feel a little helpless. Events were going to fall as they would, and his loyalties bound him.

When Connors called for another bourbon, Schrader joined him. They touched glasses and drank a toast to that plague of mankind — the unexpected.

* * *

Eddie was different when he came back with Rita. Schrader could see it right away. Malone's limp was pronounced again, and little lines of pain etched his face. The eyes that had been so bright only a few weeks before were starting to dull.

Malone and Mingo found Schrader at his house that Monday. Eddie was using his walking cane again.

"Don't you ever have to work?" Schrader joked to Mingo.

"Joe gave me some time off, when the hero here showed up." And he slapped Eddie on the back.

"Easy on the hero stuff," Eddie scoffed. "I pawned my purple heart. It bought me a bus ticket out of some little town. Don't remember where."

"The leg is acting up again, eh?" They were sitting around the kitchen table. Eddie tried to pass it off.

"It comes and goes, you know. The weather changes or maybe I ain't livin' as smart as I should, and it starts to ache again. There's some metal left in the bone. What do you got to drink?"

Schrader walked to the cabinet. "Got some pretty good bourbon and some very good tequila. How 'bout some tequila, *hombres*?"

"Right on."

"Just one for me," Mingo said. "I have to work."

"Come on!" Eddie joked. "Your father-in-law owns the damned company. Take some time off!"

"No, man. That's why I have to work harder. They've been good to me."

"A regular family man, eh?" Eddie laughed. "Aside from beating up cops, you're a paragon of virtue."

Schrader looked sharply at Mingo, who looked away guiltily.

"Some stunt you two pulled," Eddie was saying. "It makes me proud of you."

Schrader stepped to the table and poured a round of tequila. He was giving Mingo the hard eye, but Mingo still was not looking at him.

"Listen Eddie, I told Mingo that I didn't want you to know about Manley. It's nothing personal, so don't be offended. I want to keep it very secret."

"Hey! You know I'm cool!"

"Sure, David," Mingo added, glancing at him. "You know Eddie's okay. Hell, he asked me point blank if we did it. I couldn't lie to him!"

Mingo's like a kid sometimes. It's hard to stay mad at him. But Schrader felt a cold spot in his stomach. *Damn!*

"Here's to the old gang," Schrader toasted, and they drank the tequila down. It was in his mind then to tell Eddie about Logan.

"You ain't pissed, are you?" Mingo asked.

Schrader shook his head.

Eddie reached for the bottle. "Do you mind?"

"Help yourself. Don't you get a prescription for some pain killer?"

"I ran out. Rita's got something."

"Yeah," Schrader muttered. "I'll bet."

"What's that supposed to mean?"

"It means I'll bet she's got something. Any color pill you want. PCP. Heroin. How about heroin, Eddie? She got any of that?"

Eddie looked offended. "What are you talking about, David?"

Schrader watched him playing innocent and it made him angry. "I'm talking about that slut you're screwing. I'm talking about the trash I know she deals."

"You're a grand one to talk about sluts!" Eddie laughed harshly. "I never knew you to turn down a roll in the sack!"

Mingo was sitting between them nervously. He held up his hands in restraint. "Wait a minute! King's X! David, this ain't the way to tell him."

"Tell me what?" Eddie demanded.

Schrader picked up the tequila and poured a shot for Eddie and himself. "How do you feel about Rita?" he asked Malone.

Eddie looked resentful. "She's my girl now. I don't care what you think of her. She ain't as well-mannered as your girl, maybe. She ain't as educated as Adelita. But she's had a rough life. I don't like you calling her names."

"That's fair enough," Schrader told him. "I apologize. I've been helping to set her up for a drug bust."

That startled Malone. Schrader might have told him he'd joined the FBI.

Mingo shook his head. "I don't think that was the way to tell him, either."

"Why pretty it up?" Schrader shrugged. "There's a police lieutenant who's been pressuring me to help him. He knows Rita is dealing from the club. It seemed to me—knowing we might need some police good will—it seemed to be a good idea. Your girl's got all of Texas to deal her trash in. The club is my responsibility."

"My, my! What a fine little soldier!" Eddie's sarcasm was acid. "That's a great rationale, Schrader."

"Well then, forget the last part. It suffices to say that me and Mingo had plans, and the lieutenant fit in handily. And neither of us have any sympathy for junk dealers."

"So!" Eddie waved his arms loftily. "With all appropriate piety you decided to suck a cop's ass and sell Rita down the river!"

"That's right," Schrader admitted.

Mingo spoke up then. "Hey Eddie, this all changed when you started seeing her. We didn't know if you cared about her, and we didn't want the cops to get a line on you. So we're coming clean now. I was hoping, maybe, you'd keep it on the QT, but it doesn't look like you will."

"You bet your ass I won't! What the hell's got into you two, anyway? I can't believe you've turned into finks!"

Mingo looked like a friendly hound that had been kicked.

"We're *un*-finking right now," Mingo told him. "Tell your girl about this lieutenant—his name is Logan—and the matter is done with . . . But she'll still be hot whether David helps the cops or not. So you'll want to watch out for yourself."

"I can do that all right," Eddie spat. "What I can't do is figure out the change in the two of you." He shook his head sadly and got to his feet. "I need some fresh air."

"Where are you going?" Mingo asked.

"Just somewhere."

"Hell, you can't walk far with your leg hurting. Let me give you a ride."

"Just back off!" Eddie snapped at him. "Give me some space. This has been a heavy afternoon." And he limped determinedly out of the house.

Mingo looked forlorn. "This didn't turn out the way I thought," he said. "Maybe I ought to go after him."

"Let him stew. He'll get over it."

"I hate to think of him walking back to town."

"He'll go to a phone booth and call Rita. She'll pick him up."

"I think I screwed up," Mingo said. "I think he'll tell her all of it."

"We'd better plan on it, brother. And we'd better not plan on any support from Eddie."

"What are you thinking?" Mingo asked.

"Nothing yet," Schrader lied. "Don't worry about Rita. I can handle her, Eddie or no . . ." He wanted to change the subject. "You've got enough to think about, Mingo. What are you going to name my goddaughter, anyway?"

Mingo laughed and shook his head. "We still can't make up our minds. It's either Daniela Marie, or Donna Elena. If the baby is a boy, we're just going to call him 'boy'."

Schrader tried to keep the talk light, but his brain was churning. Mingo stayed awhile longer but returned eventually to his job and Schrader sat there and turned the prospects in his mind. *If Eddie tells Rita that we beat up the cop, our prospects don't look real good.*

But then, neither will hers.

Rita was surly to Schrader for a couple of nights, snapping her call drinks and giving him mean looks. Eddie would come in at closing, keep to a back table, and say nothing to David, who felt awful. Schrader was beginning to feel like an informer, and was almost ready to apologize to Rita. It turned out that he did not have to.

After Schrader came to work Jessie had left him with a lingering kiss and a promise of a sweet evening. His life seemed to be settling down. The police investigation had slackened and David was hoping for an end to it.

Rita was late and Happy Hour was briskly busy when Eddie waltzed her into the club. She flounced past Schrader smiling just so, going to change her clothes, and Eddie sat at the bar.

"Enough being mad, eh?" Malone said, holding out his hand.

"Sure, brother," Schrader replied, "I never wanted to get in dutch with you."

"I know, man. And I appreciate your being up front about the pig lieutenant. You gave up a valuable contact. Maybe I can make it up to you."

"Forget it, Eddie. I was way off base."

"Still," Malone persisted, "when something of value is lost in a bargain, one gets restitution. We're all capitalists, right?"

Schrader laughed. "What a terrible admission for an old radical."

"Times change, David. The old spirit is down the drain. Who can feed the starving? Not us. Can we fight Big Business or the CIA? Shit no! They knocked the socks off us, never mind the big talk about stopping the war. We didn't stop a damned thing! The war wound down at its own pace, after every muck-sucker but *us* made a buck off it. Time for *us* to make some bucks, eh?"

David shrugged, wiping the bar clean. "Sure, Eddie, if that's what you want." He was suddenly becoming wary. "I'm not chasing dollars, though. Some good money would be nice, don't get me wrong. But it isn't what I'm looking for."

"Oh? Just what the hell are you looking for? I know what you want, David. You want to write the Great American Novel."

"Shut up, why don't you—"

Three of the girls came to the bar, calling for drink orders. As Schrader made the drinks, he felt Eddie watching, predator-like.

When the girls returned to the floor: "I can make you the money you need," Eddie told him. "You can take a year to write, to go somewhere inspiring, eh?"

"Are you crazy, man? Rita's hot! You can't pull off a deal with the cops sniffing around!"

Eddie nodded reassuringly. "There's a way. Believe me. You and Mingo aren't the only grunts in town. Maybe after work you'll hear me out?"

"It won't do any good," Schrader told him. "I'm not messing with heroin."

"Hey, David. Junkies are gonna be junkies, whether you deal the stuff or not. Nobody else making money is asking the ethics of it. You had ethics when you fought for your country. What the hell has it got you?"

"Lay off that line, goddamnit!"

"Just hear me out, David. For chrissake, I want some things for myself finally! We gotta take them, man. Ain't no Santa Claus, haven't you heard?"

David looked around wildly, the walls seeming to close on him. Eddie's face was a foot away, his dark eyes intense, his lips pressed into a hard line. Schrader could see enough suffering in that face for a dozen men.

He sighed wearily. "All right, Eddie. I'll listen."

"That's my old sarge!"

Rita was back on the floor. She came to the bar. "Two scotch sodas, rum 'n coke — You fellas making up?" She batted her eyes and smiled prettily.

"We're family," Schrader told her. "That's a hard act to break up."

"Oh, is it?" Rita smirked. "I never had much of a family, so I wouldn't know."

"Listen, Rita. I've been trying to think of you with more compassion, but it isn't easy. You don't have many virtues."

"At least I don't fink to the cops!" she flashed. And then, smiling again, "At least, I haven't yet."

The warning was implicit. Schrader set out her drinks, and she took them and turned away.

Hours later, Schrader locked up the club and made a bank deposit, then he followed them to Rita's house. Eddie was too chummy, Rita was altogether too nice. They drank coffee, and Schrader listened to Eddie's plan to pull off a heroin deal under the nose of the police. It was a pretty good scheme.

"There's no way, Eddie." David shook his head. "I won't do it, no matter how good your plans."

"We need you for this, man! It won't work without you as a decoy."

"So sorry," Schrader said quietly, his hands folded in his lap, feigning calm. But his mind was racing. He felt trapped.

Rita was stretched prone on the couch — a sleek and carnivorous mink — and Schrader could see what was coming. "With what we know about you," she purred, "it doesn't seem you have much choice."

"That's what I was waiting to hear," David told her, and he stood as if to leave.

Rita leaped from the couch and thrust her face close to

his. "Change your mind, sucker, or I go to the cops! They're hot to find the guys who beat up their boy." She looked hard and tough, a girl who rode the river.

Schrader turned cold as stone. "Do you understand what she's saying, Eddie? Do you understand that Mingo goes down with me?"

Eddie stood but avoided Schrader's eyes. "It's your own stubbornness, man. It wouldn't come to that if you helped us out." He looked at David, and he was someone David did not know. "I have to think about myself," Malone told him.

"So now you understand," Rita taunted, "family's not so hard to break up, after all."

"Neither are people, Rita." Schrader dipped his shoulder and brought up his fist hard into her belly. She crumpled with a gasp of pain. Eddie snarled and lunged at him but, slowed by his bad leg, there was time for Schrader to kick him hard on the knee. Really hard. Eddie screamed and crumpled to the floor, his face an agonized mask. David struck a roundhouse to Eddie's jaw and his head bounced—and he lay still.

David stood hunched over Malone for some seconds, his mind frozen, and his eyes wild. The expectation of betrayal had strung him taut as a bow, and he could see but one solution—one terrible way to keep his fractured life together, to keep Mingo from jail. He had to break Rita's spirit. He had to fill her with a fear she had never known. Or kill her. But then he would have to kill Eddie. And then there would be no end to it, except his own death. Seeing it in his mind's eye, Schrader looked a long way down a dark road, and he shuddered.

His face grim, Schrader cut cord from the drapes and bound Eddie's arms behind him. He gagged him, and used Eddie's belt to tie his legs.

Rita was catching her breath, her eyes flashing defiance but her mouth slack with fear. She was too weak from the punch to stand up, and it was easy for Schrader to tie her hands. Rita's windbreaker lay on the couch and Schrader ripped the sleeve off and gagged her roughly.

Think! he shouted to himself. *Be precise! What did you learn? Show the enemy no emotion. Evoke no anger, only terror.*

He propped Rita against the couch and touched her face

gently, but his eyes were cold. "You're a beautiful woman," he told her. "But your beauty is all you have. A fleeting thing, beauty—No? I talk like my friend Mingo, sometimes. He's rubbed off on me. We've gone through a lot together, and now you would put him in jail—"

Rita shook her head and mumbled through her gag.

"Sorry, kid. Too late." Schrader tied her legs with the shreds of the windbreaker, and stepped to the kitchen. He found a deep tub and began to fill it with water, turning the faucet full to make certain that Rita could hear the sound. Once, Schrader had watched as an Arvin captain had lined up captured Viet Cong along a water-filled ditch and ordered them drowned, one by one, until the captain had been given the information he sought. The first man had died horribly, his legs thrashing as two strong soldiers held his head beneath the water. The second man in line could not babble fast enough. Later, the captain had assured Schrader that nothing was more terrifying than the thought of being drowned. Now, Schrader remembered.

It was a ten gallon tub, and water sloshed as he carried it to the living room. A glint of understanding came to Rita and panic showed in her eyes. She kicked out with her legs, and tried to squirm away. She growled and cursed through the gag. Schrader grabbed her long black hair and slapped her face. He backhanded her, bringing blood to her cheek.

Stop it! came Schrader's own voice in his mind. *Stop! Be precise! Don't make her angry, make her afraid!*

Schrader took a deep, ragged breath and watched his hands shaking. Then he yanked Rita roughly to the tub and forced her head into the water. Schrader put all his weight into the effort, locking his knees about her, slowly counting to fifteen. She came up sputtering and coughing through the gag, choking on the water in her mouth. Schrader yanked the gag down around her neck and let her draw two sucking breaths, then plunged her head into the tub again. He counted to twenty and then let her breathe, and quickly dunked her again. Rita was in a panic and growing too weak to fight. Soon, all she could do was gasp for air.

David kept at it for a long and wearying hour. He held her submerged until her heart must have seemed to jump thumping out of her throat, her lungs pulling from her ribs and knotting into a cramped fist. Then he would let her breathe, just a little while, so she would not pass out, so she would think he was finished. Then David would dunk her again, so the blood pounding in her skull would seem to explode from her eardrums. He wanted her to feel it was a nightmare. He wanted her to feel it would go on forever.

When Eddie regained consciousness he tried to struggle free of his bonds. He made threatening noises through his gag. But as the torment continued Malone became curiously subdued. His face was pale and sweaty, and his leg hurt wretchedly.

"The joke of it is, Rita," David said to her once, while he let her breathe, "the joke of it is, that I'd be a first offender and in a couple of years I'd be out of prison. And then I'd come to get you." He talked to her calmly, as though they were having a pleasant lunch together. He felt the madness just beneath his skin. "And what's happening to you now, would seem like nothing. Because then I'd really hurt you."

Schrader smiled at her. He looked like the death's head. He pushed her face under the water, longer this time, thirty seconds, thirty-five . . . When Schrader let go, between the choking and gasping breaths, she started to weep like a frightened child. It was a pathetic noise. The shell of ice that had surrounded him was beginning to crack.

In her bedroom, Schrader found a hand mirror. He walked back, held her by the hair, pulled her head up.

"Look at yourself, Rita. Look there— What do you see? You're afraid to die. You're afraid to be ugly and scarred. You don't want to be ugly and scarred, do you?"

She shook her head spastically, still sobbing. David knew she must have had a hard life. Happy children, loved and reassured, seldom end up selling their bodies and losing their souls. David felt sorry for her, and sick at himself, and he knew it was time to be done with it.

"You won't go to the police, will you, Rita?" Again came the spastic, terrified shake of her head.

With an unseeming gentleness, Schrader lifted Rita and laid her on the couch. Then he knelt beside Malone.

"Hey, old friend. Each of us knows what the other can do, eh? You might come looking for me, it doesn't matter. We have friends in common. You don't want them to know what you've tried to do. Listen to me, Eddie. I'll keep quiet about this. You can believe me or not."

David patted him on the shoulder, looking one last time at the painful, soulful eyes that so many times had burned their way to Schrader's heart. "Be seeing you, Eddie."

He drove the Fiat to Jessie's. It was very late and the house was dark. When he unlocked the door he tossed her car keys on the floor. He shut the door and while he walked home he was still trembling, and wondering, could he have Jessie then? Would she want him to touch her? It had not been great sport beating up a woman. He felt no satisfaction. Yet he had no apologies to offer.

One night in his youth he had peered through a 'scope and had learned he could not kill a human being. Yet it was paramount he pull the trigger, so what he killed became a thing in his mind, not a man at all. Schrader learned in that instant how to reduce people to objects without souls. He did not ask for that knack, it just came to him. Kill a few times and the knack might come to you. You cannot unlearn it. You have to struggle with it everyday, struggle to see people within human bounds.

Something else happened to David Schrader.

They were somewhere outside Danang. Where ever they camped a bevy of peddlers followed, and for runners and deal- ers they hired children: *Hey, Marine! You shop-shop!* Cute kids, and they had nothing. Sometimes not even folks.

A couple of them cornered the market in Mingo and David's platoon: a wary, street-wise twelve-year-old and his kid brother, a little rascal not yet four who was everywhere getting into everything. They sort of adopted him. That was common enough. When the Marines pulled out, they'd give him a few boxes of rations and some money and wish him well.

One night the Viet Cong planted a mine near the camp gate. All along the road were makeshift store fronts and shel- ters. The first truck out of camp the next morning hit the mine. Schrader was eating the slop they served for breakfast, and the explosion jarred the entire camp. It was a big damned mine. It tossed the heavy truck a good one and tore up some marines inside.

Of course, they all ran like the blazes to help them.

It was a mess: twisted and smoking pieces of truck, flattened store-fronts, the awful odor and glisten on the ground of sprayed blood and flesh. You can't see a more miserable sight.

There were plenty of hands to help their own, to get the marines out of the truck and into the aid station. So Schrader began to look around in the rubble. The little orphan was there, lying under a makeshift tin roof. Something freaky had happened. A piece of his skull, like a grapefruit half, was torn away cleanly and lay in the dirt barely attached. But he was still alive. His eyes fluttered and he was moaning very softly. He looked at David, while his exposed brain shone and shook like jello.

There was an old flattened cardboard nearby. Schrader put the boy on it, careful with the fragment of skull, and hurried to the aid station. He knew somebody could save him, but the aid station was a madhouse with only three corpsmen. There weren't enough cots for the marines and there was a mad scramble to set more up.

David stood in a corner with the child in his arms and waited for someone to notice him. One of the corpsmen stepped over and glanced at the boy hurriedly.

"He's still alive, Doc! You can hear him cry! Look at his eyes!"

The corpsman barely looked at him and shook his head. "There's nothing I can do, Corporal." And he started to hurry away.

"Wait a second, Doc! There must be something you can do? At least till we put him on the chopper!"

The corpsman turned back to him. He was an old salt. "No gooks are going on that chopper. There's just enough room for our boys. And there's no time for him now . . . Here!" He tossed half a dozen syrettes of morphine onto the cardboard. "All we can do is put him out of his misery." And he turned and hurried to his other tasks.

Schrader could never recall how long he stood there with his mouth open, the boy moaning in his arms; but at some point he found himself outside kneeling in the white sand, over him. It looked so disgustingly obscene — his little body on the filthy cardboard — the image never left Schrader's mind. The boy was three years old. David knew in his heart they could have saved him, but he was only a gook kid.

One by one he emptied the morphine into him, his hands trembling badly, shuddering each time the soft flesh gave to the bite of the syrette. Gradually, the child's eyes ceased to flutter and the moaning stopped, and David felt one last spasm beneath his fingers.

He broke down. Schrader was a hardened trooper who always did his duty, but he had never expected to do anything like that. Mingo kept him drunk for two days.

Where were you on the 4th of July, 1966? What were you doing? It doesn't matter. You were there with him that day, you were looking over his shoulder. When David killed that child something shattered in him, some irretrievable image of himself, and he was never the same again.

Now Schrader could be easily blinded to what is human in people, to do them harm. He could brutalize a woman and not feel sorry.

None of us ever said we were sorry to him.

18

Schrader was wary about Eddie Malone when he went to work the next day. Malone might have shown up anywhere, and he was easily capable of revenge. Some part of Schrader's mind rejected that, however; he thought Eddie might also want a truce.

Schrader had noticed something about him the night before, bound and gagged like he was. Eddie did not care to see Schrader's regression. He had ghosts enough of his own and as he had watched Rita's torment, Schrader thought Eddie had begun to see himself in Schrader's situation. That situation went beyond anything he'd foreseen — as Schrader's own had done — and it had served to sober him some.

That was Schrader's hope, anyway. He wanted an end to the intrigue. *Funny*, he thought, *I'm thinking of a suitable lie for Jessie.*

She wasn't behind the bar. One of the day girls was there washing glasses.

"Where's Jessie?" Schrader asked.

"Something awful happened," the girl told him. "Rita came in all beat up. I think she wanted her paycheck. She's gone now, but Jessie is still in the office."

Schrader's heart sank.

Jessie was sitting quietly at her desk. She looked up when he opened the door, then quickly looked away.

"She told you?"

Jessie nodded and busied her hands with the ledger on the desk.

"I can explain."

"Can you? Can you really? A nice pat explanation that's going to make it seem like nothing's happened?" Her voice trembled.

"Rita's no damned good!" Schrader blurted. "Eddie told her what me and Mingo did. She was going to the cops! They were trying to blackmail me into helping them with a drug deal."

Jessie stone-faced him. "It doesn't matter what they were doing. It only matters what *you* did—, you react violently to everything!"

"Some people understand that best, Jessie. That's the kind of world that Eddie and Rita move in."

"It isn't my world!" Jessie cried. "I can't stand hitting and bleeding. I wasn't raised that way!" She put her hands to her face. "You move in and out of that world too easily, David. It frightens me."

"Jessie, I'd never treat you that way. I swear. I'd—"

"Please don't touch me."

"I'm sorry—I'm sorry. Just listen to me, please. It wasn't for me! I could stand a little time in jail but what about Mingo? I couldn't let them ruin his chances! The guy's come so far. They're having my godchild. That means something to me, a kid I could help raise, do nice things for instead of blowing them up! For God's sake, I couldn't let that bitch spoil all that!" He was talking as fast as he could, thinking he might make

her see the panic he'd felt the night before. If she could only
see the disgust that was swelling in him like rotten bile.

"Oh David . . ."

"Don't look at me like that! I don't want any pity. Can't
you see that I was cornered?" He sat in another chair and they
looked at each other across the small room.

She sighed deeply. "What I see is you putting yourself in
these corners, one after another. You beat up that policeman
without even considering taking the matter to a review board.
Oh, go ahead and scoff, but it *was* an alternative! And you
precipitated the whole affair the night you played tag with the
police. Don't you see, David? You've built a world around
yourself, with your own morals, your own judgments. And
when you try to plug into the real world, something always
short-circuits somewhere."

"Don't you think I want to fit in, Jessie?"

"No. I don't believe you do. You hold everything around
you in disdain."

"Not you."

"Not yet you don't, David. But we both know what fa-
miliarity breeds."

"I respect you, honey. You have to believe me!"

She shook her head. "Perhaps I'm making a mistake. But
I'm afraid of you now. Rita was a mess. She's a tough cookie
but you did something to her, something mean and cold, and
I don't want to guess what it was. I can't live with a man and
be afraid of him, too."

Schrader turned cold inside. "Is that your final word?"

She looked at him sadly. "I feel like I'm deserting you,
David."

He stood up brusquely. "Don't be foolish. We're hardly
bound to each other. I've a few things at your place. Maybe
you could put them in a sack for me." He walked stiffly from
the office and out the back door to the alley, angry again.
Always angry again, telling her in his mind that he didn't need
her, want her and who the hell did she think she was! The
anger did not make him feel any better; it just delayed the
realization that he was alone again.

When Schrader took over the bar, Jessie was already gone.

"Did you hear about Rita?" Christian asked. "She split."

"Where did she go?"

"Who knows?" Christian shrugged. "I think she's with that friend of yours. They must have had some trouble. Somebody beat her up."

"Did you talk with her?" Schrader asked.

"No. One of the day girls filled me in. The Margarita is straight up, babe."

"And the martini is on the rocks?"

"That's right," she answered. "You feeling okay?"

"I'm fine. Here's your drinks."

"You don't look so good."

"Mind your own damned business!" He was that way with everyone the rest of the night. He'd had his fill of them all: the club, the people, their empty prattle.

It was the usual crowd, milling around and grabbing at flesh, telling the same dumb jokes and obvious lies. Schrader looked at them and was disgusted, and he poisoned them good; poured heavy drinks the whole evening through, like some crazed alchemist, waiting to see which of them would turn into toads. Booze flowed like water. He scurried back and forth from the stores bringing *more, more! Let them drink*. And he sat back smugly, maliciously, watching each failed soul grope for whatever the alcohol promised. *Let them drink! They are the whole human race to me. Damn them all!*

But it was too pathetic even for Schrader. In the end it was their dehumanizing weaknesses that made them all the more human. Their hopeless dreams became his own.

Long before closing, he called half-a-fleet of cabs, collared the men two and three at a time, and eased them out to the taxis. He put all the girls in one cab and gave the driver a twenty, and saw the last of them. Then he locked himself in the club and closed out the register. He wrote Connors a note: I'VE TAKEN MY SALARY IN CASH. SORRY. I'VE HAD MY FILL OF THIS PLACE. He put the eighty-four dollars due him in his pocket, and the rest of the money and slips in the bank bag. He set the chairs, up-ended, on the tables, and washed the rest of the glasses and laid them out neatly.

There was a knock at the front door. Schrader thought it would be Connors, but it was Lieutenant Logan, and he wasn't exactly prepared to see Logan then.

"Closing up early, David?"

"Yeah. I, uh, thought I would. Business was slow."

"You going to let me in?"

"Sure, Lieutenant, come on in."

They walked to the back and Logan sat on a stool. Schrader busied himself with the glasses.

"Is Connors in?"

"No. I haven't seen him all night."

"Good. I wanted to talk to you alone."

"Oh really? What's up?" Schrader was trying to act as if he were not ill at ease, but he didn't know that he was succeeding.

"I was hoping you could tell me that, David. I was hoping you could tell me about—" and here he took out his notebook and squinted in the dim light, "about one Edward C. Malone, from Philadelphia, Pennsylvania. And I was hoping you could tell me about our deal."

Schrader set a bottle of good bourbon on the bar, with two glasses. "I haven't had one all night," he told the lieutenant. "Join me?"

Logan looked around secretively. "You won't tell the captain?"

Schrader poured out two stiff ones. "Eddie Malone was a buddy of mine. He was getting involved with your girl Rita, and I couldn't fink on him, too. I guess we don't have a deal anymore."

The lieutenant sipped his bourbon appreciatively. "Malone has a pretty good bruise on his jaw. Is that how you treat your friends?"

"Well, he's not exactly my friend anymore. Obviously, you've spoken to him."

"He didn't have a lot to say, David. The woman was more cooperative though. We stopped them on the highway heading north. They had enough non-prescription downers to sink a ship. Not to mention the cocaine and a little heroin. That's a heavy bust. The girl got a little loose-lipped."

Here it comes, Schrader thought to himself. For one wild moment, he thought to run for it. Crack the lieutenant a good one with the bottle, take his pistol and the cash and run for the border. *People have escaped before! But it's insane. Jessie is right. I have to step back into the real world sometime. And I have to think of Mingo.*

"Did you come to arrest me?" he asked Logan.

"I've known you awhile, David," Logan finally said. "At least, I've known about you. I heard you give a talk once, let's see, way back in 1971. You kids were having a rally or something, there on the state capitol grounds, and we were all nervous about it, of course. I was a detective sergeant then. I was in the crowd."

"Did I make a speech? I don't remember."

"Well now, I wouldn't call it a speech. You stepped up there and talked about Vietnam. It was a pretty good talk. I didn't forget you. When you showed up at the club last year, well, it was like seeing an old friend again."

Schrader was getting suspicious. What else did Logan want from him? "All right, Lieutenant. Can we stop the games? Are you going to arrest me?"

The lieutenant eyed David again for a long time, and sipped his bourbon. "I lost my boy in Vietnam, David. He was the only son I had—" And he sat down his glass suddenly as if the weight of it was too much. "He was the only boy I had, all right, the pride and sum of my whole life and I wish to God I had him back."

It all began to come clear then, the doubts and questions Schrader had about this man. He looked away from him, gave him time to recompose himself.

"How did it happen?"

"Some night patrol," Logan replied, gripping the glass tightly. "They were ambushed; Jerry crawled from cover to help his buddy . . ." His voice trailed off. "He was always a brave kid. You were like that, weren't you?"

"Most of us were. Not brave, maybe, but helpful."

"My boy was a marine, too. Yep. Just like his old dad. I used to sit him on my knee and tell him the biggest lies about the war. Played it up to him. Told him about all the laughs I had with my buddies, made it seem like a great time."

Schrader poured them each some more bourbon.

"What would he have been like, David? If he'd lived, who would he be now?"

"I can't answer that."

"Would he be angry? Tell me. Would he be mad and bitter like all you boys?"

"Maybe. If he were sensitive enough."

"Would he hate me for being a cop?"

"How did you raise him, Lieutenant?"

"He respected me."

"And he joined the Marines to please you?"

"Yes." But Logan could not look at Schrader when he answered.

"Then he wouldn't have hated you, though you might have been at odds with him. You might not have understood him so well, anymore. Probably, you would have fought a few times, wasted a lot of breath on meaningless arguments. But no, he wouldn't have hated you. I'm sure he would have loved you all the more. He would have wanted you to understand the war as he did, because he loved you."

The lieutenant straightened himself then and cleared his throat. "Now about this Darnell woman and your friend Malone. There was one other officer with me when we pulled them over. A young patrolman who happens to be my cousin's boy. He was a friend of my son's. He's a good cop, not real bright but he has a good heart. That story she told isn't going any farther than us. We confiscated their drugs, and I made it clear that if I ever saw them in my town again, I'd have their asses. I'm sure they believed me."

Schrader gawked at him with his mouth open. "You mean you let them go?"

"That's right. I don't think they'll bother you. I don't know why you beat them up like that, but I have my suspicions."

"It's not important anymore."

"Remember what you told me outside the station?" he asked.

Schrader was trying to clear his head. "What was that?"

"You told me to look under my own bed. And I did. Manley is a rotten cop. He was transferred to the east side after some misconduct the department would rather forget. I've asked some questions about him and I don't like any of the answers. We try to police ourselves, David, whether you believe that or not. I expect we'll be seeing Manley's resignation soon. Maybe we can make things uncomfortable for Quigley too."

Schrader shook his head in disbelief. "You mean the investigation is over?"

"Well, it's not officially over. Tomorrow morning it will start to fizzle out. Quietly, you understand."

"And what about your heroin case? I've blown it good now."

Logan shrugged. "There are lots of punks around. I've nailed my share."

"I don't know what to say, Lieutenant."

"Don't you think you ought to tell your buddy, Calderone?"

"Right—that's right! I'll go get them out of bed."

"Thanks for the bourbon, David." Logan stood to leave.

"Yeah. Sure . . . uh, Lieutenant? Thanks for—thanks for looking under your bed."

Logan waved his hand. "Thanks for telling me about my son." And he walked out.

A cabbie drove Schrader to Mingo's house and he got them out of bed, Mingo bleary-eyed and grumpy, Adelita not sleeping well anyway. After they were good and awake he told them the news, at least as much as they needed to know: about Logan's unexpected friendship and everything that followed. But he was quiet about what Eddie had tried to do, and about the events at Rita's house. There wasn't any need to kick a dead horse. *Oh Dios Mio!* He remembered Adelita crying! *Yo no lo creo!* Oh my God, I can't believe it!

Schrader told them he'd quit the club, that he'd be out of town awhile, camping. Could he use their old truck? Sure. Adelita asked about Jessie, was she going with him? He made some excuse. *Let them find out about that for themselves. Then they would find out about Eddie, too.*

They looked so fine together then, suddenly relieved of the threat of prison. *It's good to bring them the news.* But Schrader caught himself staring—as if they were a photograph; rather, as if they were three dimensional but his own perspective was from a flat picture in black and white. He could reach for them, but he could not grasp.

After a time he left them, started their old clunky Chevy and shivered in the metal cab, drove slowly home, truck cold and gears stiff, wondering all the while if the news would make any difference to Jessie.

Jessie will be happy that I'm out of trouble, but it won't change things. She can go to hell, he thought, *I'm not going to beg her!* And he wrapped himself in a chill that was much more than the cold of the night.

But Schrader slept fitfully and late into the day. Waking up half in a dream, he expected her to be there. The flaking ceiling stared back at him mutely. He couldn't stand that house any longer. He dressed quickly and began to collect his camping gear, made up a back pack and tossed the excess gear in a box. There was a paper sack tucked in one corner of the refrigerator. He stared at it and hesitated, then stuffed the sack in the box. After he locked the house and loaded his gear, he drove the hell out of Austin as fast as he could. He knew where he wanted to go.

The day had that crystal sharp brightness that comes with the northwest winds. There was not a cloud. The old truck clattered and rattled and buffed with the wind as it rolled up and down the hills, a crow's view of Texas rising and falling before his eyes. The road led to Johnson City and Schrader turned off there, drove another hour through the winding ranch country.

He came on it kind of sudden, the oak and cedar crowding the road to blind him, but suddenly there it is like a huge red fist hammered down in anger. It was a ghost rock to the Indians, and a holy place. He could not pretend to know what it meant to them, a holy place, telescoped here in the present day. It must have been something very special. It is a great, red granite knob that upthrusts from the surrounding hills and plains, a monster rock full of caves and great cracks and surrounded by house-sized boulders like complementary jewels. Perhaps it is three hundred feet high and a ragged dome in shape, with a hollow carved out like a bowl on the very top.

The last Comanche fight in Texas was there, Schrader knew. The plaque that commemorates the battle hardly does justice to the losers. He wondered if there would ever be a plaque at Khe Sahn. To the victors go the plaques, yes, and the smugness sometimes.

I am full of contradictions. We could have won. As tough as their soldiers were, we were tougher. We were the best, but we were blunted time and again by misuse. That is as perverse a pride as I can have. How many more would we have to kill, in order to win? No, I'm glad we lost. But I hated being treated like a loser.

After two trips he'd moved his gear and water to the top.

He was panting and his leg muscles fluttered and the wind sliced the sweat from him like a razor. There were still no clouds.

He could see the land start to change from there—the rolling of the hills begins to break open into the vaster stretches of the West. The kind of country that made his eye reach and stretch for the colors and shapes it holds.

He moved his gear to the western side of the rock to the hollow with the old cave that narrows to a dark and musty crack. A thin veneer of soil covers the hollow, and a few scraggly trees struggle to grow there. Down in that bowl the wind only fluffed.

It took a couple hours to gather firewood. There were pockets of soil up and down the rock, oak and juniper clung there like lost climbers, but the going was steep and rocky and he slung his wood over his shoulder a bundle at a time.

When he finished he made a small camp. Some hearth stones were already laid, so he kindled a fire and began to boil some water for coffee. He was a little shaky from the climbing, but he felt fine, his back against a stunted oak and the small fire cracking and smelling cedar-sweet. The afternoon was getting on, and shadows were creeping into the hollow.

After awhile he laid out a bedroll and began to rummage through the box. There were canned and dried goods, coffee and tea, what remained of his bourbon and tequila. And in the sack that he'd hurriedly tossed into the box were the mushrooms that he'd found on the Pedernales. They were cured and shrunken with the same color as dried wheat. He handled the sack with indecision, weighing the whys and what-nots, and dropped them back in the box.

There was a time once, after Schrader was discharged and told to be *normal*, there was a time he had thought he'd lose his mind. He tried seeing psychiatrists, but the questions they asked had nothing to do with his problem: how do you feel about your father, do you masturbate often, are you embarrassed to see your mother undress? He had wanted to scream at them! *Don't you know we're killing a nation of people?* But in the ordered neatness of their offices, with the well-modulated professionalism, screaming always seemed so out of place . . . The first time he ate the mushrooms, though, he began to get a grip on his life. They showed him how to grasp each secret and shake it out in the light. But those times lay years behind him when he was stronger and more hopeful. He asked himself what might happen if he didn't have the strength anymore . . .

He walked from the hollow up to the rimrock. The fall was sharp and long there, with huge boulders tumbled pell-mell at the bottom, and the land stretched out with a humbling sweep. Something needed to change in his life. And the change wasn't coming on it's own . . .

Schrader walked back to his fire where the pot of water was boiling. From the sack he dropped in a small handful of mushrooms. They floated in the water and then swelled and sank and the water turned dark blue. He looked at the sack and then up at the sky and it was clear as heaven can be.

He up-ended the sack into the water, and it splashed and the fire sizzled as he poked the mushrooms down. It was an absurd amount. But something in him needed out.

19

Below him in the distance was a pond shimmering rose petal pink in the slanting light. He sat on the rimrock and felt he could touch the very fabric of the land. He *knew* that pond, knew the cold springs that fed it, drank its crystal water until it became part of him and he part of it.

What am I but water?

The landscape seemed to breathe. The setting sun was an amber, invisible force that pushed on him gently to hold him in place. The first rushes of the drug were swirling over him; he felt his muscles swell and he was so keenly alert that his eyes ached at the beauty. He saw the sun as an angry coal and it shot its last heat like barbs and the red granite shined and bled. The sky rippled orange to red-yellow to pale green to deep blue. The sun cracked, and setting, began to draw all the colors to itself. The western sky seemed to whirl and fold inward, stealing the precious light from boulder and hill and they reached with shadows to bring the light back but it danced before their grasp and he could almost hear the sun laughing.

Dusk fell like a cape, the scowling eye of the sun grew smaller and faded and the wind seemed to blow it away, or it winked, and it was night.

Schrader was alone on the rock. The rock was him.

When he returned to camp, walking lightly, he wanted to dance on his toes from the current surging through him. The fire was almost gone. There was no moon, but the stars were out so bright that he cast a shadow on the glimmering stone.

With some weathered wood he built up the fire, and the tortured trees seemed to lean toward the heat. The drug was toying with his moods. He knew he would be a slave to it.

David did not see him until the fire grew and palely lighted the hollow. Then he did see the man, sitting on a stone quite naturally.

Enos Wheeler had been a good friend. Once upon a time, Schrader had sent him to a dangerous place and he never returned. *Dear David*, the letter from his buddies began, *we hate to tell you this but Enos never made it off Hill 881*. It seemed that he was trying to make it off, when the helicopter he was on crashed with another and nobody survived.

By then Schrader was safely in the States, tour of duty done, his freedom before him like a playground.

David stared at him and grew afraid. Enos was wearing jungle gear, looking quite healthy, but older like David. *How could that be? He died when he was twenty-two.*

Schrader couldn't think of anything to say.

"Surprised to see me?" Enos asked. It sounded like Enos.

"Yes. A little surprised. But it's good to see you. At least I think I see you . . ." David tossed some more wood on the fire and it caught and the light sprang brighter and Enos was still there.

"How is it that you're older? I don't understand."

He shrugged. "You're older, aren't you? Seeing with older eyes?"

David stood there and considered, the fire licking between them as protection. Enos was as real to Schrader as his own flesh, but he knew it could not be.

"Relax, David. It's out of your hands now."

Still Schrader stared at him.

"Weren't you going to make some coffee?" Enos asked him, standing then and walking to the fire.

Schrader backed away quickly. "Yeah. That's right, I was." And he rinsed the pot and refilled it and put it on the coals. But all the while, he kept his eyes on the apparition.

Enos was looking over the camp sight. Schrader remembered Enos had always had a way of slow deliberation, looking carefully before he leaped. *I'd figured him for a survivor*, thought Schrader.

"Just a bad break," Enos said simply to the thought in Schrader's mind.

It startled him. "You mean the helicopter crash?"

"That's right. Bad luck. The hill was taking a lot of rockets. I jumped on an overloaded chopper to get back to Khe Sahn. I should have stayed in the bunker."

"Wait a minute!" David protested. "I never learned any of those details!"

"I'm telling them to you now," Enos replied, matter of factly.

"But you're only a mirage! You can't know anything that I don't know!"

"Oh? Then how did I know the details?"

"You must have made them up," David said, and then he laughed at the absurdity. Enos laughed too. *It's his same old laugh*.

Once, from boredom and exasperation, Enos had had himself sheared bald, except for one Mohawk strip of hair. It was at Khe Sahn. They were all tightly strung, almost out of ammunition, and the first relief plane in days was loaded with nothing but old Christmas eggnog. And the eggnog was sour. So Enos came whooping from his bunker, stripped naked and war-painted. "Indian no need bullets!" he'd howled, and he had danced on top of his bunker until they drew mortar fire.

The X.O. hadn't liked it much. Schrader recalled he'd had to defend Enos to the major.

"I never thanked you for that," Enos said to David then, still standing by the campfire.

"That's right. You never did."

"You were the sergeant, David. It wasn't always easy for you to be one of the boys."

Schrader said nothing. He did not like to be reminded that there had been barriers between them. *One day you were a corporal and still one of the gang, and then bang! You were a sergeant and everything changed. You were responsible for fifty-six men.*

"You want some coffee?" Schrader asked Enos.

"No thanks. I never seem to get thirsty anymore."

Schrader thought Enos was making a joke, but he didn't see him smile.

Schrader found himself pacing around Enos as he stood there, first one direction then the other. The wind moaned a different pitch on each side of the fire. Schrader was less afraid of Enos, and more skeptical. He was perfectly cognizant that the mushrooms were at work, but the ghost demanded that he accept it as real. Schrader's mood was changing again. He was getting irritated that what stood before his eyes could not be believed.

"Shouldn't we get down to it?" Enos asked.

"What's your hurry, Enos?" Schrader was still pacing, sipping the hot coffee.

Enos danced a little jig. "The night won't last forever."

Schrader smirked. "And you disappear with the sun?"

Enos looked at him half in anger and walked from the fire to the edge of its light, seeming to blend with the shadows and Schrader stared where he thought Enos was . . . When Enos touched him from behind, he jumped and spilled his coffee. It burned his hand.

"I'm here, now, because in the night you find me more acceptable. You think that I'm a dream, David, or some kind of mirage but I can prove to you that I'm real. Don't make me break you down like you did to Rita."

Schrader did not reply.

"Why don't you trust me?" Enos asked.

"Because you'd have to hate me," Schrader replied. "I sent you up there."

"I was the logical replacement," he shrugged.

"I could have sent Lewis or Williams."

Enos shook his head. "They weren't the ones for the job.

Lewis couldn't field strip a cigarette, much less an M-60. Williams was too green."

"My, aren't you a forgiving sonuvabitch!"

"I thought you'd be glad to see me, David."

"Right! I'm just thrilled! I've spent ten years trying to push you out of my mind and now here you are in living color . . . Just go away, Enos. I don't need a ghost telling me how I've screwed up my life!"

Enos shook his head. "You never took advice worth a damn."

"But you loved giving it, didn't you? Sergeant Schrader! The drinking water is muddy! Sergeant Schrader! There's rat shit in the beans! What did you expect me to do? Eat the damned beans for you!"

Enos smiled at him. "You always did the best you could, David. We appreciated it."

"Then why are you picking on me?"

"I have the right to tell you some things," he insisted.

"Not in my mind you don't! You're a figment of my imagination!" Every cell in Schrader felt drenched in the drug and he shouted his madness at the wind, glaring bug-eyed at this apparition that plagued him.

"I'm warning you, David."

Schrader laughed harshly. "You can't warn anyone! I'll wave my hands and you'll disappear."

"I don't believe I will," he replied, shaking his head. "I told you it was out of your hands."

"To hell with you!" Schrader snapped. "To hell with all the dead! You don't know the grief the living have!"

Enos only looked at him sadly and very casually stepped into the campfire. The flames suddenly billowed white hot and flared up his body and burned his clothes away. The flesh began to sizzle and split and crack like pork rind.

Schrader screamed. The sound hammered back at him from the nooks and crevices and his mind twisted painfully with the agony of the screams, Enos's screams in the helicopter, that day on the hill.

"ENOS! NO! I NEVER SAW YOU LIKE THAT!" Schrader collapsed on the ground, the smell of burnt flesh heavy on the air and he tried to close his eyes but the image was fixed in his mind, the pork rind human flesh bursting, crackling, turning black.

"Please, Enos!" he sobbed. "That's enough, please. I never saw you like that!" Schrader didn't know how long he lay on the ground, hugging himself while the night weighed on him like a blanket. It seemed like forever. He was afraid to open his eyes. But he felt Enos's hand on him.

"It's all right, David. You can get up."

He was Enos again. The odor of cooked meat was gone, the fire was burning normally.

"Don't do that again. Please." Schrader was trembling like a whipped puppy.

"I won't."

"I didn't mean that about the dead. How could I mean that? You were so fine; you were all so fine and there were so many of you . . . Look at me, Enos. I'm counting," and Schrader began a roll call of the names. "See Enos! I'm running out of fingers! Reeves and Belcher and Smith and Kott! See Enos! I'm running out of toes! Murphy and Johnson and Duffy and Gaines and Krause and poor Calvin! Goddamn, Enos! I'm just one man! How come I know so many dead kids?" Schrader was slipping over the edge then, and he fought to hold back. He didn't want to go crazy on the hill top with only a ghost to see him through, but there seemed to be no stopping. The psilocybin had him on a roller coaster. Schrader fell into the trunks of one of the trees and held on for all he was worth. *You didn't want to leave here unchanged*, he heard Enos say. Or maybe he said it to himself. When the vertigo passed Schrader was panting like a dog and clutching the tree.

He struggled to his feet, wiped snot from his nose. "For a long time, Enos, I was ashamed to be alive. Everyone I sent up to that cursed hill was killed. Everyone! I wanted to go myself but the XO kept saying no, send someone else . . . And then they would die, too. For a piece of jungle. So some generals could have targets for their bombers . . ."

The fire had gone to coals again. Hunkering, David fed it more wood and warmed his hands. The stars seemed a splash of gems on black velvet and he could have touched them, there at the center of all things, his impenetrable self.

"You think my life was wasted, don't you, David?"

"Yes . . . I'm sorry but, yes."

"And you're going to compound the waste?"

"What?"

"The past is dead. Keep your feet in it and you'll be dead, too. Walking and breathing and eating isn't living. Hiding your heart away isn't living. Twice burned is no excuse, or three times burned or a hundred! You keep coming back, my friend . . . Look at me, David. I'm dead. That's the ultimate trip, brother. There's only one place left for me and that's in your heart. You hear me? It's the only place I have, and it gets awfully cold in there sometimes . . . If you keep hallowing me in anger, man, I really will be forgotten."

For the first time Schrader noticed how cold the night had become. His flesh raised and he huddled closer to the fire, listened as the cedar popped and the wind whistled around the hollow. He had always felt he was keeping the dead somehow alive with his anger, and then he saw that it gave them only a sadder death. The wind seemed to claw into his soul and he clutched the nearby blankets and wrapped them around, feet to the fire.

"Hell, David, we were this cold at Khe Sahn."

"No one believes me when I say it snowed."

"Those little white fluffy things that fell before Christmas? Those couldn't have been snowflakes, man. I think it was some kind of chemical."

Schrader remembered Enos laughing, the wind scattering the laughter about the hollow: above him, behind him. And as his head turned to catch the sound, he vaguely recalled the stars beginning to reel. He reached for something to hold, saw Enos trying to grab for him but he was very, very far away and Enos moved ever so slowly, and Schrader had already fallen a long, long time . . .

. . . Sunlight like glass across the eyeball. The rocks mashing his muscles clung to him, tumor-like, and his whole right side was numb and palsied. Schrader struggled to his feet, croaking, too parched to groan. Birds flickered about the hollow trilling their wake up calls; sparrows in his food stash tweeting and tumbling, feathers ruffled. A slice of bread on wings fluttered from the box, fell, came apart under attack, disappeared.

He found the water bottle and rinsed his mouth, splashed

his face. Schrader's head was fine, not like a hangover, but his feet felt frozen and, fumbling, he kindled a fire. Man's mark. The birds flew to tree limbs, sad trees dripping dew, tears for Enos.

David made coffee and greased the cast iron skillet. A raccoon had been in the bacon—the meat was clawed and chewed—but he had left enough. Sizzling, it sloughed images to the breeze: sound became smell, became taste. Schrader was awakening to the hilltop. The sky was perfectly blue. The coffee was the best in the world. He tipped his cup and smiled to the rock where Enos had sat.

After breakfast he took his time breaking camp, leaving the fire until last. His morning view had been the red granite nest of the hollow, only the sky open to him. On the rim, though, the world began to take proportion and he walked the huge rock's measure, keeping to the crest, revelling in the freshness of the morning. Later, in camp, he smothered the glowing coals and re-packed, tightly and carefully this time, making one load. Leaving, he could not bear to look back.

It was a pensive drive, made gloomy by the thought of the empty house awaiting him. *Why look for another job in Austin? It's a nice town, but it seems my life has gone full circle there and still come up empty. I'll wait until my godchild is born and then hit the road. It will be good for me. I've saved a pretty good stake and I can travel: see Joe Haney and his family, move up the East Coast and visit the old gang. Then what? Canada? Europe on a shoestring? Anywhere but that drab little cottage.*

Austin was a jumble of cars and signs and people. Tortoise-like, he steered the old truck through the traffic, wishing he could tuck in his head. Finally home, he bounced the pickup over the curb and into his front yard, feeling grimy and wrung out. When he opened the door, a note dropped to the ground and he stepped over it, letting it lay in the open door.

Stripping in the bedroom, clothes in a pile, Schrader walked to the bath and turned on the shower. Then he fetched the note:

David, no one knows when you'll be back. Just in case, here's the news. Adelita went into labor this

morning, birthing room, 4th floor. I'm assistant coach!
Come if you can. We'll miss you.

Jessie

He read it again, slow coming around. *The baby!*

He was running into the building, his hair still damp from
the shower, and the cop in the entrance scowled at him. The
elevator was crowded, faces automatically going blank — second
floor, third floor — .

Mingo was in the lobby, looking out the window, draped
in a green gown with a surgeon's cap on his head. David stepped
up behind him.

"Hey, big daddy!"

"David! Good to see you, man."

"So what's the scoop? How's Adelita?"

"She's okay. Jessie is with her, keeping her breathing up.
I'm taking a break. Christ, she's wearing me out! It's nine hours
now."

"What's the doctor say?"

Mingo shrugged helplessly and sat down in a chair. "He
expected a quicker delivery because she was already dilated
eight centimeters when we got here. Ten centimeters is about
max, you know. But she's not dilating past nine or nine and a
half. She's hovered there for hours . . . Her cervical lip is
swollen, David. The baby's head isn't engaged just right, and
it's going to make things more difficult . . ."

"Is Adelita frightened?"

"Naw. She's plenty game. I'm the one who's scared . . .
The doctor's going to let her try awhile longer, but I know he's
started thinking about a caesarean."

"You've talked about that possibility for months, Mingo.
The important thing is a safe delivery, right?"

"*Por supuesto*! And the baby is fine so far. She has a good
pulse . . . But Adelita sure wants to do this on her own . . ."
He stood abruptly. "I feel guilty hiding out here. C'mon. The
Garcias are down the hall. Go say hello then get a gown and
mask and come see Adelita. The Doc is cool, as long as you
keep out of the way."

Schrader took his arm. "Did Jessie say anything to you
. . . about us, I mean?"

He looked puzzled. "No, nothing. She had lunch with Adelita yesterday. But they never tell me anything. Is something wrong?"

"No, I guess not."

"C'mon, man. Time's wasting."

Down the corridor, Adelita's father stood to shake Schrader's hand. He was a lean, good-looking man, graying, well-dressed. "*Buenas tardes*, David. It's good to see you."

"Thank you, sir, hello beautiful Senora." He stopped to kiss Mrs. Garcia.

"Oh, David. I'm so worried! Adelita should forget all these new ideas and let the doctor do things his way."

"Now mama, *no preocupado*."

"She'll be fine, Mrs. Garcia. She's tough. Have you been in the birthing room?"

"No. I'm not going in there. I'll wait here the whole time."

"Is Ramon here?"

"He's back at work now. We're swamped. When are you going to quit that lousy job and come to work for me?"

Schrader smiled. "You've asked me that for years. Be careful or I'll take you up on it."

"Any time, David. I mean that. In a couple of years you'll be licensed like Mingo. You two could make some good money subbing from me. The sky's the limit in Austin."

"Thanks. It makes me feel good that you've asked."

He heard a door hiss shut and turned to see Jessie coming from the room, green gowned and looking tired, her hair pinned up beneath the cap.

She smiled and patted *la Senora*. "Can I borrow this *hombre*?"

"You kids go ahead." Mr. Garcia sat down as he walked with Jessie out of earshot. There was a rack of fresh hospital laundry and Jessie snatched a gown and cap, tucked them under her arm. Nurses walked past with brisk efficiency, carts clattered down the hall. They looked at each other.

"One more chance?" she asked sheepishly.

"I should be asking you that."

She took his hands. "I had a talk with Adelita. It was a good talk, about how to live with men like you and Mingo.

She doubts that you would ever hurt me, David. But she warned me of the lengths to which you'd go, to protect me. That's a little frightening, too. Sometimes anger doesn't know which way to jump."

Schrader thought of Enos and the winter inside himself. "Maybe something is different, now."

"Put these on," she smiled, handing David the bundle. "Come and cheer up Adelita."

"Does it look bad?"

"Who knows? She's wearing down. All day she's gritted through contractions every two minutes, and she's kept up her discipline beautifully. But her strength is going . . . Even if the baby does start to pass, the doctor is worried she won't have the strength to push."

"And what do you think?" He slipped the gown over his head.

Jessie paused and pursed her lips. "I think she'll find the strength when she needs it . . . If only the baby's head would rotate a bit. But Adelita's so swollen . . ."

"And the baby's been engaged the whole time?"

"Just about. The doctor's concern is foetal distress. I think he'll be back to check on her soon."

"Then let's go in now."

The room was pleasant enough: pastel walls curtained gaily, furniture made of wood. There was a vanity and a mirror. Mingo had hung a Velazquez on the wall, a print of *The Fable of Arachne*. Adelita seemed to be staring at it when they came in, her eyes not wavering as she puffed her breath loudly, much as a weight lifter would. The bed was cranked high and she was sitting up, beneath a rumpled sheet, her knees up and legs spread.

"Cleansing breath now, baby. C'mon, real deep . . . That's my girl!"

She was pale and drawn, and the hair matted her head in damp little curls. She managed a wan smile as Mingo held bits of ice to her lips.

"Hey, good-looking." David stepped close and took her hand.

Her voice was a hoarse whisper. "How was the wild west, *forastero*?"

"Tame . . . There's more action going on in here."

"You betting?"

"On you, kid. Every cent."

She rolled her head back and forth on the pillow, tried to massage her groin beneath the sheet. "Effleurage doesn't work worth a damn!" Schrader heard her mutter. Then: "Please rub my back, Jessie . . ." and she turned slowly on her side and Mingo propped pillows between her legs and beneath her bulge.

David stepped back and made room for Jessie, and saw Adelita stiffen slightly and begin to inhale with some force. Mingo glanced at his watch, bent closely over his wife and listened to her labored panting.

"That's too quick, honey. *Mas despacio . . . muy bien.* Thirty seconds now. Ride this one out, baby. That's good . . . forty-five seconds . . ."

Jessie was kneading her back. When a nurse came in Schrader stepped even farther away. The nurse smiled and glanced at the chart.

". . . a minute fifteen now. Should be going over the crest. Your doing great . . . Keep it up, baby. Keep it up . . . minute forty-five. It's going away now. Slow it down. Good girl . . . Two minutes . . . Going away. Floating away . . . two fifteen . . . Deep cleansing breath, now. Real deep. Real deep, baby . . . I love you. You're doing great!" Mingo was also pale and haggard. It was long years past since Schrader had seen Mingo this tender.

"Time to palpate you, Mrs. Calderone," the nurse said. Adelita groaned wearily.

"A minute please, Senora," Mingo cut in. "Only fifteen minutes ago a nurse came and did that, and she poked pretty hard. My wife doesn't need the aggravation now."

"There isn't a recent palpation logged on the chart, Mr. Calderone."

"Can I help that, Senora? The morning shift didn't log that her water hadn't broken yet. Like they were supposed to."

"I'm supposed to palpate her, sir." The nurse seemed a nice lady. She had a friendly face.

"And I'm supposed to keep my wife comfortable. She doesn't need to be examined now by anyone but Doctor Bertram."

The nurse shrugged and picked up the chart, spoke as she wrote: "Four twenty five. Tried to palpate patient but husband would not allow it . . ." The chart clattered against the bed and the nurse stepped around Mingo, took Adelita's pulse, fluffed her pillow. "Honey, girls come through here all the time and take twice as long as you. Don't you be discouraged. Just keep swinging. You'll hit the prettiest homerun anyone ever saw."

"What's the line?" Jessie asked, still kneading Adelita's back. "The morning crew was split four to three, boy."

"Not a chance. We're five to two, girl. Wait and see. On Thursdays we're practically always right . . . I'll ring for Doctor Bertram, honey."

She was barely out the door when Adelita's contractions began again. David flopped his arms at his side, feeling useless. Jessie glanced at him. "Don't just stand there like a bump. Rub her feet and legs!"

They were clustered around Adelita when the doctor came in, frowning when he saw Schrader.

"Who are you?" He was big nosed, with glasses and a bushy mustache.

"He's my brother," Adelita whispered. "It's okay."

"Your brother, eh? I thought your brother was a Mexican," he grinned.

"Be a sport, Doctor Bertram. He'll behave."

"Just keep out of the way Mister, uh, Garcia. *Comprende?*"

David backed three quick steps into the corner while the doctor sat on the bed and Adelita shifted awkwardly to her back. The same friendly nurse pushed through the door, bearing a tray that she placed on the stand by the foot of the bed.

"I can't let you go much longer," the doctor was telling Adelita. "More pitocin won't do any good, and it looks like you're weakening."

"I don't want a C section. You said you'd go all the way with me, Doctor Bertram."

"And I want to, Adelita. Under different circumstances I'd give you a lot more time. But soon the baby may be stressed. You may not be able to stretch enough, with your swelling. And you might be too weak to push . . . I'll probably have to move you down the hall and knock you out. First, I'll try a forceps rotation. Maybe that will work. Otherwise it's a caesarean, sweetheart."

As her contractions rolled around again the doctor stepped to the foot of the bed and put on surgeon's gloves. Mingo was counting ". . . thirty seconds. Good breathing . . . Hey, Doc. How 'bout a little pushing at the height of contraction. The manual says . . ."

"Thank you, Doctor Cálderone. I've read the manual. Sure, go ahead. But gently, Adelita. You can tell if there's undue strain . . . and I'm going to examine you."

Adelita nodded tersely while she panted.

"Okay, baby, let's shift gears. Sixty seconds now. We'll switch to push breathing, okay?"

Jessie had stepped away while the nurse folded back the sheet, and the doctor leaned over to perform the examination. Adelita took some deep breaths and then held her breath, very obviously pushing with her pelvic muscles, while Mingo counted out loud. David saw Adelita wince at the doctor's touch, saw him stand abruptly and noticed the bloody brown smear on his glove.

"Meconium," he told the nurse.

"A minute thirty," Mingo said, looking sharply at the doctor. "Deep cleansing breath, baby. You got it . . ."

The nurse was hurrying out the door. Mingo nodded to the doctor and seemed to sag, his face folding sadly.

The doctor had dropped the gloves in the trash. Again Schrader glimpsed the ugly smear.

"There's some foetal discharge, Adelita. We've talked about what that might mean . . . We'll have to hurry now, and get you down the hall. I'm sorry, dear."

Something was going wrong with the baby. David's knees felt suddenly weak and he leaned against the wall, seeing the dismay in Jessie's eyes, the helplessness in Mingo's.

He knelt down by Adelita and stroked her hair, touched his lips to hers, glanced up at David with more despair than Schrader had ever seen in a face. His guts twisted. Schrader knew what fear lurked deepest in his heart. He knew why he looked secretively over his shoulder, each day of his life. *Because what a man does, comes back to him. Mr. Li would tell*

*us that . . . For every village you ever burned, Mingo Cal-
derone, for all the children you ever terrified, for the innocent
lives you took in Hue, you must pay . . .* Seeing that in his
eyes, Schrader knew why they tucked themselves away on the
fringes and minimized their lives. *The cutting edge of karma
is always about.*

But in his emotional stew, Schrader had forgotten about
Adelita. As her contractions came around again, she leaned
forward and spread her legs with a spine-raking groan, and as
she pushed the blood left her face and the veins in her neck
leaped and pulsed.

The sheet was folded back. Jessie gasped and pointed.
The doctor turned quickly to see the baby's head begin to
bulge from Adelita's womb.

"We have crowning!" the doctor blurted. "Good girl!" And
he hurried into another pair of gloves.

Adelita sucked in air two, three times, locking her hands
to the bedframe, then she held her breath and pushed again,
Mingo talking and grinning hugely while the baby's head
stretched the cervix beyond belief.

Schrader winced and his toes turned in, feeling a pain in
his own groin as a little brown head popped into the world,
sheening slightly blue, doctor's hands rotating the head then
pulling out a shoulder and in a rush, as soap slips from grasp,
out popped David's glistening goddaughter, writhing and curly
headed, the doctor hanging her by her feet and cleaning her
mouth, giving her a shake and then she spoke to them. *Wake
up world! Here I am!*

Schrader was weak against the wall, his throat dry, when
Jessie came and leaned into him. She was trembling and he
could feel her heart racing. When the nurse hurried back into
the room she stopped a moment, surprised, and then calmly
went about helping the doctor. The baby was on Adelita's belly
and Mingo was hovering over them both. After the cord was
tied and cut, the nurse took the baby gently and began to
clean and swaddle her. Adelita was still pushing, discharging
the placenta as the doctor urged her, as Mingo counted out
loud.

From the corner, they gave Adelita a high sign and she
laughed, beaming. She was suddenly radiant, her eyes spar-

kling with a brand new light. She seemed not to notice the
doctor stitching her, but Mingo was wincing, not knowing what
to do until the nurse handed him the baby.

Mingo took her, looking wonder-struck. *Mi bonita Daniela*,
he crooned, *Bienvenida, mi amor* . . . And then Mingo walked
to David and held out his daughter. Schrader was petrified.
He shook his head but Mingo pressed Daniela into his arms,
and her touch was electric.

Once in Schrader's heart there dwelled a broken child,
whose touch in the terror of his heart he recalled with a shudder. And here was another child, the finest thing a man could
ever hope to touch, and she took his heart in her tiny breast
and made it glad.

When spring came the next year, the river swelled with
rain and rippled a deeper green than in autumn. The rapids
tumbled with genuine treachery, undercutting banks, shifting
sandbars, sweeping stones and even boulders along in its rush.
But the fury was hidden when viewed from the crest, where
the eye strayed to patches of bluebonnet and primrose while
the cunning river performed its sleight of hand, dangerously
lovely in pastels.

Down the valley, just going around the bend, they were
ambling along: Mingo cavorting, Jessie and Adelita more subdued, bright prints of their halters disappearing as the river
curved away. Once again Schrader was boot to Mingo, now
that he knew all about babies. In the seconds that he lagged
behind the women, who were scrambling down the slope,
Mingo had tried to impart his wealth of knowledge: what to
do and when, and why and how. David was heavily armed
with a teddy bear and a mobile that hung over the playpen, a
rattle and a yellow duck, two kinds of fruit juice, diapers and
a jack-in-the-box that finally opened three beats after the
pop! But it was all superfluous. Daniela preferred Schrader's
nose.

He was cradling her. She was staring around at the wide
world with her mother's eyes, and David thought how nice it
would be someday to tell her about her papa, in secret little
ways that he knew, and she could be proud. That way, she
might learn a little of her Uncle David, too, and the folly of
men.

Then she looked at him in a special way, with his nose in a vise grip. Gently, Schrader kissed her soft little mouth and whispered thank you.

"Keekeegeek!" she gurgled, which meant that he was welcome.

ABOUT THE AUTHOR

While he was a marine, ALLEN ANTHONY GLICK served two tours in Vietnam, where he frequently worked with Vietnamese peasants in civilian support programs. He is a veteran of the 1968 TET Offensive and the seige of Khe Sahn. He resides with his wife and two daughters in Austin, Texas.

Special Offer
Buy a Bantam Book
for only 50¢.

Now you can have Bantam's catalog filled with hundreds of titles plus take advantage of our unique and exciting bonus book offer. A special offer which gives you the opportunity to purchase a Bantam book for only 50¢. Here's how!

By ordering any five books at the regular price per order, you can also choose any other single book listed (up to a $5.95 value) for just 50¢. Some restrictions do apply, but for further details why not send for Bantam's catalog of titles today!

Just send us your name and address and we will send you a catalog!

BANTAM IS PROUD TO PRESENT A MAJOR PUBLISHING EVENT

THE ILLUSTRATED HISTORY OF THE VIETNAM WAR

Never before has the Vietnam War been so vividly presented. Never before has a full account of the controversial war been available in inexpensive paperback editions.

Each Volume in the series is an original work by an outstanding and recognized military author. Each volume is lavishly illustrated with up to 32 pages of full color photographs, maps, and black and white photos drawn from military archives and features see-through, cutaway, four-color paintings of major weapons.

Don't miss the first four exciting volumes:

- [ ] **SKY SOLDIERS**
  by Clifton Betty, Jr. #34320 $6.95
- [ ] **MARINES**
  by General Edwin Simmons #34448 $6.95
- [ ] **ARMOR**
  by James Arnold #34347 $6.95
- [ ] **CARRIER OPERATIONS**
  by Edward J. Maroldo #34348 $6.95

and . . .

COMING IN OCTOBER 1987:

**KHE SAHN
TUNNEL WARFARE**

Look for these books at your bookstore or use the coupon below: